DESTINATION
CONNELLY

THE COLLOWAY BROTHERS #4

K.L. KREIG

To Alice,
my inspiration for Barb Colloway.

I miss you and hope
you would have been proud of me.

Prologue

Nora

Karma is king.

Karma is a bitch.

Karma is a dish best served warm. Or maybe that's revenge? No matter. Isn't revenge nature's karma anyway?

There are hundreds of sayings about how we each reap what we sow. How we each get what we deserve in the end.

But the one I think fits this situation best is: Karma has no deadline.

And as I run my thumb over the eclectic navy logo on the corner of the pristine linen paper, I know this saying couldn't be truer.

Wynn Consulting, a wholly owned subsidiary of GRASCO Holdings.

He's finally found me.

It was inevitable, really. I knew this day would happen; I just hoped to stave it off a little bit longer. Like maybe forever.

I try to stop falling into the past, to the last night we had together—the *only* night we were intimate. But as I sit here and feel memories stare me in the face, I can't push the brakes hard enough to keep from crashing into them.

"I love your eyes," I say softly, running a finger down his cheek as we lie side by side, our naked bodies entwined.

Thick, black, lashes that make me envious frame his unique hazel eyes. Eyes I've never seen on another human being. Amber encircles his entire pupil and covers the top half of his iris with flecks of bright greens and blues peeking through, but the bottom half has a thick ring of deep blue on the outer edge and is an incredible mossy green color. The contrasts are mesmerizing. Hypnotic. Otherworldly, almost. It's as if the angels knew this boy was so extraordinary, so multifaceted, so special that a singular blue or brown or green just wasn't adequate.

They also represent his carefully layered personality perfectly. The one I know he gifts to very few people—just the special ones. To everyone else, he's cocky and arrogant and confident. But with me—when it's just the two of us—he's sweet and loving and vulnerable.

"They're just eyes, princess." His gentle smile is full of adoration. I've never been happier than I am in this moment, in his arms.

"No...you're wrong. They're so much more. They're like glass windows into your soul."

"What do you see when you look in them?"

"Me."

"God, Nora," he whispers before his lips land on mine. "I am so in love with you."

My heart does somersaults. We've officially been dating for just a couple of months, but I've been in love with this man for close to a year. Tonight is the first time either of us has uttered those three oh so important words. "I'm in love with you, too," I confess, my voice soft.

His magnificent smile steals my breath, lighting me up from the inside out like I'd just swallowed a whole jarful of fireflies.

"Just a sec. I'll be right back." Kissing me quick, he jumps out of bed and rummages in his backpack in the corner of the room, letting me admire his fine ass in the process. When he slips back into bed next to me, he gently takes my hand, slides something around my wrist, and tightens it snug.

Tears well in my eyes as I look down at a red threaded bracelet. Sitting in the center is a scarlet ladybug. My watery eyes snag his and I smile. "You didn't make this, did you?" I tease.

"Hell no. I'm all man, princess." As if to prove the point, he swoops back down, taking my mouth in a fast, punishing kiss. "I went shopping with my mom the other day and it caught my eye in one of those boutique stores as we were walking by. It made me think of you. I wanted you to have something from me before you left. Something you could look at every day. Something you love. To remember me by when we're apart."

I gaze at the first gift a boy has ever given me. "It's beautiful. I love it. I won't take if off. Ever."

"You're mine now. You realize that, right?"

I tumble into his depths once again. "I was born yours. Only yours."

"Nora..." Hands frame my face; his lips capture mine once again. His kiss is tender, loving. It brims with promise and hope and the pain we both feel at our impending separation. I leave for Baltimore in the morning.

"Someday you're going to marry me, Nora," he whispers in my ear as he easily glides inside me once again on a strangled groan.

I believe him.

"I know."

I believed the words I spoke with my entire self that night. I believed I was born for him. That I was meant to marry him. Share a life with him. But it's funny how life's circumstances can completely change the path we have laid out for ourselves. In a blink of an eye, your life can be thrown on its axis and you will spend the rest of your days playing the "what if" game, which doesn't do a damn thing except endlessly torment you. I had no way to know it at the time, but everything would change for me. For *us*.

Every. Thing.

My entire life would be shattered, derailed, thrown so far off kilter it would take me years to recover. I would become lost, adrift and isolation was how I dealt. It was the only way I could cope, even if it was the wrong way.

One night, a series of events and horribly bad decisions set me on a new path. That one slight shift would change my entire world.

I would be betrayed.

I would be the betrayer.

It would ruin me.

It would change him.

It would tear us apart.

And now, eleven years later, I'm about to come face-to-face again with the first man I gave myself to. The only man I've ever let inside my heart. The man whose essence still runs wild and rampant through my blood, even though I've tried to exorcise him countless times.

Once again, because life has a fucked-up way of doing that (aka karma), I am thrown into circumstances beyond my control, and I know it's merely a matter of time before shit hits the fan and I am covered in a stench so foul I'll never be able to scrub the lingering stink from my skin.

Chapter 1

CONN

"Harder. Fuck, yes. That's it, doll." My fist grips her long bleached blonde tresses hard, setting the pace I want her to take. Right now, it's slow and steady because her mouth is pure sin and I'd let her drag me into the depths of hell as long as she kept it wrapped around my cock the whole way south.

I met Lorna at the gym a month ago in the building where I live. She'd just moved in and hadn't been warned about me yet, so I took advantage of the situation. I'm a cunning guy like that. As soon as she stumbles across the wrong woman in the locker room shower, she'll lock her abundant assets down tighter than Fort Knox. Good thing I didn't miss my chance.

I wanted Lorna the minute I set eyes on her. She's absolutely fucking stunning and has a rack I've contemplated sliding my cock between. Her lips are full and pouty, though, so it was a toss-up. The mouth won. And Jesus, am I glad. She's sucking me off like a professional. Hell, she should take out insurance on her mouth. It is *that* damn good.

Prying my head from the back of her couch, I look down at the woman on her knees in front of me. She's beautiful, yes. She has great tits and a smokin' body, no doubt. She can string a few decent sentences together in a row, so she seems halfway intelligent. Regardless of what my brothers think, I don't just tap anything with a pussy. I am a *little* more selective than that.

But I already know this first encounter with Lorna, as stunning as she is, will be my last. She's like all the others. Maybe she has a personality, maybe she doesn't. Maybe she could be long-term relationship material, maybe she'd turn out to be a whiny bitch and eating a bullet would sound far more appealing. Maybe she's my perfect "Match.com" life companion. Who knows? I don't, because I won't give her a chance to get that far. I feel nothing for her other than intense physical pleasure as she works me expertly closer to one hell of a climax.

Her eyes sweep up to mine, looking for encouragement. She doesn't need it and she knows it. I give it anyway. "You're doing great, baby," I rasp thickly. She holds my gaze, trying to see if there's something there. A spark. Hope. Maybe I changed my mind about seeing the inside of her apartment once and once only? I may be a manwhore, but I am no bastard. Before I let you anywhere near my dick, you know the score, and so does Lorna.

I don't do seconds. Ever. It's too messy for everyone involved.

I stare into her doe eyes a second longer. *Nope.* No emotional connection whatsoever. No burn in my gut. No music in my ears. No racing of my heart—other than the fact I'm getting closer to spurting down her throat.

That emotional switch was flipped to the off position over a decade ago when the girl who managed to brand her initials on the soles of my feet and the palms of my hands got on a plane and never looked back. After the way she fucked me over, you would think I hate her. In many ways I do.

But it doesn't matter how deeply she's wounded me, I still try to picture *her* face in every woman I take. I still try to imagine the taste of *her* nipples on my tongue and the feel of *her* pussy embracing my cock for the very first time.

Getting the hint, Lorna's eyes flutter before dropping again, going back to the task at hand. Sensing she wasn't quite truthful that she was okay with this one-time thing I decide it's time to reach the goal line. I guide her up and down my shaft quicker, fisting the base so I can squeeze hard the way I like it. She gets the clue, sucking harder, moving faster, running her tongue perfectly around and under my crown until my hips buck. On a growl, my seed is ripped viciously from my balls. Proving this isn't her first rodeo, she swallows every drop, not spilling a one.

My head is tipped back, eyes shut, my chest still heaving with the effort of the last few minutes when I feel her crawling up my body. She straddles my lap, the warmth of her silk-covered pussy bearing down against my semierect shaft, her bare tits press against my still shirt-covered chest. Scattering kisses up my throat and jaw she latches on to my mouth, thrusting her tongue inside. I taste myself on her and while it doesn't repulse me, it's not a turn-on for me either.

Suddenly I'm not in the mood to take this further. The vibe I'm getting from her is like epoxy, Elmer's glue. She's trying to fasten herself to me and I am the antiadhesive. I'm a slippery fucker, like glass.

Again, I'm not a bastard. I may not feel like fucking her but I'm not going to leave her with the woman's equivalent of blue balls either. So I reach between us, her pelvis now writhing, and pull aside the crotch of her white silk panties, slipping my fingers through her drenched folds.

"God, yes," she moans in my ear. Once I slide two fingers inside, she rides my hand like she grew up spending hours a day on a stallion. Feathering my thumb over her clit, I bring her to a quick orgasm, enjoying the feel of her womanly softness under my fingertips. I let her kiss me and, for not the first time, have a twinge of guilt I can't feel anything for a woman beyond the physical pleasures they bring me. That part of me has been on lockdown for over a decade.

"Gotta go, babe," I say as I lift her off my lap. I linger too long on her generous tits. She notices. *Damn.*

Her face falls, her lips turn down, and disappointment is etched over every beautiful feature. Yep...this right here is why I don't do seconds. Technically I didn't even do firsts with Lorna, and my spidey senses were spot-on. She wants more than I'm capable of giving.

"But we didn't get to the good part," she whines.

Ladies, I'm here to tell you, sticking your bottom lip out like a four-year-old to get what you want is not attractive. Have a little more self-respect than that for God's sake.

"Have some work stuff I need to take care of." It's true—I always have work to do, even though that's not the reason I'm now anxious to make my getaway. I should have seen the handmade wedding invitations and 2.5 babies floating in her clear blue eyes well before I ever walked into her apartment. But I was too focused on getting her undressed instead. I tuck myself away, zip my jeans, and make my way to the exit. I mean, door.

"I want to see you again," she says pleadingly, grabbing hold of my arm.

I stop and gently take her face in my hands, enunciating my words slowly so she'll get the message. "Lorna, we talked about this. It was a one-time thing."

She looks like someone just ran over her puppy and left it for dead in the middle of the road. It makes me feel like the hit-and-run professional I've become. That's not a great feeling by the way, and I'm not proud of it, but *c'est la vie*, as the French would say. I am what I am and I don't foresee that changing anytime soon.

Lorna's actually a nice woman. She's funny, takes care of herself, and holds an executive VP of marketing position at some local media company, which is more than I want or need to know about her. She deserves to be someone's special girl. I'm just not that someone.

"But why?"

I know my smile will come across as sad. I'm not doing it to garner sympathy from the woman whose talented mouth was just wrapped around my cock. The one I'm about to heave-ho. It's a genuine emotion that I try my damnedest to stifle. "I'm simply not capable of more. I'm sorry." And I am. Sorry. So fucking sorry to leave another victim in my jerky wake but not sorry enough that I won't do it again and again and again.

Kissing her temple, I drop my hold and, without a word, make my escape.

Lorna lives on the eighth floor. I live on the thirty-fourth. It would be much quicker to take the elevator, but I need to blow off some excess energy and make my thigh muscles burn a little since I missed out on my cardio just now, so I take the stairs instead, two by two. By the time I reach my floor a few minutes later, I'm a sweaty mess, my tee sticking to my chest and back. I feel better, though.

Just as I'm unlocking my door, I see Ella walking toward me with her arms full of bags. I run over to her, taking them from her grip.

"Why didn't you have Sam help you up with these?" I scold her. She does this all the damn time. It drives me fucking crazy. She's the most stubborn, independent woman I have ever met. It's alluring and infuriating all at the same time.

"Because I don't like to be dependent on anyone. You know that. Now shut the fuck up."

"Jesus, you're a pain in my ass, Ella."

"That's why you love me, hon."

"You're right." I kiss her cheek and we walk a few steps down the hall until we're at her door.

Ella is my next-door neighbor. If there were any woman I could remotely envision myself with, it would be her. But I don't do emotion and I don't do commitment, much like Ella. We are simply the best of friends, although we've almost crossed the proverbial line several times late at night when we've had too much to drink and the moon is bright, throwing some sort of carnal spell through the windows.

As if she's just noticing the clothes sticking to me, along with the beads of water running down my forehead, she teases me. "Make another getaway, did you?"

I laugh loudly. "Along those lines."

She unlocks her door. I follow. Her condo is identical to mine, except the layout is flip-flopped with the spacious kitchen and open main living area on the left and two bedrooms down the hallway to the right. She has a bay of floor-to-ceiling windows that mirror mine, except I have a corner space, so my windows span two sides.

"When are you going to learn not to shit where you eat?" She shakes her head in mocking disapproval. "You're going to bang the wrong woman and she's going to know where you live and go all stalker on your ass. Not smart, Connelly. Not smart at all."

I shrug. "I'm a slow learner." I drop the bags on the counter and start helping her unload groceries.

Ella and I have been neighbors, and friends, for the last year. When I first saw her, of course I wanted to do her, badly. I even considered breaking my "one-and-done" rule because this woman is something incredible.

She's beautiful, both inside and out. Petite, at most, five foot three. Tight, fit body. Average tits, but they're all natural and I'd rather have a smaller, malleable handful than rock-hard fake ones any day. She's smart, witty, and successful. You can't have a three-thousand-square-foot condo in downtown Chicago that overlooks Navy Pier if you're not doing something right with your career.

But the more I got to know her, the more I discovered there's just something extraordinary about her heart that I don't want to ruin. Like we all do, she tucks a part of herself away that should only be shared with that one special person when he comes along. I'm not that guy, so I don't want to take that away from whoever he is.

I sincerely like Ella and if we cross that sometimes-wavering line, I will lose her as a friend. I don't want that. Outside of my brothers, she's one of the few genuine people in my life who's not after something of mine, whether it be my contacts, my power, my money, or riding my coattails until they find something or someone better. When you are a young, attractive, wealthy, single man, trust me...you have a lot of sharks circling your boat, hungry for what you have, trying to take a bite, no matter how small. Many have tried before in innumerable ways.

"When are you going to settle down?" she asks after putting the last of the fresh vegetables in the crisper.

"When are you?" I retort.

"You know the answer to that." At thirty-three, Ella is three years older than me. I know she's been married and divorced, but other than that, she refuses to talk further about that relationship or any relationship for that matter. "Besides, we're talking about you, now. Not me."

My lips curl. "This is a tired conversation." And one we have all too often. Ella thinks by now I should be settling down, having babies, and building a six-thousand-foot-square-foot house by the lake. I wholeheartedly disagree with her hypocrisy.

"Well, someone needs to make you see you have more to give of yourself than just your dick. As impressive as I'm sure it is."

My smile grows wide. "Impressive, huh? Want a demonstration?" I joke, wagging my eyebrows up and down.

Laughing, she answers, "As tantalizing as that offer is, it has to be a hard pass for me, cowboy."

"Hmmm. Your loss."

"I don't doubt it." She winks playfully.

This is what I love about hanging out with Ella. We flirt, we banter, we play around and it butts right up to the edge of sinful, but that's where it stops. As much as I don't want to ruin what we have, neither does she.

"How's that big acquisition you're working on?"

14

"Almost sewn up, actually. Did you secure that big marketing campaign?"

"Sure did," she replies with a shit-eating grin on her face. The small digital ad agency that Ella co-owns was going against a big-time, well-known large firm for complete redesign of a multimedia marketing campaign for a Fortune 50 firm. It's a campaign worth over ten million dollars. Annually. She's been working on it for months and it's been an all-out dogfight.

"Did you have to sell your soul?"

Her perfectly shaped brows rise. "Pretty damn close. I had to give up my first-born."

"I didn't think you were going to have kids."

"Exactly," she winks.

I spy a box that has brightly colored cartoons on the front and after leaning over to inspect it, I see it's a design tablet.

"Take up drawing?"

"It's for my niece. She loves photography and drawing. Has a great eye for that stuff." She offers me a beer. I take it, popping off the top with a hiss. "I need to get it mailed."

"You have a niece?" I've known Ella for almost a year and this is the most I've gotten out of her about family.

"What are we? Girlfriends?"

"Well...yeah. I thought so." I laugh.

She chuckles. "Well, we're not, hot stuff. You talk about your conquests. I berate you. You ineffectively defend your manwhore actions and then we veg and watch a movie or stuff our faces with your sinful home cooking."

True. We've never talked about the secrets we hide under the surface. Yet I find I want to know more now that she's opened that door. "So, a sister or brother?"

"Sister." I get the evil eye like she knows what's coming next.

"She as beautiful as you?"

"Oh, no you don't, Conn. Don't even ask about my sister."

"Why? Isn't she my type?" I take a long pull of my hops and barley. "Is she a butter face?"

"A butter face? What the hell is a butter face?"

"You know, everything's smokin', *but* her face."

"Oh my God. No, she's not a butter face, you fucking asshole. She's stunning. And smart. Exactly why she's not your type."

"Ouch, that hurts," I say, pointing my bottle at her. "And I'll have you know the women I date are smart. Some of them anyway."

"Date?" she asks mockingly, dragging out the word unnecessarily.

I shrug, wondering why that causes a twinge inside.

"See? That right there is why you are going to stay away from my sister. Now, have you eaten?"

"No. You offering?" I ask, finishing off my drink.

She smirks. "No. I thought maybe you would offer this time. You're a better cook than I am."

"True that." We both laugh. One of the very many lessons forced on me by Barb Colloway, my fan-fucking-tastic mother. "Okay. Give me twenty minutes to shower and change then pop on over. I'll leave the door open. Fish okay?"

"Sounds perfect. I'll whip up some rice."

"You mean that bagged crap?"

"Uh…is there any other kind?" Her nose wrinkles in confusion. Ella eats processed food like it's about to be banned. It should be—it's poison in a bottle or box or can or whatever else they put it into.

"Yes. The good fucking kind."

"Fine. Then I'll bring some wine."

"Now you're talking. You have excellent taste in wine. See you in a few."

"Okay," she calls after me. I walk to the front door and let myself out.

———

As I slip inside my condo, strip off my clothes, and step under the hot spray a few minutes later, I think about Ella's question regarding the acquisition. I let my mind drift to the business meeting I have in two days with the owner of Steele Executive Recruiting—SER for short—which is the executive recruiting firm I've been doggedly pursuing for the last several months.

At first, it was just mild interest on my part. I'd heard it was for sale and I almost dismissed the acquisition after our first meeting—until I found out who "he" was, that is. From then on, I have actively pursued the company, continuing to up the stakes whenever Carl Steele has gotten cold feet, which has been several times.

With one hundred fifty employees, SER is a

relatively small organization that works with small- to mid-level-sized clients. They are highly successful and have a fantastic reputation in the industry yet don't place even a third of the executives my company does. So it's not like they are a huge competitor of mine I need to gobble up. And they could merge with a number of other smaller firms or simply dissolve; a competitor would easily scoop up their best and brightest.

No, I don't need Steele Executive Recruiting to round out my business plan or fill a competitive hole. I don't need them for technology or their talent or their paltry 5.7 million dollars in annual net revenue to add to my own bottom line. There's one reason and one reason only I want to acquire them, adding them to Wynn Consulting's portfolio, the human resources consulting company I run as president and CEO.

Nora fucking Cantres.

Do you know how many Nora Cantreses there are in the US? Surprisingly, too fucking many. I could have pulled a Gray and hired a PI to find her like he did with Livia. I could have, but my youth at first and, as I grew older, my pride prevented me from doing it. Even though I haven't hired a professional to find her, I've always kept my ear to the ground and my eyes peeled for her, nonetheless.

And this is the thing about my line of work: human resources. It's a small and incestuous community. And the subspecialties within HR? Even smaller. So a few months ago when I started hearing rumors of a "star" executive recruiter who worked for SER by the name of Nora Cantres, my interest was piqued. And when everything about her fit *my* Nora to the proverbial "T," I knew this wasn't coincidence. I had finally found her.

Some men would do anything to scourge the woman who callously trampled their fragile masculine ego from their memory banks without a backward glance. Especially one who whispered promises of love and devotion yet coldheartedly broke them weeks later.

But I'm not like other men.

I still think nonstop about the woman who devastated me eleven years ago. Do her eyes still sparkle like jewels when she laughs? Does her voice still drop low and throaty when she's turned on? Will her moans of ecstasy still dive right into my chest cavity, squeezing my heart like a gentle fist?

I hear her whispers, her whimpers, her moans, her laugh, her very heartbeat. I feel the silk of her hair under the pads of my fingers, the kiss of her breath on my cheek, the brush of her lips against mine. I imagine her sweet taste lingering on my taste buds.

Her memory has forever echoed inside of me since the last day I saw her. Yet as much as it's haunted me, there was a part of me that always held fast to that echo anyway. When it would fade, I'd sit quietly and listen until I could hear it again. I couldn't force myself to let it go, let the ties sever. If I let her memory fade, it felt like none of it was real and I had to believe it was. It was real to me anyway. Now I have to find out if it was real to *her*.

It's time for Nora and me to meet up again, but

this time, we're all grown up and in very different places in our lives. And now, *I'm* pulling the strings. I am going to reel her in and tie those fucking strings in so many goddamn knots she won't know where to begin to free herself. With any luck, she'll just give up and give in.

I've gotta hand it to my mom about now. Because she wanted "worldly," well-rounded boys, my brothers and I were in just about everything under the sun, including Boy Scouts, and I became very fucking proficient at tying knots, even earning a Knot Master patch.

Tying a physical knot isn't much different than tying an invisible one. You simply take the tools you have to work with and bend them to your will. You play, you twist, you curve, you angle, you loop, and you pull tight. You pull so damn tight, you know whatever you've bound won't come undone without a big fucking razor-sharp Ginsu.

So while I started out tying physical knots in my youth, I mastered the invisible ones in adulthood. Now I'm the motherfucking king of loops and turns and angles, bending everything and anything to *my* will, *my* benefit.

And I've already expertly started weaving a combination of them to get what I want. I started the day I heard her name. And at last, two days from now, I will come face-to-face with Nora Cantres for the first time in eleven years. It's a meeting I have requested, *required* actually. On top of Carl Steele's demands, I have a few of my own before I ink this acquisition, which I hope will be after this next meeting.

The thing is...I just give a shit about *one* of my demands.

Just one.

When I said earlier Ella was the only woman I could possibly imagine myself with, that's not entirely true. She's the only one since Nora, but from the time I met Nora when she transferred to my high school in our junior year, she called to me on every level. Nora is the one woman I have had both an unholy physical attraction to and a bone-deep emotional, almost spiritual, connection with.

So I make no fucking apologies for what most people would consider extreme, maybe even unethical, measures to get to the woman who's always had my balls firmly in her grasp. She's managed to avoid me for more than a decade, but she can't run anymore. I've made damn sure of that.

I realize that, while in just two days I'll come face-to-face with the only woman I have ever loved outside of my mother, I know nothing about her now or how much she's changed. Over a decade is a long time. People mature, evolve, and change whether we want them to or not. I know I have. As I wipe off the steam on the bathroom mirror from my hot shower and look at the reflection staring back at me, I have to wonder if Nora will like the different man she will see standing before her.

Not likely, I muse. Hell, even I don't like the unemotional, aloof man I've turned into most days.

I may not know a lot of things, but I know now

that I've found her again, I will not rest until I own Nora Cantres, thoroughly and completely.

And once I possess her, I'll have to decide what I'm going to do with her. Because along with the deep-seated love that I've never been able to squash, I also have a whole fucking boatload of anger and resentment being thrown around in that noxious sea. I'm just not sure which emotion will bubble to the surface once I see her again.

Anyone will tell you I'm not a vengeful person. I'm not exactly a graceful loser, yet I don't retaliate maliciously either. However, the need I have to hurt her so it's a permanent scar on her psyche that will never heal, the same way she did to me, keeps trumping everything else I feel for her. And with eleven years to gather steam, right now I don't know if I can stop acting on the revenge brewing inside me, waiting to be unleashed, waiting to blow.

Or if I even *want* to.

Chapter 2

Nora

"I really wish you'd reconsider the offer, Nora."

"No. And I'm done talking about it, Uncle Carl."

He sighs heavily, taking a seat in the empty chair across from my desk. With dark circles under his eyes, he looks more tired than usual and his color is off. I make a mental note to ask him about his health when he's done grilling me for the hundredth time. He's almost the only family I have left. I can't lose him, too.

"Nora, it's a good offer. You'll have stability, build a good nest egg for the future and I want that for you. I want you to take the offer."

He is correct. The offer is generous. Since I live and breathe the executive recruiting world, I'm intimately familiar with generous compensation packages. There is no doubt this falls into that category. While the base salary is the same as I'm making now, my bonus potential is substantial, more than doubling what my uncle pays. Plus, the profit-sharing percentage rivals that of a senior-level executive and all of my relocation expenses will be liberally covered, including an unheard of housing allowance to cover the sale of my existing home.

It's a dream offer, actually. One I should take and quite frankly, one I would encourage *any* of my clients to accept. In fact, I was only one of six employees of Steele Executive Recruiting who even received formal, long-term employment offers from the company trying to purchase SER, so I realize I should be jumping all over it.

But I can't, because it's also too good to be true. I am not an executive within SER. I am a recruiter, plain and simple. Just one of many. I may be a damn good one, but there's no vice president title behind my name, so there's no reason I should have even been on anyone's radar screen to begin with, let alone be given a compensation package worth well over a quarter million dollars annually.

"I would have to move, uproot my life here. I don't want to do that. I don't want to leave you."

Another catch in the agreement. I would be required to move to Chicago. There could be worse places to live I suppose, but moving is only a small part of the reason I can't agree to this.

The offer letter is signed by Camille Hayes, GRASCO Holdings' Vice President of Human Resources and of course, *his* name isn't anywhere on the document, but his stamp is all over it. I could smell it a mile away the minute I opened the fancy ivory linen envelope it was couriered in and reviewed the terms of the agreement.

Wynn Consulting is in a different league from SER. They're the big fish in the HR consulting world. Our little company is but a drop in their bucket, so why Connelly Colloway has any interest in buying my uncle's company may be a mystery to many, but it's not to me. That was made even more apparent by the ridiculous offer sitting on the corner of my desk.

So, no. I am not, and will not, take this offer. While it can set me up financially, it will destroy me personally. I need to run far and fast in the complete opposite direction from the sinfully handsome, womanizing CEO of Wynn Consulting. I need to stay away from Connelly Colloway for so many reasons, not the least of which is if he ever finds out what I've done...well, I just can't go there.

"Nora, there's a contraption now called the phone." I snort but can't crack a smile. He leans forward, pinning me down. "Besides, that's just an excuse. Not even a good one at that. You're not even seriously considering this offer, so spill. What's going on here?"

I look away, unable to hold his penetrating stare. It's always been like that with Carl. I could always pull a fast one over on my parents, but never him. There is no way in hell I am going into details about my past with Connelly, because I would have to get into so many things and I just can't. As close as we are, there is so much Carl doesn't know about me. So instead of lying, which I'll be caught red-handed at, I deflect.

I'm good at that.

"I don't understand why you're doing this. Brad or Greg could easily take over running SER. You don't need to sell. If you're tired of working, you can just go part-time. You built this company from the ground up. You know you'll never be happy running to the senior center every day, playing poker, hitting on the old gray hairs, and drinking smoothies full of kale."

His smile is full of something bittersweet, I think. I wish I knew why. Something's been going on with him for the last few months and no amount of cajoling has convinced him to spill the beans. He sounds as tired as he looks when he speaks. "It's time, Nora. I'm getting to be a tired old man and besides, I'm starting to like kale and I'm ready to play a lively game of poker and give those little old ladies a run for their money. Who knows? Maybe I'll even find myself a wife before I kick the old bucket."

My mouth turns down. "You're barely sixty, Carl. What's really going on with you? I didn't even know you were thinking about selling your company."

And I have to admit, that hurt. Carl has been more of a father to me than my own, so when I had to hear from a client, of all people, that he was in discussions with Wynn to sell his business, I was sure the client was misinformed.

Turns out it was *me* and that stung. Still does.

"There was nothing to tell before. It was all just exploratory until the last meeting when Wynn made me an offer I couldn't refuse. I need this, Nora. I need to make sure my company and my employees are taken care of. I need to make sure *you're* taken care of." He says the words with smooth practice, but I can tell they are full of carefully constructed half-truths. "Come now, we're going to be late," he says, as he stands.

I stare at him, feeling defeated. This is the only job I've had since I graduated college. I've risen quickly in the company without feeling like it's been handed to me because of my skills and savvy working with the upper crust. I'm proud of what I've been able to accomplish. Now I feel it all slipping from my grasp and I'm in the dark as to why.

With a resigned sigh, I grab a notepad and make way around my desk, stopping in front of him. "I wish you wouldn't do this. I'd step up. Do anything you need me to."

Uncle Carl grabs hold of my shoulder, pulling me to him for a hug. "I know, Ladybug."

"You haven't called me that in years. I think I outgrew that nickname when I was ten," I say, trying to smile. Uncle Carl isn't really my uncle. He's my godfather and my father's best friend, but as far as I'm concerned he's family. He's been part of my life for as long as I can remember, attending just about every holiday, every birthday, my graduations. He's never been married and doesn't have any children, so I'm as much family to him as he is to me.

"Never. You'll never be too old for that." He kisses my forehead before releasing me. "You sure you won't reconsider?"

"I'm sure." My decision is steadfast and final.

His lips thin and he nods. "Then I will let *you* explain that to their CEO, who has personally flown in to meet with the SER team this afternoon."

Oh.

Shit.

"What?" I whisper, taking a step backward. *Tall, dark, and handsome is here?* In *my* building?

My legs suddenly feel like rubber and I lean against my desk so I don't crumble into a heap on the floor. I had intended to politely decline the employment offer during our little "meet and greet" with Camille Hayes from GRASCO Holdings this afternoon then return to my office to polish up my resume.

I have no doubt it won't take me long to find another job. I intend to stay on here as long as they'll allow it without a contract, but I'd already assumed that wouldn't be long since I'll now be considered competition. They certainly don't want "trade" secrets walking out the door with me, a possibly disgruntled ex-employee.

"I thought—" I stop to swallow the lump of anxiety now sitting thick in my throat and try to send calming thoughts to my now racing heart. "I thought Camille Hayes was supposed to be running this meeting?"

He just shrugs.

"You're really going through with this, aren't you?" I croak.

I've thought a lot of things the last few weeks since I found out about the potential sale of SER, the main one being that this whole thing was going to just blow over and Carl would come to his senses before the path he's headed down is irreversible. But with Connelly here, the situation is grave. Any chance I've had that this is going away has just fizzled with a loud and resounding pop.

If Carl is truly moving ahead with this sale, and I'm losing hope by the second he's going to change his mind, all it will take is Carl's signature and approval by the GRASCO board to make everything official. Then SER will become wholly owned by Connelly Colloway.

Fucking hell. This is really happening.

Carl nods, taking my hands in his. "Yes, Nora. I am. I've been trying to tell you that. I know you have a lot to consider, but *please* listen to what they have to say before you just say no. Okay?"

I swallow hard. It hurts on account of the lump that still sits firmly in the middle of my neck, growing bigger by the second, but now it's turned into full-blown panic.

I nod, unable to speak.

With that, Uncle Carl leads me out of my office, down the hallway, and directly into the mouth of the lion's den where I have no doubt the king of the jungle himself is lying in wait, ready to pounce the second his prey enters. It's also 100 percent clear to me who that prey is.

And it's not Uncle Carl or SER.

On the long walk down the hallway to where I will finally meet up with the past I've been trying so hard to outrun, I think I get a glimpse of what a death-row inmate feels like on that slow walk to their final minutes.

Along with pure, utter terror has to be gut-wrenching remorse that you should have done things differently so you wouldn't have ended up in this position to begin with.

I know I have remorse, regret. Bucketfuls of it. I have many things I'd redo, given the chance.

So many.

Unfortunately, I have no genie in a bottle and real life doesn't grant wishes for seconds or do-overs. You get one shot to not fuck things up beyond all repair. Too bad I've already blown mine.

Chapter 3

Nora

When Uncle Carl and I walked into the boardroom a few minutes ago and my eyes landed on Connelly, I had a hard time catching a breath. It felt as though the wind was knocked straight from my lungs.

Lord have blessed mercy.

The real-life, grown-up version of Connelly Colloway was so much more handsome than I could have ever imagined. The pictures online have done him a complete injustice. Now, I understand why he has women swarming all over him like bees to nectar.

He is sexy as hell, oozing carnal sensuality in a way he didn't before.

I've got to be honest, I may not have kept in contact with Connelly all these years, but he's never been far from my mind. It was especially hard to ignore him when his sexy, day-old scruffy GQ face was splashed all over *Forbes* magazine a couple of years ago as one of Chicago's newest, most successful and eligible bachelors, along with his other two brothers, Gray and Asher.

Connelly isn't a celebrity, but he's a hard man to escape. He's often quoted in some sort of business article. And his picture has graced the Internet more than once, often with a beautiful woman dripping like an expensive jewel from his elbow. I've never seen him with the same woman twice. Even when we were young, he had an affinity for the girls and it's clear that hasn't changed a bit. In fact, he's grown into quite the all-star player.

With our eyes locked on each other, I have to force my feet to keep their forward motion toward my seat. I have to remind my knees they aren't made of Jell-O so I don't melt into the carpet. And as I slide into my chair, the questions I've tortured myself with all these years come racing back: Did I make the right decision so long ago? Am I still making it now? I go round and round, making myself dizzy with doubt.

But I *always* end up in the same place I started.

Connelly was my first boyfriend. My first love. My first everything and I walked away from him. For good reasons then. For valid reasons now. There is no room in my complicated life for a playboy who has obvious commitment issues. *Still.* People would just end up getting hurt. I've had enough emotional agony to last ten lifetimes. I don't need to go inviting it in personally. I did that once before with him.

I used to wish my life had ended up differently. It didn't and I've long since stopped wishing. Wishing doesn't change a damn thing anyway. It keeps you frozen, tethered to yesterday's sins and broken vows. Having no choice, I've accepted my lot in life and moved ahead.

I have to say, though, in this moment, I *wish*. I wish for things I'd long stopped wishing for. I wish that I was *his*. I wish I could go back in time and make different choices. I wish he had loved me the way I loved him. The way I *still* love him, even after all this time, even after everything he did to us.

I wish.

A pointed question my way makes my wishes turn to mist, coating my skin with a slick film of faded dreams and what-ifs. Just as well. I need to move ahead with confidence and hope, not look behind with longing and regret.

"Uh, my apologies. Could you repeat that?" I glance at Carl to see a frown turn down his face. It's not at all like me to be mentally absent during a meeting, especially one as important as this one.

Well, it's important to Carl. It's just a nuisance for me. It irritates me how every other one of my colleagues in here acts like rays of sun have just been blown where it doesn't normally shine. Maybe it has. Personally, I rather like sunshine warming my skin, not burning my ass.

"Of course. I asked if you had any general questions on the proposed employment contract?" Camille Hayes asks sweetly.

Camille is a very beautiful woman. The type I've seen time and again pictured with Connelly. As I look at her, I wonder if she's been in his bed, had his lips on hers, had his talented hands bringing her to a quivering climax over and over again. The thought of it makes me irrationally jealous. Anger marches through my veins, mostly aimed at me, but that doesn't stop me from taking it out on her anyway.

"No." I snip harshly, earning me a vicious glare from Carl.

"Have you even reviewed it?" a baritone, throaty, panty-wetting voice rumbles close to my ear. Hot breath slides over me and slithers down, down, down until it lands with powerful longing at the base of my spine.

God in heaven. His voice.

It's haunted me more than I care to admit.

Carl and I were the last two to arrive at this meeting and there were only two chairs left: one across from Connelly and one conveniently next to him. Carl, the bastard, took the one right across from him, forcing me to sit next to my former love who I abandoned so long ago with a lie that burned my lips as I forced myself to speak it.

So...talk about *awkward*.

But the plus to sitting next to him is that, except for the brief moment our eyes locked when I walked into the room, I have succeeded at avoiding direct eye contact for the last thirty minutes, while he and Camille have droned on and on about how great this merger will be for both companies and our clients and how excited they are to have our exceptional talents combining to make Wynn Consulting an unstoppable force in the recruiting industry.

Blah frickin' blah.

Now I have no choice but to give him my full

attention. I will not let him intimidate me any more than he's already trying to do. His larger-than-life presence alone makes our largest conference room feel like we're sitting in a closet on top of each other.

Again with the wishes.

Turning to face him, I am stunned speechless for a moment as our gazes collide. Helpless, I'm sucked into the deep pools of his stunning hazel eyes where memories of our time together float on the greenish-brown surface. They are eyes I could never get enough of once upon a time. Eyes that still haunt my waking thoughts and torment my dreams. They are eyes I see every day.

"Yes, I've reviewed it, Mr. Colloway."

A ghost of a smile tilts his bitable—so goddamned bitable—lips. A memory slams into me: those lips wrapped around my aching nipples as he rocked into me, bringing me to a shattering climax. Even as inexperienced as we were, no man has ever felt as right inside me as he did. But then, other memories flood me like a tsunami and I have to slam the steel gates shut fast before I drown under their crushing weight.

"Then surely you have questions, Ms. Cantres." Why does the fact he used my formal name cause a twinge of hurt in my heart when I just did the same thing to him? "You review and negotiate employment contracts daily on behalf of your own clients. Certainly there's some point you want to discuss. Negotiate, perhaps?"

Yes, there is actually. How about the fact you're an arrogant asshole who thinks he can waltz in here and just buy me off like I'm in some desperate need of a job. I'm not, by the way. I'll be snatched up within a week, tops. Hell, I can even leverage his own offer to get a comparable one from someone else.

Besides, I would never negotiate the specifics of an employment contract in front of my colleagues, so I have no idea what in the hell he thinks he's doing. Asshat.

"There *is* one point I'd like to discuss, now that you bring it up," I retort, turning my body toward his.

I don't miss the slow gander of his eyes down my frame. I suddenly wish I'd worn more than a low-cut blouse and a tight pencil skirt that's hitting me midthigh. Like perhaps a full coat of armor. But I'm not even sure that would have stopped the heat of his gaze from penetrating my skin like warm, thick dark chocolate. It makes me feel hungry.

Very, *very* hungry.

For moments, I can think of nothing else but scraping my teeth over his sexy-as-sin scruff. I want to run my fingers through his short jet-black locks and use a fistful as leverage to pull him to my waiting mouth, reacquainting my tongue to the taste of his. Thoughts of him demanding everyone to leave so he can bend me over this long oak table and have his wicked way with me runs on a distracting loop.

I yearn to see for myself if he is as fit and toned underneath his tailored, no doubt custom-made, impeccable charcoal suit as it appears. The stark white of his dress shirt sets off the tanned flesh that is decorated in a light dusting of dark hair peeking through the top two buttons he's so generously left undone.

Shit, that's new.

"Go on," he cajoles with a slight wave of his hand, a smug smirk now turning one corner of his mouth. He leans back, places his elbows on the chair arms, and laces his fingers together, resting them on his abdomen. Crossing one leg over the other, he looks very much like the successful executive he is. And he knows exactly how he's affecting me.

Bastard.

Well, two can play this game and this is a game I play very, very well. I slowly uncross and recross my long, pale, toned legs. For a moment, his eyes snap to them and flare.

Gotcha.

"Do you plan to close the Cincinnati office?" I ask, trying to hold in my own smile at the small victory I feel.

He looks a little surprised at my question before responding, "There are no immediate plans for office consolidation, no."

I think about his answer for a minute, contemplating my options. If that's true, then maybe there's a sliver of hope I can make this work. I could live here, working for his company and further my career until I can find a better position at a competitor. At least then we wouldn't have to be in the same building. Maybe I'd just have to see him at the occasional holiday party. I could probably make that work and still manage to keep my private life private.

Yes, this may be a solution.

"Then I don't understand the requirement to relocate to Chicago. If you don't plan to close the office, I could continue to work from here instead of having to uproot my life, leaving my home and my...*friends*."

I don't miss the flare of his nostrils at the mention of the word "friends." A bigger part of me than I want to admit revels in the idea he's jealous a man may be in my life. I also didn't miss the glance at my left ring finger when I walked through the door earlier. He's so glaringly overt it's almost laughable.

"I require all of my executives to be located at headquarters, which is in Chicago. It's a lovely city." He starts casually swinging his foot back and forth, intimating he's already bored with this conversation. I don't miss the fact that his black, shiny loafers probably cost more than I make in a month.

My eyes find his again and I let my lips tilt in victory. "Well, that's solved then. I'm not an executive. I'm just a recruiter."

At this juncture, I *should* be leaning slightly forward, but not too much that I seem aggressive. I *should* have my arms draped over the lifts of my chair, not closed in front of me. My face *should* be just warm enough so that I appear open and agreeable.

I *should* be, but I'm not. I'm not agreeable and I'm not open. Instead, I lean back in my chair and cross my arms. It pisses me off he's reduced me to acting like a petulant child. Crossing your arms makes you seem defensive and closed off, but I can't help the instinctive need to protect every part of myself from his hot, knowing stare.

When he speaks, his tone has a clear bite he doesn't even try to mask. "Is *that* the issue, Ms. Cantres? Were you hoping for a promotion out of the acquisition? I thought we made a very generous financial offer."

My face flames with embarrassment as my mouth drops open.

What the ever fuck? How *dare* he!

I'm rendered speechless for all of two seconds before my temper fires red hot, courtesy of my matching hair and half-Irish heritage as my mother used to say. "Why you—"

"Connelly, maybe it's a provision we could take offline and revisit." Good ol' Camille Hayes, who probably has a damn PhD in psychology, saves the day, interrupting what would have been a career-ending sentence. For a top recruiter who's known to keep her cool under pressure, I am unraveling at the seams within a span of two dozen words from this infuriating man—a man who has changed more than I could ever have imagined.

His playful attitude has been completely transplanted by cool and aloof.

And am I just making shit up or did she sound a little too familiar with him when she said his name? If possible, my anger spikes even more.

"No." He doesn't even look at her when his harsh response slices the air like a bullwhip. "*That* particular term is nonnegotiable." His gaze pins me down, daring me to argue.

I want to. Jesus, do I want to lay into him hard and bruising. But I don't. I can't or else I will explode and I may very well ruin this entire acquisition.

Say...that's an idea.

But even as I think it, I look over at Carl who knows right where my devious mind is going. I don't miss his quiet pleading not to screw this up for him. That deflates my fight, so I take a deep, cleansing breath and turn away from Connelly in silence, facing the table again without another word.

The room falls still for a few tense moments before Camille breaks it by asking the same question to Rob, our marketing VP. He answers immediately, asking a question about finding elderly care assistance for his ill mother, who he would have to leave behind if he decides to accept Wynn's offer.

For not the first time, I can't help the resentment that bubbles at Uncle Carl for putting everyone in this position. Surely he doesn't need the money, so that makes me wonder what's behind this sale.

The next twenty minutes tick by painfully slow. Every minute seems like ten. My eyes flick to the clock and just thirty-two seconds have passed since the last time I looked. At least I made it longer than the twenty-one seconds that mocked me before.

I fidget, leaning to the left so I can escape the

heat of Connelly's arm. The smooth bastard has shifted in his chair, scooting it closer to mine. Being this close to him makes my blood boil with need I haven't felt in years. It's just another poke to ratchet up my ire at this whole fucked-up situation I can't believe I've found myself immersed in.

When I heard Connelly had taken over as the CEO of Wynn Consulting a couple of years ago, I knew it was only a matter of time before we ran into each other. Recruiting is a small world, executive recruiting even smaller. For the last two years I've tried to keep my head down and my private life even more private, but my luck has run dry. Not that the well was deep to begin with. Lady luck seems to fuck me at every opportunity she's given for some unknown reason.

The scrape of chairs and seated forms rising signal the meeting has adjourned. Thank God...I can make my escape. But of course, Mr. I'm-an-all-powerful-executive-and-irresistible-sex-god won't make it that easy. Just as I reach the door, I hear a dark voice call, "Ms. Cantres, a moment alone, please."

I stop in my tracks and sigh deeply, dropping my head as everyone else files out past me. Brad, our chief operations officer, lightly clamps my shoulder as he passes. I flash him a tight smile I know doesn't reach my eyes.

"You okay?" Carl asks. He stops beside me, concern pinching his thick graying brows.

"Yes, fine," I whisper.

Throwing a glance over his shoulder at

Connelly, he gives me a quick smile and a squeeze of my hand before closing the door when he exits, leaving me alone with this man for the first time in more than ten years. I'm both terrified and thrilled.

With my back to Connelly, I try to regain my cool, to fortify my resolve against what I know will be a merciless assault.

My wishes rush back, except this time, I wish I could stop the memories pelting me like heavy rain soaking into my thirsty pores. They'd been hidden in the shadows of my mind, fading, but crashed front and center with a reverberating, ear-piercing boom when I laid eyes on him an hour ago. The ricochet is now whisper soft, but I'll hear it until my dying breath.

Then I feel him behind me. I'm unable to stop my eyes from falling shut as the warmth of his solid, masculine perfection cloaks my entire body. I'm *barely* able to suppress a moan when hot breath tickles my ear, making me shiver with desire. The low voice that follows is seduction. Sin. Pure temptation.

It's trouble.

And it will take me down.

"It's good to see you, Nora."

Chapter 4

CONN

Jesus fucking Christ. When Nora walked into the conference room, I was stupefied. Struck dumber than an ox.

She is absolutely breathtaking. Has grown from a beautiful teenager into a drop-dead gorgeous goddess of sex and lust. Her one-of-a-kind red hair now has golden highlights woven throughout. When we were in high school, she kept it shoulder length. Now it runs down her back in soft, flowing waves. I can't help imagining what it would feel like underneath my palms as I used it as leverage when driving into her from behind, making her sob my name as she unravels all around my cock.

Her pale skin contrasts harshly against her piercing green eyes, which sparkle like emeralds framed by thick, inky lashes so long they almost reach her dainty eyebrows. She's curvy in all the right places, but I would venture to guess she doesn't like them, as most women with curves don't.

I don't understand that. A woman is supposed

to look different from a man. She should have flared hips, thighs that touch at the juncture of her womanhood, and an ass you can hang on to when you're pulling her closer to sink your cock deeper into her snugness. I like women of all shapes and sizes and am an equal opportunity kinda guy, but my preference is what's hidden underneath Nora's professional, but hot-as-sin attire.

When she sat next to me, I wasn't sure if I was relieved or pissed that Carl sat across from me, forcing her to take the one remaining chair. Her inebriating scent, a heady combination of vanilla and honeysuckle and Nora, has filled my lungs with every breath. I had to stop myself several times from closing my eyes from the celestial pleasure as my blood carried it through my veins, nourishing parts of me I didn't know were emaciated.

But I had also looked forward to visually soaking in everything old and new about Nora during the meeting, even though I could tell within two seconds of walking through the door that she would do everything she could to avoid me, just as she has all this time.

Wasn't wrong about that. Her body language is like a bullhorn shouting, "back the fuck off or you may end up tasting your balls in a way you never thought possible." Too bad for Nora I'm kind of hard of hearing when it comes to things I don't want to accept. She should know that better than anyone.

I didn't know how I would feel after seeing her again for so long, but *fuck*...it is not what I wanted.

I wanted to hate her.

I wanted to crush her.

I wanted to tie her to me like she did me to her so long ago, then cut her loose so her broken pieces would scatter helplessly to the wind like mine did. I don't *want* to want her. I don't *want* to imagine keeping her forever as if she's the ultimate prize I've been striving for my entire life. But I fucking do. And she is. And with just one glimpse of her, I already know I'm not strong enough to walk away.

My heart is chained to hers. If I'm honest with myself, it always has been.

I realize now that I've craved this woman on a conscious and subconscious level for eleven long, lonely years. I haven't wanted to, but I have nonetheless. And I know this craving I have for her is so unstoppable, uncontainable, and uncontrollable I just need to take take take. I need to ravage, pillage, and tear her apart from the inside out so I can put her back together again, fitting her jagged pieces perfectly to mine. I need to make her crave me on the same biological level as I do her.

My brother Luke's words from many months ago come rushing back with crystal-clear clarity. At the time, I thought my younger brother was full of shit, thinking with his dick because he'd found his one and only. But now, I understand what he meant.

"Finding that elusive woman who will plug holes you didn't know you had in ways you can't possibly comprehend is fucking priceless. And I guarantee

when you find her, you'd give up every last thing you own to make her yours."

Prolific words spoken right there.

I want Nora. Correction...*need*. Crave. I hunger and thirst for her. And she will be mine, no matter the price. I would do any-fucking-thing to have her. I would sell my soul to the very devil himself right here, right now if it guaranteed she'd agree to be mine, and I wouldn't bat a single eyelash. Spending eternity in the fiery pits of hell and brimstone is a small price to pay if I could spend the next sixty years with her by my side.

This time, I'm not going to walk away so easy.

I made that mistake before. I will not do it again.

"Take a seat," I say quietly. I think we've been standing here for a solid five minutes, neither of us moving a muscle. The only sounds in the room are the muffled ones of chatter on the other side of the closed door and our slightly labored breathing. Regardless of what she wants me to believe, she is as affected by me as I am by her. Yet she'll go to her death fighting it for some damn reason. It makes me wonder what else she's kept from me.

When I step back, giving her room to move, she avoids eye contact and walks to the opposite side of the table but doesn't sit. Instead, she grabs ahold of the back of the rolling office chair, her grip so hard her knuckles turn white. I take a seat in my original chair, crossing my legs to hide my straining erection. For good measure, I place my folded hands on my lap after gesturing to the seat once more.

"No, thank you. I'll stand."

I smirk. I swear Nora's heels have ten-inch spikes embedded in them. When she unleashes them, she digs them in so damn far it's near impossible to get her to budge. With great effort, I managed once before. Now, it will be no different, except I'm older, savvier, and a helluva lot more experienced.

Patience trumps pigheadedness.

Every.

Single.

Time.

And I've got a motherfucking truckload of it.

"What's the *real* reason you don't want to move to Chicago?"

Regardless of what she tried to make me think earlier, her last name is still Cantres and I see no diamond circling her wedding finger. That makes her fair game in my book.

"What are you doing, Connelly?"

"Answering a question with a question. How very Nora-like."

"You don't know anything about me anymore."

Her eyes burn, reminding me of hot coals. God, I have fucking missed her and how she used to challenge me at every turn. No woman has ever made me work more for her affections than Nora did. It was one of the things that made me fall hard and fast for her. She didn't roll over to my demands. She didn't fawn all over me like the other girls in my school. I actually had to *work* to be friends with her. She did her level best to stay away from me, but I wore her down once.

And I'll do it again.

"I know you better than you know yourself. Better than anyone, princess."

"Don't call me that." Her voice is hard and clipped.

"I seem to remember you used to love it," I deadpan.

I let the corner of my mouth turn up as I study her. Do I want to know why she dumped me? "Claimed" there was someone else just a few weeks after she left Detroit? Do I want to know why she refused my phone calls? Never returned an e-mail or letter?

She told me she was mine.

She told me she was born for me.

She told me she would marry me someday.

Then she threw me away like week-old rotting trash smelling up the garage.

So, *fuck yes*, I want to know. I want to know it all.

Then you'll have some confessions of your own, I remind myself.

My stomach flips at that thought, knowing there are things I need to tell her I don't know how to say. We have a lot to talk about, probably a lot to confess, but we'll get there in due time. At the moment, I need to focus on convincing her to accept the job at Wynn so I can move her near me and begin phase two of my plan.

We have a silent stare-off until she breaks eye contact, looking down at the table. Sighing heavily, her gaze sweeps back up. When she speaks, her voice is soft, almost defeated. I feel a twinge of remorse, but not enough to make me stop my pursuit of her. "Why are you doing this?"

"I'm not sure I understand the question."

Her back straightens and it looks as if I've brought out the rattler in her. "Well, let me see if I can paint this crystal clear for you, *Mr.* Colloway," she bites with venom. *Yep, her tail's shaking. Hard.* "Why are you buying my uncle's company? Why are you offering me a job that will pay me twice what I'm making today when you surely have enough talented recruiters in your own firm? Why are *you* here today, when you could have sent Camille by herself to work out the details of employment contracts? And why are you here *at all* before the acquisition is even closed? It's not a done deal yet."

I ignore her questions, asking one of my own.

"He's not really your uncle. Why did you never tell me that?"

"Jesus!" she yells, her hands flailing before falling to her sides. "That's beside the point." Her forehead creases. "And how do you know that anyway?"

Nora and I officially dated for all of two months before she moved. I'd met her parents, of course, but I'd only met her "Uncle Carl" for a brief few seconds at her high school graduation party. I never knew him by anything else other than her uncle or bothered to pay attention to his last name, if she even told me. Not many teenagers are interested in their own extended families, let alone that of their girlfriend.

So when I met Carl Steele for the first time, he

looked familiar but I couldn't place him. I thought nothing more of it until I had dinner with a business colleague and long-time friend Samuel Makey when I was in Louisville for a leadership conference in late April. Sam's the VP of human resources at Regency Commerce, a medium-sized real estate company we've been trying to land for the last year. He's also a friend of Carl's.

And guess who I've been trying to steal them from?

In an innocent conversation over prime rib and single-malt Scotch almost four months ago now, Sam unknowingly turned over every single card I needed to win this poker match. I have a true royal flush, and for you nonpoker players, nothing beats that, baby.

"I'm thorough in my homework, Nora. *Very* thorough."

Her face blanches. Tendrils of secrets float in her jeweled eyes. I want to latch on to each one, pulling them from the abyss. I need to learn each and every one she's hiding from me because it couldn't be clearer there are many.

"Is this a game to you?" she says bitterly, her forehead wrinkling in anger.

I narrowly avoid laughing, but I can't hide my smile. I'm relaxed and calm and I can tell my casual demeanor just fuels her raging fire. "I don't play games, Nora." I do, but *this* isn't a fucking game. Not by a long shot.

"Don't pretend for a minute that's not what you're doing, Connelly. You're taking your bruised high school ego out on me by using your power and money to control the situation without any regard for the consequences."

Remorse flashes in her eyes before it's gone, replaced again by her fiery ire. I loved that about Nora back in the day. She would get worked up at the drop of a hat and I was always cool, calm, and collected.

At least that's how I appeared on the *outside*. Inside, it's a different story. I just don't show it. I want to control everything and I've become very, *very* adept at getting what I want while leading people to believe the outcome is irrelevant to me. I lure them in with my indifference, then go in for the easy kill. But right now, I'm a coiled snake, ready to strike, because her comment just pissed me. The fuck. Off.

She is the one who dumped *me*.

"I think *your* ego is a little self-inflated, doll. This is a business decision, plain and simple." It's not, but there's no way in hell I'm tipping my hand just yet.

Her teeth clamp together. "Arrogant and cocky as ever, I see?"

"Some of my best strengths," I retort snidely. The anger and bitterness that beg to be unleashed smolder just beneath the surface. I work to contain them. Blowing up right now would be akin to throwing water on a grease fire, and I need to control this thing arching between us at a slow simmer until I'm ready to turn it up to a raging boil.

"Traits you probably hate in your kids, I bet."

She's fishing. I smirk but remain stoic and silent. She looks away at being caught.

"I'm not taking the offer."

"You will," I state plainly. Yes, I'm *that* confident. Extending employment positions for the five executives we met with earlier was Carl Steele's requirement in this acquisition. In case you haven't figured it out yet, *Nora* is mine. And I won't lose her—or this deal.

"You're un-fucking-believable."

"Nora, Nora," I say, tsking. "That's not very professional."

"Funny, I thought this was entirely personal."

It is. "Not *entirely*."

Standing there with her mouth agape for a few moments, I can tell she's trying to decide what to do next. Back in the day, when we'd get into an argument, she'd stomp out of the room. I wonder if that's how she still reacts when she's so mad she can't speak.

I watch with pure enjoyment as she heads for the door. Same tenacity, same short fuse, same Nora, only more lovely and definitely all woman now. My words halt her and I suppress another smile. "I expect your signed employment agreement on my desk within twenty-four hours."

Shaking her head, she pivots slowly back around. Her emeralds blaze like the pits of hell. Hot and furious. I try to discreetly adjust my hard-on. I cannot believe how much her fierce spirit still turns me on. "That will *never* happen."

I stand and walk to her until we're a half foot apart. At six two, I'm not that much taller than Nora's five-foot-seven frame right now, what with her three- or four-inch heels bringing her nicely in line with my mouth. A mouth I want to swoop down, poach, and possess.

"Never say never, princess," I tell her softly, using the endearment I had for her long ago.

She tips her head up glaring at me in defiance, her jaw set in a hard, insolent line. "Never is the only word that applies in this particular situation."

"What can I do to change your mind?" I don't like the pleading tone I hear in my own voice. I know Nora doesn't miss it when her demeanor softens slightly.

"Why me, Connelly? You can have any recruiter here. Why me?"

There are so many answers to that question.

It's always been you.

I didn't realize how dead inside I've been without you until today.

I won't be satisfied until I possess every last shred of you, until your very breath is mine and mine is yours.

Instead, I lean forward and let my lips brush the shell of her ear when I rasp, "I don't think you're ready to hear the *real* answer to that question yet, Nora."

When her breath hitches, a memory slams into me: her making that same noise the first time I entered her. Christ, I am a masochist. Being this close to her without my lips or my hands on her is sheer torture. Her smell is driving me bat-fucking-mad. Existing in a hush, the heat of our bodies blending into the other's, we're both suspended in the past.

Remembering.

Wanting.

Aching.

The tenderness of the moment makes me want to wrap her in my arms and carry her to the closest bed so I can spend hours reminding her how good we were together. With great effort, I pull myself out of the clutches of the past and back to the task at hand.

"I think you should talk to Carl before making your final decision," I tell her quietly, pulling back just enough to grab her eyes again with mine. They're wild with want, her cheeks tinged ruddy pink with desire. Just looking at her steals my breath like it always used to.

The warmth of the moment ices over when her feisty comes roaring back with resounding force. "I already have," she spouts tersely. Goddamn her stubborn ass.

"Do it again, Nora."

"Stop this, Connelly," she beseeches. "It's not too late. Just walk away from the deal. Please."

Jesus, her begging just about undoes me, but I want this too badly. I want *her* too much and while this is a good business decision for Wynn and GRASCO, I also know it's the only way I'm going to get close enough to make her mine again.

"Can't do that, sweetheart."

"Can't or won't?"

"Irrelevant."

She stands there, stony. Angry. Pissed as fucking hell. But she's also as turned on as I am. I spent months studying her, learning her telltale signs. And those are signs I will never forget. There are so many things I've never forgotten about her and basking in her presence again soothes my soul like nothing else I've known. Jesus, I have missed her.

"Am I free to leave now or are you going to block the exit again?"

"I never blocked the exit, Nora. You've always had free will here."

"Hmm. I wonder why it doesn't feel like it then." Her jaw ticks in anger. That twinge of remorse returns, because she's right. I've made her a generous offer, yet I've also taken away her choices. She may not quite realize that yet, though she will all too soon. I can only imagine how she'll react when she finds out the corner I've backed her into.

I move to the side, letting her pass. As she skirts by her arm brushes mine leaving her energy behind on my skin. It penetrates through my suit jacket and dress shirt and now crackles on my forearm. I want more of it. I want it blanketing every inch of my naked flesh. I want her energy tied to mine so we ache without the other.

With a huff, she yanks open the door and leaves without another word or a look back, the heavy oak automatically closing behind her. The soft sound of the latch clicking resonates in the now-deserted space.

I blow out a long, frustrated breath. I knew this would be a challenge. Everything with Nora always was. I realize from her perspective I'm waltzing in here trying to scoop up a life she's built and rearrange it, but I get the distinct impression she doesn't have the whole story either.

Her "uncle" came to me first. *He* pursued this merger initially. I'll admit I became aggressive about making the merger happen after I found out his connection with Nora. But that was after the fact. Carl Steele has gotten cold feet a couple of times, but that's to be expected. He's selling his blood, sweat, and tears and regardless of the circumstances, it's hard for any successful man or woman to sell their legacy. I also happen to know why he's being forced to sell. A fact I'm betting Nora's not privy to.

All of that is irrelevant, though, as I told her. After seeing Nora again, I would just as soon set myself on fire than willingly walk away from her.

She belongs with me.

She always has.

She always will.

Now I just need to make her see that.

Chapter 5

Nora

"Hi. I'm Connelly."

I slide my eyes to the god-like basketball stud who just glided into the open spot next to me like it was reserved for him. He's tall and filled out for a junior. The light facial hair he's sporting makes him look as if he belongs on a college campus instead. I'm surprised to see he's far more graceful than I ever thought someone of that height could be, but I shouldn't be. I've seen him on the court. He's like liquid nitrogen. Fluid, steamy, and definitely dangerous to the touch.

Connelly Colloway is sinfully handsome. He's a talented athlete. Smart, I hear. Aaaand he has a quite a reputation with the ladies, of which I will not be one. The last thing I need is to get involved with a boy who's probably had his dick wet by most of the girls here. I have grand plans for my life, one of which doesn't include getting an STD.

I shudder.

Nope. He needs to go. He's temptation sent by Lucifer and his intent is very clear. Drag me down into his dark den of depravity with him. Well, Lucifer, consider this mission a fail, because he's a sinful lure I will not fall victim to.

"Yes, I know." *I turn my attention back to my peanut butter-and-jelly sandwich. Childish, maybe, but I don't think you're ever too old to enjoy one of your favorite food groups. Fat and sugar. Yum.*

"You know, you'll have to stop eating those once you're my girlfriend."

I guess his ego is right up there with his womanizing. He doesn't seem to get the subtle hint I'm not interested. I laugh and swivel back toward him. "Wow, I'm not sure where to start with that comment."

Looking at him up close and personal is definitely a mistake. A big, fat, mother of all mistakes I wish I could undo. His smile is disarming. I mean, completely mind erasing. I'm disgusted by the tingle it sends to the dark, unbreeched area between my legs.

"I'm allergic to peanuts, you see." *He nods toward the delicious goodness I hold in my hands. Skippy and Smucker's grape jelly slathered between two pieces of the softest white bread man can buy.*

"I'm sorry for you, but I don't see how that's my problem."

He leans over close to my ear as if he has a secret to tell and doesn't want anyone else to overhear. "It's your problem, Nora, because if even so much as a fragment of a peanut touches my tongue, my throat closes and I can't get enough air to stay alive. And that would certainly kill the moment."

"What moment is that?" *I hear myself stupidly*

ask, enjoying the way my name sounded rolling off his tongue waaay too much, along with the fact he even knew my name in the first place. He hasn't moved back, even a fraction of an inch. When I feel his nose nudge the delicate skin underneath my ear, I shiver and close my eyes, forgetting we're in a lunchroom full of gossipmongers. That, and I'm the new girl in school with the hot class president and basketball team captain whispering sweet nothings in my ear and looking at me as if he wants to eat me for lunch instead of the burger in front of him. I'm pretty sure I just made an entire school full of enemies—all female—with claws that will be razor sharp by next period.

Fabulous. Three weeks into my new high school and I'll already be ostracized because someone I have no interest in won't take no for an answer. Well...maybe I have a little interest, but I certainly won't act on it. Connelly Colloway is a life-altering bad mistake.

"Our first kiss, of course," he breathes. The confident words dance on my skin, enticingly, making me feel every bit of the schoolgirl that I am. I immediately envision his lips on mine. Would they be as pillow soft as they look? Would he be gentle or demanding? Would the first touch of his tongue on mine bind our souls together forever as I fear it could? Well...it could mine. Doubtful this playboy has the ability to bind anything except maybe his dick. At least I hope he wraps it up. Not that I care because it will never get close enough to me to matter.

When he pulls back, the whites of his teeth blind

the rest of my common sense into the far recesses of my mind and, wow, suddenly I don't remember why it would be a bad idea to like this guy.

"Hey asshole, you beat me to her," a throaty voice says on the other side of me. Connelly and I hold our heated stare longer than appropriate, but he breaks it to look over my shoulder at our intruder before I'm ready to let it go.

"Yep, so you can piss off, Alan."

"Like fuck. Hi, I'm Alan Johansen. Star center and all around good guy. And I don't have near the reputation of this one, so your virtue is safe with me." He gestures with his chin to Connelly and a wink to me.

I don't believe for a nanosecond my virtue is safe with either one of these stunning, egotistical men.

"Wow. It's starting to stink in here with the shit that just poured out of your mouth. Bet it tastes bad, too,," Connelly jibes, but there is a definite bite to his tone. It sounds a lot like jealousy. I find myself wondering why that makes my skin heat.

I recognize the guy to my right as one of Connelly's teammates. He's handsome, no doubt, and seems just as cocky and self-assured as the one to my left. Though I know they aren't brothers, with their dark hair, same height, and same build, they sure could be, except for the unique, startling hazel eyes God blessed Connelly Colloway with.

As I sit between these two vying for my attention as if I'm the last female on earth—or fresh meat—I feel a magnetic pull toward Connelly like I have with no one else before. I know I could easily fall head over heels for him if I let myself. Which I can't. He's a heartbreaker, that one.

I spend the next ten minutes trying to dodge pass after pass being tossed at me faster than a Harlem Globetrotter before I excuse myself and spend the rest of my lunch break out on the grassy lawn, bundled in a jacket to shield myself against the cool spring wind. I may be cold, but at least my thoughts aren't clouded with testosterone and something I'm not all that familiar with...acute longing.

With a glass of Merlot in my hand, I sit quietly on my patio and reminisce in the darkness of night. I've been an absolute wreck since this afternoon. All the love I have felt for Connelly still lies right underneath my thin skin just waiting for it to be split open so it can bleed, finally running free. I was able to keep it locked down, dormant...until I walked into that conference room today and saw his arrogant ass sitting there.

Now, against my will, all those latent feelings wash like tidal waves through my heart and I let loose the tears I've been holding back all day. His smoldering eyes were full of hurt, anger, and lust. But it was the longing I witnessed that almost broke me.

When I first met Connelly, he appeared to be the classic cliché I despised. Cocky and full of nothing but himself and silky smooth lines. The kind of guy who worked and worked until he got into your pants, but once he did...bam. You were now just another tally in the "win" column that he and his buddies would brag about.

After that day in the cafeteria, I avoided his relentless pursuit. For months I was successful. The thing was, though...I wanted to be around him. I crushed on him. Big. Time. Arrogant or not, he was still the guy every single girl in school wanted to snag so they could hang pictures of him in their locker and walk down the hall between classes hand in hand. Maybe even sneak off behind school to make out whenever they could. They wanted the right to call him "my boyfriend."

And why wouldn't they? In addition to being gifted athletically, he was wickedly handsome and had a magnetic personality. Everyone—eventually including me—was helpless to its pull. He was witty. A leader in every single way. Intelligent and undyingly loyal to his friends, his team, his family. His smile was infectious. His deep laugh carried down the hall, making everyone smile when they heard it.

He was the classic overachiever you wanted to hate, but he made it impossible. Teachers, coaches, and students alike loved him, revered him even. I never heard a bad word spoken about Connelly Colloway, even by the girls he left behind like a trail of crumbs. He was genuine, big-hearted, and just plain likeable. He might as well have had a halo circling his head and a monument resurrected in his honor. That's how loved he was. Hell, who knows? I haven't been back to Dowling High since I graduated, so maybe one sits outside on the grassy lawn right now.

So while all of this was undeniably attractive and I wanted to be friends, I didn't think I could just be friends, so it was best to keep my distance.

Besides, we both had plans. Lives to live elsewhere. He had a basketball scholarship to UCLA and I was attending Dartmouth. But the biggest reason was I knew in my heart of hearts what I was feeling for Connelly was no high school crush. He was the type of man who would kiss your soul leaving behind an invisible imprint, forever marking you. A forever love you'd be helpless against. We would be a country apart and I didn't want to fall in love with him just to have to leave him after graduation.

But what I had with Connelly was undeniable—inevitable, really—from the very moment he whispered his cocky, confident declaration in my ear at lunch that day. In our senior year, Connelly turned his pursuit of me into a full-time job. Our attraction grew and thickened until it couldn't be contained anymore. I finally caved. Or he wore me down, more likely. We started out as friends. And a few months into our "friendship," my resolve crumbled some more.

I let him kiss me.

That was the beginning of the end for me. Once his lips touched mine, I knew we could never go back to anything before that. I knew I never wanted to.

Then it happened. A mere two months after that life-changing first kiss, my brilliant father accepted an Endowed Chair position at Johns Hopkins University and we had to move. Again. So in a decision I would soon come to regret, I gave not only my virginity but my very spirit to Connelly in one night of passion that I've yet to match.

If only I knew then what I would find out just weeks later. That Connelly wasn't the person I thought he was. That he was every bit the player everyone said he was. That he didn't deserve my trust, my love, or my heart.

Or that his selfish actions would lead to my own moral demise.

As our gazes greedily drank each other in today, guilt and hurt ate me up from the inside. My stomach now feels like someone opened my throat and poured undiluted acid inside it. For the millionth time, I'm wondering if I haven't made the biggest mistake of my life by shutting him out so long ago when maybe I should have talked to him instead.

That terrifies me more than anything, because after seeing that longing in his face, I fear the answer may be yes. I think I fucked up royally. I can't go back and undo it and I can't come clean now. It's too late. Too much water is under our bridge. He made mistakes, yes, but so did I. I have betrayed him in the absolute worst possible way. With each passing year, it becomes more and more apparent.

I hate myself for it.

But I'm trapped. Chained to my lies with no hope of escape. Gasping for air that won't come because it's all been sucked out by my dishonesty and treachery. My carefully constructed world made up of noble intentions and reinforced with layers of evasion and excuses is rapidly crumbling around me, the structure sinking under the weight of my own selfish duplicity.

Lies.

Secrets.

Betrayals.

If you invite them in, they have a way of winding their poisonous tentacles through every word, every action, every part of your life until you start to mistake their deception for truth. It's amazing, really, how much we can convince ourselves into believing the altruism of our own lies.

But lies are lies, secrets destroy, and betrayal can cost you everything. Connelly may have betrayed me, but anyone on the outside looking in would say my betrayal is far worse. They'd be right.

If Connelly finds out the secret I'm harboring, it will destroy him and in turn, he will destroy me. My entire life. And I wouldn't blame him. What I've done is simply unforgivable. I can make every excuse under the sun for my actions, but deep down I know they have been self-serving and not at all altruistic, as I've pretended.

I rub my chest, trying to ease the pain and sorrow I feel sitting heavily there. I let sadness wash down my face, unchecked. And I allow myself a few more moments to enjoy the memories before I tuck them away again.

Then I strengthen myself for what needs to be done. As much as my entire being has missed

Connelly, like an essential part of my body has been removed and I still feel that phantom pain, it's too messy to have him in my life. Which is why I have to say no to this once-in-a-lifetime opportunity. Regardless of what Connelly thinks, I will not be accepting his offer. I can't. As with so many years ago, I am once again steadfast in my decision to turn Connelly down.

But this time, I can't waver. This time, I can't let his subtle seduction tactics, sweet-talking promises, or arm-twisting dominance sway my resolve. Because if I do, I stand to lose the one thing I have left that really matters to me.

And I will never let that happen.

Chapter 6

Nora

"Mr. Trammal—"

"Bill, Nora. Remember?"

I clear my throat, glad we're having this conversation by phone instead of in person so at least I'm not forced to hide my facial expressions at his lame seduction attempts. "Bill, yes, of course. How are you today, *Bill*?"

"Extremely busy, but I always have time for you, Nora."

Bill Trammal is the thirty-three-year-old brilliant, and I mean *brilliant* CEO of Project R&R, a company that develops bioconductor software for analysis and comprehension of genomic data generated by wet lab experiments in molecular biology. Now...ask me if I have a clue what that means. If I did, I would have followed my father into medical research instead of Carl's footsteps into human resources. As luck would have it, I don't have to understand the ins and outs of genomic data and software coding to find the right chief financial officer for his company.

He's also made it clear he'd like more than a professional relationship. I've made it clear I don't. Bill is handsome in a nerdy sort of way, I guess—if you look long enough at him and he's in the just right light and you place your beer goggles firmly around your eyes. But he's just not my type. Not many men are.

Because you compare them all to Connelly. You always have. It's not fair for mere mortal men to have to live up to demigod status.

"Well, I won't take up too much of your time. I talked to Mark Longley about your offer and he has a daughter with some special needs."

"I'm sorry to hear that. Does that mean he's turning down the offer, Nora?"

"No. But he does have some stipulations. Unfortunately, his fifteen-year-old daughter has cerebral palsy and they'll need some modifications to any new home they purchase in the Columbus area. Home modifications are not generally a covered benefit by insurance companies, so he's asking for a stipend of twenty-five thousand dollars to cover the costs."

For the next few minutes, we talk about the requirements of his CFO candidate and I try to keep my thoughts on business instead of drifting to Connelly and the way that suit hugged the outline of his erection so damn perfectly. It was thick and long and I swear I saw it twitch once. He did a miserable job trying to hide it when he sat haughtily in that chair. My core tingles as I remember how I slipped my vibrator inside last night wishing it was him pulsing against my walls instead of silicone powered by four AA batteries.

After Bill goes silent again, I make a suggestion. "What if you counteroffered, upping it just to put him at ease? He would know you're serious about working for Project R&R and you'd get the candidate you want."

Bill Trammal may be a brilliant man, very book smart, but this should have been sewn up weeks ago. Getting him to make any sort of decision on this position is like pulling teeth from a chicken.

"Yes, yes. That's not a bad idea, Nora."

I barely stop myself from sighing. The constant tacking on of my name at the end of each sentence has grown irritating, like nails on a chalkboard over and over and over again.

I hear a noise and look up to see Uncle Carl peeking his head in my doorway. I wave him in, knowing I'm just about done with *Bill* here, but putting my finger to my lips so he knows to be quiet as I'm on speakerphone. He soundlessly slides into the seat across from me.

"I would also suggest adding a clause to reimburse him after he's incurred the expense and we can add an extra condition that he has to reimburse Project R&R if he voluntarily terminates employment or is let go due to performance issues within a two-year period of time."

Silence. Carl and I exchange glances and I roll my eyes while he smiles. He knows how challenging Bill Trammal has been.

"He is still the candidate you want for your CFO position, correct, Bill?"

"Yes, of course, Nora."

"Then I assume I can discuss your counteroffer with Mr. Longley?"

"Yes, yes, of course. Great ideas, as usual, Nora."

"Okay then. I'll talk to him and circle back around with you soon."

I punch the speakerphone lightning fast, disconnecting the call to avoid Bill asking me out. Again. It never fails. Carl's laughing before my finger leaves the button.

"Good reflexes."

"I've been practicing."

"It's paying off."

"Thanks," I reply with a big grin. I grab the yellow folder from the edge of my desk, making assumptions as to why Carl is here. "Did you want an update about the Gemini position?"

"No, actually. I was wondering how your *private* meeting went with Colloway yesterday?" he asks tentatively.

I settle into my chair and shut the file in front of me. I didn't have a chance to talk to Carl again, as "instructed" by Connelly because...well, because I chose not to. I already knew I wouldn't be taking the job, no matter how much goading he does.

"It was fine."

"Fine? Just...*fine*?" His forehead wrinkles as his bushy brows furrow.

"Yes. Just fine."

He regards me before speaking again. "He told me this morning you turned down the offer again."

"Carl, we've talked about this."

He looks at me sternly, putting on his best pseudo father face. "I want you to take the offer, sweet girl. If not for yourself, I want you to do it for me."

That's a low blow. He knows I'd do anything for him. I just...I can't do *that* and I can't tell him why. I know he thinks I'm just being stubborn, but I'm not. I'm protecting myself and the little I have left in this world I love.

"I can't, Carl," I say softly.

"Mira's there. You can spend more time with her. Get to know your sister better."

Mira is my *half* sister, my father's daughter from his first marriage. She's three years older than me, single, lives in Chicago, and is very successful and downright beautiful, both inside and out.

Mira and I were never close. In fact, I'd only seen her a handful of times growing up, because if my father didn't have enough time for his current family, he certainly didn't have time for his former one. We reconnected at our father's funeral a few years ago.

"I don't have to *live* there to get to know her better. We've talked a lot on the phone lately."

My gaze flits to the silver picture frame sitting on my maple desk. Carl's eyes follow and his mouth turns down. That picture was taken just days after we moved to Baltimore all those years ago. It was taken just before everything in my life changed.

Sighing heavily, he stands and paces, rubbing the silvery strands on his head. "Nora, there's a one-year noncompete clause in the sale agreement that I've agreed to for all directors and above. It specifically includes you, too."

My blood runs cold as my brain tries to catch

up to what he just told me. "What?" I choke, not believing my ears. "Why in the hell would you agree to that?"

"I didn't have a choice, Nora! I tried to leave you out of it, but Colloway wouldn't agree. He can't have half the staff quitting on him after the sale. One of the reasons he's buying this business is because of the talent I've been able to secure. Regardless of what he says, it's hurting Wynn and you're our best recruiter. Our business has tripled within the last twenty-four months, and most of it's because of you."

I scoff. "You're being ridiculous. That's not true."

"Nora, it is, and you know it."

"It will never hold up in a court of law. We each have to give our signatory for that type of stipulation." I'm grasping at strings that are quickly unraveling but I don't have any other choice. I *cannot* work for Connelly.

"I assure you, it will hold up. And even if it doesn't, you'll spend more than a year going through the legal system. *Jesus*, I'm trying to secure your future here. Why are you fighting me on this?" he huffs in frustration.

"By handcuffing me? You know that means I can't get another recruiting job for one year. What the hell am I supposed to do in the meantime for income?" It's not like I'm poor with no money in savings, but I can't afford to be without a job for an entire year until the clause expires either. Goddamn him.

He stops, looking at me pointedly. "Take the deal he's offering."

"It's not that easy, Carl."

"It *is* that easy, Nora. Why are you making this so damn difficult?" He raises his voice, almost yelling, and now I know something is wrong. Carl has not once, in all the years I've known him, raised his voice to me.

"I could ask the same question." Uncomfortable silence thickens into a sea of foreboding I can scarcely see through. "What else?"

His eyes snap away before returning to mine. I see loads of regret hanging in them. Then he takes a deep breath and crushes my world knowing there's no way I can say no now. "I need the money from the sale, Nora."

My heart sinks and my head falls back heavily against my chair. "How much?" I choke through the lump of anxiety swelling my throat.

I love my Uncle Carl, but he's a gambler. Not in the seedy, loan shark, someone's-gonna-break-your-kneecaps-unless-you-pay-up kind of way, but in the get-rich-quick-and-risk-everything-you-love kind instead. He finds penny stocks he's convinced are going to turn him into an insta-multimillionaire, even though he doesn't need the money because he has a very successful business. Which he nearly lost once before six years ago because of this shit, mind you. He's been taken for a ride more than once. It's an obsession, a rush he's told me he was done with time and again. Guess that was a lie.

He averts his gaze, embarrassed. "Enough." Which means *everything*.

"Fuck, Carl," I curse lowly.

"I'm sorry, Nora." He means it, but it's not nearly enough. This entire acquisition now rests squarely on my shoulders. Carl has to sell or go bankrupt. If I refuse to agree to the employment terms outlined by Wynn, not only will I be out of a job, but the rest of the one hundred and fifty people who work for my uncle will be standing in the unemployment line, or worse, embroiled in some type of scandal that's no fault of their own, their resumes now tainted because they worked for SER.

No pressure there.

I think of my admin, Vicky, a single mother of three. Recently divorced, barely making ends meet with the bills she's now sacked with from her loser husband who hasn't paid a dime of child support and left her drowning under a mound of credit card debt.

I think of Brandon, another fellow recruiter who's getting married in a month and how he and his fiancée, Patricia, are paying for their entire wedding themselves.

I think of Ronnie in accounting who is less than a year away from retiring. She needs her job to maintain her health insurance until she turns sixty-five.

I suspiciously wonder if Connelly knew all of this and if that's the "thorough research" he's referring to instead of what I originally thought— my secret that I've held tight to. It seems quite coincidental my uncle's financial trouble coincided with an out-of-the-blue offer from Wynn. I don't believe in those types of coincidences. Although it makes me angry either way, I'd rather have this be the "secret" he's ferreted out than the ones I'm hiding.

"Yeah, me too," I mumble, knowing I am well and thoroughly fucked.

Your day of atonement has finally almost arrived, Nora. I knew it was coming. I knew it was inevitable. I just never imagined, in my wildest dreams, that my hand would be forced quite like this or that it would be done by both of the men I love.

Chapter 7

CONN

"What crawled up your ass and died?" Asher asks over the mouth of his coffee cup. He blows on it for a few seconds before taking a careful sip of his black coffee.

Other than the fact it's been two days since my meeting with Nora and I don't have her signed employment agreement on my desk yet? Not a fucking thing.

"I don't know what you're talking about." I take a taste of my cappuccino to keep myself from saying anything else to add fuel to Asher's fire like *shut the fuck up.*

He laughs, popping a chunk of blueberry muffin in his big mouth. We met for breakfast this Saturday morning because Alyse was attending a Pilates class and Asher had some free time. He and Alyse were married a month ago and ever since, he's been pretty preoccupied with his new wife. Hell, since he *reunited* with Alyse, he's possessive and obsessed, almost never leaving her side. I have to say...I miss my best friend. Not that I'm jealous or anything. I most certainly am *not*. Not in the least.

"I call bullshit. You haven't been acting like yourself for the last few weeks. What gives?"

"And how would you know that?" I growl, pissed that he's called me out on my sour mood. "You've barely come up for air since you got married."

A devilish grin eats up my twin's face. "See, now I *know* you're hiding something. The Conn I know would be giving me a high five instead of sounding like a jealous little bitch baby."

"I'm not fucking jealous." I may be. Just a little. *Christ.*

I hate these crazy, nonsensical feelings racing through me. I'm nervous, anxious, and worried. All of which I'm not used to. I don't know what to do with the noxious stew brewing inside me. It needs an outlet or I'm going to blow. I have an inordinate amount of patience, but when it reaches its end, watch the fuck out. You do not want to be in my warpath because it's downright ugly. I get that trait directly from my mother.

Asshole laughs. "I think you are. You know I can feel your emotions, right? Just like you can mine."

That's the thing about twins or at least with mine. It doesn't matter how far away we seem to be from each other, I can sense when Asher has extreme emotional swings. High anxiety, extreme sadness, or happiness. Unfortunately, that works both ways and he can easily tell I've been under some high stress myself lately.

"How's that acquisition going?" he prods knowingly.

Wynn Consulting sits under GRASCO Holdings, a company my brothers, Gray, Asher, and I own and run. Gray is the GRASCO chairman of the board and Asher is the CEO of another subsidiary under GRASCO, Colloway Financial Consulting. The GRASCO board, which all three of us sit on, needs to approve any and all acquisition activities. My brothers, along with the other three board members, have been supportive, albeit wondering why the hell I've set my sights on them.

I regard Asher quietly, wondering what he suspects. I've not said a word to Asher about Nora working for SER, but he knows something is askew. Surprisingly, he's kept his mouth shut about the whole thing, not questioning why I'm hell-bent on owning a company I don't need but want desperately. Guess that was bound to end sometime.

"It's going."

"Run into a snag?"

"Nothing I can't overcome," I announce with more assurance than I feel as doubt slithers its way through me, undermining the confidence I had when I set this all into motion months ago.

I'm usually the guy who thinks of plans A through E because you don't know when your first four plans will fall through and you'll need the fifth one. That's the one no one thinks far enough ahead about to orchestrate. That's why I win a hell of a lot more than I lose.

I plan.

I scheme.

I win.

Period.

I'll eventually win SER, but I could care less about them. What I care about is getting Nora back into my life. My bed. My future. I will stop at nothing until I have her.

"Don't doubt that. You're not one to lose when you want something."

"No, I'm not." I'm man enough to admit I'm not the most gracious loser and if anyone knows that better than me, it's Asher. In my book, if you're not first, you're last. The second place podium is lower than the first for a reason. I don't know a damn person who competes in anything: sport, careers, life, where they set out to be *second* place.

"You seem to want this company pretty badly. More than I think I've ever seen you want anything." He holds my stare, daring me to deny it. I give him nothing and he adds, "So who is she?"

"Who's who?" I ask, feigning ignorance. I take a gulp of my too hot cappuccino, burning my tongue in the process. Shit...that hurt.

"Really? That how we're playing?" he responds with a chuckle, raising his brows in challenge.

"Isn't it about time to get back to the wifey?" I chide, trying to change subjects by pissing him off. Asher and I are two peas in a pod when it comes to doing shit like that.

He doesn't take the bait, the fucker. "Cut the shit, Conn. You're wound tighter than a fucking top. You're moody, short-tempered and preoccupied. Hell, you're acting like..." He stops midsentence narrowing his eyes as if he's just solved a brainteaser. And knowing Asher, he probably has. Then a broad grin splits his lips. Kinda how I'd like to do it about now, except mine would involve a fist and blood. "You're acting like Gray did. Well, I'll be damned," he drawls, his cocky smile broadening. "You've found her."

"Know what I think?" I once again rush to change the subject, not quite ready to talk about Nora. Not until I know I have her. That way if for some reason I lose her, I can suffer my humiliation alone. Losers like to tuck tail and hide their shame from others. Not that I'm used to being on the losing end, so I can only imagine that's how they would feel.

Knowing exactly what I'm doing, Asher laughs loudly, drawing the attention of two striking women in their mid-twenties sitting in the corner of the small café. When they giggle—*annoyingly giggle*—my eyes flick to them and back to Asher, my dick not even twitching.

Even just a few days ago, I'd have been making eye contact, smiling, flirting, drawing them in. Getting into one, or both, of their panties, would be like taking candy from a fucking baby.

So easy.

Too easy.

But since seeing Nora again, I have zero interest in any woman who doesn't have haunted emerald eyes that hold tight to secrets of the past, honeyed red hair that lightly caresses the blades of her shoulders, or curves that rival Marilyn Monroe's. Even *thinking* of Nora makes me harder than titanium.

Jesus, I'm fucked ten ways to Sunday. I knew it the moment her footsteps faltered when our gazes violently collided two days ago, but can I be the man she needs? Can I give her what she wants and deserves? After spending so many years being emotionally unavailable and in more beds that I even care to count, am I even *capable* of intimacy? Of tenderness? Of selflessness?

Do I truly think I can start over again with a woman who ruined me before?

I don't know, but I want to try. *That* much I do know.

"If I give you the house at Mackinac Island this New Year's Eve would that persuade you to keep your opinions to yourself?" Asher quips.

"Hell no. I plan on winning that fair and square on Thanksgiving, asshole. Last year was a fluke and nothing more. And I think Alyse's magic pussy has you so whipped you're looking for things that aren't there, brother."

My twin regards me silently, a slight curve tilting his lips, but anger burns hot in his eyes. I'm not sure, but I may have just earned my own fist to the face. Asher is fiercely protective of Alyse and I understand why. What I said borders on disrespect, yet I have nothing but respect for my twin's beautiful wife who has made him happier than I've ever seen him.

"I'm going to do you a favor and ignore the chum you're intentionally flinging, but know this, Connelly. You're not as cagey as you think you are. I'm the motherfucking expert at avoidance. I'll be here whenever you're ready to talk." He rises and pushes in his chair before pinning me with a heated glare. "And you ever mention my wife's pussy again, I'll take great pleasure in laying you flat on your back, you fucker."

I grit my teeth and nod tightly, knowing I'll have to apologize later, but still feeling too surly to do it right now. I throw two twenties on the table, exit the small café, and make my way to my office.

An hour later, I'm reviewing the final SER acquisition paperwork, fuming that I don't have a signed employment agreement on my desk yet from Nora Cantres. With every hour that passes, my irritation at her stubbornness increases. My fingers itch with the urge to make her acquiesce to my demands. My cock twitches with the need to board GRASCO's new private plane, fly to Cincinnati, throw her over my shoulder, and haul her ass back, swinging and bellowing. Hell, I would even take great pleasure in binding and gagging her if necessary. After I strip her naked of course.

My world-famous patience is nearing its end when my phone rings, dragging me from the multiple plans I'm formulating to get what I want. Seeing it's our attorney, I quickly answer knowing it's about SER.

"Harold."

"I got a call this morning from Carl Steele. He has one final condition to the sale."

I hold in my angry sigh. Fucking Carl and his stipulations. It's taken me months and a few strategically placed discussions to convince him selling his business to Wynn was the right—*the only*—decision he could make. If I could get away with stealing his company out from underneath this sorry excuse for a man and a business owner, I would. So far he hasn't held up his end of the bargain. I'm not in the mood to give him anything else until I know I'm getting what *I* want, but Nora has to sign the agreement of her own free will or it will never hold up.

"What is it?" I keep my voice calm when I feel anything but.

Harold hesitates. I shake my head knowing this stipulation is going to be a doozy. "He wants written assurance that you won't close the Cincinnati location for three years or lay off any of the employees at SER during that time."

"What?" I laugh. "Is he out of his ever-loving mind? He wants employment agreements extended to *everyone* at SER? He can't negotiate what happens to his business *after* he sells. No fucking way. Forget it."

Harold ignores my unusual outburst, continuing. "There's one more thing."

"Oh, I can't wait to hear this," I say on a chuckle. Leaning back in my smooth-as-butter Italian leather chair I grab my stress ball, tossing it in the air. I effortlessly catch it with each pull of gravity on the sponge. "Go on."

"Carl wanted me to pass along that Ms. Cantres has agreed to execute the employment agreement if you agree to this condition."

I freeze, the forgotten globe falling to the floor. It bounces across the room, where it stops against the leg of my cream-colored sofa. I think back to the conversation Nora and I had in the conference room about whether I intended to close the Cincy office and my response that I had no immediate plans.

Then I smile.

This is not Carl's requirement. It's Nora's. In addition to being beautiful with a stellar professional reputation, she's a shrewd businesswoman, too. The selfless side of Nora I've witnessed many times when we were just kids is once again showing itself. I'm glad to know it's still there underneath her irritating stubbornness.

"Done."

"Connelly, my professional advice is to reject this condition. We have a solid offer on the table. This term limits your ability to effectively and efficiently integrate SER into Wynn. There are obvious areas of overlap and agreeing could be an expensive financial mistake."

I grind my teeth, pissed that Harold's insinuating I'd make an intentionally poor financial decision for Wynn or GRASCO. As much as I want Nora, I would never do that to myself or my brothers or our company that we've busted our asses to build together. And essentially all she's done is ensure that SER employees remain stable and that Wynn employees are the ones affected once we start thinking consolidation of functions and duties. Her beauty is breathtaking, but her intelligence is sexy as fuck. She senses how much I want this so she's making me work for it. Classic Nora.

"I said agree to the terms, Harold."

"Connelly—"

"Harold, I respect and value your opinion, but do what I'm paying you to do."

"May I suggest an added clause?" he responds tightly.

This time, I let my sigh free. "Not if it costs me the sale."

"This should be acceptable. It seems the concern here is for the continued employment of the SER associates, so I would offer a stipulation that we agree to one year and if business conditions change that require loss of employment, Wynn will provide a minimum of one-year of severance to any affected associates."

"Make it one and two years of severance." Per the terms of a severance agreement, once the recipient is gainfully employed, severance ends. So this gives us time to develop and execute a solid integration plan and gets Nora what she's asking—financial security for people she cares about. And, of course, garners me what I want.

Her.

"Of course."

"And you can tell Mr. Steele that as soon as I have Ms. Cantres's signed employment agreement on my desk, we have a deal."

I can tell he's irritated when he hangs up, but I don't care. I can't help the slow smile that creeps across my face. I think maybe Nora has been underutilized as just a recruiter, even though she's excelled and has been highly successful in that role from everything I hear. When she works at my company, I have no doubt the sky's gonna be the limit for her. The thought of her leading by my side, like the queen she is, makes my heart pound in excitement.

I stand and retrieve the ball, tossing it toward the net hanging from the back of my closet door.

Swish.

Picking it up, I aim and let the spongy roundness roll off the tips of my fingers again.

Swish.

My bum knee may have fucked up my college basketball scholarship, but after tens of thousands of hours practicing, I can still hit a three-pointer with consistent accuracy. Unless I'm having an off day, I always win when I challenge my brothers to a *friendly* game of HORSE. And since my off days with a ball in my hands are few and far between and my brothers can't resist a bet any more than I can, I always rake in the dough. But with all of my brothers now paired off except for me, we don't get to play as often as we once did.

Swish.

Swish.

As I sink basket after basket, I let myself bask in the first win in my not-so-elaborate game plan. A few more legal formalities and Steele Executive Recruiting will be mine. Very soon, Nora will be here in Chicago working for me and I will put the second portion of my plan into motion. The first part was the hard, messy one.

Swish.

The second one, folks, is the simple one: getting her into my bed and keeping her there. I excel at many things, but getting a woman to willingly open her legs? Piece o' fucking cake. Nora was the one and only exception. But that was then and this is now. Regardless of the cold shoulder she gave me earlier, she's still very much attracted to me. I know once I have her between the four walls of my business, getting her between the thousand-count Egyptian cotton sheets on my bed will be a breeze.

I've already begun tying a continuous, complex string of knots and loops that will be wound so tightly Nora won't know where she begins and I end. Despite what I thought a few days ago, that I didn't know what I'd do with her once I had her bound to me, after setting my starved eyes on her again, I know *exactly* what I'll be doing with her. And I'll be doing it repeatedly because I also know sampling Nora once will not be enough to sate the starvation that's cramped and twisted my insides for years.

The need to ravage, claim, and strip her physically, emotionally, and spiritually raw so all she will know is me is too powerful to push away or ignore. For the first time in years, I want more than one meaningless night between the thighs of a woman whose name I won't remember and sometimes don't even bother to ask for.

Swish.

Ten in a row.

Nora Cantres will be mine again, and there is nothing or no one that can possibly keep her from me.

Swish.

Not even her.

Chapter 8

Nora

"Oh my God! It's so good to see you, sweetie!" Kamryn Winthrop screeches in my ear as she squeezes the air from my lungs.

"You too, Kam. It's been a long time."

"Too long," she whispers.

In the early summer before fifth grade, when my father accepted a research position at UCal's San Diego branch, my family moved from the icy cold of the Northeast to sunny La Jolla, California. We lived in a fancy, gated community filled with old people and even older money.

I hated it.

Until I met the person who would become one of my best lifelong friends.

Kamryn Winthrop.

It was a hot summer day. I was practicing my golf swing in the front yard with a nine iron and Wiffle balls. Most ten-year-olds are riding their bikes or going to the pool or even still playing with dolls, but not me. My Uncle Carl had me on the greens at the age of four, telling me that every young woman should "never rely on a man for happiness, money, or carrying your ass on the golf course."

I swing sure and swift only to watch my ball slice, missing the fake green I'd constructed in the middle of the grass by winding three jump ropes together. "You're doing that wrong," a squeaky voice yells from across the street.

"And how would you know?" I mumble, not giving that tiny squawk the time of day. I didn't know one girl my age who even knew what golf was, let alone understood the mechanics of a proper swing.

I rear back, striking the small white globe again, watching it sail through the air to my right, once again missing the green.

Darn it.

"You're pushing it," miss know-it-all yells, a bit closer now.

Who the heck does this girl think she is anyway? I've been golfing for six years already. She probably doesn't even know where the ball's supposed to land, let alone what type of club I'm holding.

"You need to close your grip just a tad and follow through with your swing. And you're not rotating your hips and shoulders all the way," the disembodied small voice calls again; but this time, she's practically right behind me.

I drop my club angrily and whirl around to meet the most striking set of blue eyes. They would hypnotize you if you stared too long. They're attached to a tiny human being with hair so blonde

89

it looks dipped in bleach and a face so beautiful she resembles what I imagine an angel would look like.

"And who are you? Greg Norman?"

"No." She smiles like the cat that ate the canary. "Clearly I'm JoAnne Carner."

That was it. That short exchange solidified our friendship for life. That little wisp of a girl and I bonded over a love of golf and hatred of absentee fathers.

Holding me at arm's length, looking me up and down, Kam tells me, "You look fucking hot, woman."

I'm sure my blush complements my hair. I hate how easily my skin flushes bright pink. It's hard to hide a damn thing when your body visibly betrays you. "Thanks. I've gained a few pounds since college, but..."

"Girl, shut it. Any hot-blooded man would cut off his right nut at a chance to do you. Besides, you know my motto."

"Fuck ducks who cluck," we both laugh in unison.

Kamryn has always been drop-dead gorgeous, even when she was just a kid. Classic natural blonde beauty with striking eyes and curves in all the right places. But the thing I've always admired most about her is how she embraces who she is, flaws and all. While so many of us incessantly focus on our imperfections, she has a take-me-as-I-am-middle-finger-to-the-world attitude that I envy. I care too much what people think about sometimes.

"Thanks for meeting me for breakfast."

"My pleasure. I would have been upset if you hadn't called. So, you excited about your move to Chi-town?" Kam asks after we put in our breakfast order.

Last week, the acquisition between Steele Executive Recruiting and Wynn was finalized, and all my hopes that this deal would fall through went up in a plume of black smoke. Carl signed, GRASCO held a special board meeting, and a few simple swipes of the pen later, SER became a wholly owned subsidiary of GRASCO Holdings. So I'm now in Chicago for a couple of days for a planning meeting at Wynn that starts at one this afternoon and doesn't finish until tomorrow at five.

I haven't seen an agenda, but I have no doubt I'll have to spend the next thirty-six hours trying to keep my libido in check, because as involved as he's been to date, I also can't imagine that Connelly doesn't have his hands all over this meeting.

"Uh..."

"Hmm, there's a story there. Spill."

"Still golfing?" I divert, squirming a bit in my chair. It doesn't go unnoticed by Kam, judging by the wag of her perfectly sculpted eyebrows, but she doesn't press. Yet. It's coming, I'm sure.

"Not as much as I'd like. Too busy with the job. We just secured a new exclusive spring line at Macy's," she announces as I longingly watch her bite into a flakey croissant that was delivered moments ago.

Damn, I wish carbs didn't have a nonstop express line right to my thighs and ass.

"Wow, Kam. Just...wow. That's incredible." In addition to being extraordinarily beautiful and a junior league LPGA champion two years in a row, Kam has an uncanny eye for fashion. I have no doubt she could have gone on to be a JoAnne Carner, one of the most famous and successful LPGA players of all time, but her interests lay elsewhere. When she opened her own fashion design company at the young age of twenty-one, I also had no doubt she'd be wildly successful.

"Thanks. Now, back to you and your evasion tactics."

"I'm not evading." I shift my eyes and feel the warmth rise, heating first my cheeks, then my ears.

Kam laughs boisterously. "God, my friends are all terrible liars. Have I taught you nothing?"

"It wasn't for lack of trying," I reply, laughing myself, remembering how much trouble we got into for the four years we were neighbors.

"Do you remember that time we snuck out when you were in the eighth grade and rode our bikes down to Brantley Bennington's house for that teen dreams concert they were having in their basement?" Kam asks, wiping buttery crumbs of goodness from the corner of her mouth.

"The Kiss concert where they made drums out of ice cream buckets and aluminum foil and played tennis racket guitars?"

"The one and only." Kam's laughing so hard now she can barely speak. "And do you remember how Ricky Hamilton serenaded you with *Beth* and how his tongue was almost as long as Gene Simmons's and how he tried to stick it down your throat in the bathroom?"

"How could I forget? He slobbered more than a Basset hound. It took me days to get the taste of beef jerky, Dr. Pepper, and mint out of my mouth. To this day, I won't eat or chew anything wintermint."

I got into so much trouble that night. When I tried to sneak back in the house, I found my window locked up tight so I had to use the front door to get back inside. I practically ran into my mother, who had moved a wingback chair right inside the door so there was no way I could sneak around her.

Grounded for an entire month.

But it was *so* worth it.

"God, we were bad."

"That we were. I swore my dad took that job in Maryland to get me away from you."

"Me?" she shrieks. "You were just as bad, Lucy."

"I beg to differ, Ethel."

We giggle loudly at our childhood nicknames, mine being ever so obvious. We're drawing the attention of the entire little café Kam chose for breakfast, but I don't mind. I've never had a girlfriend like Kamryn and I didn't realize how much I missed her.

Maybe moving to Chicago won't be so bad after all. I just have to find a way to stay far away from Connelly.

"So, you'll be working for Conn Colloway then?" Kam asks, eyeing me with keen interest.

Surprised, I look up from the scrambled eggs I'm pushing around on my plate. I've told Kam very little about my move. Just that Wynn Consulting had purchased the company I work for and that it required me to move to Chicago. "How did you know that?"

She shrugs her shoulders like it's no big deal. "I know him."

"You know who?"

"Connelly."

See...this is exactly why I wish I had a better poker face and a different heritage than half-Irish, half-German, which makes for a mighty explosive combo, by the way. My temper is always balanced on the edge of a blade.

I have a lot of cuts.

"You know *Connelly*?" I ask carefully, trying for nonchalant. I know by the squeak in my voice, though, I just ended up in a virtual sidewalk face-plant instead.

Her mouth turns up. "Seeing green, are we?"

I open and close my mouth a few times, trying to gather my wits before responding, because she's absolutely right. The shades I'm seeing are getting progressively darker with each second that ticks by.

I've never seen a picture of Connelly with Kamryn, not that I've scoured each and every one of them, mind you, but she fits his type perfectly. Blonde, beautiful, and buxom. And if I had, I have to admit, I'm not sure I could be sitting here now, knowing that one of my best friends has been intimate with the man I've never been able to forget, the man I'm foolishly and hopelessly still in love with after all this time.

"I have no idea what you're talking about." I manage to push the lie that feels as heavy as a two-ton boulder off my tongue. I'm sweating from the effort.

"You know," she starts, leaning back in her chair before crossing her long, lean legs, "I remember when I got a phone call from a very distraught Nora soon after she moved to Baltimore. Something about the guy she'd fallen in love with in Detroit was...what was it?" She taps her temple a few times. "Oh yes...a 'two-timing, cheating, lying son-of-a-bitch fucker who I wish I'd never met.' That sound about right?"

The other thing I forgot to mention about Kamryn is that she has a memory like a steel trap. If she says that's what I said, then that's what I said. Word for word.

Damn her.

"I don't see what that has to do with Connelly Colloway."

"It has to do with Conn because *he* was the two-timing, cheating, lying son-of-a-bitch fucker."

Now I'm starting to panic for a whole host of different reasons.

"And how would you jump to that conclusion, Kam? I never told you his name." It was hard to keep in touch in high school, so Kam and I only talked every few months. She knew there was a boy I was crushing on, but that was about it. And the last thing I wanted to do when I unloaded on her about my failed whirlwind romance was to remember Connelly's name, let alone speak it.

Her perceptive smile pisses me off. "You never told me his whole name, but you did tell me his first name. Maybe you don't remember during your little blubbering rant, but that's a pretty unique name. And do you know how many Connellys I've met in my lifetime?"

I say nothing. Instead, I'm twisting my fingers together under the table, internally freaking the fuck out.

"Two. The other was a Scottish actor with horse breath and an Albert Einstein haircut. Don't ask." She puts up her hand just as I open my mouth.

"And do you know which one lived in Detroit about the same time as you and had a redheaded girlfriend in high school who's considered 'the one that got away'?" she continues.

My fingers fall lax. "The one that got away?" Why does that statement simultaneously excite me and piss me off?

"That's the story *I* heard."

"From who?"

"His twin brother's wife, Alyse."

"Asher is married?"

"Oh, yes. All the Colloway brothers have dropped like flies within the last year. Except Conn, that is. He's still making the rounds, pining away after the long-lost redhead." She shoots me a grin before taking a sip of her now-cooled coffee.

"Pining away?" I parrot incredulously. "Now, you're just making shit up, Kamryn."

"I'm not. I heard this redheaded beauty broke his heart."

"Broke *his* heart? Are you serious? Well, someone apparently doesn't have all the facts. I'm not sure how *I* could have broken *his* heart since I found him in bed with another girl not two weeks after he professed his undying love to me."

Her mouth turns down slightly. I hate the sympathy I see staring back. "I don't know, Nora. I'm just telling you what I heard."

"Well, you heard wrong," I say through gritted teeth, no longer stewing because she knows about my connection with Connelly but mad as hell he would lead people to believe *I'm* the one who broke *his* heart.

It pisses me off I am being blamed for our breakup. True, I may not have confronted Connelly about his cheating ways when I broke it off, but I was gutted from the inside out after what I'd witnessed. I couldn't stomach listening to excuses and groveling, so I lied instead. Cut us off at the knees by telling him there was someone else. It was easier to let him think it was me than have him banging down my door begging forgiveness. And I knew he would. He was tenacious like that.

It was a horrible time in my life. I went into a deep depression. I unenrolled in college and spent months in bed reliving a torturous night I wasn't even supposed to be a part of. I had come back to Detroit to surprise him for his birthday, but the surprise was on me when I found him with a naked woman sprawled all over his equally naked body. I have never felt more betrayed by anyone than I did in the moment I heard her moaning his name.

Once a player, always a player and everything I've been able to find on him throughout the years has only reinforced my initial perceptions of him, reminding me why I kept my distance then. Why I need to keep it now.

Then why do you feel so damn guilty, Nora?

"Oh, and in case you were wondering, I haven't let him dip his wick in my pond."

My eyes widen as they snap to hers. My pulse starts to race. "Haven't *let* him? Did he ask?"

She doesn't reply, but her face says it all. Of course, he's asked. He's probably fucked half the city of Chicago by now and propositioned the rest.

Pussy-hopping bastard.

I have to admit, a big part of me hurts to see him casually churn through the female population as if they're easily expendable. It shouldn't. It's none of my business anymore. But I'm also not sure if it would hurt worse to see him happily married with a family of his own either, so I'm trying not care either way because caring makes me invested.

And getting invested in Connelly Colloway is something I cannot allow myself to do, especially after this little revelation. It just reinforces my resolve to stay aloof and as far away from him as possible.

Chapter 9

CONN

"How long will the integration take?"

"Everything is business as usual right now," I answer truthfully. I haven't given one thought to assimilating SER into Wynn yet beyond getting the handful of executives and Nora to Chicago. My only plans have revolved around how soon I can get Nora tied to my bed and sated. Once that happens, I can move on to the SER acquisition specifics. Besides, fully integrating two organizations can take months, years even, and those kinds of changes need to be strategically planned and executed, not rushed.

"Will our duties change?"

"No, not in the near term, but that will inevitably happen in some departments. We'll all need to work together when it does." My gaze flicks to Nora, who's sitting stone-faced; her eyes won't meet mine. We've been having a discussion about the combination of our two organizations for almost two hours now and she's yet to ask one question. "We'll give plenty of notice before they do."

"How will new recruiting cases be assigned, Mr. Colloway?" Jeanine, one of my top recruiters asks innocently enough. Jeanine is a good employee, but she is as bloodthirsty a woman as I've ever run across. I don't miss her jealous glance in Nora's direction, though. Neither does Nora.

I can see the marking of territories has already started. Nora remains passive, but gives an almost imperceptible shake of her head, like she expected this. Then her eyes finally meet mine for the first time since she walked through the door nearly two hours ago.

She's waiting on my response as anxiously as Jeanine is. Thank Jesus I'm sitting down because I have to mentally talk my cock into deflating as I stare into her bewitching jade eyes.

Fuck. I want her so damn much, it's hard to think straight. The second she walked into the crowded conference room at five minutes to one, dressed in a conservative, but curve-hugging peach dress, the ache I've felt in every part of my being intensified. It throbs now, almost out of control.

"We'll make those decisions as they come up," I reply to Jeanine, but my smoldering gaze never strays from Nora's, my mind whirling with one wicked, sinful thing I plan to do to her after the other...once I get her underneath me. Which will be tonight if I have my way.

My answer hits with a resounding thud in front of Jeanine. Out of my peripheral, I see she does a piss-poor job of hiding her annoyance. If she's unhappy now, her talons will really unleash when I announce that Nora will be assigned to one of our biggest and most important clients who called yesterday to let me know their CEO is retiring and they need to replace her. In the past, I would have assigned a case like this to Jeanine. I will be giving it to Nora instead.

And I'll be personally overseeing it.

"Next question," I say when Nora finally looks away.

The insecurities and anxieties continue to be lobbed for the next hour and a half. I continue to watch Nora, but she never makes eye contact with me again. My annoyance spikes. It's getting harder and harder to tuck it down.

Your evasion is going to fucking stop, princess.

"Once again," I start, anxious to end this so I can get a minute alone with Nora. "A warm welcome to our new SER family. I have no doubt our Wynn family will be nothing but gracious in welcoming you all. And to that end, you're all invited for a celebration this evening. We'll have cocktails and heavy hors d'oeuvres starting at six-thirty. Lydia will have the information on your way out. I expect to see you all there."

Everyone rises and starts chattering, but the one person my attention is riveted on is Nora. I watch her effortlessly chat up Brad Harding, the SER COO. Their heads are close together and with the heated way his eyes graze over her body whenever she looks away, he is either intimately familiar with her or he wants to be.

Irrational hate burns through me, and my vision instantly fogs with violent, possessive jealousy.

She.
Belongs.
To.
Me.

I've done nothing for the past two weeks other than soul-searching, allowing myself to remember and, more importantly, deal with the deep hurt I've held inside for years at her bullshit breakup phone call. After seeing her again, after I've acknowledged that all I want is her, all I've ever *wanted* is her, and all I will *ever* want is her, I now want all of that resentment, hurt, and anger gone.

I'm tired of being buried, suffocating under its oppressive weight.

I *want* to forgive her. I want it all washed away by the pure love and raw ache I've always held for this woman. Eleven years, wasted. I've fought hard to forget her, all the while secretly pining away for her instead. I may not know the real reasons she left me, and I know that's an inevitable conversation we'll need to have. We both have confessions. We both need to clear the air so we can look to the future unencumbered, but I find I'm not even sure I care what the answers are anymore because I'm not letting her go.

Ever.

And I'm sure as hell not letting some other man move in on *my* turf right the fuck in front of me.

Oh, fuck no.

"Nora, can I speak to you for a minute?" I bark when I see her moving toward the door with his mitt at the small of her back. That possessive gesture is implied universal guy code for letting every other cock in the vicinity know "this woman's with me, stay in your steel cage, fuckers," and I swear by all that I own if Mr. Operations doesn't remove that hand in the next two seconds I'll break it the fuck off.

No one has the right to touch her but me.

Not now. Not ever again.

They both turn their heads. Harding must feel the sharp, cutting sting of the daggers I'm visually hurling; he drops his hand not a moment too soon.

Nora turns back to him, saying something I can't hear before he gives me a tight smile, then leaves with everyone else. Once the last person has shut the door behind them, she shifts to me, irritation written all over her beautiful face. She's not even trying to hide it.

Well, join the fucking club, sweetheart. Water's a sweltering, unforgivable hundred twenty degrees right about now. I push the boil below the surface, keeping my outer pretense calm.

"You know, if you keep calling me after class, people will start thinking I'm the teacher's pet."

Her smart comment instantly grounds the electricity crackling the air, making me chuckle. I let an amused smile curl my lips. "You are."

No sense in sugar coating it any longer.

I want her.

I need her.

Fuck...I *will* have her.

Her aloof façade slips for a moment and I glimpse a genuine smile. The first I've seen from her in so many years. Christ, it's so heady it's as if pure, undiluted oxygen was just pumped directly into my bloodstream.

"Brilliant counterproposal you made, by the way."

She watches me contemplatively for a few heartbeats. She's trying to figure out how to respond. "I'm not sure what you mean."

I tamp down my smile. "It was a smart move, Nora. You should own it."

An impish smile curls her glossy lips. "You seemed desperate," she finally counters. That's all I would get from her, but it was an admission nonetheless. And I was. Desperate. Desperate to get my hands on *her*.

"Desperation implies recklessness, and I assure you I am anything but reckless. I just know what I want, I know how to get it, and I make no apology for it."

Cocking her head slightly, she asks, "Did you want something, Connelly, or did you just want to lord your power over me again?"

Did I mention how I've always loved that she uses my full name while most everyone else just calls me Conn? Every time those three syllables roll from her tongue, I start to swell.

A ghost of a smile crosses my face. "You know what I've always loved about you, Nora?" I ask, slowly closing the distance she's intentionally tried putting between us.

I don't miss the widening of her eyes at my specific choice of words. I could have used any number of adjectives besides loved. Liked.

Admired. Respected. But I chose that one with intent. And it didn't escape her perceptivity.

"My feistiness?" she replies a little nervously. Good, I want to keep her on her toes. Actually, I'd love to keep her on her back. Naked. Legs spread.

"Mmmm, yes." I nod absently. "That always made me stone fucking hard." I luxuriate in her sharp intake of breath at my bold statement. *Oh, princess, I'm only getting started.* "But that's not what I was thinking just now."

With every step I take toward her, she shifts uncomfortably. I have to give her credit, though. She doesn't move an inch, holding her ground. I'll bet those stubborn spikes are firmly rooted, even as bad as she's itching to rip them from the floorboards and flee. But her mulishness is no match for me and *my* resolve. I'll shred her righteous determination into so many goddamned splinters they'll all be embedded in *me*. Lost to her forever because I'm not fucking giving them back. Then I will own her, just like she owns me, whether she realizes it or not.

I stop right in front of her, our toes almost touching.

Breathing deep, I take her perfumed scent into my lungs. Standing this close to her, it's hard to control myself. My fists open and close at my sides, when all I want to do is brush her hair aside and nip the graceful length of her neck before sinking my teeth into the crook, marking her. I want to dig my fingers into her hips and yank her roughly into me so she can feel for herself how hard she makes me.

Fuck it, I decide. Self-restraint is overrated.

Reaching up, I frame her cheek and run my thumb over the plush lower lip she's painted with berry-red gloss, smearing the stickiness on my finger.

"Stop," she breathes unconvincingly. Her body tenses, but she makes no move to pull out of my grip. In fact, I think I may even feel her lean into it. Her words and her actions are a veritable contradiction.

I drop my voice to just above a whisper, ignoring her weak request. "What I loved is how your expressive eyes always told the truth even when your lying mouth didn't. And that hasn't changed. One. Bit."

My gaze drops to her lips. I watch her little pink tongue dart out to wet them. I groan softly, unable to hold it in.

"Connelly, I work for you now. This is wro—"

"And do you know what I see floating in them now, princess?" I continue, steamrolling right over her pathetic protest. Snaking my free hand around her waist, I tug her into me, pressing her pelvis into my throbbing erection. I just about come on the spot when her eyes fall shut and my name escapes her lips on a low exhale. I deserve some fucking award for not ripping off her clothes right now and pounding into her with the raw primal lust that's screaming *"claim mark claim."*

Leaning down, I torture myself further by skating my lips over her cheek, punctuating each word with light kisses down her jaw. "Desire.

Craving. Biting hunger that eats at your resolve to deny me."

Her breath catches hard and fast. It's sweet, sublime acknowledgment that makes my cock twitch.

Darting my tongue out to lick the delicate skin underneath her ear, I pull her closer, let my hand cup her curvaceous ass. I tease the seam between her globes. Her breathlessness tests every last shred of restraint I'm hanging on to. My fingers are bruised and bloody with the amount of sheer will I'm tapping into right now.

"I can almost hear your silent plea begging for my mouth, for my touch, for my cock, Nora. Mine. *No one* else's."

"No..."

I pull back and grasp her face between my long fingers. Her emeralds remain squeezed shut, intentionally denying me the truth I know I'll see in the shadows.

"Look at me."

She shakes her head. I tighten my grip, my infamous control slipping. Who the fuck am I kidding? It's been nearly gone since the second I saw her again and I don't think I'll be able to reclaim it until I reclaim her.

I haven't been the same since this woman walked out of my life. I've loved her with every part of me all these years. What I feel for her is that once-in-a-lifetime, soul-destroying, I-can't-live-a-fucking-second-without-this-person love that my brothers talk about, but I denied believing in.

Until now.

"Open your eyes, Nora," I growl, my incensed tone leaving no room for argument.

When she finally submits, they blaze hot with everything I've described and then some. She knows I see it.

"Are you wet for me, princess?" I growl, breathing deeply. I know she is. Her intoxicating scent lands on my taste buds, making my mouth water. It's driving me fucking mad.

"This is not foreplay, Connelly." Her eyes are dark and stormy, but transparent as glass. And I see right through all her bullshit.

"Tell me, Nora, if I slide my hand underneath your skirt right now and run my fingers along the seam of your panties, will I find them soaked with...foreplay?"

Her lids drop briefly before opening to meet mine again. *Yeah, that's what I thought, sweetheart.*

"Now who's being unprofessional?" she chokes, swallowing hard.

"Oh, this is entirely fucking personal, and I think we both know that. Don't we?"

Her chin is still firmly in my hand and her eyes dart back and forth between mine. She opens her mouth to lie to me. Again. I can feel it. See it. Taste the bitter fumes before they tumble from her deceitful lips. And I want to punish her for it until she confesses the truth, then comes all over my cock.

"Connelly, what we had is over."

Lies. Every word.

I've spent a lot of time studying people and

their superficially innocent signs of dishonesty. While some people won't shut the hell up and would rather listen to themselves talk for hours on end, I'm that quiet sleeper in the corner who doesn't say much. I'd rather spend my valuable time observing others instead. Listen to what's *not* being said. Silence is the most powerful tool in the arsenal of communication. At the end of the day, that skill garners me far more than plugging empty space with unnecessary bullshit.

So, you noticed how she deflected instead of answering the goddamned question, right?

What you didn't see were her eyes as they darted and dilated ever so slightly or her lip as she tried—and failed—not to bite it.

What you didn't hear was her steady voice lacking conviction as her breathing turned labored.

What you didn't feel was the minor shift of her feet as the lie fell hard and flat by her toes. It's nearly impossible for the body to follow along with a lie, and if you watch close enough, the signs are recognizable, even to the untrained eye. But most people don't pay close enough attention because they are either too busy talking or thinking of the next thing they're going to talk about instead of observing.

Nora's never been able to pull one over on me.

Not many people can.

"No lies. No more fucking lies, Nora. Here's a little honesty for *you*, princess." My hand slips into her silky hair, fisting it tightly while my other starts kneading the generous flesh in my palm. I force her head back, capturing her smoky eyes with mine so she can't look away. Her lids fall to half-mast. She's so damn turned on, she's panting.

I'll take that damn award now.

"With every breath I take, I still smell you. I still taste you on my tongue. I feel your very spirit wrapped around my soul. I have *never* stopped thinking about you, Nora. I can't get you out of my fucking head. I've tried. God knows I've tried everything I can think of to eradicate you because it's been excruciating to have your memory taunt me when I couldn't have you. But nothing has worked. No amount of alcohol or denial or women or success or wealth will remove your permanent brand from me. You're singed into my brain, my bones, my goddamned DNA."

Bending my head, I nuzzle her ear, her neck. "You were born for me, Nora. Only me. Just like I was for you." I use her very own words from so many years ago. Ones that rattle around in my skull constantly.

I'm nibbling my way back to take her mouth when she snakes her hand between us, pushing her palm against my chest, fruitlessly trying to stop me. "Connelly, what are you—"

"Taking what's mine," I murmur against her wet, parted lips before she can finish. "Taking what's *always* been mine."

Then I don't just kiss her. I claim her.

I lick, I taste, I possess. I conquer, drawing her soul into me. Taking it hostage.

My kiss is long and sensual and full of promises I want her to hear. To believe. To trust.

She fights me at first. Not physically, but

emotionally, mentally. I can tell the instant her barriers collapse because when she starts kissing me back—*really* kissing me back—I feel it everywhere.

My mind.

My blood.

My cock.

My very fucking soul.

Her touch soothes the ache I've buried deep in my marrow. It's real and heavy and burdensome and the intense relief I feel is so damn good, it's liberating.

"Nora," I rasp between bites of her kiss-swollen lips. Palming her face between my hands, I shift her so I can gain better access and she responds by moaning and running her hands around my waist, up my back, pulling me closer by her fingernails.

I'm basking in the feel of her lips on mine again, feeling as though I've finally come home. But before I know what's happening she's breaking free from my arms and running toward the door, disappearing before I can do a damn thing but curse, try to catch my breath, and calm my raging, angry erection.

"Go ahead, Nora," I murmur, my voice hoarse. "Run while you can. Because this is the last fucking time you're getting away."

Chapter 10

Nora

"Nora, hi. I wasn't sure if you were coming or not," Brad says the instant my feet hit the second-floor landing.

Neither was I. I am now officially half an hour late, which is not the way to start off on the right foot at your new job, even if it is a social event. But I couldn't talk my legs into walking out of my hotel room. When I finally did, I lingered at the luxurious entryway of the Renaissance for nearly ten minutes before I could make myself leave the safety and comfort of anonymity.

"What can I get you to drink?" He sets his hand at the small of my back and guides me over to the makeshift bar in the corner of the low-lit room. I haven't forgotten the murderous look Connelly had on his face earlier today when he saw Brad's hand in the exact same position. Taking a quick look around, I breathe a sigh of relief when I notice he hasn't arrived yet. I don't need another ridiculous display of male dominance in front of my new peers, especially from the owner of the company.

"Uh…" What I want is a double whiskey, neat and undiluted and strong as hell to calm my raw nerves, but instead, I say, "Just a glass of white wine is fine."

I need to keep every single wit about me this evening. While numbing my anxiety seems like a pretty stellar idea right now, it won't be in about an hour when the full effects of eighty-proof alcohol strip away my defenses.

And right now my defenses are just as raw and brittle as my nerves.

I stop short of the bar so Brad is forced to leave me to order my cocktail. Connelly may be late, but Murphy's Law is a merciless beyotch sometimes. I just know if I'm standing at the bar with my back to the entrance and another man's body part is touching mine, a scene right out of *Fight Club* may ensue.

Brad returns with my fruity drink. I take a long, deep gulp while working to keep a respectable distance between us.

"Thirsty?" Brad asks, eyeing me as if he knows what's running through my brain.

He doesn't. Trust me. Even I can't catch the end of one frayed thread in my unraveled thoughts.

His touch.

His declaration.

His possession.

Your lies.

Your deception.

Your betrayal.

It's all running on an unforgiving loop through my goddamned head, the words and thoughts and

113

feelings blending and swirling together until they're a massive blur. Until I don't know up from down. Until I don't know what the hell I'm going to do.

"Parched," I settle for, taking another unladylike swallow.

"So...what did our new boss want this afternoon?"

Me. He wanted me.

"Just buttoning up some outstanding terms of my new employment with Wynn." My gaze instinctively drops with my lie but snaps right back up at his statement. I do not miss the protectiveness in his tone.

"You two know each other."

Oh, we know each other, all right. Intimately. And I'm not sure what the hell I'm going to do when I see him here after he vomited his "honesty" all over me earlier, crushing my determination to stay away under his heartfelt confession. What I *want* to do is drag him into a dark corner and beg him to fuck me until I forget my name, forget every reason why I shouldn't want him and forget why I left him in the first place.

I can't, but *sweet baby Jesus* do I want to.

"Who?" I feign, looking around the room.

"Nora." He lowers his voice as a few Wynn employees crowd around us trying to erase their sad problems with their own poison. Gently grabbing my elbow, he maneuvers us over a few feet for privacy. "We've known each other far too long and far too well to play this game."

I look up at Brad, all six foot four, two hundred twenty taut pounds of him. With gray eyes, sandy hair, and a somewhat crooked nose that's just a tad too big, he's handsome in a roughhewn sort of way. In college, he was a linebacker, playing for the Florida Gators and was nearly drafted by the NFL. He was an undrafted free agent for a couple of years before he gave up on his professional sports dream and put the business degree he'd earned at UFL to good use.

He's smart and kind. Charismatic. He's trustworthy, successful, and treats me like a desired woman. He would be a good husband. Just for someone else. Not me. We've worked together now for three years and for the past two he's been unrelenting in letting me know he's all but in love with me. Maybe he is.

I *want* to reciprocate his feelings, but unfortunately, when I look at him, I don't get tingles on my skin or flutters in my stomach. My pulse doesn't race with desire nor does my body light up with lust. But that didn't stop me from inviting him into my home and into my bed after the Christmas party last year and subsequently breaking his heart when I made him leave right after the act.

I rationalized it by telling myself I'd had too much to drink, but the truth of the matter was...I was lonely. Hurt. And insanely jealous.

A few days before, I "happened across" a picture online of Connelly at a fundraiser with a stunning blonde. His arm was wrapped around her perfectly tiny waist and her perfectly painted lips were pasted against his perfectly happy cheek. Connelly's tux draped perfectly over his fit body, and Barbie's perfectly perky boobs were pressed against his perfectly buff chest. The roundness of her perfectly shaped ass was the perfect landing spot for Connelly's perfectly manicured hand. Hell, they looked like the perfect couple who could live a perfect life in a perfect house with perfect pets and have perfectly fucking perfect babies.

Yep. They were dripping perfect, perfect perfection, so I did what I do best.

Make mistakes.

I sigh, the memory jogging all the reasons why giving in to this insane desire I have burning for Connelly is a supremely bad idea. "It was a long time ago," I answer almost too softly to be heard.

He nods, his lips tightening. Reaching up, he runs a finger across my cheek. It's a comforting gesture, one friend to another. He sees more than I want him to when he makes another very observant statement. "Now, things are starting to make sense."

"What does that mean?"

"He hurt you."

I open my mouth to deny it. The last thing I want is people knowing about our past. I can't, though. It's true. Connelly hurt me terribly, but I've made my share of bad decisions and I can't sit here and shovel all the shit into his pigpen and stay clean. I'm up to my ears in it. Shit's everywhere and it's getting deeper than ever.

I'm now like a sitting duck mired in a deep shit pile of its own making.

I'm in hell and I've never been more aware of that than I am now.

"I'm far from blameless."

"Hmmm," he says thoughtfully, looking over my shoulder before mumbling, "Somehow I doubt that."

You'd be so wrong, I think. So very wrong.

Then I feel *him*. I wish I could stop the intoxicating warmth from spreading throughout my bloodstream like a drug was just shot into my veins. I feel the weight of his stare heating my flesh, sending tingles on the fast track to my core where the desire I'd managed to settle to smoldering embers before now flares to life with renewed potency, burning me from the inside out.

Brad's eyes return to mine and he runs his free hand down my arm, giving my hand a squeeze, which in retrospect may have been a career-ending move for him. But kudos to him. He knew exactly what he was doing and who was watching. He did it anyway, uncaring about the consequences. I may not be in love with Brad, but he's a good man. He's been a good friend to me, even when I haven't been to him.

Taking a fortifying breath, I turn around to see Connelly standing tall and regal and composed across the room, his face stoic and impassive as he watches us. Connelly's always had the best poker face of anyone I've known, never letting his eyes express what's going on behind them or his body show the emotions crawling underneath his skin. It's admirable and irritating all at the same time.

Damn, he looks good. His suit jacket is shed, so

now he's sporting just gray dress pants and the lavender button-down from earlier, which he's managed to make look ultra sexy by undoing the top button and loosening the tie so it hangs haphazardly down his sculpted chest. The sleeves are rolled up enough to showcase his strong, masculine forearms. He holds a highball glass with amber liquid in one hand while the other is draped casually in his pocket, thumb hooked outside. Two men are on either side chatting him up. In an instant, I recognize them as his brothers, Gray and Asher.

But he's not paying attention to anyone except me. While I register that Brad is still right at my back, talking to someone else, the rest of the noisy crowd falls away and it's just the two of us.

Hazel eyes kiss my skin as they slide slowly down my curves, stopping for long lengths in all the right places. My parted lips, the swell of my breasts, the juncture of my thighs, the long expanse of my bare legs. By the time they land back on mine, they are no longer cool but smoldering with fire and hunger. I feel almost singed by their intensity.

As a woman, there's not a headier feeling in the world than being visually undressed by the man you desire—the man who will fuck you until you melt into a sated pool of bliss in his arms. Except maybe *actually* being undressed by him.

"Nora, I wanted to personally welcome you to Wynn," a raspy female voice drawls in my ear, breaking our thrall. I already know all too well who that voice belongs to and she's a goddamned viper lying in wait for her prey. She is as unprofessional and cold-blooded as they come and has a cutthroat reputation that well precedes her. How Connelly doesn't see through her bullshit and fire her ass is beyond me.

"Thank you, Jeanine. It's great to be here." I paste a plastic smile on my face as I turn toward her, but not before I notice Connelly's eyes widening just a bit like he's worried about a catfight breaking out.

He shouldn't be. My venom comes in the form of poison-tipped words, not razor-sharp claws.

"I'm sure it is." With a smirk on her stiff Botox-injected lips, her eyes slide briefly to Connelly before returning to me. She's baiting me, seeing how I'll respond. It would be a shame to disappoint. It's not like we're going to be besties anytime soon anyway. I have standards.

"It's nice to finally meet the *infamous* Jeanine Anderson."

"You mean famous, don't you?" she responds with thinly veiled vitriol, her synthetic smile not reaching her eyes. It's not her fault, really, given the fact her red lips are swollen to almost the size of a peach. Jeanine is a tall woman, probably five foot nine, and she may be striking on the outside with her olive skin, dark chocolate eyes, and long, sleek black hair, but ugliness on the inside always dims outer beauty. I could tell within thirty seconds in her presence that her insides are full of rot and fakery.

"Ummm...no. I chose my words very carefully."

Her fake smile falls—*I think*—and she attempts

to thin her lips, but it's an effort in futility. "I think you have your sights set a little too high, sweetie."

"All right, I'll bite," I reply in amusement after finishing the last of my Pinot Grigio. This is the most fun I've had in weeks. Who knew it would be so easy to get under her skin? "What, pray tell, are my too-lofty goals?"

This time, she turns fully toward Connelly and waves. You know, the kind of head-slapping, nauseating wave that high school girls do where they scrunch up their shoulders and wiggle their fingers like the rest of their arm doesn't function properly?

Yeah, that one.

He acknowledges her with a slight dip of his head but does a poor job of hiding his irritation. I smile inwardly. Or I guess it's outwardly, because when the childish display is over and my attention swings back to Jeanine, I think my throat would be ripped out by now if she were a vampire. Lucky for me, she's not. But just in case, I'll be stopping at the corner market on the way back to my hotel to pick up a garlic string.

"He's undeniably hot, but he's a once-and-dump kinda guy."

Despite my best efforts, my jaw clenches and my quick temper flares. I take a couple of deep breaths, trying to drive away the red mist that just showered me in deadly thoughts. Thoughts that will get me hard prison time in an unflattering orange jumper if acted upon. And no matter what they say, orange is not the new black. But I've gotta be honest, I'm having a very difficult time because it never occurred to me until right now that Connelly's maybe wet his dick with most of his staff as well. And although I can't imagine him with the likes of her, I guess I shouldn't be surprised either.

"And who exactly are we gossiping about now?" I finally manage to ask, proud of the way I controlled my voice. And my fists, because I'm feeling all kinds of violent right now, despite the fact I have not a violent bone in my body.

"Don't play coy, Nora. He may be interested in you because you're the new pretty little plaything, but I guarantee you Connelly Colloway, CEO and playboy extraordinaire, is not marriage material. But if you're looking for a great fuck for the evening you couldn't pick a finer, well-bred male specimen."

"Sounds like you have firsthand knowledge," I fire back. The words feel hot as pokers on my tongue.

Her slow, malicious smile is nothing short of victorious. After luring me smack dab into the center of her minefield, I took that final fatal step myself and felt the explosion rattle my entire body. The shrapnel lodged itself deep in my soul— I feel each agonizing slice keenly.

Why does it seem as though I need these painful reminders of why I should stay far, far away from the only man I've ever allowed myself to love?

Because you're a slow fucking learner, Nora.

"Best I've ever had." She winks, then leaves me standing alone, watching her generous ass sway in her too short, highly unprofessional, almost see-through white dress.

That bitch. I was played. I knew it and I let her do it to me anyway.

I don't want to look at him, but my head turns of its own accord anyway. Connelly's gaze is darting between Jeanine and me. He's now not even trying to hide behind his cool demeanor. His jaw is tight, he's grinding his teeth, and his eyes have gone slate hard.

Ignoring him, I make my way through the crowd, back to the bar. "Whiskey, neat. Make it a double. Hell. Might as well leave the whole damn bottle."

The cute young bartender—Chad, according to his name tag—quirks a smile. I'm sure he's heard this a thousand times before. "Bad day?"

"You could say that."

"Work or relationship?"

"What makes you think either?"

"There are only three problems that drive people to ask for a bottle full of liquid painkillers. Work. Relationships. Or money."

"What makes you think it's not money then?"

"I'm observant." He chuckles, which lightens some of my anxiety. I smile. Nodding to the wall behind him, he asks, "Any preference on brand?"

My eyes float over the bottles of mind erasers stacked behind Chad just waiting to be consumed. I don't drink whiskey that often, and it all tastes like gasoline to me anyway, so I ask, "It's all covered by Wynn, right?"

"Yes, ma'am." He winks conspiratorially.

"Then I'll take the most expensive one you have."

I feel his body heat blanket me right before his husky voice rumbles in my ear, "Get the lady a Scotch, Chad. The Dalmore 25 year." By his light chuckle, he doesn't miss the shiver that works its way from the top of my head down the length of my spine, slowing to a leisurely stop in the center of my core where it settles, firing up that slow burn.

Chad nods, ignoring me now that the big man with the black Amex is here giving orders.

Bastard. Damn him and that unspoken guy code.

"I don't like Scotch," I snip. I don't face Connelly, keeping my eyes straight ahead on the bottle Chad just pulled from under the bar. It has a beautiful twelve-point bull splayed across the front and dark amber liquid sloshing inside. By the looks of it, a glass of the undoubtedly expensive malt has already been poured. One guess as to who's drinking it.

"Scotch is whiskey, babe."

Oh. Well. Who the hell knew that?

Connelly hasn't moved, his warm breath caressing my right cheek with each exhale. One-half step back and we'll be melded together, back to front. It's intimate and highly inappropriate for a business setting. But even through my hurt, I have to fight to keep from leaning back into the comfort of his broad, muscular frame anyway. His left hand meets the bar top, all but caging me in, his thumb intentionally brushing over my pinky.

Back and forth.

Back and forth.

Every hypnotic stroke sends a fresh flood of desire buzzing through my veins.

I should be pushing him away, yet all I can think of is pulling him closer. His touch lays me bare, opens my insides, strips me empty of all thought and reason. Just like this afternoon, until my self-preservation instincts kicked in and I fled.

"I'm not your babe," I reply belatedly. I take a healthy drink from the glass that Chad sets in front me. He's now shoving warm bottles of beer into a cooler of ice, trying not to pay attention to the scene about to unfold right in front of him. *Try harder, Chad. You're not fooling anyone.*

"By the way, I thought I should clear up the fact that I don't have any children," he whispers seductively.

My eyelids suddenly feel heavy and fall shut. I need to get the fuck out of this situation. I turn toward Connelly, placing my elbows on the wood surface behind me, leaning back. He doesn't move an inch. "You're in my space."

"Your space?" A smile plays at a corner of his mouth. I want to slap it off as much as I want to kiss him stupid. I look around the room to see that we're attracting more attention than I'm comfortable with, including that of his brothers and the slut in the white dress who's now looking a little green around the gills.

My inner bitch smiles at that, but I keep my outside cold, because if I don't I won't get out of this encounter with an unscathed heart or ego.

I tilt my head up and look Connelly hard in the eye. "Yes. My *space*. My *personal* space."

"Personal space?" He laughs low and deep, the sound rolling lazily over me, making me dizzy. And wet.

He fucked Jeanine. And countless others. Remember that.

"Yes. My personal space," I punctuate each word, trying not to raise my voice and draw even more eyes to us.

But Connelly clearly doesn't care that he's unprofessionally draped over one of his new employees. He leans closer, eyes dancing with mirth and challenge. "And what is *that* exactly?"

"God. Are you obtuse? That space that's...personal. You. Are. In. It."

His panty-wetting smile is charming and enthralling and I can see why women crawl on their knees for one night alone with him. Hell, I'm about to drop this second and unzip him in front of everyone, damn the consequences.

"For a woman who's so intelligent, Nora, you're not being very articulate right now."

Gah...

He moves back slightly but, as if in challenge, stays just on the edge of my little comfort bubble. I feel like I can breathe for the first time in five minutes. They may be shallow breaths, but air is air.

Taking a sip of his cocktail, he watches me intently before saying, "You know there's a clause in the employment agreement against theft of company property."

Huh? "Did someone pilfer a Bic after today's meeting?" I raise a confrontational brow.

"No." His voice hardens. "Someone's trying to pilfer something much more valuable than a fucking pen."

My lips turn up. I have no idea what the hell he's going on about. "A pack of Post-it notes or a gold-plated paper clip perhaps?"

"I don't give a shit about office supplies, Nora."

"I have no idea where you're going with this annoying conversation, Connelly."

"Oh, I think you do. But I'll spell it out for you so we're both singing from the same songbook here. It's you, princess. I'm talking about you."

I laugh in total disbelief, shaking my head. "Me? You bought my uncle's business, so I'm considered company property now?"

He cocks his head. It should look arrogant and haughty, but on him, it's sexy as fuck. "You belong with me, and I own the company, so in a way...yes."

I take that back. Arrogant and haughty are the perfect adjectives to describe his egotistical ass. Oh, and domineering, pretentious, smug. I really could go on and on.

"Oh my God. You are absolutely delusional."

Leaning in, he sets his empty glass on the counter right behind me and whispers in my ear, "Au contraire, princess. I'm thinking clearly for the first time since the night you gave me your virginity. Fuck, I can still feel you writhing under me as I rocked into you, Nora. I still feel your breath on my neck as you told me you loved me.

Over and over again. And I cannot get the taste of your silky release out of my mouth."

Mother of all things dirty.

Pure lust warms my body like an electric blanket on high. I swallow hard and will the pace of my heart to slow. When I speak, my voice cracks with the longing I want to subdue but can't. "Connelly...stop it. This is not the place."

"What did Jeanine say to upset you, baby?" His voice lowers with concern, all playfulness evaporated like morning dew in the hot sun. What vanished along with it was my lust at the mention of that bitch's name.

Turning my head, I throw back the rest of my overpriced Scotch, relishing the fumes now burning my nose and esophagus, before slamming the heavy crystal a little too hard on the bar.

"What's the matter? Worried your reputation preceded you? Well, that ship has already sailed, Connelly. That happened eleven years ago, and I should have done myself a huge favor and listened then."

He straightens, taking a step back. His hand drops to his side, leaving cold in its wake where it had been touching my arm only moments ago. I'm pissed at myself that I want it back. "What the fuck is that supposed to mean?" he says, his voice tight. And is it guilt or feigned confusion now creasing his thick brows?

"Everything okay here?" A throaty male voice interrupts. Fantastic, the "company pilferer" couldn't have worse timing.

"This is a private conversation," Connelly grits

through clenched teeth, not even bothering to look at our party crasher.

I glance over Connelly's shoulder to see Brad tower several inches above him, looking all protective like a papa bear. Connelly's broad and fit and undoubtedly ripped underneath his dapper suit, but he played basketball while Brad ate running backs for lunch. You do the math.

"I'd like to hear from Nora if you don't mind."

Connelly slowly pivots so he's facing Brad. I don't miss the fact that, even through his loose dress shirt, his muscles are rippling in an effort to contain his irritation. When he speaks, it's with such a sharp edge, I'm surprised to find Brad's not bleeding out from the verbal blade. "I do mind. Excuse us."

Steely fingers wrap above my elbow. Connelly pulls me to his side, weaving us through the room to a back staircase leading up to another floor, which is closed off with a purple velvet rope. But that doesn't stop him from trespassing anyway, ushering me up to the dark space with his hand still firmly around my arm.

"Jesus, Connelly, have you lost your damn mind?" I spit when we've reached the last step. Yanking loose from his grip, I pace to the other side of the very small room. It looks to be another entertainment area. For VIPs, perhaps. Through the blackness, I can tell furniture lines the walls, but I don't stop to take inventory.

"What the hell is everyone going to think?" I practically screech, leaning against the far side wall for support. "That you've dragged your new pet back here to fuck her?"

"Nora, stop," he scolds, stalking toward me slowly as if I'm some rabid animal that will attack if he moves too fast. He couldn't be more right. I want to hurt him like he's hurt me. Tenfold.

"Is that what happened with Jeanine?" I rant, unable to keep the suffocating pain from leaking out. It needs a place to go besides just sitting in my gut, rotting my insides, making me hemorrhage with a heartbreaking ache I have no right to feel but do anyway. "Did you drag her into the storage room at a corporate get-together and fuck her brains out before returning to brag about your latest conquest to your executive buddies?"

"That's enough," he growls, as each step brings him closer.

Backlight spills golden rays around his tall, broad form, making him look like a dark angel of temptation rising directly from the fires of the underworld. He's so damn alluring, even this deep hurt I have inside me can't squelch my unerring want for him.

I hate myself for being so weak.

Needing to keep our distance, I back into the shadows as he moves toward me, stopping only when the back of my knees hit the edge of smooth leather. "Did she scream your name and pull your hair as you went down on her or was her mouth too full with your cock to talk, because I gotta tell you...if it were me, I'd do anything to shut her the fuck up."

"Don't say another word, princess."

Adrenaline flows hot as lava through me, fueling me on. My chest heaves and my stomach churns with the agony ripping through me at the thought of him with her. With the others.

I've been with a total of five men since we parted ways, yet if bed hopping were an Olympic sport, he'd have a dozen gold medals displayed proudly around his neck by now.

I hurt so much I can barely breathe.

"You're not denying it," I continue unfazed, trying not to fall apart completely. "So it must be true."

He's now right in front of me, legs spread on either side of mine. As I try to get away, I move backward but forget I'm trapped against something. Instead of making my escape I fall over the arm and onto my back, landing on a soft buttery surface.

In a flash, Connelly takes advantage and is looming over me, strong arms pinning mine down on either side of my head, powerful thighs caging me. The hardness in his groin presses into my core, making me pathetic and needy. My pulse thunders like bongo drums in my ears, partly out of anger, partly out of desire.

Why do I have to want him so much?

"I'm just going to say this once, so listen closely. I didn't fuck Jeanine in any way, shape, or form, and I wouldn't get my double-wrapped dick within ten feet of her so if that's what she told you, then she a lying, conniving bitch."

His nose is less than an inch from mine, our ragged breaths sparring.

"Are you sure? Maybe you just don't remember. There have been so many, I imagine it's hard to keep them all straight."

He ignores my low blow, a slow grin spreading his sensual lips. "That look suits you, princess."

"What look is that? Animosity?" I spit, wishing I hated his pet name for me, but I don't. God, I *love* it.

"Jealousy."

"I am not jealous," I huff, trying not to blink or look away as the lie trickles out. I think I almost manage to fool myself, but not Connelly. Even in the dark I can't hide from him.

"Again with the lies, princess. If you weren't jealous, you wouldn't give a shit if I'd fucked Jeanine." I scoff at that, wishing it sounded more convincing. "Now it's your turn."

"What's my turn?"

"To tell me you didn't fuck the Florida gator."

"You're cutting off my circulation." I squirm to get free, but Connelly knows exactly what I'm doing and his fingers clamp tighter. I wish I could tell you that his body blanketing mine didn't make me feel safe and cherished and at peace for the first time in over a decade, but you'd see right through that bullshit, just like Connelly would.

"Tell. Me."

I want to tell him that it was all his doing. That I only slept with Brad because, even though I had no right, I was jealous when I saw pictures of him and perfect Buxom Barbie. I want to tell him that had he kept his dick in his pants all those years ago we may be living a very different life, together. But I don't. I don't say any of those things, turning my head away from his intense stare instead.

131

"I'm going to fucking kill him," he growls, lowering his hot mouth to my now-exposed throat like he had an open invitation.

But do I stop him? No.

Do I encourage him? Shamefully, yes.

"You belong with me, Nora. Me," he declares between openmouthed kisses and possessive nips. When he grinds his pelvis into my sex, I moan his name, shifting my hips upward with every downward thrust of his.

"I know it makes me a hypocrite, but I hate the thought of his hands on you," he rasps gruffly. His hands travel down my sides, thumbs grazing my painfully erect nipples on their descent. "It makes me fucking crazy with jealousy, and I haven't experienced jealousy since high school."

I have. With every smile you gifted another woman or possessive arm wound about her waist.

All of a sudden, he stops all movement and I whimper.

Whim-per. Like a pet that was cheated out of its promised treat.

Palming my face with one hand, he slides the other between us, cupping my aching pussy over my panties. It feels so right, I have to fight my eyes to stay open. Running lithe fingers along the edge of the damp material, he teases and prods. "This, here? This. Is. Mine. We clear?"

My voice is suddenly gone, like an escaped convict. I mean to protest, but I find myself nodding my agreement instead.

"I'm going to kiss you now, Nora. Long, deep and

very fucking thoroughly. And when I'm done you're going to remember well who you belong to."

I've never forgotten, I think. *Never.*

Without waiting on a response, his lips smash to mine. His kiss is rough and desperate. Possessive. A declaration. It is long and deep and thorough just as he'd promised. My toes curl and my belly unfurls in desire. I may have bruises by the time he's done, but at this moment, I couldn't care less.

I want them.

I crave his dominant possession.

I *want* to be his, even if only for a few short minutes.

I don't stop him as his greedy lips work their way down my clavicle and strong hands grasp my hips, squeezing hard before snaking underneath my thong-bared ass, pulling me tight against his pulsing cock. Running his palms slowly down my bare legs, goose bumps trail behind as he grabs my ankles and clasps them behind his back.

In this position, I'm exposed, vulnerable, and literally seconds away from one hell of an intense orgasm. One that's been building since this afternoon. With the next flex of his hips, I gasp at the feel of the thickness that's hitting my sweet spot perfectly. His finger slips between my cheeks and follows the thin string south to my embarrassing wetness. We both moan loudly the second he circles my soaked opening, pushing in slightly before dragging my juices all the way back up my crack.

"Fuck, Nora." His voice is thick with passion. "I want you. I *need* you so badly I'm in agony." His entire body moves relentlessly against mine now, fucking me like we have no barriers. I wish we didn't. I want to feel him moving inside of me. I want to know if the memory I hold on to is real or something I've just trumped up in my lonely mind.

"Connelly...God," I pant, clawing at his ass so he keeps hitting the small bundle of nerves I need to send me flying apart. His mouth takes mine again, almost violently. I love it. Every raw, unguarded second of it.

Gripping my hip, he holds me in place as he continues to drive furiously into me. "That's it, princess. Come for me," he grunts against my lax mouth.

My orgasm hits me with the force of a hurricane. I'm viciously swept up in the maelstrom of pleasure that Connelly's every touch and every kiss have produced inside me. I bite his shoulder to stifle my cries, and he chants my name as shudder after shudder of pure bliss works its way through me.

It's mind-melting pleasure I've never felt before, and he's so damn talented he created it even with a barrier of linen and silk between us.

I've lost all sense of reality and am about half a second away from ripping off my clothes and begging him to take me on a rough, hot ride when laughter from down below penetrates the sexual fog that's fuzzing my head. It reminds me where I am...and what I have to hide. And why I can't do this.

"Connelly, stop," I pant. "We have to stop."

"Fuuuck." His forehead goes to mine and he pinches his eyes closed. Working to catch his breath, his jaw ticks in impatience. "I'm getting tired of that word, Nora," he tells me, his voice low and gravelly and breathless.

"Get off me. Please." I push. With a frustrated exhale he finally lifts his heavy bulk. I tug my dress down and right myself on the couch, ignoring the hand he's holding out, palm up. It is steady and calm while both of mine are shaking like an 8.2 Richter is raging through my body.

It is. It's called passion.

Something I haven't really felt since my one night with him.

Shit. Shit. Shit.

I sit there, eyes cast down, confusion and horror driving aftershocks through me. Sensing my turmoil, Connelly remains quiet, letting me gather my thoughts, not pushing me for once.

"We can't do this, Connelly." My shaking voice is outright wishy-washy.

"And what exactly can't we do, Nora?" His is soft and cajoling and patient. It twists my insides into knots.

"This. You. Me. Us!" I wave back and forth between us, still unable to raise my eyes to his. If I do, I'll be lost. Again. And I want to be. I want to get so fucking lost in him I don't need food or air or water. Just him. But I can't afford to.

"Why, princess?"

"Why what?" I ask, exasperated, trying desperately to smooth the wrinkles in my dress. Anything to avoid looking at him, falling again.

His movements are slow and precise when he squats down in front of my seated form. Gently he places his index finger under my chin and lifts it so I'm forced to make eye contact.

And I was right. The genuine confusion on his handsome face about my manic outbreak is starting to chase away my determination again. I barely catch it fast enough. I'm hanging on to it so damn tight my muscles burn.

"Why can't we do us?"

So many goddamn reasons. Too many. "It won't work," I say simply. Simple is always, always better. When you start talking too much, you say too much.

He nods his head, but I know he's about to argue. He's so damn calm, it's as if the last twenty minutes never even happened while my heart could win a hundred-meter dash about now. "And why do you think this won't work?"

Because you can't commit and if I have you in my life, I need a whole heap of commitment you're not capable of. Because I'm a horrible betrayer. Worse than Judas. I'm a Benedict Arnold. But I don't say any of that. I don't give him the truth. I just hedge. "It didn't before."

"We were teenagers, Nora. I'd like to think both of us have changed and matured since then."

"That's the problem, Connelly," I tell him softly, standing so he's also forced to stand and take a few steps back. "I *have* changed."

136

I walk around him only making it down two steps when his question floats heavy in the air in front of me, stopping me in my tracks. I consider lying. In the end, though, I don't. I don't think I can feed more hurtful words past my deceit-cracked lips, each one stinging worse than the one before it.

"Is it him? Harding? Are you in love with him?"

I've only ever been in love with you. "No."

"Is there someone else then?"

Not in the way you think. "No."

When he speaks again, his hot breath dances across my nape and I moan at the feel of his hands lightly settling on my hips. "Then you should know that I will move heaven and earth to make you mine again, Nora. It doesn't matter how much time it takes. It doesn't matter what I have to do. How many rocks I have to move or oceans I have to part. I'll use every ounce of my infinite patience to wait out whatever struggle you have going on inside of you because we belong together and you know it as well as I do."

When I feel his nose nuzzling the underside of my ear, my knees almost give out. "I love you. I have *always* loved you, Nora. You are lodged so far inside me I can't possibly get you out and I'm fucking done trying. And you should also know that I'm very adept at hearing the unspoken and I heard the words you *didn't* say loud and crystal clear, baby."

Chills.

I have them everywhere.

Walking away after he confessed he still loves

me is by far the hardest thing I've ever done in my entire life, but what other choice can I make? Before he can say another word, I flee down the stairs, his second fervent profession of the day clanging loudly behind like empty tin cans tied to my ankles.

Chapter 11

Nora

I look around the place I've called home for the last six years. Sealed boxes are stacked everywhere, waiting for the movers to arrive. I need to run a wet mop around the baseboards of the hardwood floors to get rid of the dust balls lining the corners. The windows still need to be cleaned. All final bills have been paid, all good-byes said, all memories packed away, ready to be shuffled to the next stop in life's journey.

You'd think after moving around so much during my childhood I'd be used to it by now. Strangely I'm not, even though this hasn't felt any more like a home than all of the other places I've lived. It is the place I've lived the longest, though: the house I moved to after I left my father's home in Baltimore.

Baltimore. The place my life started falling apart.

As a genetic researcher, my father's life was work, not us. His sequencing and genotyping research was widely published and regarded. His position at Johns Hopkins was the realization of a lifelong dream. Because I was the good little daughter, I never complained when we had to move or when he missed my plays or concerts or volleyball games. I understood how important his work was to him and to others.

But once we moved to Baltimore after I graduated high school, he was a ghost. Many nights he didn't even bother coming home. I became more and more resentful, especially when my mom was diagnosed with stage-four lung cancer thirteen months after we moved. Nine months later, we were burying her. She suffered greatly and because of my father's new position, I was her primary caregiver at one of the hardest times in my own life.

Thank God for Uncle Carl. He flew in from Cincinnati as much as possible to help, even taking a leave of absence toward the end when she was put in hospice to live with us until she passed. Had it not been for him, I don't think I would have made it through those dark days.

After my mom died, I turned angry and bitter. I unfairly blamed all the bad in my life on my father. Had he been home, where he should have been, maybe my life would be entirely different. Maybe I would have been a high school psychologist like I'd planned. Maybe he'd still be alive because he'd have no reason to be on that plane. Maybe my mom's cancer would have been caught earlier because he would have realized something was wrong well before she did. And if not, maybe at least she could have died with the comfort of a loving husband, instead of a distraught daughter and distressed family friend by her side.

Maybe I'd be married to Connelly and I'd be living a very different life.

See? Irrational. I know, yet I can't help the way I felt. *Still* feel. Except now, alongside the anger and bitterness that have their claws buried deep in me, I harbor immense guilt for feeling that way, because my father and I were still not on the best of terms when he died suddenly.

"Everything all packed?" a familiar male voice calls from behind me.

I smile sadly, not turning around to face Carl. I'm still pretty fucking mad at him, so I've been avoiding him as much as possible these past weeks. "Yes," I reply tersely.

It's been three weeks since I signed my life away. Okay, so maybe that's a *tad* bit melodramatic, but that's what it feels like nonetheless. I've done nothing—and I mean *nothing*—but lie awake in bed every night reliving every syllable of Connelly's genuine confession and every second of his male display of dominance from our meeting and the party two weeks ago.

It left me wanting him even more than I have all these years.

It flayed every emotion open so now they're raw and exposed.

"I'm so—"

"Don't say you're sorry. Not again."

He takes a deep breath. I hear him blow it out slowly, the movement catching my hair. "You're doing the right thing, Ladybug," he says quietly.

"Well you didn't give me much of a choice, now did you?" I retort.

Sighing, he speaks after a few silent, tense beats. "You're right. I fucked up, but what's done is done. I'd honestly like to say if I could go back and make different decisions, I would, but..." He leaves his sentence hanging. We both know the truth. He wouldn't. "I don't want you to leave mad at me, Nora. I just couldn't bear that. Please." The last few words are choked, thick with remorse and shame and sorrow.

My vision blurs as I try to hold my emotions in check. I will not let this break me. I am far stronger than my life's circumstances. It took time, maturity, and soul-searching, but I know I can handle whatever life throws at me and then some.

"I'm mad at the situation. I don't want to have to start over again."

I can.

I will.

I've done it time and again.

I just don't *want* to.

Here, it's all too easy to bury my head in the sand and try to justify my lies and actions, but there's also a part of me, bigger than I want to acknowledge, that's also excited about being around Connelly more, even if it will lead to my demise.

"You know, sometimes life takes us to places we don't think we want to go, but it's exactly where we need to be because that's where our next great thing will happen."

I snort. "Is that some Robert Frost or Walt Whitman quote?" I never gave a crap about boring English lit when I was in school. Still don't. I'd prefer a good, smutty romance novel to poems and sonnets any day.

He chuckles, stepping beside me before throwing an arm around my shoulder and tugging me close. "No. It's a Carl Steele original."

"You should have it burned onto a plaque or something," I say, wiping away a stray tear before sinking into his hold. It's a sign of forgiveness and acceptance for everything he is and everything he's not. No one's perfect and I should stop expecting them to be. God knows I'm so far from it, it's just a blip on the horizon now, unattainable.

"There's my girl." His lips lovingly touch my temple. "Have you talked to Mira?"

"Yes. She hooked me up with a real estate agent who found a nice rental house in LaGrange. It's in a good area, close to good schools and the train for easy commuting downtown. I think I'll talk to Camille about telecommuting a couple of days a week. That would definitely help."

"I'm sure they'll be flexible."

"I don't know," I mumble. "Connelly Colloway doesn't seem like the flexible type to me." In fact, he seems downright ruthless these days in order to get exactly what he wants. He's made it perfectly clear it's me, and that both thrills and scares the shit out of me for more reasons than I want to explore right now.

Carl huffs. "Let me know if you have any trouble, Nora, and I'll take care of it." A few beats later, "So, I heard you have a new assignment. One from Wynn."

"Who told you that?"

"Nora, these people are like family to me. Just because I've sold the company doesn't mean I don't know everything that goes on."

"Rick?"

He chuckles. "He's got looser lips than a Saturday night special."

"Oh my God. Where do you come up with this stuff?" I smile, snaking an arm around his waist. Even though I'm mad at him, I'm going to miss him like crazy. "I'm sure this new assignment is going over like a lead balloon about now at Wynn. I understand it's a pretty big client of theirs."

"Well, the only thing that's constant is change. Get on the horse or be left staring at its ass. It's pretty damn simple."

I chuckle again. I love Carl's crazy euphemisms.

"Kinnick Investments is a pretty big deal. They're a multibillion-dollar conglomerate."

Yes, they are, and I have to wonder why I was assigned this client instead of Jeanine. "Wow, you really do have the scoop."

"CEO's retiring, I hear."

"Yeah, but that's suspicious. She was just hired less than three years ago and I heard their latest acquisition caused their stock to plummet and has investors upset. She was a little too employee friendly versus Wall Street friendly."

"Just up your alley."

I've had several clients like this over the years. The board of directors seems to take no culpability for either their approvals on their CEO choices or their acquisitions. The CEO is always sent down the river, the designated fall guy for a poor business decision or drop in stock prices. Always. They make the big bucks for a reason, and it's because their performance is under constant scrutiny, their ass always on the line.

His heavy hand squeezes my shoulder. "Your mom would have been proud of you, Ladybug. Of everything you've accomplished."

Would she? I used to think so. I'm not so sure anymore. No one outside of her, not even my dad, knew my deepest secret. She never once judged me for my decisions, hard as they were, but I think now she might. I think now she'd tell me how wrong I've been all along.

A sudden melancholy washes over me. "I miss her," I choke.

"So do I." His voice is full of the kind of sorrow that only comes from losing someone you deeply love. Friends since elementary school, Carl had a special bond with my father, but I think he had a special spot deep inside for my mother. Her death was as hard on him as it was on me. Maybe even more so.

"Why have so many bad things happened to me?" I ask wistfully, feeling the full weight of all I've lost in life. It's rhetorical and pathetic and full of self-pity. I try not to wallow in that muck too often. It gets sticky there.

"Not everything has been bad, Nora," he reminds me.

We gaze out the three bay windows that

overlook my decent-sized backyard, watching the one good thing in my life, outside of Carl, play on the swing set we spent an entire Saturday afternoon putting together six years ago now. Hawk, our five-year-old Basenji, runs back and forth, nipping at her heels and toes when she swings past him. Her squeal spurns him on.

"No. Not everything," I concur quietly.

As I watch my daughter play and talk and sing to herself, like I used to do at her age, all I see is *him*. Now more than ever.

I see his beguiling eyes.

I see his innate intelligence.

I see his magnetic charisma.

I see him in her every single day.

I see the girl that, as she's grown older and older, can be mistaken for none other than the spitting image of her father.

I see the daughter I've kept from him for all these years, because of my anger, hurt, shame, and fear.

I see my entire world falling apart if he ever finds out what the hell I've done. There isn't even an "if" anymore. There's just "when." It's only a matter of time now. The sands of the hourglass are falling faster and faster, gravity tugging hard at the tiny grains that will lead to my demise when the last one hits bottom.

He thinks he loves me; but he will be full of nothing but hatred when the truth comes out. I've been racking my brain for the past two weeks on how to come clean because I know I have to. It's time. It's *past* time.

I justified my actions early on by convincing myself I wasn't even sure she was his. But when it couldn't be denied any longer, I came up with new excuses. He didn't want *me* to begin with, so why would he want *her*. Hell, he didn't even want children. *That* I knew for a fact. I've told myself I couldn't possibly stomach his rejection again and I'd never put my daughter through his rebuff either. I've used his commitment issues and womanizing as rationalization to keep him away from us.

But after spending two solid days with him, all I feel now is guilt.

Profound, gut-twisting, soul-tearing, unforgivable guilt.

Guilt for my mistakes.

Guilt for sleeping with another man the night I was betrayed out of hurt, despair, and spite.

Guilt for letting pride and fear keep me from doing the right thing when it stares me in the face every single day.

Mostly, though, I feel guilt that maybe, just maybe, I've misjudged everything, depriving not only Connelly of his daughter but my daughter of her father.

I know it won't matter to him once this comes out, but I actually decided to tell him. Twice before. But both times it was as if the world was working against us in the cruelest of ways again, so I left well enough alone, thinking our lives were meant to be without him.

But now. Now...

"I love you. I've always loved you, Nora."

Could I have been wrong all this time? Would Connelly have wanted us? Would he have absolved my transgressions? Could I have forgiven his? Would we be the perfect happy family now had I just shown up with his daughter in tow, begging for his forgiveness?

I don't know. I guess I never will.

A part of me has always held on to the fantasy of Connelly Colloway. That we would one day reunite. That one day he'd be mine and that maybe we'd be happy, living the life together I'd always daydreamed about.

The small part of me that still hopes for such things is the young and foolish one, the teenager who fell madly in love with an unattainable ideal of life and happiness and the man she thought was utter perfection in every way except the one that really counts.

Fidelity.

The woman in me is still irrefutably in love with Connelly, regardless of his commitment issues. I've never stopped, even through the hurt, pain, and cheating. My heart beats only for him. I have no hope of erasing any part of him from me without erasing a part of me, too.

But the pragmatist in me knows a life with him is not reality. All our future holds is anger, bitterness, and resentment.

As I stand here watching Zel, the one person I love more than life itself, genuine fear coils deep in my gut. Connelly will hate me once this comes to light, but I've never thought about the rest of the fallout. How will Zel take this news? That I've perhaps unfairly kept her father from her and it was all my doing. Not his. I've never once thought about the fact that she may not forgive me and I may lose my daughter, too.

It's true what they say about hindsight. It slaps you square in the face with the sting of undeniable clarity. You wonder how you couldn't have seen the answers plain as day before. And what I see right now makes me utterly sick with regret.

What have you done, Nora? What the hell have you done?

Chapter 12

CONN

I hear footsteps straining behind me on the dock, but I don't turn. I don't move. I take another swallow of the drink in my hand and watch my bare feet ripple the lake water with each swirl.

I love spending time at my mother's house. Sometimes, when things get too hectic at work in the city, I just come here for a Saturday and unwind. Spend it with her. We shop the farmers market. Go to a matinee. Sit on the patio, listen to the crickets, and talk about Dad and how much we both miss him.

My childhood home is quiet and peaceful. Serene. Filled with happy memories. And this weekend it's bursting with family since we're having our annual "end of summer" Labor Day celebration. Even though my brothers and I all live in the same city, Gray, Asher, and I in the same downtown building even, I cherish getting together with my entire family here. Especially more now that it's expanded with fun, spunky women who keep my brothers on their toes. I love seeing my mom interact with her daughters-in-law and coddle her new twin grandbabies, Gray's kids.

Barb Colloway is the greatest human being on planet earth. Selfless, loving. The most forgiving person I know. I like to think I inherited a few of my good qualities from her.

The wood creaks beside me. When another pair of male feet quietly joins mine, I still don't look. Instead, I enjoy the sun setting behind the trees and the way it makes the almost black water look like glass. It makes me ache, reminding me of Nora's secret-filled dark eyes and how fucking much I miss them. And her.

Nora loved our lake. We spent many a night at the end of this dock hanging our feet in the water. Talking. Laughing. Flirting.

It was here she showed me the mole on the inside of her upper thigh, almost right where it meets her honeyed center. Fuck, I was achingly hard that night.

It was here she told me how she wished she wasn't an only child. It pained me I had built-in best friends and she had no one.

It was here she told me she wanted a minivan full of kids and donated a penny to the bottom of the lake for good luck. I secretly wished I would be the one to give them to her as the copper sank out of sight.

It was here she confessed she'd always felt like a part of her was missing...until she met me. I twined our fingers together and told her I felt the same.

And as the sun set one warm evening, casting her in a golden glow that I swear to God made her look as though she'd just been dipped in light and sent down from heaven as a gift to me from The Man himself, it was here that I almost confessed I was so madly in love with her I couldn't see straight. Instead, I kissed the shit out of her until we were breathless and lost to lust.

Jesus, she is one stubborn woman. When we first met, she wouldn't give me the time of day. I wore her down, but it took months to move past the friend zone. She denied she felt more when I knew she did. From the word go, though, I wanted it all. I was patient when maybe I should have pushed instead. I have to wonder—if I'd pressed harder, faster, tied her heart and her body to me sooner, would she be sitting beside me now instead of my brother? And I have to wonder if it's too late.

It's been two weeks since the incident at SER's welcome party. Two long, endless, torturous weeks without her face, her touch, her smart mouth. Because of the new assignment I gave her, we've talked on the phone a couple of times and through e-mail briefly. But she's short, closed off. All business. It's pissing me off for so many reasons, not the least of which are the ulcer-inducing, unfamiliar feelings I have rolling around inside of me.

Now that I've seen her again, tasted her again, felt her underneath me again, I'm in absolute and utter agony without her. I ache all over. But this is far more than just a fucking horrific case of blue balls. God knows I had those for the rest of the night after she fled until I could make it back to my condo and jerk off to the musky scent of her still on my hand.

No, being without her now is more than just plain old discomfort. It's downright malaise. I feel weak, almost ill. I'm anxious and in a constant piss-poor mood. I'm miserable and, in turn, I'm making everyone around me miserable. Or trying my fucking hardest to.

I'm totally out of sorts. I am usually easygoing. I make people laugh. I'm the voice of reason. I'm the fucking life of the party.

But I have turned into something I swore I wouldn't.

Pussy whipped. Just like my brothers.

And I fucking hate it.

"Beer?" Gray finally asks, handing over a frosty bottle of Sprecher's Black Bavarian.

"Nah." I pick up my peach Snapple and finish it off, setting the empty beside me.

"Wow, you have it pretty fucking bad, Conn. Tea leaves instead of hops or malt?"

I have no comeback, so I just shrug. It's not often I turn down a cold brew, but I haven't touched a lick of anything in two solid weeks that will fuck my head up any more than it already is.

I can't. I already feel so close to the edge of desperation, the last thing I need is something to exacerbate it. So instead, I've been hitting the gym daily, sometimes more than once, trying to put the brakes on my fucking pity party and get my game back on track.

Nora moves to Chicago this coming week. I need to be ready, because if I feel like this now, I cannot imagine how I'll feel if she continues to reject me. I can't even stomach that thought. There is no world I can live in without Nora as part of it.

Getting her in my bed is proving to be a harder feat than I originally thought.

"So...the redhead is back, huh?"

I snort. "Why are you down here, Gray? I thought the fact that I bit Ash's head off earlier when he asked me to be his errand boy would have clued you all in. I'm feeling kinda antisocial about now."

"Drew the short end of the stick," he deadpans.

At last, I give in and turn to see he's smirking, casually waiting for my reaction. I chuckle, scrubbing a hand over my stubble.

"Shit. I'm sorry. I've been a dick for the past couple of weeks."

"Weeks? Try months. Like six."

"It hasn't been that long, asshole."

"Pretty damn close, brother. Red have something to do with it?"

"Not *something*." Grabbing the tea bottle, I begin to pick at the label, feeling slight relief at the chance to get this hefty weight off my chest. Ash has prodded but, not ready to talk about it yet, I've told him to fuck off. "Everything."

"How come I never knew how you felt about this girl?"

Gray was in college by the time I started hanging out with Nora, and after...let's just say I didn't really talk to anyone about her crushing blow to my heart or ego.

"Heartbreak is best buried deep, rather than staining your sleeve."

"Yeah. I know that better than most."

I nod, not knowing how to respond. I watched Gray go through years of heartbreak and loneliness without his now wife, Livia, by his side. It was hard to witness. The entire time I empathized. I'd silently walked ten miles in his shoes, but it wasn't until I saw Nora again that I realized just how bad the hell I was ghosting through all these years truly was.

"I've never been able to forget her and I can't figure out why," I finally confess.

Gray laughs, deep and loud, as if he has a secret I'm not privy to. "And you won't. One of life's unsolved mysteries, Conn. But does it matter why anyway? Shouldn't all that matters is...you can't?"

"I don't know. I guess."

Silence wraps me in her memories...

Her head tilts to the clear blue sky and her nose crinkles slightly before she sneezes loudly.

"Why do you do that?" I ask, genuinely curious. She does it all the time.

"Do what?"

"Look at the sun and sneeze?"

"Because it makes me."

"The sun makes you sneeze?" I laugh. "You're making that up. I've never heard of such a thing."

With a broad smile on her lips, she faces me. My

breath catches with how beautiful the reflection of the lake is in her bright green eyes.

"It is a thing. It's called photic sneeze reflex and up to thirty-five percent of people have it."

"Really? That's weird." The random facts she knows about so many things always blow me away.

"You're weird." She's laughing now, pushing on my chest playfully. She has no idea how much I love it when she touches me, even in play.

...before Gray tugs me back to the present, damn him. "She's the one, then."

I nod, feeling immense relief to admit it out loud. "There's not room for anyone else. There never has been."

"What does she want?"

"I wish I knew. She wants me...that much she can't hide. But she's running. I just can't figure out what or who from," I reply quietly. I hope it's not me, but my fear is it is.

"Are you sure you want to know?" says the man with firsthand experience.

I don't know. *Do I?* Is it possible to move ahead without knowing? Do I want to unearth the type of secrets that Livia kept from Gray? Ones that may destroy me? Destroy us? "I guess I don't know."

"Do you love her, Conn? I mean...truly love her? Or is she just another challenge to you? A revenge fuck perhaps?"

My head snaps to Gray, ready to chew him a new asshole, but I stop short of my verbal lashing because as much as it pains me to admit it, I deserve it. Regardless of my "honorable" intentions in all of my sexual escapades over the years, the simple fact of the matter is I have used women all of my adult life. It wasn't with malicious intent; it was self-preservation. But the reasons don't matter, I guess. They don't change facts.

"She is the *ultimate* challenge, Gray. She always has been. But this is not about revenge or winning. I want her. Period. I am so fucking in love with her I don't know what to do about it. I'm feeling a whole shitload of emotions I'm just not used to, that I've tried so hard not to feel for too many years. It's hard to process it all, you know?"

He nods. "Love makes men crazy. Possessive. Animalistic, really. The truest form of my base self is how I feel around Livvy. It's like she strips me down to my primal level with one bat of her eyelashes and I would do anything for her. Be anything she needs. The one thing I would never do is let her go."

How right he is. Honestly, if I could get away with tying Nora to my bed and keeping her there for the rest of my life, I'd do it. At least until she agreed to be my wife.

My *wife*.
What.
The.
Fuck.
Am.
I.
Thinking?
That you are nothing without her. Less than nothing.

"What happened between you two?" Gray asks. He picks up a pebble lying next to us and throws it into the water where it lands with a plop. I watch the waves ripple from the center outward, getting wider and slower the further they stray from the epicenter of the disturbance.

That's exactly how I feel. The ripples from loving Nora were always present, softly lapping my insides, no matter how much time passed from that day, no matter how far away I got from the epicenter. But now I'm right smack inside the hotbed again. The waves are choppy and unforgiving and I think her rebuff may be my punishment for the way I've lived my life over the past decade without her.

"She dumped me just weeks after she moved to Baltimore with her family. Gave me some bullshit about meeting another guy. That we'd never work long-distance. I didn't buy it but she refused to talk to me again. I never understood it. Still don't."

After a few beats, Gray says, "She wouldn't have found out about that girl at your birthday party, would she?"

Color me fucking stunned.

"What did you say?"

Gray shrugs. "Listen, Ash swore me to secrecy, so don't tell him I said anything."

"That fucking traitor," I breathe, unable to drum up true anger.

Regardless of how hurt I was that Nora just up and left me, I know I'm not blameless here. In fact, I think karma may have bit me and bit me good. I made one horrible mistake, one night long ago.

But that's all it takes to reshape your future. Just one single moment of weakness. Just one lapse in judgment. Just one.

I drift back to that all-day party Alan threw for me for my nineteenth birthday just two weeks after Nora left. His dad was at a conference. His mom had taken off for the weekend with one of her torrid lovers, which was her norm, so he had the run of his parents' million-dollar home. There must have been more than a hundred underage kids there. I still don't know how the cops didn't bust us. Alan told me he went through ten kegs and countless bottles of liquor. Whatever your poison, it was available at that party, including pot, X, coke even.

I was depressed, lonely, and miserable without Nora. I begged her to come back and celebrate with me. All I wanted was to spend the day with her. But she said her mom hadn't been well and she needed to stay home, so as the day went on and turned into night, the more shitfaced I got. I don't remember much about anything after seven o'clock in the evening.

What I do remember, however, was waking up the next morning in one of Alan's four guest bedrooms with the worst hangover I have ever had and an unknown naked girl draped over my equally naked form. A couple used condoms strewn on the carpeted floor were like blinking neon signs advertising our indiscretions from the night before.

As much as I wanted to deny otherwise, it was obvious they were mine. My skin was sticky with sweat and bodily fluids. But I didn't remember a fucking thing. The night was a total blank. Still is to this day.

I'll never forget sitting there on the edge of the bed gripping the mattress until my knuckles screamed, staring my crimes right in the face. Panic ran rampant through my blood. I was sick with shame and disappointment in myself. Even though I couldn't scrape a memory together, I wanted to call Nora to confess and hoped she'd find it within herself to forgive me. Instead, I called Ash to come pick me up, hoping like hell I would wake from that fucking nightmare.

But I didn't and I never would. Nine days later I got the "it's not going to work" phone call.

Then a few weeks after that, still mourning my loss of Nora, said girl confronted me with a pregnancy scare. And I was scared shitless, let me tell you. My whole future hung in the balance because I slept with a girl whose name I didn't even know. I made her—Meredith Lee—pee on a stick in front of me, which showed she was, in fact, pregnant. I was reeling. Was it mine? We'd used protection, right? Fuck, how could I be sure? That night was blacker than black.

After that, I became a little reckless. I drank and drove one night, uncaring about the consequences. Slammed into a hundred-year-old oak just two blocks from my house. Totaled my car *and* my knee. Luckily no one else was involved and thanks to Asher for covering up for me, no charges were filed, but my life and my basketball career were both fucked.

As I lay at home recovering from my ACL repair, Meredith came to see me again and gave me yet more life-altering news. She'd had a miscarriage. As horrible as it sounds, I was relieved. I'd made a terrible mistake and I couldn't imagine paying for it for the rest of my days tied to a woman I didn't care about.

I didn't drink again until I started college at UCLA the end of that summer and I have never been that drunk again. One blackout was one blackout too many for me, thank you the fuck much.

I've thought about that night often. Wondered if Nora found out somehow. But I keep coming back to the same answer. No way in hell. There were exactly four people who were privy to what happened. Asher, Alan, Meredith, and myself.

Though she was upset, Meredith was just as relieved about the miscarriage as I was. She was headed off to London that fall to start vet school at University of London's Royal Veterinary College and a baby didn't fit into her plans either. Asher would never breathe a word. He was my twin, my blood. He'd protect me until his dying day. And Alan was Alan. He wasn't blood, but he was my brother by proxy.

One night, one bad choice altered my life forever. Does Nora know? Fuck. It makes me sick to think maybe all this time she has and that's the reason she left me.

"It didn't mean anything. I don't even remember a single second of it," I tell Gray softly.

"Connelly," he sighs my name heavily,

reminding me of exactly how I think our father would react. Disappointment is etched all over him.

Shit. I deserve it. I was eaten up inside trying to figure out how or *if* I would break the news to Nora. How do you tell someone something you don't even remember yourself? But then Murphy's Law struck. I probably got what I deserved.

I've been pissed at Nora all these years, but truth be told, had I been given an opportunity to confess, chances are high Nora and I would have been over either way. But if she knew, she didn't give me that chance. And therein lies my hurt. It may be selfish and unwarranted and may not have changed the outcome, but if *that's* the reason she left me, I at least deserved a chance to explain and apologize and grovel for forgiveness until she gave it to me. I wouldn't have let her walk away. As it was, I shouldn't have.

"Did he like Nora?"

"Who?" I ask, thoughts still clouded by yesterday's mistakes.

"Alan."

Alan. Yes. I'm pretty damn sure he was in love with her, too. "Who wouldn't like Nora? She was a dick magnet."

"And Alan knew about this whole cheating thing that happened?"

I nod slowly. Alan was the *only* one I could confide in. Although Asher knew about my indiscretion, he never knew about the pregnancy scare. I was too embarrassed to tell him.

"And you trusted the friend who's been jealous

of you your entire life not to say anything to a girl *he* also liked? Who *you* won over him?"

I shake my head furiously. "Alan wasn't jealous of me, Gray," I reply with utter confidence. "And he knew how much I loved Nora. He would never do that to me."

Alan Johansen was my best friend outside of Asher. We met in kindergarten when another kid on the playground pushed him down and called him a retard. I'd watched him get picked on for almost two weeks before I stepped in and laid down some of the kids' own medicine on him. He was never bothered again. I gained a lifelong friend.

Alan was loyal. A good friend. Still is to this day.

"The fuck he wasn't, Conn. Star basketball player, class president, National Honor Society inductee, and girls trailing after you like baby ducks? Everyone saw it but you. I think more than anything he was jealous of your bond with your brothers. Your parents. Your family. You had everything he didn't. And he wanted it."

Alan had his issues. We all do. But a shitty home life doesn't make a traitor. I never sensed jealousy from him. Ever. Alan spent a lot of time with my family, even vacationing with us a couple of times, but I never got the feeling he was jealous of what I had.

Was he?

Alan stabbing me in the back would be akin to one of my brothers doing it. At the time, I just couldn't see that happening, but talking about it out loud for the first time more than a decade later, I now hear how the whole story sounds. And if I were Gray, I'd draw the same conclusion.

I think back to Nora's feisty comment at the cocktail party about my reputation preceding me and how that ship sailed eleven years ago. It dripped with raw hurt that couldn't be faked. Could she possibly have meant Meredith?

Did my best friend betray me?

"Yes, I did trust him."

"Maybe that was a mistake."

"Maybe," I mumble, doubt poking the smallest of holes into the indignation I've held fast to all these years.

Fuck. Could the blame for losing Nora this entire time rest on *my* shoulders? Could one night of drowning my sorrows and wallowing in self-pity have caused me to end up relationship phobic and in an endless string of beds belonging to women I don't give two shits about? Is it possible Alan betrayed our friendship, our brotherhood, and ratted me out to Nora?

I don't believe it, but even if he did, I'm not sure it makes any difference. In fact, I know it doesn't. It won't erase the last few years and all the bad choices I've made. It won't change that night.

I may not know how we ended up where we are today, I may not be able to erase past mistakes or change history, but this I do know: I have one hell of an uphill battle to win back the woman I know I *can* live without—because I've done it this long—but who I simply don't *want to* live without anymore.

I was dead-on when I told her she belonged

with me. But I am hers and I belong with her, too. Hell, I more than just belong *with* her, I belong *to* her. I always have, and it feels freeing to finally cut the macho bullshit and admit it.

Pussy whipped. Right here.

Oh well...own it, right?

Feeling lighter than I have in weeks, I tell Gray, "I'll take that beer now."

Laughing, he relinquishes his hold on the now probably warm brew. "Get ready for the ride of your life, little brother."

"That sounds like a warning."

"It is. It won't be easy."

"Nothing worth having ever is," I mumble, taking a deep pull from the brown glass bottle.

I decide right then and there I'm going to come clean. Whether Nora knows about the past or not is irrelevant. *I know.* I need to do right by her. Strip my soul bare and confess all my past sins so she sees I mean business.

I will pursue her to the ends of this earth. And this time, I mean to keep her.

Chapter 13

Nora

I smile at Kam's text. Kam knows about Zel, of course, but like everyone else, she doesn't know who her father is. I *may* have led her to believe it was a fictitious rebound. The same fictitious guy I let Connelly believe I'd left him for. And at lunch a few weeks ago, after I was positive she hadn't fit the pieces together, I mentioned I needed to find someone to help out with Zel—getting her to and from school and to the tutor three times a week. One of the hardest parts about moving is getting everyone into a routine and, Sunny, the part-time nanny I had in Cincinnati was an absolute gem. She was in college, lived just down the street, and loved Zel like her own sister. It killed Zel to leave Sunny, and in turn, it killed me.

However, I think Landyn Monroe, the niece of one of Kam's friends, will work out perfectly. She just recently moved to Chicago for grad school. She needed a job. I needed her. The night I had her over for an interview, Zel and Landyn instantly bonded over their mutual love of the Chicago Blackhawks and their hate of the Detroit Red Wings. Carl turned Zel into a hockey nut. She's a die-hard fan. And while she was sad to leave her friends and Sunny behind in Cincinnati, the only home she remembers, moving to the city where her favorite team in the whole world hails from had her excitedly packing boxes the night we talked about it.

Me: fab. zel loves her
Kam: i knew she would.
Me: thanks for recommending her. u saved me
Kam: anything for you babe. drinks soon? want u to meet some friends
Me: can't wait.
Kam: gtg. luv u lucy. so glad ur here
Me: back at ya ethel

"Knock, knock." I look up from my cell to see Brad taking up most of my open doorway with his broad frame. He looks handsome today in his black slacks and white-collared button-down. They have a pretty casual dress code at Wynn, but Brad can't seem to swap out his dress shirts for polos. "Have a minute?"

"Yes, sure. Come on in."

He closes the door and slides his large frame into the navy-blue padded seat across from my desk. It's almost too small for him. When I laugh, he knows exactly why.

"Getting all settled?"

"Getting there," I reply, looking around. I had all my files shipped and they arrived earlier in the week. I have one more box to go through before everything will have a home. What is it about that one lone box that never seems to get unpacked?

"All moved in at home?"

"Now that's going to take a bit longer," I say with a smirk. "The kitchen's completely unpacked and I've cleared a path through my living room. That's about it."

"You should have taken me up on my offer. We'd have everything done by now."

My mouth turns down slightly. "I appreciate the offer, Brad, but I'm pretty much a pro at moving. Besides, Carl came for a few days and helped with the hard stuff, like putting together shelves and beds."

He nods, but I can tell he's still disappointed. Looking around, he takes in my own private space. It's an office. Nothing special. Four walls that hold a desk, a few chairs, and some filing cabinets.

"Nice view," he nods to the wall of windows behind me.

Oh. And a kick-ass view of the all-glass Thompson Center.

I smile. "It is." I've seen Brad's office. He has a nice view of office buildings. And even though the Thompson Center houses governmental offices, you can look at it and pretend it's being used for something more remarkable than wasted taxpayer dollars.

"I'm not surprised," he states plainly. Throwing one elbow over the back of his chair, he rests one ankle on his opposite knee and waits. He doesn't sound upset or judgmental, just matter-of-fact. Brad and I have spent a lot of time together at work and socially, so I can read him pretty well. Right now, he looks relaxed when he's anything but.

My forehead wrinkles in confusion. "What are you not surprised about?" I ask, leaning back in my own seat.

"That you got the best office out of the SER transplants."

I chuckle before I realize he's dead serious. I study Brad's eyes and facial expressions for a few long seconds. He doesn't look away. I've never been an office snob and he knows that. I took the office I was assigned, but if he'd asked, I would have given it up. Not that I'll complain about the view, but all I've ever needed was a door, a desk, and a computer.

"I didn't ask for this, Brad. I didn't even want this sale to happen. I didn't want to move here, uproot my life. I didn't want to take this job, and I did everything within my power to stop it. You know that. So what's this really about? Because I know it's not about square footage or views of the Chicago Loop."

He breaks our locked stare briefly before returning his eyes to mine. Then I see it. Or he's not able to hide it any longer, one of the two.

Jealousy.

"Brad, don't—"

"I don't want to see you hurt again, Nora. I..." He huffs in frustration, stands and paces a few

169

steps toward the door before turning back to face me. "I don't want *him* to hurt you again and I'm watching this whole thing unfold in front of me like some goddamned tragic Broadway play. He's a manwhore, Nora. I've heard stories about the infamous CEO of Wynn Consulting for years! He can't commit. Hell, he doesn't *want* to commit. He fucks anything that walks and he likes it that way. He can't be what you need, what your daughter needs."

"Stop. Right. Now," I say through clenched teeth. I don't want to hear him voice my own thoughts, my own questionable rationale, or anything else I've used to keep Connelly away from our daughter and from me, but I certainly don't need to hear it at work where Connelly could drop in unannounced at a moment's notice.

"I love you, Nora." His voice is ripe with pain and sorrow for all he wants but knows he can't have.

"Brad, please..." My tone beseeches him to stop before this conversation goes to places that won't end well for either of us. I care about Brad. Not in the way he does me, but seeing him torn apart like this makes me feel as if something in me is missing and that's why I can't give him what he wants.

But it's not rocket science to understand you can't give away what you don't have. And my heart hasn't been my own since I was a junior in high school.

"I know. Christ, I know." He throws his hands up in defeat before they drop with a slap to his thighs. "You're not in love with me, I get it. As much as I want you to be, you're not, because it's *him*. It's always been him. The attraction was tangible between you two at that party and everyone saw it, Nora. Hell, the room heated twenty fucking degrees the moment his eyes landed on you like you were the whole menu for the night. It *gutted* me to watch you with him knowing I can give you everything you need but nothing you want, and he can give you nothing you need, but everything you want. He'll break your fucking heart. Again."

I stare at him. His chest heaving, his face flushed, his heart breaking into pieces right before me. I open my mouth, not sure what I'm going to say when he puts his hands on my desk and leans toward me, pinning me with sad, knowing eyes. "He holds you in the past while life marches on around you without your participation. You're still in love with him, Nora." His eyes track to the place on my new desk where my picture frames sit and then back to me. An obvious one is missing. "And now I understand why."

My lungs seize and my mouth is gaping in disbelief at the conclusions he's drawn when a disembodied male voice calls, "Am I interrupting?"

Oh shit.

Oh.

Fucking.

Shit.

Neither of us answers. Awkward silence stretches on as Brad stays as is, eyes volleying back and forth between mine. After what seems like an hour, but is probably mere seconds, he slowly straightens, facing our boss. He's still blocking my line of sight to the door. And Connelly.

"We were just finishing up," he responds tightly.

Oh shit. Shit. Fuck. Shit. How much did Connelly hear? And why did I not hear him knock? Oh my God. Connelly *cannot* find out this way. I need to tell him my way, in my own time, not have him overhear some overheated argument from a scorned male whose affections I can't return. Anxiety sits like a ten-ton mass of twisted steel in my stomach, holding me down, making me nauseous.

What did Brad say? My mind works backward. Did he mention Zel? Fuck, I don't remember.

"I need a moment of Nora's time," Connelly says calmly, taking a few steps inside where he finally comes into my peripheral. Even out of the corner of my eye, it's plain to see the man exudes power and control. He's always carried himself with confidence and ferocity. All of those traits are what attracted me to him in the first place, but the grown-up version of them is magnetic and thoroughly irresistible.

I don't look at him, though. I can't. I'm worried—no, not worried...*terrified*—terrified as hell about what I'm going to see on his face.

Anger?

Confusion?

Hatred?

It doesn't matter, I decide. Because nothing I'm picturing could prepare me for what I do see when

I force my eyes to his. Ready for my penance, I am completely taken aback instead, my breath catching hard in my throat.

They are full of undeniable love and sweet affection.

A sweat of blessed relief dots my forehead and my lungs fill with much-needed oxygen. *Thank God. Thank God.*

"Of course you do," Brad mumbles flippantly. "I'll talk to you later, Nora."

But I don't respond. I barely hear the door close, our heated gazes locked hard on each other. His eyes smolder. His scruffy face is sexy as hell. His sharp inky-black tailored suit molds to him with perfection. He looks every bit the playboy he is, which should turn me off. It does the total opposite instead. Once again, I'm free-falling into the irresistible sensual pull that is Connelly Colloway.

Damn him. I am doomed. My heart will never be free of him.

Never.

"Hi," he says softly, lulling me deeper into his sticky web of false promises.

"Hi," I parrot dumbly.

I've seen Connelly exactly twice since I started in the Wynn corporate office almost two weeks ago. Once was at a one-hour staff meeting the Monday afternoon I started when he spent five minutes kicking it off before he left, leaving me to wonder why he'd hardly even glanced in my direction. The other was yesterday in the hallway as we passed each other.

That time he left me burning with desire. He was with Asher, who politely nodded at me while Connelly's blazing stare practically disintegrated my panties into liquid. But other than just saying my name on a low, sexy rumble, he walked right on past. I had to force myself not to look back at the taut ass I'd held in my palms as he made me come undone several weeks ago with a few thrusts of his fabric-covered hips.

"May I sit?" He gestures to the seat Brad vacated.

A relieved smile tugs at my mouth. "Well, since that's the property of Wynn and you own the company, I guess you already own that chair so you don't need my permission to sit in it, do you?"

His deep chuckle rolls over me like gentle ocean waves. It's light and refreshing and it feels so damn good, I find myself laughing along with him.

"So you're saying I don't need permission to take anything that's company property then. Is that it?"

Remembering our heated exchange about me being his property, laughter dies on my lips as his gets louder. "You're too easy. God, I have missed you, Nora." My pulse skyrockets at his devastating smile. I want to say the words back, but I can't force them out. He takes a seat in the guest chair and crosses his long, lean legs, his warm hazels never straying from mine. "Not many people dare talk to me the way you do, you know."

"Well, I know how you much you like a challenge," I reply, proud of myself for my witty comeback.

His amused smile drops, replaced with a desperate hunger that causes my sex to clench in anticipation. Uncrossing his legs, he leans forward with his elbows on his knees, hands linked and dropped between them. "You're right. So you also know that I don't back down until I've won."

Oh.

Wow.

Our eyes clash in a battle of wills and unspoken words, but I hear every one of his clear as day. I always have.

I want you.

I love you.

And I'll stop at nothing until I win you.

I'll admit it; I lost the game of chicken and am the first to break away, stupidly straightening the pile of resumes on my desk, giving myself a few seconds to gather my frayed wits.

By the time I've summoned the courage to look at him again he's already assumed the same relaxed position as before, his desire tempered to a slow simmer.

I wish I could say the same.

I wait for him to mention Brad and the conversation he walked in on. I know he heard something, I just don't know how much. Instead, he dives right into business. I internally sigh at the small reprieve I've been given.

Heated eyes leave mine and scan my small space. "Nice picture." He nods to the framed abstract Zel drew. It looks professional and more than one person has said I could probably sell it. But she made it for me this year on the anniversary of my mom's death, using my mother's favorite colors of blue and yellow. There's no amount of money that would make me part with it.

"Thanks," is all I can manage.

"We have a dinner meeting set for tomorrow evening with Alred Kinnick, Chairman of Board of Kinnick Investments. I'm sorry for the last minute notice, but he had a late cancellation and could fit us in. We need to take the opportunity because it may be a while before he can meet again and he's anxious to get this CEO recruitment started."

The only word I heard in that entire sentence was..."We?"

"Yes. *We.*" He tamps down a smirk, but barely. "I realize we didn't discuss the particulars and I don't often get so involved in executive recruitments, but Alred is an old family friend and he can be rather..." He pauses, contemplating his choice of words. "...*challenging* to deal with, so the first meeting will be together. If he's comfortable with you, then you can take subsequent meetings without me unless he wants me more heavily involved."

I'm a little incensed, but try to hold my voice steady. Not once did my Uncle Carl have to accompany me to a client meeting. "Why give this to me if you don't trust me?"

"It's not a matter of trust, Nora. I would have accompanied whomever I assigned to this case."

"Oh." My indignation quickly deflates. "Okay. Does Jeanine know?" Jeanine and I have mutually avoided each other since I arrived, but I have to believe she knows about this assignment and is pissed as hell.

His face hardens when he responds tersely, "I don't report to Jeanine. She reports to me."

Alrighty then.

"Do I need to make dinner reservations somewhere?"

"No. Lydia, my admin, will take care of that."

"All right. Anything else?"

The grin is back. And a sudden bad feeling starts in the pit of my stomach. "We need to prep before the meeting. I have a full afternoon so it will have to be over dinner this evening."

Dinner? Alone?

Oh, hell no. Dinner will lead to personal conversations, maybe even another orgasm, and while my body's already preparing itself for the latter, I'm not mentally prepared at all for the former. Besides, I would have to find something to do with Zel last minute. I look at the clock and note it's already after two. "Dinner? No. I can't. I have other responsibilities, Connelly."

Disbelief raises his brows and twitches his lips. Settling his hands on the arms of the chair, he pushes his long, lean frame up and starts walking toward the door as if he didn't even hear my protest. "It wasn't a request, Nora. This is an important meeting and there are some things I need to get you up to speed about prior."

I open my mouth, still trying to formulate a believable reason I can't stay when he turns and holds up a palm. "I already know your argument, Nora, but this is business. I'll have dinner catered in instead if it will make you feel better. Be in my office at six sharp. Please," he tacks on at the end.

And with that small concession he quietly exits, leaving me to stare at the blank space he just occupied, wondering two things.

One: how am I going to dodge the inevitable personal questions and, two: how in the hell am I going to get my riotous hormones under control so I'm able to get through two hours alone with him without ending up naked on his desk? Or his chair? Or against the damn wall?

I have no answer to either of those, but I have exactly three hours and forty-five minutes to figure it out.

Then I pick up the phone to call Landyn and beg for what will probably be the first of many favors.

Chapter 14

CONN

Another glance at my watch shows it's 5:45. Fifteen minutes until I see Nora again. Fifteen fucking long lonely minutes. It feels like a month has passed since I've last seen her and it hasn't even been four hours.

I go back to staring out of my corner office window, lost in thought. It's an unfortunate, common occurrence for me as of late and a development I'm none too happy about. I'm not as much of an asshole at work as I have been to my brothers, but I am short-tempered and moody. I'm distracted.

Having Nora here, right under my nose, but not being able to touch her like I need to, or take her the way I want to is sheer fucking torture. I am desperate for her, which is one of the reasons I have stayed far away from her these past two weeks.

I wanted her to get comfortable here, let her guard down a little before I pounced on her, but that plan was just chucked out of my thirty-two story window the second I set foot into her office and heard Brad I'm-about-to-fuck-up-his-college-football-face Harding talk about how much he wanted her and how I would do nothing but hurt her.

What gutted me the most, though, was to hear that she's in the exact same place I am. Stuck in memories. Floundering in the past. She hasn't been able to emotionally move on any more than I have and that makes me again wonder again why she left me in the first place.

She loves me.

She knows it.

I know it.

Apparently the former Chief of SER Operations knows it, too.

Does she know about Meredith? Maybe I just blurt it out over dinner tonight so we can put our past to bed once and for all. Then I can bend her down and fuck her over my desk until she tells me I'm forgiven and admits she's mine.

The thought makes my cock throb and jerk in sweet, aching anticipation.

I shouldn't chase after one of my new employees so blatantly. It's highly unprofessional. I'm probably violating a dozen human resources policies right now, but I. Do. Not. Fucking. Care. I'm so far from caring what anyone else thinks, it borders on irresponsible.

I'm too far gone on Nora. I cannot think straight and I will mow down any fucker who gets in my way as I claim what's rightfully mine. And, employment contract or not, Brad Harding is walking a very fucking thin tightrope right now.

Nora may not want him, but he wants her, and I can already tell he's one tenacious bastard. He's fighting for what he wants, just like I am. Under any other circumstance, I'd commend him for going toe-to-toe with the man who signs his paycheck. Cheer him on even. Except in this case, all I'm ready to do is cut off his balls and feed them to him one by one until he admits defeat.

"Sir," Lydia says, interrupting the mental visual of taking apart my competition piece by piece. Probably a good thing—it was becoming more realistic by the minute. "Your *dinner* is here." She almost asks it like a question. I'm sure she's confused as to why I have my sister-in-law delivering a meal. "Should I have her bring it in and set it up now?"

"Yes, thank you." She turns to leave when I add, "And you can go home for the evening, Lydia."

Typically, I would have her stay for a late business meeting in case I needed anything, but I don't want anyone within hearing distance of my office. She nods slightly, no doubt knowing why I'm cutting her loose early.

"Have a good night then."

I plan on it.

I grab my sister-in-law in a bear hug when she walks through my door. "Thanks, Livia. You're a lifesaver. I owe you one."

"No problem." She laughs. "It's a strange request, but hey, whatever help you need to land your girl, count me in," she quips. "You're just lucky I had Brit for the afternoon already. She cooked all this for you."

181

Brit is Gray and Livia's part-time nanny to their three-month-old twin boys. Good kid.

"God bless Brit. Maybe that means things will go my way tonight."

"I hope so, Conn. You need a good woman."

"I just need the *right* one," I mumble, finally believing it's true.

My pocket vibrates. Checking my phone quick, I see it's Ella.

Ella: hey asshole. u free tonite?

Ella and I occasionally have dinner and drinks to unwind at the end of a particularly tough day, but I'm not free tonight. In fact, hopefully, I won't be free for the next eighteen thousand nights. Heck, maybe I'll introduce the two. I think with their strong personalities and cutting wit, they'd get along well. And Nora could probably use a friend in her new city.

Me: sorry. 'fraid ur stuck with bagged rice or canned soup
Ella: shit. fine. b that way
Me: i'll make it up to u sometime
Ella: hold u 2 it.

"Competition?" Livia asks, spying my phone, clearly seeing Ella's name.

Women. They stick together, no matter what. And it seems Livia's siding with Nora even before she's met her for no other reason than because she's captured my heart. I don't even have to tell her; she already knows I'd never do this for just anyone.

"No. Just a friend."

Her hand goes to her hip and she cocks a brow.

"Really. She's just a friend. I'm allowed to have a female friend, aren't I?"

She scrutinizes me. It makes me uncomfortable, like the jackass I know I am when it comes to women. "You are. You just...don't."

True. Ella's the exception. I turn my attention back to the bags and start unloading. "There's more to me than meets the eye, Liv."

"I'm starting to see that." She surprises me by reaching up and placing a kiss on my cheek.

"What's that for?" I ask, rubbing the damp spot.

"You're a good guy, Connelly. Underneath your playful, laissez-faire attitude you have a squishy, soft romantic side. I knew it was there, you just needed someone to peel back the layers so it could be found."

"Shhh. Don't tell anyone. You'll ruin my rep." I wink.

She twists her fingers over her mouth, locking my secret inside. We quickly unload in silence. Once everything is set, we say our good-byes not a second too soon.

I'm just sitting down at my desk when Nora knocks lightly, standing at the entrance of my office, waiting. She's trying hard not to, but she looks nervous. I have to admit I thought she may be a no-show, finding some lame excuse that she couldn't come, so it's a relief to see her here.

Standing, I don't say a word. I just walk slowly

across my speckled carpet until I'm right in front of her. I unashamedly drink her in from head to toe. She looks so damn beautiful in her classy form-fitting navy dress and nude pumps, but all I want to do right now is see the sheath in a puddle on my floor and feel her heels burn into the muscles of my ass.

I've thought of nothing else for the last few weeks but how she felt shuddering in my arms as I dry humped her to climax. My mouth waters when I remember how sweet her lips and skin tasted under my tongue. I've masturbated almost daily remembering the hitch in her voice and how sweet my name sounded on a breathless exhale as she fell headfirst over the sharp ledge into ecstasy before she bolted faster than a jackrabbit.

She left me with the worst case of blue balls I can ever remember having, but given the choice of living that night over again and having it end the same way or not living it at all...bring on the sweet agony of denied release, because I'd do it repeatedly. I'd do anything for her.

When my gaze trails lazily back to her face, it's flushed. "You came." Now it turns a deeper shade of red and I know we're both remembering the exact same thing. I don't even bother trying to suppress my grin.

"I thought I was summoned," she sasses. Her face is defiant, but her voice is delightfully breathy.

"You don't seem to take orders well." Her eyes widen and her cute little mouth falls open. Bending my head, my lips brush her lobe before I nip it, whispering huskily, "But I intend to change that."

"Connelly—" She starts to protest, but I'm done listening. I don't want to hear that she's changed or that we can't do this or that I'm in her damn personal space. I don't want to hear any more excuses.

I only want to hear her say *yes*.

Yes to me. Yes to us. Yes to everything I want from her.

"Hush, princess. The evasion stops now," I growl lowly before kissing her cheek.

Her breath hitches and it takes everything in me not to shove her up against the wall, rip off her panties, and pound into her like a madman. Instead, placing my hand at the small of her back, I usher her inside before closing and locking the door for good measure. My office is in the corner of the thirty-second floor. It's rather secluded, but there are likely still people milling about somewhere. Since I'm known for working late, I wouldn't want anyone barging in with an urgent issue that can't wait until morning.

"Have a seat." I nod toward the round oak table in the corner that contains the spread I've put together for my "meeting" with Nora. And once she gets a good look, I hope I score some points. God knows I'll work my balls off to earn every one of them.

She almost reaches the table when she stops short. I'm trailing far enough behind, mostly because I wanted to ogle her ass, or otherwise I would have run smack into her.

"What is all this?" she asks with genuine surprise, before turning to me with wide eyes.

"It's dinner." I shrug like it's no big deal; yet I'm dying inside to know what she's thinking. I don't usually eat this stuff, but Nora does. Or at least she did once upon a time.

"But this is...this is freezer crap," she says on a small laugh, turning back toward our fried feast of mozzarella sticks, chicken nuggets, pizza rolls, mini corn dogs, crab Rangoon, and skinny fries, which used to be her favorite. There's even something I don't recognize. Raviolis maybe? Fuck all if I know. None of it looks appetizing. I did ask Livia to add a salad, but other than that, the entire table is full of fat- and calorie-laden fried breading.

Yum.

"It is," I reply quietly against the column of her neck, letting my breath dance over her. Taking a chance, I place my hands lightly on her hips. She surprises me by sinking into my hold. My semi is now at full attention and I swallow a groan. "I don't know if you still eat this stuff, but I remember how much you used to love freezer crap night back in the day."

Nora and her mother used to have "freezer crap" night about once every other month or so. They'd make an entire unhealthy meal out of nothing but frozen shit you accumulated to eat on lazy nights. It was "their thing," she would tell me. She invited me a couple of times, but I always declined. Even back then, I ate healthy. But I'll eat it tonight. For her.

She's quiet for so long I'm convinced I've missed the mark. Then she turns in my arms. I know I've hit a home run when I see tears. "I can't believe you remember that."

I frame her face. Look deeply into her watery eyes. "Nora, there isn't a single thing about you I've forgotten. I remember everything. Every like. Every dislike. Every laugh. Every smile. Every freckle. Every conversation. Every minute I spent with you is forever burned into my memory."

She smiles and I can't tell if it's a happy or sad one. I think both. "Thank you, Connelly. You have no idea what this means to me."

Her eyes dart to my mouth and when they return to mine, I can read her emotions perfectly. She's full of longing and want. When her tongue peeks out to moisten her lips, the thin thread of control I've been grasping snaps in two.

"I'm going to kiss you," I announce, low and gruff.

"Conn—"

"Be quiet, Nora. It's just a kiss."

"O...Okay," she says on an exhale.

Her eyes flutter shut before my mouth reaches hers. Suddenly I wish I hadn't promised it was only a kiss, because the moment our lips touch, she willingly opens to me. This isn't a kiss of control or power. This isn't a kiss of dominance or jealousy or claiming.

It's the heady kiss of mutual desire. It's the one I've longed for her to gift me with for nearly a month.

Christ, she feels so good.

Groaning, I deepen my strokes but keep it soft. Languid. Tongue twisting with mine, she follows my every lead. Her body melts into me. Her hands grip my waist like she needs something to hold her up. Kissing her long and thoroughly, I worship her mouth the way I want to do to the rest of her body, savoring her taste, her warmth. I soak in each ragged breath, every tiny moan. I make them mine.

Her acquiescence makes me want to ravage her, but more than that right now, I need her to know how fucking much I love her, so after another few seconds, I do the right thing before I can't anymore.

I stop.

Her rosy chest heaves and her eyes are still closed when I pull back. As slowly as they fluttered shut, they open. They're dilated, dark and hazy with desire as they bounce back and forth, silently questioning why I've stopped.

Fuck. I'm asking myself the same damn question.

"Dinner's going to get cold," I tell her. My voice is heavy and thick, just like my cock. She thought going out with me to a restaurant was too intimate, but I assure you, her virtue would have been far safer in a public space rather than alone with me in *any* private space.

"Oh. Yeah, okay."

Placing a chaste kiss to her now puffy lips, I guide her toward a seat, pulling it out for her. She mumbles her thanks while I proceed to grab a couple of everything and set a plate down in front of her.

"Salad?" I ask, immensely enjoying the way she's watching my every move like she's trying to figure out my motives. They are entirely dishonorable, I promise.

"Uh, sure."

After I get her all settled, I grab my own plate and fill it just as I did hers, with a bigger portion of salad. With all this fried food, I'll have the heartburn from the gates of hell later, but I don't care. Then I pour us each a glass of the Cabernet I asked Livia to bring and take a seat across from Nora.

"Bon appetite," I say, holding up my drink.

"Bon appetite," she mimics quietly before taking a small sip. She holds my stare for a few more moments before leaving me bereft by breaking away. I hate that I feel so damn needy I want all of her attention focused on me. I'm not that guy. I'm not possessive or covetous or attention seeking, but I almost feel like I've had a damn personality transplant around her because I'm feeling every single one of those in spades right now.

I understand so much better why my brothers act like lunatics about their women. Being with Nora has brought out every single caveman tendency I never thought I possessed but apparently do. I guess I wasn't immune after all.

For the most part, we're quiet as she tries a bit of everything. It's not uncomfortable for once. It feels...right. Easy. Like a missing part of me has been put securely back into place. I know for the first time since I last laid my eyes on Nora, I'm exactly where I'm supposed to be. The panic I once felt about someday calling this amazing woman my wife has vanished.

I'm content, I finally realize. That, too, is a foreign feeling, yet one I'm embracing. Isn't it strange how one person, out of the billions on this planet, can change your outlook on life entirely?

Just one.

The *right* one.

Suddenly you're thinking about things in a whole new light. Your path bends, your dreams shift, and the steadfast future you planned for yourself without her now looks dull and lifeless, dark and full of profound loneliness. But you are strangely okay with it all. That's how much this *one* person means to you. For her, you're willing to upend every brick you've spent your life laying and lay new ones...*with* her.

"How did you do this?" she asks, after polishing off every last bite.

"Do what?" I push my plate of half-eaten fried junk away and grab my wine. I'll be starving later, but I'll live.

"This?" Her arms spread as wide as her smile and my chest puffs at her happiness. *I* did that. "Who has freezer crap just lying around, and more importantly, who did you get to bring it to you?"

My mouth turns up. "I have connections all over this city, baby."

That makes her laugh. A genuine, relaxed, happy laugh.

I feel such intense love for this woman at this very second, it's hard to even understand myself, let alone explain. I want to drop to my knees in front of her and beg her to come back to me, demand that she give us a fair chance. A real chance. But I do none of those things. I know I need to *win* her love, not demand it. I briefly wonder if now is the time to confess my sins, then quickly decide against it. I don't want to ruin the only relaxed moment we've experienced in two months. So instead, I refill her wineglass.

"Trying to get me drunk so you can take advantage of me?" she quips with sparkling eyes and a cheeky grin after taking a sip.

I set down the nearly empty bottle and pick up my own glass, my face replicating hers. "That depends."

"Depends on what?" The brilliant smile that lights up her face steals my thoughts and air at the same time.

"If it will work?" I wag my brows and wink.

Her eyes close as she laughs. I feel time slow as I sit there taking in her beauty and everything that is Nora. The sound of a real laugh is as brilliant as the authentic joy on her face.

"No. It won't," she replies, still chuckling. But, once again, I detect she's not being entirely truthful.

"That's too bad. I'll just have to find something else that will."

Her smile falls and she gazes at me thoughtfully. I

wish she'd tell me what she's thinking, but Nora holds her thoughts very close to the vest, more so now than ever. Her emotions, not so much, though, and that will work in my favor during my quest to win her back.

"You done?" I nod at the food still littering my table. The cleaning people will hate me tonight, but all I give a shit about right now is that I've made Nora happy. Score one for me.

She dips her head once.

"Good, then grab your drink and let's sit on the couch. The smell of this fried shit is making me nauseous."

Her eyes bounce between the couch and me and, once again, the nervousness returns. But I also see obvious longing. With wine in one hand, I hold my other hand out to help her up, relieved she doesn't reject me like last time. Pulling her right into my "personal space," I tell her lowly, "It's just a couch, Nora. Not a bed."

Then it's my turn to chuckle when she replies breathlessly, "Beds are overrated anyway."

"Damn straight they are."

She stands there, hand in mine, unmoving. Staring. Clearly wanting. If I pushed her against the wall right now I could be inside her in less than ten seconds. And she'd let me. I have no idea when this about-face took place, and I'm sure I'll kick myself to hell and back for what I'm about to do because I've wanted nothing more than to be buried inside her sweet pussy for a goddamned month. But I walk with her hand in mine to the couch, gesturing for her to sit.

As much as I want to fuck her, I want to talk to her more.

For a while anyway.

———————

As I suspected, she takes the far end, so I sit in the middle. I'm not crowding her, but I'm not letting her put three feet between us either.

"Thanks again for dinner." Her gaze drops. When it returns to mine, it brims with sadness and heartbreak.

"You're welcome." I frown, confused about her sudden change in mood. "I thought it would make you happy."

"It did," she quickly answers. "It did, Connelly. More than you know. But it also makes me...sad at the same time."

"Why?"

Her gaze falls again. We both watch her finger trace the rim of her glass over and over, the musical sound from the rhythm filling the silence.

I didn't want the night to go like this. I wanted to get reacquainted with the woman I once lost. I want to start over again, not spend the night cemented in history we can't change.

"Nora, I'm sorry," I say softly, not having a fucking clue what just happened or what I'm sorry for other than making her upset. I'm mentally preparing myself for our past to be split open, the entire sordid guts of my unintended betrayal exposed for my rightful judgment, but the next words out of her mouth couldn't have shocked me more.

"My mom died of lung cancer a few years ago. I just miss her, is all."

Her mother died?

"Jesus, I had no idea. I'm..." I scrub my face, not knowing what to say. How did I not know this? "I wouldn't have done this had I known."

She puts her hand on my forearm. When she looks up her tears destroy me. "I'm glad you did. It brought back good memories, too. It's okay. There's no way you could have known."

I couldn't have, but I should have. I should have been there for her, helped her with the funeral, helped her carry her grief. I vow right then and there to be by Nora for the rest of my life, no matter what. Even if she doesn't want me like that, I won't let her go through those heart-wrenching events alone ever again.

I take the wine from her hand and set both of our glasses on the small end table next to the sofa. "Come here," I croak, holding my arms open. She hesitates just for a moment before sliding into me, sighing as she melts against my chest. The feeling is sublime. Nothing has ever felt as good as having a willing Nora in my arms.

Stroking her silky hair with one hand and lacing the fingers of our other hand together, I ask, "Did you want to talk about it?"

"I thought this was supposed to be a business dinner?"

"That can wait." The truth of the matter is I could tell Nora what she needs to know ten minutes before our meeting tomorrow. I just used it as an excuse to spend time with her. I knew she wouldn't say no. Well...I wouldn't *let* her say no.

"Did you...did you want to hear about it?"

I tug on her hair gently until her head tilts back, mainly because I don't want to stop holding her other hand. "Of course I do, sweetheart."

Her sad smile dives straight to my heart, squeezing it tight. This woman completely owns me. I would do anything to take away her sadness. "Okay." She settles her head in the groove my shoulder, flexing her smaller fingers between my bigger ones, gathering courage as she stares off into space. I tighten my other arm around her shoulder, pulling her closer, letting her know it's safe to let go. This time, I'll be there to catch her.

"Well, she was diagnosed a little over a year after we moved to Baltimore. She'd been having back pain for months, even before we left Detroit and no one could figure out what was wrong. Eventually they found a suspicious spot on an X-ray and after a PET scan, they found eight more. Stage-four metastatic adenocarcinoma lung cancer."

"Nora, sweetheart." I have no words that will make the loss of her mother easier. I know from my own father's death a few years back that losing a parent is a hole that will never be filled, no matter how much time passes.

"Did you know the number one cause of cancer-related death in women is lung cancer? It kills more women than breast, uterine, and ovarian cancer combined. A useless fact I found when pouring over the Internet in search of any type of hope." She squeezes my hand tighter and I let her continue at her own pace. "She was never a smoker, which also is apparently irrelevant when contracting lung cancer, and by the time they found it, the cancer had spread to her liver, her kidneys, her bones, and her brain. She was in a lot of pain. She suffered horribly. I think that was the worst part of it all, you know—watching her literally die right in front of my eyes, suffering but trying to be brave for me."

"Nora, God. I am so sorry." Sorry seems utterly inadequate, but I don't know what else to say. My father died, but at least his heart attack was quick and not long-suffering—a fact I was probably not grateful enough for at the time. "How did your father handle it?"

She tenses. "How did he handle it? Like he did everything else. He threw himself into work, forgetting that he even had a family. Do you know he wasn't even there when she died? I was holding one hand and Carl was holding her other."

Her father always did live in his own little bubble. And where was I when Nora was going through ten kinds of hell? I was undoubtedly fucking some random woman while she had to grieve almost alone. I couldn't hate myself any more than I do right now, even though I know it's totally irrational.

"I wish I could have been there for you," I say quietly, kissing the crown of her head.

She's silent for a long time. When she tilts her

head, her eyes sparkle with unshed tears. "I'm sorry, Connelly."

Her apology hangs thickly in the air like an opaque curtain I need to pull back. I don't want to yet.

"What are you sorry for, princess?"

"Everything. I'm sorry for everything."

I'm sorry for the same thing.

She searches my face for forgiveness. I hope she sees it. I know we can't create a new story, a new us, without it. And that's all I want to do right now.

Forget the past.

Forget the hurt.

Forget the rejection.

Forget the reasons we both left us behind.

I reach up and palm her cheek, feathering my thumb right underneath the fullness of her bottom lip. "I'm sorry, too."

With the half-mast doe eyes she's giving me, all I can think of is kissing her, ripping off her clothes, and taking her with the ferocity I've felt building inside me for weeks. I force myself steady, letting her lead. But I'm here to tell you...one touch of my lips to hers and it's all over. I will have her underneath me tonight, filled with both my cock and my quasi knots, because once I'm inside of her that final knot is fastened. I will not let her walk away from us.

"Connelly..." Barely audible, my name goes straight from her lips to my cock. The surrender in her tone feels like a snug fist, squeezing my dick from root to tip. I feel pre-cum soak my briefs as my breaths quicken.

"What, Nora? Tell me what you want."

Wetting her lips, her eyes drop to my mouth and she whispers huskily, "Kiss me. Please."

"Fuck," I mumble, knowing straight where this will lead, even if she doesn't. This will not be an innocent kiss. It will be pure, raw, out-and-out passion and claiming. And I won't stop with one fucking kiss. I won't stop until she's crying out my name in utter euphoria over and over again. "Are you sure this is what you want?"

"Yes," she pleads, breathless.

"I'm warning you now, princess, if my lips land anywhere on your flesh again, I'm not stopping with a kiss. I won't quit until I have all of you."

Her chest expands rapidly, with excitement or fear I'm not sure. "We...we can't have sex. Not here."

I grab her hips and pull her astride my lap, settling her hot pussy snug against my hard-as-stone erection. One hard thrust has her head falling back fleetingly on a rough exhale. "Good, because I don't want to have sex with you, Nora."

Her brows furrow in confusion. "You don't?"

Grabbing her bare thighs, I squeeze gently as my hands trail upward, raising her dress until I expose the tiny pale pink panties scarcely covering her sex.

Fuck. *Me.*

They're already drenched. I have to tear my eyes away before I turn into a complete Neanderthal and ravage her right now without preamble.

"No." My voice is gravelly with lust. Kneading

the soft flesh on her hips and thighs, I hold her smoky eyes and begin to tell her in great detail what I want from her. What I will have from her. "Sex is just a physical act. A few inches of penetration. Lust. Gluttony. Pleasures of the flesh, the sharing of bodily fluids, and a physical release that can be had with anyone, anytime without emotion or attachment."

I would know. I'm the master of emotional detachment.

Letting my thumbs slip under the silky fabric, she bucks and I curse under my breath at the feel of her velvety wetness on my fingertips. Jesus, she's soaked. My cock is in absolute agony with want for her, but I tell him to be patient because I'm nowhere near done yet. I'll fill her mind with every carnal thing I want to do to her. Then I'll act on them.

"No, that's not what I want at all. What I want from you is far more than a simple physical act, Nora. I want your heart, your mind, your spirit, your passion. Your complete and total surrender. I want to rejoin our souls, where they belong. I want to steal your heart and hold it captive." I run a thumb, now wet with her desire, along her lips until she opens up for me. Taking it inside she swirls her tongue around, tasting her desire. *Fuuuck.*

I palm her nape, pulling her face to me until our lips are a hairsbreadth apart.

"I want to dig into the deepest recesses of your mind, find what makes you tick now, and turn it up a hundred fucking notches until you beg for mercy. I want to fuck you hard and rough, then make love to you softly and sweetly. I want to ruin you then save you."

The thumb dancing along her pussy brushes against her clit, avoiding direct contact and, perched at the doorstep of pleasure, she can barely keep her eyes open now, so I deliver my final declaration. "I want to start over, Nora. I want to make you mine again."

"Wow," she pants. "Uh...that's a whole lot of wants."

A Cheshire grin stretches my face. "Oh, there's much more where that came from." I drag my wet digit down toward her opening and tease, and my Nora tries to remain unaffected, even though I read the burning desire all over her face.

"Is there now?" she squeaks when I dip inside her snugness briefly.

Christ. I love her like this. Even all worked up, she can still give as good as she gets. She is the absolute perfect woman for me.

"Fuck yes. Look at me." With a tug on her hair, I force her eyes to mine, which had drifted shut. "I want to feel you, lick you, taste you, bite you, touch you, suck you, worship you, and fuck you until you cry for more. I want to do things to you that you don't even know you want. I want everything, Nora. Everything. I always have. The only problem is, princess, I just didn't realize that I had nothing until I laid eyes on you again."

"Connelly..."

Maybe I shouldn't have tipped all my cards so soon, but what the hell. I want her. I want it all from her and I want her to know it. Pulling her to my mouth, I rasp gruffly against her parted lips, "You have five seconds, sweetheart. Five. And if you don't tell me to stop after five seconds, my fingers are going to be buried deep in this pussy, and I'll swallow my name as it falls off your tongue when you orgasm all over my hand."

"Oh God." Her soft plea is nothing but air.

Our eyes are locked and in my mind, I'm silently counting. I've made it to three when she grabs the hand now resting on her hip, places it against her belly and guides it underneath the delicate barrier that's keeping her from me. She runs our joined digits slowly through her soaked lips and pushes one of hers and two of my fingers easily inside of her.

"Oh fuuuck, Nora. You are deliciously wet," I rumble, watching her pump our joined hands in and out of her tight pussy. My hips jerk, my cock pulses, and my balls are cinched so tight they're screaming bloody murder. The panties, which were sexy moments ago, are now the most hated piece of fabric on planet earth, so I take care of that in short order by snapping the flimsy strings. It flops between us and I leave it, only caring it's now out of the way.

"Christ." I'm riveted, watching our hands working her together. My cock twitches madly as Nora rubs her bare pussy back and forth on me while fucking herself with our fingers, adding to the sheer eroticism.

I think we've established by now that I like to be in control, but I've honestly never seen anything sexier than Nora taking charge, using me to pleasure her, which, in turn, sure as fuck pleasures me.

Hooking her thumb around my hand, she drags our fingers out and circles her clit. Pressing down with her middle finger on mine, she moans and writhes under our combined touch before lifting them to paint my lips.

"Holy shit," I breathe in complete and total awe right before her lips capture mine, licking herself off of me before I even get a chance. When her tongue slides into my mouth and I taste remnants of her, I crack. Max limit reached. It's time to take the reins back, because if I don't, I will unzip and viciously take her. I don't want our first time after so many years to spiral out of my control.

With one arm around her waist, I stand to deposit her on the back of the couch so her feet are resting on the cushions. I drop my eyes to the ruined panties now laying beside her toes. Shit. They're so damp with her arousal I may be able to wring them out.

"Take off your dress," I command gutturally. Undoing my cufflinks with ease, I throw them in my pants pocket before reaching for the small discs down my front. Complying readily, Nora stretches behind and unzips, letting the dress fall to her waist. She's wearing a matching pale pink push-up bra, which perfectly cups and rounds her ample breasts. I wish I had the patience to enjoy it, but I fucking don't. "Everything, princess. I want you completely bare for me."

Our smoldering gazes never waver, never drop while we disrobe. In less than fifteen seconds, she's naked and ready and...Holy. Fuck. I am thunderstruck by how mouthwatering she looks sitting there, waiting for my next instruction.

Perched in the spot where I left her, she watches me intently as I drink my fill of her perfection. Her back is pressed tall against the wall, her toned, pale legs are held tightly together and her green orbs are half-lidded with unquenched desire.

I'll be taking care of that right fucking now.

"Legs apart." They open, but not far enough. "All the way." She spreads them wide and my knees almost give way at the creaminess soaking her bare lips.

Her long hair lies in soft waves, stopping right above her dark, puckered nipples. The deep flush of desire spreading across her skin is like a siren's melody, drawing me to her. Jesus, she reminds me of a regal queen, a Greek goddess on a throne and I'm her minion. She could tell me to do anything for her right now and I would. No questions asked.

I'd maim.

I'd kill.

I'd burn cities to the fucking ground and bring her back my spoils.

For the first time in my adult life, I have a thorough understanding of the absolute power a woman has over a man...and why we simply don't give a shit.

I palm my cock, stroking slow and long, letting her eyes wander over my nakedness. She swallows hard as she watches me for a few beats. When her eyes jerk back to mine, I swear to fucking God I just about come. No woman, and I've been with a lot, has ever looked at me with such a potent combination of longing and love before. It's a heady goddamned feeling, especially since it comes from Nora.

"Like what you see?"

Her burning eyes blaze into me. "It's acceptable," she retorts smartly; a small smirk turns her gorgeous full lips.

"You're gonna pay for that."

"I hope so." Her eyes darken and quietly summon me to her.

"Nora, I want you so fucking much."

I'm torn between wanting to take her hard or fuck her slow.

Both. I'm going to do both.

When she runs a finger deliberately slow and teasing through her spread lips and trails it all the way up the line of her curves before it disappears in her mouth, my cock gushes. Fucking gushes. "Then what are you waiting for?" she husks, twinkling emeralds daring me to take action.

I won't disappoint.

Kneeling on the buttery brown leather, I pick up a foot, run my tongue along her instep, and gently bite her heel, enjoying her gasp of surprise. "Tell me what you want," I cajole between lazy openmouthed kisses up her calf, the back of her knee, her inner thigh. Each one pulls a tiny breath from her lungs. Each breath makes my cock pulse angrily. I stop when I feel the warmth of her pussy radiating on my cheek and look up the length of her gorgeous, flawless body. "Tell me what you want or I stop."

Her mouth curves slightly. "I want you to make me come."

She sucks in a sharp breath and her hands grip my hair when I nip the sensitive flesh at the junction of her pelvis before swirling my tongue to soothe it. "Then what, Nora? What do you want after that?" This time, I trail my tongue up and down the sexy trimmed patch of reddish hair above her slit before letting it circle her clit, feathering ever so lightly.

Jesus. She tastes so damn good I could live here.

Using my hair as leverage, she tilts my head up. "I want you to make me come again while you're fucking me. Now stop teasing."

Hot. Damn. "I love a woman who knows exactly what she wants and isn't afraid to say it."

"Connelly, please. I need you," she begs sweetly.

Need. Not want.

Need.

That one word sets me into motion. I've thought of nothing else for the last few weeks but how her nipples will taste now or how the hot junction between her thighs would melt in my mouth, on my tongue like the sweetest of spun sugar. And I'm not waiting any longer to find out.

Holding her legs all the way open, I rasp, "Hang on, princess, the ride may get bumpy." I dive into her warmth, taking my first long lick of her honeyed center and groan loudly. "Nora, my God. I could eat you for days."

"Don't stop," she pants, her hips gyrating seductively, calling me back.

"Not until you beg me to."

Dropping back down, I spread her to find her hardened clit with my tongue. I hear her head thud against the wall when I draw it into my mouth and suck, lightly at first, then progressively harder, paying close attention to each and every one of her clues. The firmer I suck, the choppier her breaths become, the more my scalp stings from her fingernails and the faster her legs quiver. And the second I thrust two fingers inside her tight, drenched channel she explodes in my mouth on a sharp cry.

Jesus Christ, it's pure nirvana. Memories of her taste flood me. I can feel her writhing underneath my hands, my mouth, my cock just like it was yesterday.

"Are you okay?" I ask, sliding into her scorching heat, my eyes rolling in my head at how fucking good she feels.

"Yes. Don't stop."

"Are you sure, princess? You feel tense." I stop and, levered on my forearms, look into her eyes. "Don't lie."

"It stings a little, but I'm fine. Please, Connelly."

"You sure?"

"More than."

"Okay."

"Kiss me."

"Try to stop me."

After years of not being with a woman more than one fleeting time and never even having the desire to, I'm ravenous. I know I will never get enough of Nora. She's the one I've been waiting for. I knew it when I first saw her walking down the Dowling High hallway when I was seventeen years old.

I knew it then. I know it now. I've known it all along.

"Connelly," she calls brokenly, over and over again as I bring her to orgasm repeatedly. She rides my fingers and my tongue for long minutes as I wring every ounce of pleasure from her body that she'll give me. I don't let up until she pleads for me to stop. Even then, I don't want to. My fingers are drenched and I know her essence will linger on my taste buds for days.

Pressing soft kisses to her now swollen sex, I delay while she catches her breath before I pave my way up her slightly rounded stomach, slowing for a dip in her belly button. When I reach her full breasts, I stop for a sample, biting and sucking, and more memories assail me.

"You have the most perfect tits I've ever seen," I murmur when she removes her utilitarian white bra.

"They're too big," she laments, trying to cover them.

"I have big hands. And a big mouth," I quip.

She laughs, but only until I suck one puckered nipple into my watering mouth. Then moans fill the darkness.

"I need you inside me, Connelly. Now. Please." She's tugging on my hair, trying to get me to move faster, but I don't want to. Screw hard and fast. I need to make love to her, taking my sweet-ass time. Every second I touch her, I feel her life force bleeding into me, making me whole, complete, filling those places I didn't remember were empty.

Grabbing her waist, I lower her onto the couch so she's stretched out underneath me, arms drawn overhead. Red hair is splayed haphazardly underneath her and her hazy eyes sparkle like moonlight.

I run my eyes over the length of her, taking note of every curve, every line, seeing nothing but perfection. She's simply captivating. Mesmerizing.

Squeezing the base of my cock hard, I will my seed to retreat or this night will be over too damn fast, and I've waited far too long to be with her again for me to shoot my load within seconds like I'm eighteen again.

"Nora," I croak. "You are so ungodly beautiful."

When her entire face softens, I see the love she has for me shine brighter than a beacon in the black of night.

"Please."

One word.

Soft.

Sweet.

Surrender.

One six-letter word completely undoes me.

Reaching down, I grab a condom out of my wallet and when I finish rolling it on, Nora's gaze has cooled considerably. Spreading her legs, I wrap her gorgeous limbs around me and cover her body with mine so we're skin to skin. I hover above her, her head pressed between my hands.

"Tell me what you're thinking," I demand. Rocking my body against hers, I savor it when her eyes briefly drift shut in pleasure. My thick shaft slides easily between her thighs, and I'm groaning at how fucking fantastic her heat feels against me, counting the seconds until it cocoons my entire length.

"I'm wondering how often you've done this," she whispers, eyes latching on to mine, vulnerability bleeding out like an open wound.

I'm not sure what "this" she's referring to, but I'm sure as hell not going to ruin the moment by talking about other women, especially ones that don't mean shit to me. This right here is all that matters.

Raining kisses over her lids, her cheeks, her jaw, I whisper against her lips, "I assure you, Nora, what I'm about to do with you, I haven't done with any other woman since you."

Nora was the first and the last woman I will ever make love to. She was my first, just like I was hers. We never talked about it and she never knew that I'd not been with another girl before. I was the guy who helped build up his own player reputation and I didn't want to fess up that I had no fucking clue what I was doing just seconds before stripping her, making her mine. Before her, my reputation was just conjecture. After her, however, I took it to a whole new level. I've not been ashamed about that until just now when I've held her in my arms again.

"Are you trying to tell me you haven't made a pretty big dent in Chicago's female population?" she asks, tightening her legs around my waist angrily.

Ouch. I deserve that but fuck if it doesn't sting anyway.

"Remember what I said about sex, princess?"

Twining our fingers together I shift my hips, positioning myself at her entrance and push. Inch by agonizing inch, I sink inside her scorching heat.

Holy shit, she feels good. She feels like mine.

Eleven years, erased.

When I'm buried balls deep I pull out just as slowly, watching her mouth go slack. God almighty, I am never going to last.

"Yes," she pants, tilting her pelvis so I can go deeper. I do on a loud curse, gritting my teeth against the need to chase my own orgasm, which is just within reach already. Her tight pussy is squeezing me like nothing I remember feeling.

"This is not that. And everything I want from you, you've always had of mine. My heart, my spirit, my very fucking soul has always belonged to you, Nora."

Her beautiful emeralds mist and she whispers my name on a broken sob.

The only woman whose eyes I've looked into when I'm taking her is Nora. Connecting with another person on that level when you're having sex turns it into something far more than physical. It's intimate, affectionate, flaying. You're putting yourself into the most vulnerable position possible. Pouring the entire contents of my heart out while Nora's gaze never strays from mine, I've never felt more exposed than I do right now.

"You were made for me, Nora. Every part. Your mouth was shaped for mine. Your curves fit my hands flawlessly. Your pussy cradles my cock like it was molded just for me. Made for me to fill you perfectly. Own you completely. You belong to me in every way. You always have."

I never stop moving or talking. I need to keep her grounded with me at the same time I drive us higher and higher, our sweat-covered bodies straining to get closer. My hips thrust at a steady pace and we fall into a familiar rhythm, a seductive age-old dance, but it's one I've only ever danced with her.

Kissing her deeply, I run my nose along hers, my voice hoarse with emotion when I tell her, "This is not sex, princess. This is love."

She clamps down around me. Hard. "Shit." I breathe through the need to just slam into her taking what I need, wanting to give her everything instead. I snake my hand between our undulating bodies and rub circles around her clit.

Bowing her back, she moans, "Connelly, I'm going to come."

"Fuck yes. Give it to me. I need to feel you come around my cock again."

I've been balancing on orgasm's sweet edge since I slipped inside my rightful mate, but when I feel Nora's legs quiver and her walls clench tight around my thick length, it takes everything I have to fight it off so I can just watch her unravel beneath me.

With her eyes clenched shut and her mouth open in a silent "O," she lets go, convulsing in my arms, squeezing my fingers and my cock so tight they both hurt. I watch bliss wash over every feature of her exquisite beauty until finally I can't hold back any longer.

Letting my forehead fall to hers, all muscles go taut as the last of her climax rips mine from deep within me. It comes from a place so far inside, I've never felt anything like its dreamlike release.

After we catch our breaths and I stop twitching, I roll to the side so I don't crush her. Pulling her into me, I clutch her tight, sighing when her arms go around my waist as she snuggles close.

I feel so fucking good.

Light.

Free.

Content.

Hooking a finger under her chin, I tilt it so I can look into her soul when I tell her with words everything I just told her with my body.

"I love you, Nora. I have never stopped."

Moisture turns her eyes to crystal. Then my heart soars when she tells me what I've longed to hear for weeks. Hell, who am I kidding? I've longed to hear it for years.

"Neither have I."

Chapter 15

Nora

Sitting in my car outside the Marcor Heliport, I am freaking the fuck out.

Full meltdown has initiated as I hear the walls of my carefully constructed life crack, the small fissures creating weaknesses in my already shaky foundation. The structure is creaking and wailing and will soon disintegrate down around me, leaving rubble and ash and memories where my life once stood.

I've made a lot of mistakes, but last night had to be the topper, the pinnacle of all my fuck-ups. I believed every single word Connelly spoke as I let him make love to me. I believed them and I let them lull me into imagining there would be—*could be*—an us after I shatter him with the truth. I fed into my own lies and I hate myself for it, now more than ever.

Last night, I lost total control. On the short elevator ride and walk to Connelly's office, I had a stern talk with myself. I was steadfast, resolute in my armor, my shields locked tight. Determined to keep things between us professional.

But the second I knocked on his door, I knew I'd made a huge mistake. I'd overestimated my ability to resist his magnetic pull. There is no way I can avoid my heart's true desire when I'm around Connelly. As I stood there while he perused my body like he had every right to, like he owned me, I decided I was going to confess. Purge all the wrongs rotting my insides and hope for forgiveness. Pray he would understand.

When I saw the dinner he'd pulled together in such short order, however, I was dumbfounded. It was considerate and sweet and utterly romantic, even if he didn't mean it to be. It came from the selfless, vulnerable boy I always remembered instead of the ultra smug, I'll-stop-at-nothing-to-get-what-I-want man that I now know and I just couldn't do it. I couldn't ruin the moment. I couldn't take all the effort and thought he'd put into the night and trample it like it meant nothing.

Because it meant everything.

Then, when he held me in his arms, let me tell him about my mother, and he listened—*really* listened—I heard genuine regret that he wasn't there when I needed him, I chucked the white flag high in the air, consequences be damned. For a few precious hours, I put all the hurt, the guilt, the remorse aside and took what I desperately needed: what Connelly *wanted* me to have and what I wanted to give him in return.

Love.

Devotion.

A good memory to erase the bad ones in the past and those yet to come.

But lying in his arms after he'd lavished indescribable pleasures on me, all of it came rushing back like a tsunami against my will anyway, the burden so encumbering, so suffocating to carry alone that I almost caved right then and there in the safety of his arms. But once again, I couldn't do it. I couldn't crush the hope my selfish actions had just given him. Had given *me*.

"Are you cold?" he asks rubbing his hands rapidly up and down my arm, genuine concern for my well-being lacing his tone.

"No." His body heat burns me up from the outside while my betrayal scorches my innards. My entire being is on fire. I feel as if I've been thrown directly into the pits of hell, the agony debilitating.

"Come home with me."

"I can't, Connelly." I feel absolutely sick, dinner rolling around in my traitorous stomach, trying to push its way back out. I'm paralyzed beneath the weight of my deceit and lies. Unable to move. Hardly able to breathe.

"I'm not letting you run, Nora. Not this time."

"I'm not running. I...don't you think we're moving too fast?" Shit...I need more time to figure this out. I just found him again; I selfishly don't want to give this up already, but my time is now out. I have no choice.

"As far as I'm concerned, we're not moving fast enough. I've wasted enough time without you. I'm not wasting a second more."

Still naked, he rolls on top of me, desire stirring anew in my belly at the feel of his raw masculine perfection pressed against my bare flesh from head to toe. Pinning me with his open and exposed stare, he asks, "You love me, yes? Please tell me you love me, Nora."

Cupping his face, I confess softly, "Since before I even met you." No hesitation, no qualms, no lies. It's the truest thing I've said to him in weeks.

His brilliant, victorious, megawatt smile simultaneously lights me up and shreds me to ribbons.

"But there's so much about each other we don't even know anymore," I whisper more to myself than to him. My secrets swirl like deadly poison in my belly, a boiling mixture of regret and guilt. My eyes prick with reminders of my deception.

"Then we'll learn. I love you and nothing will change that, Nora. Nothing."

As he presses his lips to mine once more, I think, you're wrong. God help me because I don't know how our love will be able to survive the resentment and hate he'll feel for me once he knows.

A knock on my window makes me squeal and jump, dragging me back to the darkness of my deceit in the light of a new day. I look up to see Connelly's face outlined through the fog of the driver's side glass. I've been sitting here so long the entire inside of the car is now coated with obscurity. I wish I could stay encased in it forever. But I can't. My days of anonymity were always on a countdown clock to annihilation.

Taking a deep breath, I open the door, cold rain pouring inside the car.

"What are you doing, princess?"

Planning to run.

"Waiting for you," I lie.

Fact is, I was contemplating running...coming up with any plausible excuse not to spend more uninterrupted time with Connelly. I need some space to get my emotions back on lockdown and my thoughts in order and that will never happen by spending nearly twenty-four solid hours alone with him.

He holds out a steady hand. I pull back like it's a viper ready to strike.

While last night sits hard in the pit of my stomach, the reason I'm on panic's razor-sharp blade right now has little to do with that and everything to do with the fact that the dinner meeting with Kinnick Investments is in Memphis, not Chicago. And since it's a nine-hour drive to Memphis and I didn't know until last night when Connelly walked me to my car that we were meeting at the Chez Phillippe, the renowned French restaurant located inside the historic Peabody Hotel, I couldn't very well drive. I have no idea why I thought we'd be meeting in Chicago. My only excuse is that every time I'm around Connelly, my brains get scrambled. I become a blazing hot mess.

"Come on. I'm getting soaked," he says, wiggling his hand for me take it. I set my palm in his, mine slightly shaking, and join him under his huge golf-sized umbrella, burrowing closer to shield myself from the chilly sideways downpour. He starts us toward the hangar when I stop, water pelting me, drenching my business suit.

I'm barely holding my shit together. I cannot get on that plane. I cannot.

"My bag." I gesture toward my practical Ford Focus, stalling for time.

With an arm around my waist, he hauls me back under his protection, kissing me hard and quick on the lips. "Ham will get it," he says, moving us forward across the wet concrete until we're in the safety of the large, cavernous hangar. Well...safe from the rain anyway.

Connelly briefly lets me go to fold the dripping umbrella and instructs someone who looks like he could bench three of me to get my bag. I almost turn and run when he places his warm hand at the base of my spine, right above the curve of my ass, pushing me toward the stairs that could take me to my death.

With each step I take toward the small white jet that has GRASCO emblazoned across the fuselage in crisp, navy-blue letters, my vision fades, my stomach violently churns. It becomes harder and harder to suck air through my restricted airway.

"Nora, what's the matter? You're shaking like a leaf."

When he told me about dinner in Memphis, I didn't tell Connelly I couldn't do it. I didn't tell him I'm now illogically petrified of something I once loved to do. I didn't tell him of my father's death. I was a complete emotional wreck from our lovemaking. By the time we'd reached my car, I was barely holding my tears inside as he kissed me goodnight and held me in his arms, telling me again how much he loved me.

"Nothing," I choke, forcing my feet up the six narrow metal steps.

I keep reminding myself it's just a little over an hour in the air. One hour there today, one hour back tomorrow. Two hours of my life. Statistics show only one in over twenty-nine million dies in a single airplane crash, I tell myself. And if we do crash, I have a 24 percent chance of survival. I convince myself this is far safer than driving nine hours on the road with a bunch of idiots distracted by texting and crying kids.

When we step inside, the smell of new leather hits my nostrils and I freeze. Unwelcome thoughts pummel me from all sides.

I wonder if this was what my father experienced just before his demise. Did he ogle over the fancy interior of a small, private jet? Did he sink into the soft-as-silk leather seats and gaze out the small round portholes wishing he'd done things differently as life passed him by while he spent it cooped up in a lab? And as the plane went down, did he regret not being there for me, my daughter, my mother?

"Nora, baby, what's wrong?" Connelly gently coaxes in my ear, rubbing his hands up and down my freezing cold limbs. I lean into his comfort, needing his strength.

"I don't really like small planes."

I like life.

"I thought you loved to fly?"

"I used to," I mumble. Trying to be strong, I force my body to one of the plush, buttery-colored leather chairs. When I take a seat, my fingers fumble with the belt and then his are there, pushing mine away so he can buckle me in tight. When he's done, I keep my watery eyes on my lap. He grabs hold of both hands.

"Nora, look at me. Sweetheart, please," he cajoles after I hesitate.

When our eyes connect, I immediately feel safe and loved and cherished. "First, this is a Gulfstream five fifty, one of the best and safest private jets money can buy. I have a pilot and a copilot, and between them, they have over one hundred and fifteen years of experience flying in both in the military and the private sector and over twenty thousand hours of flying time. That may not sound like a lot, but it can take pilots their entire careers to reach those milestones, if ever. Phil and Ham know what they're doing. You're safe. I promise."

"You can't promise that."

"I can promise this. I've only just found you again so I'm not going to let anything, even the Messiah Himself, take you away from me just yet."

"Connelly," I breathe. I love this man so very much. I have no idea what I'm going to do when his eyes are full of contempt instead of love.

"It's okay, princess. I'm here. I won't let anything happen to you."

The way he says those words with such conviction, such *sympathy*...

"You know," I whisper.

He nods slowly, squeezing my hands. "I just found out this morning."

"How?"

"Google's a pretty powerful tool."

Yes. I suppose when a renowned researcher and three of his colleagues meet their fiery deaths where pilot error was to blame, it would make the news. I don't know. I didn't watch TV for weeks after that. I didn't pick up a paper. I didn't look at the World Wide Web.

I grieved.

I pitied myself for all I'd lost. And not just my father. I relived every loss, every mistake, every choice. Every time I felt I was pulling my life together, fate dealt me yet another cruel blow. I felt defeated, doomed. It was wrong. I knew it then and I know it now, but the only way I could survive my seemingly never-ending string of pain and suffering was to turn inside myself and shut everyone else out.

"Ah." I take a deep breath, blowing it out slowly. Connelly waits patiently, his gaze full of affection. I treasure it then tuck it away. I know my expiration on it is rapidly approaching. "I was going to tell you. I just…I…"

I didn't know how without completely breaking.

"I know. I'm sorry, Nora. I'm so fucking sorry you had to go through all of this shit alone. I should have been there."

His sincerity slays me. The hurt he feels because I hurt cuts me so deep I feel the unintentional sharpness of his words slice my heart like jagged glass. It's excruciating.

I decide in that very moment that I'm going to get through this trip, this meeting, these next twenty-four hours with Connelly and then I'll come clean. I'll tell him everything. I owe him that much, even if it means I'll lose everything in the process.

"Sir, we're ready to take off. You'll need to take your seat now," a deep, masculine voice calls from behind me.

"Thanks, Ham." He looks back at me. "You okay?"

"It's still raining." The torrential downpour has lightened up, but it's still coming down pretty hard. The wind still howls angrily as if it knows my devastating secrets.

"They wouldn't take off if it wasn't safe. I don't have a death wish, either."

"We'll climb quickly, ma'am, and be above the storm in just a few short minutes. It will be smooth sailing to Memphis after that."

Clutching Connelly's fingers tightly, I nod, not realizing the guy named Ham is still standing behind us.

"Need my hands back, babe. Gotta buckle up. You can have them right back, promise." Panic must be written all over my face because he leans up to kiss me. It's slow and sweet and when he teases my seam open, his tongue touching mine, it immediately floods my core with want. And it also does its intended trick. I let go of his hands to frame his face instead, wanting to deepen our connection.

With his lips stuck to mine, I feel him shift and

move, but I don't let go, my body straining to stay fused with his. I hear the sound of his seatbelt latch. Then he does as promised. His hands are back, covering mine.

Breaking our lip-lock, he pants, "We need to stop or I'm going to take you in the lavatory and fuck your brains out the minute we reach cruising altitude."

His words send a zing of lust straight to my nipples and clit, hardening both so the only thing I can think about is getting him inside me again, even though I know it's wrong.

My eyes roll briefly to his groin and his hardening erection before rising to meet his. "Okay."

He groans as if my agreement caused him physical pain. "Nora, for the love of God, don't tempt me."

"Why?" I ask. I don't blink. I don't move. I don't look away as I watch hunger tighten his face and thirst cloud his vision.

"Is that what you want?" he asks gruffly, now stroking my bottom lip with his thumb, fingers wrapped around my jaw.

His touch. God. It weakens me and strengthens me. It burns me and soothes me. A single press of his skin to mine brings me absolute and utter peace but sends a rush of desire barreling through me like a freight train.

"Have you done this with anyone else?"

His eyes snap to mine. Then they turn positively ravenous. They are dark seas of desire I fall helplessly into every time I look at him.

"No." His voice is low, seductive. Unmistakably sinful. And indisputably inviting.

"Then yes." I push those two words out on a puff of air that I didn't even know I had left in my lungs, my breaths now coming in shallow gasps just imagining being the first woman he takes thirty thousand feet in the air. If I'm going to go out with a bang, I might as well be enjoying the hell out of it. Or fuck out of it, as it were.

"Nora," he says with a growl, hazels arresting me, searching for truth in my words. "You are so damn perfect."

Everything else fades away. I don't know how long we sit there, staring at each other, the air thickening and heating around us. All I do know is my stomach hasn't stopped flipping since I set my hand on his back in my car. Next thing I know, he's popped out of his seat and is undoing my safety belt. I'm in his arms while he carries me through the small space. It's not until now that I register we're smoothly sailing above the clouds below. Moving through the galley, he drops me to my feet before opening the lavatory door, ushering me inside.

Shutting the pocket door, he says nothing while he shimmies my skirt up and skims my damp panties down my legs. Tapping my feet, I lift each one so he can remove them. After taking a deep whiff, he stuffs them into his pocket and wags his brows, which makes me laugh.

"A souvenir?"

Flashing a quick smile, he quips, "Hell yes."

But his smile fades and my laughter dies as

voracious hunger for each other wraps herself around us again. Palming my nape, his mouth takes mine. Swift. Hard. He owns it. Devours it. Consumes me. This is the polar opposite of his tenderness last night and I love every single second of it. This is the domineering man I've craved since the minute I laid eyes on him a month ago.

"Turn around. Hands on the mirror," he rumbles. His face is fierce and filled with aggression.

I hesitate too long. He grabs my hips, turning me toward the small sink until our mutual desire collides violently in the reflective glass.

He looks like he wants to eat me.

God, how I want him to.

I jump when the plane shudders slightly. His fingers tighten, digging almost painfully into me.

"Eyes on me, Nora."

I obey. I *want* to obey. I want to relinquish complete control to this man.

Reaching around, he undoes the two buttons on my moist blazer and removes it, hanging it on a hook behind him. Next is my silk blouse. His movements are sharp, clipped, hurried. At last, he removes his jacket, but nothing else.

I take the opportunity to glance behind me in the mirror, taking in the enclosed room. It's surprisingly large for an airplane bathroom. I even spot a small shower behind us.

"You're not following directions. Don't look away."

"You—"

"And no talking. Just watch, listen…and feel." The

last whispered word drips seduction over me like a gentle rain shower, drenching me in delirious longing.

Taking my hands, he places them above me on the cool glass, pressing them hard and flat like he's trying to glue them into place.

"Don't move, princess," he rasps against my lobe before biting hard, making me shudder. Coarse whiskers brush against the column of my throat. I need them between my legs instead.

Our gazes bolt tightly together. He draws his fingertips down my limbs, barely touching. Teasing, taunting. At the same time, he steps into me. Heat warms the chills of anticipation running down my back.

"You are absolutely exquisite."

Awe threads his low words, setting my very blood on fire.

Palming my breasts with his large hands, he kneads and plumps before tugging down the white lace demi cups, groaning when his eyes drop to my taut nipples. Taking each between his thumbs and forefingers, he twists and pulls. When he pinches them hard, I gasp, my head falling back to his shoulder.

Hot, openmouthed kisses land on my throat, my shoulder. I've never been so damned turned on before. Pressing my ass against his fabric-covered, rock-hard erection, I squirm, silently begging him to take me. Now. I can't take much more.

"I want to fuck you, Nora."

My chest heaves, the blush of my need deepening. "Hard."

I rub my thighs together, needing desperate relief.

"Rough."

My breaths are choppy and uneven; oxygen is sacred.

"Dirty."

Every nerve ending is alive. Exposed. His mere touch is almost excruciating.

"Bare." He nuzzles my ear, whispering, "Nothing between us, princess."

I freeze.

"I'd never put you in danger, Nora," he adds swiftly.

Connelly's been with a lot of women. I don't know this for a fact, but I have to assume all of the rumors I've heard and read online have at least some shred of truth to them. Without more than a second's hesitation, though, I give him my silent permission. I shouldn't, I know this, but I want to feel him take me without any barriers as much as he does.

He's mine as much as I'm his, if only for a short while.

With victory sparkling in his eyes, his hands skate down my sides, slowly gliding over my bunched skirt, then the smooth curves of my hips before he grips them with bruising force. One hand holds tightly to me while the other disappears behind him. I hear the mechanics of his slacks being worked and suck in a sharp breath when the other dives between my legs.

"Shit, Nora. You are so ready for me," he grates,

227

leisurely pumping a single finger in and out, spreading my unerring need all over.

I squirm. It's not enough. I need more.

"Last night I branded your soul," he continues, his voice a hoarse whisper. "Today I'm branding your body."

That's all the warning I get as he grabs my hips, cocks them back and slams inside me in one savage thrust.

Oh, fuck.

"Jesus, you feel incredible. So fucking good. Fuck, Nora." His voice is hard and rough. Like his grip. Like his cock.

My head falls forward and my eyes fall shut until he orders me to open them. My lids are heavy, the intense pleasure in my core drawing them closed.

"Eyes," he barks, never letting up on his ruthless assault.

With great effort, I comply. And the second I do, I connect on an entirely different plane than I have with another human being. Ever.

It's intense.

It's passionate.

It's feral.

It's soul stealing and life altering.

"I love you," I blurt, unable to keep the words in any longer. I admitted it last night, but I never said those three little words I've only ever uttered to him.

He freezes midstroke, eyes going wide. "Say it again," he demands thickly. He squeezes me hard, his cock pulsing inside me with the need to pillage. "Again."

"I love you. I love you, Connelly."

His eyes close in pure, utter rapture and my breath is stolen for an entirely different reason.

Can you recall a specific moment in your life with such vivid clarity you'd swear it just happened yesterday, but in reality it was days ago…months ago…years ago, even?

This is one of those instances. The sheer joy I see right now on Connelly's face is the same way he looked when I told him I loved him for the very first time. I've never forgotten it, just like I will never forget this. Another selfish maneuver on my part, but I need him to know how much I love him before I destroy him.

When he starts thrusting again, it's brutal and merciless, with single-minded intent. "Scream my name, Nora. Come apart for me."

I have never come on demand and I've never come from penetration alone. It always, *always* takes me a while to get my engine revved, and I always need clit stimulation, yet this is different. Even before he uttered his command, I was there.

The coarseness of his clothes abrading the backs of my thighs, the firmness of his strokes inside my swollen sex and the ferocity of his stare have already thrown me headlong into the most intense orgasm I've ever experienced at the hands of anyone.

As my body shudders under his touch, I feel myself float. I hear myself cry his name. I watch myself reduced to nothing but a swirling liquid mass of gratification as he brands me his.

Then Connelly is following on a string of muttered curses.

"Oh, fuck, yes." He tenses, growls, and pours his seed into my womb in a few hard thrusts, his head thrown back, his face tight and strained.

I watch the man who always held tightly to the reins of control lose it because of me. My femininity swells with pride.

Sagging against me, Connelly's lips dance lightly on my shoulder, tickling. Our sweat mingles while his semen trickles down my inner thigh. I am utterly replete. Sadness tries to shove her way in, shattering the moment, but I heave her out. I need to bask in this feeling in case I never experience it again.

"I love you, Nora. God, I love you so damn much," he mutters before taking my lobe gently between his teeth. The reverent words sink through my skin, staunching the hemorrhage that's slowly been killing me.

I reach around and press his head against me, holding his cheek to mine. "Not more than I love you."

As our bodies cool and our breaths even out, I know although this was the most violent, swift coupling I've ever experienced, the hollow place inside me that's been empty is finally gone.

I only wish it could last.

Chapter 16

Nora

Within two minutes after sitting down at a secluded table in the dimly lit Chez Phillippe, I understand why Connelly wanted to accompany me to this meeting. He warned me on the ride from the airport to the Peabody that Alred Kinnick is "old-fashioned." Said he's challenging to please, hard to work with.

What I see he really meant was that Alred Kinnick is a misogynist pig who disguises it under artificial Southern charm and feigned interest. He leaves an instant bitter taste in my mouth, but I paste on my own fakery and forge ahead as I always do with men like this. Men who think a woman's place is doing their laundry before sticking their ass in the air solely for their pleasure. I wonder how Kinnick Investments ended up with a CEO who doesn't have a ball sack hanging between her legs and I have to believe it wasn't this man's doing. Now things are starting to make more sense. I also wonder how Connelly knows such a jackass. They seem pretty tight.

"So, this is your new star pupil, eh, Conn?"

Connelly's face tightens almost imperceptibly. A brief glance at I'm-stuck-in-the-stone-ages shows he's clueless. I contain my eye roll. Asswipe doesn't even bother looking at me when he speaks, a fact Connelly doesn't miss.

"Nora is one of the incredible talents we acquired with the SER deal, yes." He takes a casual drink of his Scotch, neat, but irritation wafts from him in rolling waves. His annoyance fogs over the entire corner of the room. Sometimes, I think I'm the only one who can pick up on Connelly's subtle clues. That thought makes me smile to myself.

"Well, I'd say you've done very well, son. She's fine. Very fine indeed," he purrs.

What the fucking hell does that *mean?*

"What are you looking for in a CEO, Mr. Kinnick?" I ask, trying to get back on task. The faster this meeting is over with, the sooner I can get the hell out of his cloying presence. I already know this is one position I'll be working my ass to fill quickly. Like tomorrow.

Kinnick's beady black eyes meet mine for the first time since we sat down. "Please, Nora. Call me Al."

Oh, I could call you a lot of things, but Al would be at the very bottom of my very long list, asshole. I smile. It feels thin and condescending. I hope Mr. Clueless doesn't catch on.

He doesn't.

"Minimum fifteen years experience in an executive position. An ideal candidate is one who's been groomed within his or her own company and touched all major areas: finance, research and development, acquisitions and divestitures. Background in investments is a must. Of course, education is..."

I listen to the pudgy, red-faced, gray-haired chairman of the board drone on for several more minutes, nearly oblivious to what he's saying. It will be a repeat of what I've heard hundreds of times before anyway.

Instead, all I can think about is the man sitting next to me, watching me, and how my heart is racing so fast because of nerves, I wonder if I'll need a defibrillator soon. I think I saw one hanging on the wall on my way in.

I force myself back to the conversation instead of remembering what it felt like to be completely owned by Connelly just mere hours ago. And just in time, too, because both men are looking at me, waiting for my response.

"With all due respect, Mr. Kinnick, that's just a resume. What are your short- and long-term goals for Kinnick Investments? Do you have a target stock price you're aiming for? Do you want to expand further into the global markets? Are you looking for a puppet or a leader? Do you want a groundbreaker or steadfast, long-term leadership? This will be the fourth CEO in ten years and that's a lot of upheaval for any organization to endure. So the question isn't about what Ivy League school your next CEO attended or how many letters he or she has behind their name. That's all a given when I look for the right fit for my clients. The question really is where exactly do you want your next CEO to take Kinnick Investments in the future?"

I'm not sure where my tirade came from. While these are the typical questions I ask, I usually find a more politically correct way to frame them besides just blasting them out like a firing squad, but God. Damn. This arrogant prick set me off by virtually ignoring my mere existence until just moments ago.

I chance a glance at Connelly and the look on his face can be described as nothing short of pride. Unabashed pride. I flash him a quick smile before turning my attentions back to the old codger sitting across from me who drinks too much and probably has limp-dick syndrome, which he seems to be trying to make up for in other ways.

Just when I'm sure I've blown it, a slow, appreciative smile forces his dried lips open. I then know I've hit the nail square on the head. "I think I like her." He's speaking to Connelly, but his impressed eyes never leave mine.

Next to me I hear Connelly say quietly, "Me too."

My heart skips a beat. That soft acknowledgment from Connelly means more to me than any words of praise this douche across from me could ever say.

———

"That guy is an egotistical jackass," I say, punching the up arrow, *hard*, on the elevator, wishing it were Kinnick's eyeballs instead.

"He was impressed. That's hard to do."

"You mean for someone who has tits?" I scoff. I don't know why I'm so irritated. The rest of the evening went well. Compared to the first ten minutes, you'd think I'd always been part of their special little group. No fucking thanks. I'd rather eat nails.

He chuckles, placing his hand on my back. That seems to be one of his favorite spots on me. I can't believe how much I like the feel of it already. "Yes, that's what I mean. They're very nice ones, by the way," he whispers in my ear, heat flowing like magma through me. I want him. Again. And again. That's practically all I could think about through dinner as if having sex twice in the last twenty-four hours hasn't been enough.

"How do you know him?" I prod, trying to tamp down my libido. It's only eight-thirty, but I'm emotionally exhausted and physically drained from not sleeping a wink last night. I feel a migraine coming on. I need sleep.

"He's an old friend of my father's. I would say he's a nice guy once you get to know him, but that would be a lie. He's a grade-A bastard."

"Then why assign this case to me? I could do with fewer bastards in my life."

The steel door finally parts and we enter. Connelly punches the button for the fourteenth floor. I reach toward the panel to push my floor, eight, when he yanks my hand back, using it to tug me into him.

"What are you doing?" I ask on a short breath as he pins me between the wood paneling and his rock-hard body.

One look from Connelly could always make me pant, make me wet, make me submit to his every wicked whim. One touch, though...one touch and I crumble helplessly.

"Answering your question. I assigned you to this case because I wanted to spend time with you and I knew this was the only way you would let me."

I frown, anger rising to the surface. I open my mouth to give him a piece of my redheaded mind when he adds, "And because I knew if anyone could handle that chauvinist, you could, Nora. *I* was impressed. You are as brilliant as I've heard."

And just like that, my fury deflates like a balloon that's had the knot loosened.

"Thank you," I mumble.

Pressing his groin into my belly, he grasps my wrists in one hand and raises them above my head. Lowering his mouth to my neck, he rumbles between wet kisses, "Every word made me harder. I need to be inside you again. I can't fucking get enough of you."

"God." I pull in a sharp breath when he sucks painfully on the swell of my breast. Heat licks along my skin, racing straight between my legs.

"You're coming back to my room."

"That's kind of presumptuous, don't you think?" I pant, eyes rolling in the back of my head. I burn everywhere.

Every woman has her favorite place to be kissed. For some, it's as simple as the mouth. For others, it may be her inner thigh, behind the knees, or a nip on her lobe. For me, though? It's definitely the neck. And with each warm caress of Connelly's lips and hot swirl of his tongue, my willpower unwinds like a tossed spool of thread.

"Is it?" he asks. His free hand travels down my leg until it reaches the hem of my skirt. I groan when it slips under and slides back up, reaching my bare pussy. My bare, *wet* pussy. Talented fingers skim across my sex and the light scrape of his dull nails fires the burn in my core into a raging volcanic eruption.

I barely had time to get freshened up and call Zel after we checked in. I completely forgot my panties were currently being held prisoner in Connelly's suit jacket pocket until I sat down at the dinner table. At one point during the meal, Connelly slipped his hand inside, palming them, sliding a shit-eating grin my way when he subtlety brought his fingers to his nose. I was instantly wet, pressing my thighs tighter to keep moisture from staining my skirt.

"I have my own room," I tell him, even though we just passed the floor where mine is.

"Not anymore," he replies in a husky tone, right before he captures my mouth in a scorching kiss at the same time he thrusts two fingers inside me. I'm wet, so damn wet, and he slides in easily.

"Ahhh," I moan loudly.

"That is so sexy to know I do this to you."

He kicks one of my feet to the side, spreading my legs wide. Oh-so-achingly slowly, he finger-fucks me, thumbing my clit. Everything around me falls away as I let pleasure consume me. All I know is him. All I need is release.

I can taste the sweet kernel of my climax when suddenly I'm being pulled from the steel box and dragged down a hallway. Everything else is a blur, darkened by this growing need inside me.

"Connelly—"

"No more objections, Nora," he demands gruffly, his grip tightening as if he thinks I may bolt.

I won't. Not this time.

He stops in front of a double door and pulls out a key card. The gold-plated sign on the wall indicates we're at the Presidential Suite. When he silently ushers me in, I don't even get a chance to look around before I'm being scooped up in his strong, sinewy arms and carried through the biggest, most luxurious hotel room I've ever been in.

"I was just going to say I need my stuff." I lean up, running the tip of my tongue under the delicate skin behind his ear. The throaty, sexy rumble he makes causes my nipples to tingle.

"Taken care of."

"Wow. That's kind of intrusive. What if I'd said no?"

Walking through white French doors, he deposits me onto the plush carpet of a massive-sized bedroom decorated in muted yellows and pumpkin oranges. A chandelier hanging from the ceiling above the king-sized bed throws soft light around the interior, setting the sultry mood perfectly.

"I can be very convincing."

Yes. You always have been.

I feel the same aggression coming off him as I did earlier when he took me in the plane, so I expect he'll rip my clothes off and ravage me. He does the complete opposite.

Craddling my face in his big hands, he just gazes at me quietly for the longest time. It's soft. Tender. Loving. It almost ruins me. He's searching for something I don't want him to find. If he does...this fantasy I've foolishly immersed myself in will all be over. I know my time is almost up anyway. I'm panicking at the need to hold on to it just a little bit longer.

"Are you real?"

My eyes prick.

I nod because I can't speak. His question stole my voice.

"I love you so much, Nora. It's terrifying how much I feel my very breath will die if you walk away from me again. I'm trying so damn hard to tie to you to me forever, but I feel like I'm one crumbling step away from losing you. I can't lose you again, Nora. I just fucking can't. I can't."

The bottled-up emotion in his unsteady, desperate voice, as if he's seconds away from cracking, slays me. I want to dissolve at his feet and weep and beg for forgiveness I'll never deserve.

I try to speak.

Impossible.

I try to swallow.

My mouth is bone-dry. Even if I could, it would never get past the lump of betrayal sitting hard in my throat.

Suddenly the last thing I can do is lead him on

any further. I need to do the right thing. For once. I must get this unbearable mass of guilt off my chest that's holding me down, threatening to drown me in self-reproach.

"We should talk," I manage to choke. I try to step back so I can think, breathe. I need to wrap my arms around my middle and try like fuck to hold myself together while my confession breaks him apart.

He starts nodding his head but tightens his hold. "You're right. We should. We need to. And we will. Just not tonight."

Connelly's always been so perceptive. He knows something's wrong. Something big. Something that will kill the us he's trying to rebuild.

"Bu—"

Swooping down, he swallows my objection with his mouth, pushing the others back in with his tongue. Then we're on the move again. The softness of the down comforter pillows my back; his bulky weight causes me to sink farther into the feathers.

"Not tonight, Nora. Not tonight. I need one more day before we break open old wounds and unleash old ghosts that can never be put back. Please, not tonight, princess. Just let me show you how much I love you."

His voice is barely there at the end.

He sounds scared.

So am I.

I reach up and cup his cheek, willing the tears away. "Okay. Okay, not tonight."

"I need you. So goddamned much." His raspy words were unnecessary. Voracious desire is written on the hard lines of his face, threaded in every gritty word. It shines brightly in his brilliant eyes.

"You have me. I'm yours." *For as long as you'll keep me.*

He rises on his haunches, first undressing me, then himself. He lowers back down, sinks his hands into my hair, and gently pushes inside me, our eyes air locked so tight even gravity itself couldn't tear them apart. It's the most defenseless and real moment I've shared with anyone.

As Connelly sweetly makes love to me, worshipping my body with gentle touches and showering me in reverent words, we both know this is different. Tomorrow when the sun rises, casting an inescapable spotlight on our sins, everything will change.

We both know it.

We both feel it.

We're both ignoring it in a desperate attempt to soak in each precious minute we have left together that's not tainted with cloaked truths and hurts from a time long ago.

Our past, which has always been nipping at our heels, has finally caught us.

Time's up.

Chapter 17

CONN

It's nearly four in the morning and I still haven't closed my eyes. When we returned from dinner at eight-thirty, I spent hours making love to Nora and even though I feel both sated and starved, I know she needed sleep. I think I let her drift off sometime past midnight after she couldn't keep her eyes open any longer. The woman I've loved, lost, and have somehow found my way back to again is currently draped over my naked body like a soft blanket, dead to the world. The fact that she willingly spent the night wrapped around me, trusting me, is a genuine gift—one I will not take for granted.

I tighten my hold, wishing I could crawl into her.

I've never been happier.

Yet here I lie, hours later. Wide awake. Fucking terrified that true happiness I once thought unattainable is about to be blown to smithereens for the second time. This all feels too good to be true and usually, that's a bad fucking sign.

She wanted to talk. I should have said yes. I saw the veiled skeletons swirling like bony dream-killing monsters in her green eyes and I just couldn't do it. I didn't want to ruin a perfect evening. I wanted to bury my head in the luxury of denial a little while longer before we opened the history book and turned to the pages containing our past sins.

Over these past few weeks, I've bared my soul to her. I may not have shed all my transgressions, but I've bled every single emotion I have in me. I've held nothing back. Not a fucking thing. I've flayed my insides open time and again, spilling my deepest inner feelings. I've told her things I've never spoken of to another person, not even my twin, my closest confidant.

But she hasn't done the same. She has the worst poker face of anyone I've ever met, but getting her to admit what's going on inside that pretty little head of hers is the biggest challenge I've ever faced. I want to know what she's thinking. I need to know what she's feeling. I need assurances she wants there to be an us...that she's willing to try.

I love her.

She loves me.

Of those two things, I have no shred of doubt. None.

But I have secrets.

So does she. Hers are secrets she's trying to run from, though. Mine, I'm ready to bleed.

I have a gut-wrenching feeling she knows mine already, but I have no fucking clue what hers is. I want to know, yet I don't. I need to know, yet I'm scared to hear them because secrets destroy. They obliterate trust. Ruin lives. Shatter futures. They challenge your capacity to truly forgive. They test how bottomless your love really burns.

What will happen to us once our transgressions are revealed? Absolution? Resentment? God forbid...the end? Can a love that has never died be snuffed out by the admission of our weaknesses? Can I have a future with the only woman I've ever let into my soul, the only person who will ever carry my heart in the palm of her hand?

I hope so. I want that. I want freedom. I want forgiveness. For both of us. I want a life with her. I want to wake up with her in my arms and go to bed with my cock pressed snug between her ass cheeks. I want to slip inside her inviting heat morning, noon, and night. I want her silky hair wrapped around my hand and her soft lips captured between my teeth. I want her fingers intertwined with mine as we walk down the street. I want to start our own traditions, like freezer crap night. I want my possessive claim wrapped forever around her left ring finger.

And I think I may even want kids. Kids...*Me*. The man who arrogantly professed just a few months ago that a wife and kids weren't in his fifty-year plan, but now it's practically all I can think about.

I selfishly want it all.

I want my happily fucking ever after with my soul mate.

Nora was right. I have a lot of wants.

But will I get them? Is wanting everything too much to ask?

I guess today we'll find out. It's time to rip off the Band-Aid and let the past bleed scarlet until every iniquity we've committed against each other is lying in a dark puddle at our feet.

Then I can only pray we'll be able to walk away clean and pure.

Hand in hand, together.

No other outcome is acceptable.

Chapter 18

CONN

I woke Nora up this morning with my tongue in her pussy and her breathless moans ringing in my ears. I made love to her last night, but this morning I had an overwhelming need to mark her body, inside and out. I wanted her to feel me with each step she took. I wanted the imprints from my crushing passion for her to be carried around like prizes for a week, teasing her every time she glances in the mirror.

She looked at me expectantly after she came down from her tongue-induced high, but I put her off once again. I don't want to head down that rabbit hole yet. We'll be lost in it soon enough. As long as I have her here, tucked away with me alone, I'm going to keep living in my little fantasy world that everything is fine and nothing can shatter it.

But the clock is ticking louder and faster. I hear the fucker tick-tocking in my ear and I need to fasten those final knots, creating an unbreakable, load-bearing connection that will be able to withstand any tension we place on it.

We have an hour and a half before we need to leave for the airport. I intend to make full use of every one of those seconds.

"A hotel room with a doorbell?" she asks mockingly when we hear the chime echo through the massive suite.

"Nothing but the best for you." After a quick, hard kiss, I pick up a robe from the chair, leaving her lounging naked on top of the messy sheets. I glance back and catch her appreciating my ass with a satisfied smirk on her face.

I flex both cheeks before saying, "It's all yours, princess." I enjoy her laughter following me all the way to answer the door. Sliding my arms through the sleeves, I let in room service. After providing a generous tip, I wave them out and roll the cart into the bedroom with the goodies I ordered.

"What did you get?" she asks excitedly, leaning against the cushioned headboard. She covers herself with the sheet and just chuckles when I scowl.

Sitting on the edge of the bed, I pull her to my mouth. She melts under my tongue like cotton candy. I'm instantly hard. Again. Especially at the thought of how I'm about to eat my breakfast.

"Lay down, my beautiful girl." I kiss her softly while tugging down the fabric she's using to conceal herself. She lets it fall.

"But I'm hungry."

"And you'll eat. I promise."

"You've changed," she announces once she's splayed out against the stark white sheets. It makes me stone hard that she obeys me readily, but that she has her own mind and isn't afraid to use it. The dichotomy is a total turn-on.

"How so?" I ask retrieving the tie I threw on the chair in the corner of the room.

She glances at it and back to me without so much as a flinch before responding. Fuck, I love her. So damn much. "I mean you're still cocky and arrogant, don't get me wrong."

I smirk when she gives me a cheeky smile. After I ditch the robe, I sit back on the mattress, my knee touching her bare hip. Starting with the tip of her curled middle finger, I run a finger lightly down her turned-up palm and continue my path on the inside of the arm she has curved over her head. Her eyes darken and become heavy. I have a hard time not stroking my cock as I watch her desire for me deepen and spread.

"And?"

"And..." She clears her froggy throat. "You seem edgier. Like every character trait about you is sharper. Honed, I guess. You seem to have this deep-seated need for control."

I think about that for a few seconds as I circle her dark, puckered areola and twist her taut nipple, pulling a soft moan from her throat.

I am all of those things. Life has sharpened me. Why deny it? I've always had the uncontrollable need to win, but since Nora walked away from me, that's become laser focused. Losing Nora changed me in ways I still don't think I fully understand.

"You make those sound like bad things. Control is actually a very good quality, princess, as you're about to find out."

She tries to laugh but it comes out strangled. Probably because her nipple is now caught between my teeth. "You want to control me?" Her hand tangles in my hair. She arches her back to get closer.

I release her tasty bud with a pop. "That would be like controlling air. And I'm a lot of things, but I'm not a fucking sorcerer."

"Oh, I don't know about that," she groans as I take the other straining bud into my mouth. "You do pretty magical things to me."

Good to know.

"Time to eat," I growl, dragging my tongue up between the valley of her breasts before thrusting it between her lips, taking her in a bruising kiss.

I kiss her until she's putty in my hands. She puts up no resistance when I thread my tie around her eyes and knot it carefully, but snugly, on top of her red tresses.

"What are you doing?" she asks breathlessly, her hands going to the fabric now stealing her sight. I pull them back.

"Eating breakfast."

"While I'm blindfolded? That hardly seems fair. I'm hungry, too."

I whisper against her lips, "Trust that I'll take care of you, Nora. I'll always take care of you if you let me."

Her entire body relaxes and a soft smile graces her lips. Suddenly I wish I hadn't covered her eyes. I want to see them sparkle with love. "Okay."

"One more thing...don't move, princess, or I'll stop," I husk. "And I don't think you're going to want me to stop."

Her only response is to lick those luscious lips.

Uncovering several trays, I remove a piece of sliced fruit. She flinches at the first touch of coolness against her skin but is silent as I run the juicy flesh down the column of her throat. I continue between her breasts straight down her torso stopping just short of her slit, which is already exquisitely wet.

"What is that?" Her breaths have already quickened.

I don't answer. Instead, I trace the wet trail I left behind with my tongue, starting at her mound, working my way back up. When I reach her mouth, I suck her bottom lip between mine before kissing her softly. I gently twist my tongue with hers, letting her taste me.

"What does it taste like?"

"Mango."

I smile against her mouth. "Very good."

Holding the lush tropical fruit to her lips, she opens and takes a bite. "Mmm...that is so good."

I pop the rest in my mouth and reach for the next thing, changing it up. This time, I draw circles around the inner wrist of her right arm, working my way up to the crook of her elbow before repeating the entire process over again with my tongue ending up twined with hers.

"Watermelon."

"You're a fruit connoisseur, I see," I say lowly. I feed her a bite of the dripping melon, licking a stray droplet that trickles down the side of her face.

"It's going to take a long time to eat breakfast this way," she teases.

"That's the point, sweetheart."

"The sheets are going to be a mess."

"Don't give a shit if they're ruined."

"Okay, then." She smiles wide. It's contagious. "Continue. I'm starved."

I reach for the next thing and lift her leg so she's spread open to me. "Fuck, Nora," I curse, taking in the milkiness between her thighs. She's coated. "This turning you on, princess?"

"This is the sexiest thing I've ever done." Her hips shift slightly upward. I almost abandon the rest of what I have planned, her wetness beckoning me to sink inside. Quench the ache deep in my balls.

"Me too. And before you ask...this is another first."

Happiness lights up her face so bright I'm almost blinded by it. I've never seen a thing more beautiful than she is.

When I touch the next piece to her inner thigh, she jerks. "That's warm."

"It is." I draw a line north, to that sweet spot where her inner thigh meets her delightfully wet pussy. Once again I follow the same line I painted. Unable to resist, I circle her pebbled clit lightly, drawing it smoothly into my mouth. I lave gently until her moans grow louder and more insistent and then I retreat. She tastes like milk chocolate and me. Best fucking combo ever.

"Connelly, please." Her body undulates beneath me. Fuck. I can hardly stand this slow, deliberate torture myself.

"Not yet, baby," I murmur, palming myself to take the edge off. "I want you hot, wet, and wanting. Aching so badly for my touch, my kiss, my heavy cock that you'd gladly sell your soul for me to relieve your physical agony."

I tap her lips with the berry until she opens. "Oh God," she moans in delight. "Chocolate. And strawberries. Delicious."

"It's more delicious on you. Trust me on that."

My eyes are tracking down her gorgeous, writhing body when I notice a cluster of light moles just right beneath her left breast that I haven't seen before. I dip my finger in the crème fraîche and trace a line between them. When I'm done it looks like a stick figure, minus the head and arms.

"That's Cancer," she says quietly.

A rush of terror washes through me at the mention of that word. "What?"

"No, no..." she scrambles at the panic threading my voice. "The zodiac sign. Cancer."

I look at the headless figure again while I tell my heart to slow down. I just found this woman again. I can't lose her. "Hate to break it to you, princess, but the zodiac sign for Cancer is a crab."

"I know."

"Well, what I'm looking at is about three moves away from a win at hangman," I chuckle before bending over to lick the cream off.

"Yes, but those five stars are all you can see of the Cancer constellation in the summer sky with the naked eye."

My gaze drifts over her mountainous breasts in time to catch her wetting her lips. I want them wrapped around my throbbing dick.

"I'm a Cancer, you know." I don't know shit about astrology, but I at least know what my sign is. Women seem to dig that for some reason.

"I know," she replies softly.

Something in her tone catches me. I sit up, my eyes falling back to the line of tiny imperfections on her otherwise perfect body. When I connect the dots again, she shudders under my light touch.

Possessiveness swells hot inside me. I'm not usually into portents and all that crap, but I have no doubt this is one. Nora is my soul mate and this affirms it. "It's a sign, then. That you're mine."

Her smile. Magnificent. "I always knew I was destined to end up with a Cancer, and when I met you..."

Suddenly I don't want her eyes shielded from me because I feel like this is a pivotal moment for our future, so I slide the garment off and stare into her bright green eyes when she blinks them open.

"When you met me, what?"

Running her finger along the scruff of my jaw, she has so much love in her eyes when she says, "I knew I was done waiting."

"Nora." My throat constricts. I feel intensely conflicted right now. Anger and hurt that she left me try to crowd out the incredible love I have for her, taking center stage. Bitterness that we lost out on a decade together twists my gut into tight knots. But genuine fear that I'll wake up tomorrow and this will all be a dream is what's truly terrifying. "Do I have you, Nora? Really have you?"

253

Water rapidly fills her eyes before spilling over and running into her shiny hair. "You have me for as long as you want me."

I cover her body with mine and wipe away the streaks with my thumbs. "There will never be a day that goes by that I don't want you, Nora. Not one. Don't leave me again. It will completely break me this time."

"Me too."

My stomach growls, but I ignore it. I have expended so many calories over the past twelve hours, but the need to have her again outweighs every other human need I have. She's a craving I'll never satiate. A hunger I'll never assuage. I need to be inside of her, feel her snugness squeezing my cock. "Are you hungry?"

My cock throbs against her pale thigh. Her hips are undulating now, along with mine, her need mirroring mine exactly. "I can wait."

"Are you sore?"

She smiles, and I feel temporarily taken back in time to when I asked her that during our only night together. "A little, but I'm good."

Every encounter with every single woman has been hollow, lonely. Except for *her*. With Nora, I felt connected to another human being in a way I've not been able to replicate again. And that intimate connection right now is more vital than breath or food. I shift, lining up my shaft with her opening and drop my forehead to hers. "God, I'm sorry. I need you again, Nora."

Small fingers delve into my hair and tighten. Her warm, sweet breath scatters over my face when she whispers, "Don't be sorry. I need you, too."

That's the only green light I need. Just as I have for the countless time over the past two days, I slip easily inside her inviting wetness and warmth and begin rocking slow and steady.

The fluid writhing of her body under mine does me in, though, and I break. I kiss. I bite. I mark. I suck and lave and hold her hips tight in my grasp, fucking her fast and furious until she's coming all around me.

I destroy her for anyone else.

I would fuck this woman all the way to my grave if I could, but I can't possibly halt the orgasm that her spasming walls violently rip from the depths of my very being. As the rush of fire shoots up my spine and through my limbs, I feel almost reborn. It's the most cleansing climax I have had in my thirty years.

Minutes later when we've caught our breaths and her luscious curves are pressed against me in a sated puddle, the confession she makes covers me in an agonizing spray of whys, reminding me that as much as I want to, outrunning the past can only ever result in exhaustion.

"There's never been anyone else. In my heart, I mean."

I let my fingers drift up and down her arm, taking in a deep lungful of her heady unique scent, memorizing it. "For me either," I tell her truthfully.

Tilting her head up she catches my stare. I see mysteries begging to be unraveled, threatening to wreck us. "I have things I need to tell you."

But here's the thing about running...it's really mind over matter. Sheer, raw will over brute physicality. And I am famous for my sheer, raw grit.

"I know. Let's wait until we get home, yeah?"

She smiles, but it's thin and doesn't reach her eyes. "Yeah, okay."

"I love you, Nora. You should know that I'm never letting go."

"Promise?" Even her tone holds thin filaments of secrets. Perhaps even fear.

I press a kiss to her forehead and hug her tighter, trying like hell to meld her flesh into my flesh and her bones into mine so she becomes a part of me I would die without. "Yes. I promise."

Promises. They're like bull's-eyes. A big fat fucking black mark square between your eyes, just waiting for something or someone to come along and take you out. They are slippery, tricky fuckers that are hard to hold on to, even for those with the best of intentions. When you make them, you are 100 percent certain there is nothing that will or can make you break your oath, the vow you swore above all other things you'd honor.

But then something completely unforeseen, wholly unimaginable comes out of left field that tests your pledge, stretches your commitment. Makes you reevaluate where your loyalties lie and whom you can trust.

That "thing" will undermine everything you believed in, will dissolve the trust behind the promise in the first place, and sometimes that "thing" is just a misunderstanding.

More often than not, though, that "thing" is betrayal.

Chapter 19

CONN

Ella: have a pkg 4 u
Me: that a euphemism for something?
Ella: god, do u always think w/ur dick?

I laugh, feeling in a pretty good fucking mood. Better than I have in weeks. I tried to bribe Nora to come home with me so we could spend the rest of the weekend lounging in bed, nude, binge watching *The Little Mermaid*, to which she laughed so hard she had tears in her eyes. But she said she had things to do and needed to get home. We agreed to have lunch tomorrow, though and to talk. But not before I get her naked and twisted in my sheets. Hell, I may just tie her up so she has no choice but to stay this time.

Me: last time I checked, I'm a guy
Ella: that's always ur excuse
Me: b over in 10

A few minutes later, I'm knocking on Ella's

door. It's early, still not quite ten in the morning. Nora and I landed just shy of an hour ago. I miss her like hell already. After our marathon bout of sex, we cleaned up and rushed to the airport. This flight went better for her. While we didn't make the mile-high club again, between talking about my brothers and their newfound women, we made out like a couple of horny teenagers, especially on takeoff and touchdown, when she was most scared. It was fucking heaven, actually.

"Hey, come on in." Ella bounds back through the condo toward the kitchen, calling behind her, "Just be quiet."

"Be quiet? Why?" My eyes shift down the hall toward the bedrooms. "Your Coyote Ugly sleeping it off?"

"God, you are such a dick." She hands me a soft golden package containing a Grease T-Birds T-shirt I happened across on eBay. Nice gag gift for Asher. "No, my *niece* is still sleeping."

"Your niece is here? The one you bought that design thing for?"

"One and the same."

Remembering she said she had to mail the gift, I ask, "She visiting?"

"She lives here now." She shrugs and I know that's all I'll get from her tight lips.

Ella's phone rings. She swears under her breath before she puts it to her ear. "Hey, sorry," she says without even so much as a "hello."

I hear a loud female voice coming through the speaker. I can't make out what she's saying. I try not to eavesdrop but my ears perk at Ella's response.

"I know. Sorry, change of plans. I took her to *The Little Mermaid* last night at the Shakes and then we hung out on the pier for a while. We were both beat. I planned to bring her home when she woke up, but she's still sleeping."

More noise comes from the other side before Ella laughs.

"For Christ's sake, she's fine. Unharmed. Unpierced. Unmarred. Totally sober. What kind of aunt do you think I am?"

Pause.

Ella scowls. "There is this thing called the Internet. I used it. Plus a colleague has a nine-year-old."

I hear laughter and Ella's frown disappears.

"Are you sure? I can bring her over, no problem." She pauses. "Okay, see you in a few."

"Your sister?"

"Yes. She thinks she'll come home to a tatted, hungover child. I may have tatted her, but it's just a henna. Coffee?"

"Uh...sure. Got nothing better to do." Although I do. I have a shitload of e-mails to catch up on and quarterly financials to review, but for the entire last two days, I've done nothing but spend time inside of Nora. I should spend the whole day working, only for the first time in my career, I find I'm not hell-bent on getting back to the grind.

"Don't you want to shoo me out before your gorgeous sister arrives?" I tease, taking a tentative sip of the hot, strong brew. Not that I give a shit about anyone else besides Nora, but I can't pass up the opportunity to needle Ella.

Gazing at me, she replies, "No."

"No? Not that long ago I could have sworn you'd gouge my eyes out if I so much as looked at her."

"I did not. Besides, you look...I don't know." She tilts her head and narrows her eyes like she's just noticing something about me she hasn't seen before. "Different. You look relaxed. Dare I even say...happy? Someone special perhaps?"

If you told me smiling would trigger a stampede of wild boars that would crush me to death, I still couldn't have stopped it. "Yeah." I laugh. She's something special all right.

Before she can ask another probing question, which I'd willingly answer, I hear a small voice call from behind me, "Hi, Aunt Mira."

"Mira?" I ask, confused as hell.

She shrugs. "My full name is Mirabella, but my father always called me Mira. At work I go by Ella," she tells me as she quickly rushes around the kitchen island toward the child behind me. When I swivel in my stool all I can see is Ella's back and small hands around Ella's waist.

"How did you sleep, Ladybird?" Ella/Mira croons while hugging her niece.

In an instant, that nickname sucks me back in time.

"Morning, Ladybird," I tease, leaning close to smell her perfume.

"Ladybird?"

I wag my eyebrows. "Yeah, I did some research

on ladybugs, princess. Do you know in Europe they call them ladybirds?"

She smiles. It's brilliant and mind stealing. "You researched ladybugs? Why?"

"Because they interest you, and I'm interested in what interests you."

Her mouth softens and for the first time I see our future in her eyes, not just my own.

Have you ever had a heartbeat, just a single second in time, that seemed to completely stop? It's frozen, and as much as you want to press that damn fast-forward button so you can skip this point in time because you know it will change everything, you can't. You can't, because that's your life-altering moment. The one that's meant specifically for *you* to live.

I thought I'd had one of those already. The night Nora broke up with me over the phone.

But now I know I was wrong. *This* is that moment for me.

This is my game changer.

Had Ella not used that nickname, I probably would have missed it. I would have given the child a cursory glance and ran for the door, kids not really being my thing. But the second Ella mentioned "ladybird" my entire world came to a grinding, thunderous, fucked-up halt when I zeroed in on what circles the little girl's wrist.

A ladybug bracelet.

And not just any ladybug bracelet. It's the exact replica of the one I gave Nora the last night I saw her.

Random snippets of memories and conversations, completely out of order, pummel me so fast my head buzzes. It sounds as if a hundred thousand bees were just let loose to torment me. Puzzle pieces snap together. Ice crawls up my spine. My limbs feel cold, numb. My breathing labored.

It's for my niece. Really has an eye for that stuff.

Dinner? No. I can't. I have other responsibilities, Connelly.

We should talk.

Someday you're going to marry me, Nora.

I have things I need to tell you.

There's never been anyone else. In my heart, I mean.

What are you sorry for, princess?

It's beautiful. I love it. I'll never take it off.

Everything. I'm sorry for everything.

You're mine now. You realize that, right?

"Conn? Connelly? Hey…" I feel a sting on my cheek, but it barely registers as I now stare into the most angelic face I've ever seen.

She's small, no more than four and a half feet.

Her hair is a stunning hue of coppery brown.

Her lips are full and pink.

Her cheekbones high and sharp.

Her nose is small, pert, a perfect size for her tiny round face.

But it's the eyes…her unusual hazel eyes that truly do me in.

They are mine, only a hundred times more beautiful.

There is no mistake. No doubt.

She is a perfect combination of her mother and father.

Nora.

Me.

She is mine.

Fuuuuuuck.

I have things I need to tell you.

...things I need to tell you.

...we need to talk.

If I wasn't sure that this beautiful little creature in front of me was mine, the next words out of her mouth solidified it for me, another memory almost knocking me over.

Holding her hand out ever so politely, the child's hazels—*my* hazels—never waver from mine. "Hi, I'm Hazel. But my friends call me Zel."

"I love your eyes," Nora says, running a finger down my cheek.

Hazel.

Jesus Christ.

I have a daughter.

I have a daughter and her name is *Hazel.*

Chapter 20

Nora

I stand in the living room of Mira's downtown Chicago condo in absolute horror and utter confusion. I can hardly catch a speck of air as I watch my daughter put her hand in her father's for the very first time. I see the thrall and confusion on Connelly's face as he blindly takes it. And I'm well aware of my sister taking in the entire scene as if she's just stepped into the Twilight Zone.

Welcome to the fifth dimension, because there is no fucking possible way I can be witnessing what I am unless I'm lost inside of its unknown vastness. It's like I'm watching a movie in the weightlessness of space, the scene before me unfolding so slowly my heart races. The way she's looking at him, I wonder if Hazel is putting things together just like Connelly is. She's a very intuitive little girl, a trait she clearly inherited from her father.

I had tried twice over the last twenty-four hours to tell Connelly about her. Both times he put me off. I should have tried harder. I needed to have control over the situation, over my words. I had to frame the message just right to minimize the fallout and make him understand I did what I thought best at the time. This is the worst possible way he could have found out because the only way this can end is...

...utter annihilation.

And just like that, the spell is broken as Zel realizes I'm here and runs across the room to throw herself into my arms. But I can't look at her. I can't even listen to her as she starts babbling a hundred miles an hour about what she and her aunt Mira did while I was out of town.

All I can do is watch Connelly as he sits there, dumbfounded, staring blankly at the spot where Hazel just stood. His brows are creased. He blinks slowly as if trying to convince himself he just saw a hallucination.

But he didn't.

In slow motion, his head pivots my way, yet he still doesn't look at me. His eyes never leave Hazel. He's watching her talk, her little hands flailing everywhere, but like me, I'm sure he's not hearing anything she's saying. Seconds drag on like days while I wait for the other shoe to drop, all the while wondering why the hell I'm in my sister's condo gaping at Connelly.

"Uhhh, what's going on here?" Mira whispers.

I can't. I just...can't. My voice is ice covered, like my heart.

The only reason I can come up with for Connelly being here is...but...my *sister*? The thought of Connelly stroking or kissing or thoroughly dominating my sister's body the way he did mine for the past couple of days almost buckles my knees with unimaginable agony.

I can't fill my lungs with enough life-giving oxygen.

And he's here a mere hour after he left me.

Anger stirs and once again, I harden the walls he effectively managed to tear down over the past few weeks. I knew he wasn't trustworthy. I knew it was an impossibility for him to commit to one woman. I knew I shouldn't have opened up to him, let him into my heart again.

Now I remember why.

When his eyes finally rise to mine, they are full of confusion and disbelief. And hurt. Which quickly morphs into a fiery rage I've never seen in him before.

With the utmost control, he rises from the kitchen stool and stalks in my direction. A stealthy panther on the hunt. Out of my periphery, I see Mira volley back and forth between us and I hear her ask again what's happening. I ignore her.

"Mommy, this is Aunt Mira's friend, Connelly. Isn't he pretty?" She whispers the last part as Connelly comes to a stop in front of us. Zel is constantly trying to hook me up with men, always pointing out the "pretty" ones at the grocery store or the movies or the Humane Society. She has no idea that the only "pretty" man I would ever want is now full of loathing and hatred for her mother.

"Hazel, I need a moment with your mother." Connelly's jaw is plank tight, which, other than his eyes, is the one indication of how hard he's working to control himself right now. But he surprises me when he looks down at her and softens his voice considerably. "If that's okay with you?"

"Sure. Take all the time you need," she singsongs traipsing off into the kitchen, leaving the three of us standing there in a little semicircle.

"Okay, somebody better tell me what the hell is going on," Mira sneers on a low whisper.

"None of your business," we both answer at the same time, our eyes locked on the other.

"Aunt Mira, will you make me pancakes?" Zel yells from the kitchen. That little shit knows exactly what she's doing, but little does she know it will never work with this man. Not now. Not ever again. Unable to stand the condemnation in Connelly's eyes any longer, I turn to see she's already poured a glass of orange juice, making herself right at home.

"Sure will, buttercup."

I look at Mira, knowing she doesn't cook a thing that doesn't come out of the microwave. She even burns toast. "You know how to make pancakes?" I ask with doubt.

Her shoulders rise and fall. "No, but it can't be *that* hard, can it?"

"How about some instant oatmeal? You have that?"

"Nora, I got this. Go...do...whatever it is you two need to do."

Before the words even leave Mira's mouth, my elbow is in Connelly's painful grip and he's ushering me to the front door.

"Where are we—?"

"Do. Not. Speak." His growl is low. Terrifying.

He leads me down the narrow corridor, the elevator to my right mocking my escape. About now, I'm wishing I'd taken Mira up on her offer to bring Hazel home. As much as I've tried to prepare myself for this moment, I know I can never fully be ready.

When we reach the far corner, he opens another condo door before dragging me in behind him, slamming it shut. The instant we're in what I would guess is his living room, which seems to be a mirror of Mira's only backward, he lets my arm go like it's venomous and starts pacing while stabbing his fingers through his hair. I have to push down the memories of doing that just hours ago when he was fucking me so hard I couldn't see straight.

I hold in a sob, knowing I'll never have that again. I knew it when we boarded that plane and left Memphis.

Finally stopping a foot away, he glares deserving daggers into me. I don't think he'll hurt me, but that doesn't stop the "fight or flight" instinct from coursing through my veins. My feet ready to run. "Please tell me I did not see what I think I just saw." Each word is punctuated hard. Each feels like an invisible fist to my gut.

"I was going to tell you," I respond quietly. Lamely.

"Going to tell me!" he roars, his entire face turning a dark shade of red. "When the fuck were you going to tell me? When you asked me to walk her down the goddamned aisle at her wedding?"

His anger rains down all around me. It's sharp as arrows, piercing my skin, leaving trails of remorse and shame behind. Guilt that I let things go this far eats my insides until I think I may just bleed out right here on his perfect ivory carpet.

"Connelly, I—"

"Jesus. Fucking. Christ, Nora! You mean to tell me all these years I've—we've"—he waves back and forth between us—"had a daughter and you didn't have the fucking decency to even tell me? How could you do that?"

I feel myself buckling under the weight of my lies and deceptions. I knew what I was doing. I didn't have definitive DNA proof but the older Hazel got the less I needed it. Deep down I *knew* the truth. I could see it in her captivating smile, hear it in her melodic laugh, feel it in her boundless love. I knew it in my soul. Hazel is as magnetic as Connelly and she's his as surely as I once was.

But the surer I became she was his, the more scared I became at the same time. After so long, how could I go to Connelly and say, *"Hey, surprise, Daddy! Sorry, it took me years to figure out she was yours."*?

I couldn't.

"Did you want to get away from me that bad, Nora?"

"It wasn't like that," I whisper lamely.

"Wasn't like that? Then what the fuck was it like, Nora? I had the best night of my life and then I never fucking saw you again. You told me you loved me. We created a life and you…you…fuck! How could you do this?"

Every muscle is his body is vibrating as he stands there, his hard gaze boring holes into me. It burns so much. I deserve every bit of the fiery hell I've now found myself in.

This would be the time, Nora. Tell him what you did. Tell him what you saw. Tell him why.

But the words crawling up my throat get stuck in the back. They won't budge, no matter how hard I'm pushing.

As if reading my mind, he whispers brokenly, "There really was someone else, wasn't there?" He slumps into a leather lounger and hangs his head between his hands, mumbling. "Ah fuck. That's the only thing that makes sense. You didn't know if she was mine, did you?"

"Connelly…" *Tell him. Tell him. For the love of all that's good and right, tell him, Nora.* But acid slowly dissolves the confession that was stuck, so I stop talking and swallow down the vile fragments instead.

Seconds, minutes, maybe years pass. I feel as though time has frozen us in perpetual purgatory. Connelly certainly doesn't belong here, but I do.

When he finally lifts his head, the naked, brutal pain ravaging the depths of his being shames me. Pain that my selfish actions caused. Just hours ago we were in each other's arms, professing our love and promises of a future I knew we could never have, but held out hope for anyway. His raw agony shreds me. I begin to softly cry.

"Don't you fucking dare," he grits furiously.

Standing, he walks to the kitchen, pulls out a bottle of amber liquid and a tumbler. He pours himself a healthy amount, drinking it all in one swallow before repeating the same process two more times. A glance at the clock shows it's early...just half past ten.

"That's why you didn't want to move to Chicago. You didn't want me to know." His voice is eerily calm and monotone now as he stares at the cupboards, a full glass of alcohol in hand, his back to me.

It's not a question, so I don't respond.

"Is this what you were going to tell me in Memphis?"

Now he just sounds ruined.

"Yes," I answer on a sob.

The silence is deafening. Thick and nauseating. I want to throw myself in his arms and have him hold me, comfort me. It makes me mentally crumble in a heap to know I'll never know the feel of him again.

Tossing back another glassful, he fills it up yet again before facing me. The water I see in his eyes makes me cry harder. "What hurts the most is that you just walked away from me, from what we had, without a fucking backward glance. I was in *love* with you, Nora. Every single part of me was yours yet you got on that plane and I never saw you again. You left me behind like yesterday's trash, like the time we'd spent together meant absolutely nothing to you. Like that *night* meant nothing to you."

"It meant everything," I mumble almost

inaudibly. *It meant more than everything and then you destroyed us.*

"You're a fucking liar!" he spits on a thundering boom. "You clearly hopped from my dick right onto the next guy's so goddamned fast you didn't even know whose fucking kid you had!"

Quicker than a lightning bolt, his accusation stirs an angry fire deep within my belly. Instead of fighting it, I harness that energy, using it as a shield, because how. Fucking. Dare. Him. He had his dick in someone else first.

"Oh, that's rich, coming from someone whose zipper gets used more than the revolving doors at Macy's."

He stiffens and slams his glass on the counter, sloshing his precious liquor over the edges and onto the black granite. His eyes would burn me into a pile of ashes if I stood any closer. Hell, that's probably what he hoped for.

"You wanna know why I am like I am, Nora? Why I can't commit? Why I *fuck* a different woman every night of the week? Well, take a look in the mirror, sweetheart. Take a good, long, hard fucking look and the answer will be staring back in those lying fucking eyes of yours."

I shake my head, fury hazing my vision. "Your manwhoring ways are *not* my doing, Connelly. You couldn't keep your cock in your pants even back in high school. You wouldn't understand the words fidelity and commitment if someone read the definitions to you slowly from the goddamned dictionary."

With each word his face pinches further and I

don't miss the fact he's curling and uncurling the fists clenched at his sides. But that doesn't stop me.

"You want to know the real reason I didn't tell you about Hazel?" I continue, panting my rage. "I need a father for Hazel, not some fucking asshole who's going to come home smelling of women's perfume, her panties stuffed in his suit pocket. Children need stability and role models and commitment, and you have none of those qualities."

"You never gave me that fucking chance!" he bellows so loudly I know the floors above and below us had to have heard.

"You didn't deserve it!" I scream back, the reverberation stinging my vocal cords.

Several loud knocks rap on his front door. "Go away," he yells, turning his attention back to his mind eraser, swallowing hard.

"Open the fuck up, Connelly," Mira's stern voice resonates through the now quiet space.

I head to the door, not waiting for Connelly's permission. This has spiraled so far out of control, I'm afraid our hurtful words will cut so deep, they'll leave permanent scars. He needs time to digest and we both need time to cool off.

"Are you okay?" Mira asks the second I pull open the heavy wood. She's grasping my shoulders and searching my face and body for wounds, but she won't find them on my flesh. Mine are all hidden so far inside they'll never heal.

"I'm fine." I'm the furthest fucking thing from fine. Just looking at my sister cramps my stomach knowing she may have been intimate with the man I love more than I will ever love another.

"Butt out, Ella," a dark menacing voice behind me growls. Fresh tears well at how much I want him to wrap his arms around me right now. I'm so alone.

"You can fuck off, Conn," she growls back, unfazed by the waves of fury I feel painfully thrashing my back. "You're going to have the cops here in about ten minutes if you don't knock it off." She stands there pinning us both with her steely glare. "Now, I don't know what's going on between you two, but it doesn't take a genealogist to guess it's about that little girl in the next apartment, who also has ears by the way."

"Point made. Now go," Connelly gruffs.

"I'm not leaving without Nora." Mira looks past me, staring down the angry bear behind me with zero fear.

A hot, pungent wash of alcohol reaches my nostrils when he blows out a long frustrated breath. But what cuts me to the quick are his callous, heartless words that I will carry with me for eternity, even in death.

"You can fucking have her. There's nothing here for her anymore."

Chapter 21

CONN

"He's here!" I hear my twin yell to someone.

I sigh, knowing it was just a matter of time before they found me. It's what we do. One of us spirals out of the sky in a plume of smoke and ash and the others are there with a fire hose. It's what I love about us. Our camaraderie, our bond. The fact we know when someone needs the other without even asking.

But as much as I love it, I hate it equally when I'm on the receiving end. I'm not ready for purging yet. I've barely wrapped my own mind around the fact that I have a daughter. A child who has grown up without me. Who doesn't even know I'm her father, for the love of Christ. I can hardly breathe when I remember the only woman I've ever loved has committed an incomprehensible betrayal, completely fucking me over in the process. Days later, I still cannot wrap my head around it. Any of it.

My heart feels shredded. Black. My mind a jumble of unanswered questions. I can't handle

Ash right now. I can't handle anyone. I'm so goddamned furious, I could drown Nora's duplicity and deception in a bottle—or twelve—of Macallan. Hell, I was well on my way in my apartment the other day when I stopped cold; if I'd let myself sink into the warm oblivion of alcohol, I may never have found the surface again.

I did that once. Look where I am because of it.

So I came here instead, hoping fourteen-hour days of manual labor would drive me to exhaustion and help me find the clarity I need.

It hasn't.

Nothing can, I've decided.

For the three days, I've been here trying to work out what the hell my next move is, all I've managed to do is to get myself in over my head in a completely different way.

I sit back on my haunches, my eyes glazing over the mess before me. The uncovered subfloor and broken stone pieces in the corner mock me. With each inhale I take in dust and failure. I seem to remember laying tile was a bit easier than this.

"Home improvement time?" Ash drawls from behind me.

"Yep," I answer plainly, not bothering to make a move.

"Phone broken?"

Nope. Just had it off.

"I left instructions with Lydia."

"Out of the office due to a death in the family?" he snorts. "Rather cryptic don't you think? And how come I didn't know about this little family mishap?"

Damn her. "She wasn't supposed to tell you that." She was supposed to tell my brothers I'd been called out of town on an emergency business trip and she didn't know when I'd be back. She was supposed to tell everyone else of a family death so they'd leave me the fuck alone.

"She didn't," he says lightly, stepping around me into the debacle I've created. "Got a call from Fred Callahan wondering where he could send flowers in condolence."

Shit. Didn't think that all the way through.

Brushing my dusty hands off on my dirty jeans, I roll back to my heels and stand, my aching thighs protesting the entire way up. "How'd you find me?"

"Mac." Good ol' trusty Mac. Our Mackinac Island groundskeeper. "He called on Saturday because he saw a light on in the house and wasn't aware anyone was coming. When I couldn't get ahold of you, I put two and two together."

I raise my head and take my first look at my twin. I wonder if he'll be able to see the anguish raging like a storm in my soul. I wonder if I look different on the outside now that I'm a father. "So you've known I've been here for three days?"

He nods, eyeing me carefully. He's trying to work out the puzzle of my disappearance. I don't run. I face challenges head-on. I'm the levelheaded one. I talk problems out. I see reason, believe in the whole "don't go to bed mad" theory. I yank other people's heads out of *their* asses for them. I'm not generally the one with my head shoved up my own or in the damn sand.

But for the life of me, I can't work this mess out.

I want her pain, her suffering, her pride.

I want to absolutely fucking ruin her.

Most of all, though...I want my life back the way it was.

Don't I?

I don't know and therein lies the problem. I don't know which way is up, down, or sideways. Part of me wants to rewind to just a few days ago when I was blissfully happy and ignorant. Another part of me wonders how long Nora would have gone without saying a word had I not caught her red-handed.

Out of my periphery I see my other two brothers saunter up and hang out against the wall opposite the bathroom I've been trying to remodel. *Trying* being the operative word.

"This an intervention?" I ask with a little derision, pissed they can't just leave me be.

"That depends," Luke brogues, stuffing his hands in his jeans pockets. "You need one?"

"What I need," I start, "is some help putting in this goddamned floor."

The three of them exchange a look like I've just asked them to each donate a kidney to the black market. But in true Colloway brother spirit, without a word they shrug off their coats, roll up their sleeves, and we get to work in utter silence.

Five hours later we all stand back, admiring our handiwork. It would have taken me another week to get this damn floor laid and quite honestly, I'm not sure I didn't need the time. Now my excuse for being here has just run out. The upstairs bathroom countertop has a chip in it. Maybe I could replace that.

"I don't know about anybody else, but I need a fucking beer," Luke announces, making his way to the kitchen.

"Grab four," Gray yells after him.

"Don't you guys have somewhere to be?" *Like with your happy, perfect families?*

"All right. I've kept my mouth shut long enough," Ash drones. "What the fuck is going on, Conn?"

"If I wanted to talk about it, you'd know by now," I retort hotly, pushing my way past him and Gray. I stride into the kitchen and grab an open bottle of beer, chugging half the contents in one swallow.

"It wouldn't have anything to do with Nora looking like she had to just bury her puppy, would it?"

Christ. Just hearing her name almost causes my knees to buckle in anguish. Yet why does part of me feel vindicated and elated that she's suffering just as much as I am? No...there's no way in hell her pain equals mine. *I* was the one left in the dark. *I* was the one fucked over, not her.

"Not sure what you didn't understand the first time, brother." I find myself slumping into a chair wishing I was anywhere else but here right now.

"I understand when emotions get too hard for you to handle, instead of numbing yourself with alcohol like normal people do, you numb yourself with a hands-on project," Ash challenges. Can't deny that one. My mother has a whole new set of cabinets in the garage she never needed or wanted when I found out I'd never play basketball again.

"I also know a brother suffering when I see one," Gray adds with concern, sliding into an empty space across from me.

"Look," I breathe in and out heavily, "I appreciate your concern. I appreciate you all driving out here to check on me. Truly I do, but I'm just not ready to talk about it yet."

"This is about Nora, though, right?"

"What part of I'm not ready to talk can't you wrap your head around, Ash?"

The corner of Ash's mouth ticks up. I look away, not even able to drum up the energy to fire off a threat about wiping it off.

"Do you remember what you told me when I'd run to New York after I found out Livvy had been married?" Gray asks me pointedly. I don't remember the exact words, only the gist. Gray was an emotional wreck. He needed support, but he also needed a goddamned kick in the pants. He needed the truth. Suddenly I don't like where this is going. My situation is nothing like the one he and Livia went through.

Before I have a chance to say a word, Gray continues. "You told me I had that gleam I'd been missing back in my eyes since I reunited with Livvy. You told me to talk to her. Find out the truth. Even if it wasn't what I wanted to hear that I'd at least have closure. You were right. Without you pushing me to make that first step, I'm not sure I would have Livvy right now. Since Red has

281

been back in the picture, *you* have that gleam, Conn. I've never seen one on you before. Whatever's going on, you need to face it, not run from it. Face it so you can end it, no matter what that end is."

I snort at his insinuation there's actually an ending for me here. There is no end, only the beginning of a new life I'm nowhere near prepared for.

Asher's phone rings, interrupting us. He answers immediately, talking soft and soothing. His tone is filled with love and concern. I catch a few words here and there, but the one that sticks out is "nauseous." When Ash gives us a look—a worried but thrilled look—as he asks Alyse if she's eaten anything, I know something's up.

"Alyse sick?" I ask when he hangs up, the temporary diversion from my own problems welcome.

My twin's face lights up like a kid on Christmas morning. "Uh...yeah," he answers sheepishly. "Has been for the past eleven weeks."

"Eleven weeks?" I parrot on a panic before my brain catches up.

"Well all be damned, Ash. Congrats," Gray beams, standing to clasp him in a bear hug.

"Thanks, man. I was going to tell you guys next week after we passed the magical twelve-week mark. I wanted to tell you before, but Alyse wouldn't let me."

Holy shit. I'm dumbfounded. Alyse is pregnant. *Pregnant.* My twin is going to be a father, just like Gray. Just like *me*, I remember.

A rush of intense emotion courses through me and I'm not sure which I feel more acutely. Happiness for my brother or envy that he'll get to experience something stolen from me.

I never got to watch Nora's belly grow or comfort her if she was sick. I didn't get to watch my daughter being born or rub Nora's back through hours of excruciating labor. I didn't get to experience sleep deprivation or the joy of rocking my innocent newborn to sleep.

Nora's selfishness caused me to miss Hazel's first words, her first steps, her first day of school. Teaching her to count or how to read. I never had the chance to comfort her when she had a cold, punish her for a temper tantrum, or leave money under her pillow when she lost her first tooth. I don't know the first thing about my daughter and she sure as shit doesn't know me.

I'm not sure how I'll ever forgive Nora for this cutting treachery. I honestly don't know if I have that depth inside me.

Seems taking myself out of Chicago for a few days has provided me absolutely no more answers than when I came. I didn't expect it would.

I realize I've been too silent while Gray and Luke give their congratulations, so I mumble, "Congrats, Ash."

"Wow, that came from the heart," my twin replies snidely.

"I'm sorry," I say, before he lays into me. I try to muster more enthusiasm. "I'm really happy for you two, brother. Truly. You both deserve this."

He nods, replying softly, "Thanks. Alyse has been

an emotional mess. Cries at fucking commercials for Christ's sakes. And I'm not talking about those dogs or cats that have been abused or kids in third-world countries who are undernourished. I'm talking about Kleenex commercials, Conn. Tissues. I'm not sure how I'm going to get through these next few months." He scrubs his face with his hand. I want to laugh but there's no possible way I could force my lips in the upward direction.

"Be lucky you have that chance," I mumble.

"What's going on, Conn? You forget to wrap it up and get some woman pregnant?" he retorts on a chuckle.

My head snaps in his direction. I swallow hard a couple of times before I can speak. "Why would you say that?"

His laugh dies a quick death when he realizes he's hit smack in the center of the bull's-eye. "Oh, shit. You're kidding me."

I purse my lips. Unable to admit. Powerless to deny.

Luke chokes on the drink he's taking. I see a few drops filter through his nose and drip onto the countertop. Any other time I'd give him shit because that has to burn like a mother. But I don't. There's nothing funny about what I just silently confessed. He coughs a few times to clear his lungs and then the room drops into a deafening hum.

"You have a kid?" Ash breathes in astonishment.

I nod. I don't know what else to do.

"With..."

He leaves the question congealing between the four of us. It feels claustrophobic and sticky. It's fair, I guess. I've been with a lot of women and even though I've been extremely careful, always suiting up, accidents happen. Hell, I've even had a couple of women try to shake me down. One went to the press with her bogus story, which later turned out unfounded.

But I wasn't exactly careful with Nora that first time, was I?

Why, oh why, does this feel so much better than the last time? Then it hits me.

"You don't have a condom on," she gasps on a choppy breath at the same time I realize I'm riding her bareback. Christ, it feels good. So damn good.

"Shit. I can't stop, Nora. I'll pull out." She doesn't protest so I don't stop.

I pulled out all right. I'll never forget how Nora looked with my come strung all over belly. Apparently I wasn't fast enough, though. Welp...guess cat's out of the bag now. May as well go all the way. "Nora," I practically whisper.

You could hear a pin drop a state away before all three of my brothers curse simultaneously, "Fuck."

Ash and Luke come sit down with Gray and me. It's awkward. I thought maybe once I confessed it out loud it would feel real. It doesn't. And the last three days of trying to cope have just evaporated like a glass of water in the sun.

Then Ash starts peppering me with questions I have no answers to. He sounds as confused as I feel.

"Are you kidding me, Conn?"

"I wish I was." Why does saying that make me feel bad? It's one thing to have a woman come to you telling you she's knocked up; it's quite another to see that life standing, breathing, *thriving* right in front of your eyes. Saying I wish I was kidding is akin wishing she wasn't here. I don't even know her, yet I already know I could never wish a piece of me wasn't walking the earth. I can't believe I ever did before.

"Are you sure it's yours?"

"She. *It* is a she. Hazel. Her name is Hazel. And there's little doubt she's mine." She has my eyes and Nora's smile. She has Nora's nose and my little cleft in her chin. I could already tell she has cunning and intelligence. *She loves art and photography.* I grasp at anything I can remember about my daughter in the five seconds I had with her.

"You've met her?"

I try to laugh, but I choke on a sob inside instead. "You could say that." I lean forward, clasping my hands between my spread knees. I hang my head, developing a sudden interest in the hardwood flooring beneath me.

Like they do every two seconds, my thoughts drift to Nora. It seems a lifetime ago that I held her in my arms and made promises I may not end up being able to keep. I love her and hate her equally. And I hate that I still love her after everything she did to me. To us.

Fuck. Me.

The pain inside me is debilitating. It hasn't waned an ounce.

After my heart-to-heart with Gray over Labor Day weekend, I finally came clean to my twin about the real reason I bought SER. Because I found Nora again. Because I never got over her. Because I didn't want to live without her anymore. He supported me. Encouraged me, even. Now I don't have a clue what I want. Or what I'm going to do.

Shit. Could things be more fucked?

"She's ten. Or at least I would guess she is," I add absently.

"How? Well...I mean...I know *how*...but why? I mean...why? I don't understand why she would do that. What would make her keep—?"

"Ash, stop. I don't know. We didn't get that far in our verbal mudslinging." Except we did. The fact she didn't know if Hazel was mine is still nearly debilitating.

Asher takes a deep breath and blows it out slowly. My other two brothers are as stunned mute as I was when I first found out.

"I don't know what to say," he says after a few quiet moments pass.

"Me either." I lean back and force my gaze to the ceiling, willing the burning I feel behind my lids to recede. I thought I understood what it meant to have your soul ripped from your body before but that was a walk in the fucking park compared to what I'm feeling right now.

"What are you going to do?" Luke asks.

"I don't know that either. I don't know much of anything right now. I'm kind of numb, actually." *Not numb enough, though,* I think.

"You need time to process this, Conn. Don't make any rash decisions."

"I know."

"And you need to get a DNA test. Make sure she's yours," Gray adds.

"Yeah." I'd already thought about that. But I don't need a mouth swab to prove she's mine. I looked into her soul and saw my reflection. The same thing happened when I looked at Nora the first time.

My chest hurts so bad it's hard to drag in a full breath. I find myself unconsciously rubbing my breastbone, trying to ease the throbbing ache underneath.

"And you need to talk to Nora. Talk. Not yell. If she is yours, you have some real shit to figure out. Regardless of how this went down and how you feel about Nora, she's still her—Hazel's—mother, so you won't be able to avoid her forever."

"I know, Asher, but...Jesus, I can't even stomach the thought of looking at her deceitful face right now."

"Yeah. I get that. But you want to be part of your daughter's life, right?"

Opening my eyes, I look at Asher. My very best friend since the very second we were conceived. We shared a space in our mother's womb. We slept in the same room until we were ten, even though there were plenty of bedrooms in our house. We learned to ride bikes together, and he got mad when I caught on quicker than he did. We liked the same girl in fourth grade. Sarah Humphries. We agreed we were both going to marry her when we grew up until our mom told us only one man and one woman could be married. Except in Utah. I didn't understand that at the time, but we secretly planned to move there so we could both have her.

He's the only person who's seen me cry. Twice. The day Nora left me and the day we buried our father.

"Yes." I can hardly breathe.

Make that three times now.

His face softens sympathetically before he closes the space between us, clasps my face between his hands, and leans his forehead against mine while raw pain bleeds from my heart and soul.

He never says a word. Like a good brother should. He lets me grieve all I feel I've lost and celebrate the newness I've found.

With my brothers' silent, steadfast support, I begin to come to terms with how much my life is about to change. There's just one part I can't figure out: where does Nora fit in now?

I may not be able to imagine living without the woman I love, but I sure as fuck don't know how I can live *with* her either.

Chapter 22

Nora

I'm lost. The fog thickens, turning from a murky gray to blacker than tar in an instant, cutting off my vision. The air is thick and cloying with the repercussions of every bad decision I've ever made. It sits heavy on me, a massive weight I can't escape. It's become me.

The wind picks up, whipping angrily around me, slashing at my thin skin with uncontrolled ferocity, leaving behind invisible wounds that will never scar because they perpetually seep with unending pain.

I have no one.

I am alone.

The sky suddenly opens wide. I'm pelted with black, icy rain. Stuck in a blinding thunderstorm without protection. I stand helpless, feet rooted to the ground, watching the deadly lightning edge ever closer. One second, I see the light of my demise, the next, I'm plunged back into suffocating blackness. I don't know which I prefer. Freedom from my unending suffering or the shroud of darkness so no one can bear witness to it, including me.

I'm soaked physically, drowning emotionally.
I'm dead inside.
The storm stops as quickly as it started and the clouds part, but light never follows. Color never blinds. Birds don't harmonize. Heat doesn't penetrate my chilled flesh. All I hear is silence and I finally realize where I am.
Hell on earth.

I wake with a start, shaking uncontrollably. Tears stream down my face. Sobs catch in my throat. I can't gulp enough air to slow my heart rate.

"Mommy," a timid voice calls from my doorway.

"Yes, baby," I reply after a few shallow breaths.

"Are you okay? I heard you crying."

Fuck no. I'm not in the same universe as okay. I'm barely holding myself together with gum, string, and chicken wire.

"Fine, Zel. Just a bad dream is all."

"Do you want me to sleep with you? That always makes me feel better when you do that."

Oh God. I love my daughter so very much.

"That would be great," I choke on a whisper. Pulling back the sheets, she slides in beside me with her stuffed papi bear, which she carries everywhere.

Regardless of my feelings for my father, my daughter loved her papi dearly. His death was hard on her. She was only a newborn when my mother died, so she never knew what a wonderful woman her nana was. I had kept a few pieces of clothing of my father's and last Christmas had them made into a tiny suit that would fit on the bear. The buttons on the vest are from a costume pearl necklace of my mother's, so each of them is represented on the stuffed animal. Zel treasures that thing like its gold.

"Was somebody chasing you?" my daughter asks innocently as she throws her arms protectively around me.

Yes...my penance.

"Something like that."

I can't help it. I cry softly hugging my daughter to my chest. She's my rock whether she knows it or not. If it weren't for her, I'm pretty damn sure I would have fallen apart when my mom died. But she was helpless and needed me and I held it together for her. I lived for her and her alone. I still do.

"It's okay, Mommy," she soothes, stroking my hair. "It was just pretend, like a bad movie, remember?"

My words, coming back at me. Except she doesn't realize that mine wasn't "pretend." My hell is all too real and wholly inescapable in consciousness and unconsciousness. It has been for the entire week since I last set eyes on Connelly, his cutting words still stinging sharply days later.

Seven days.

One hundred sixty-eight hours.

Over ten thousand agonizingly lonely minutes.

I continue to show up to work every single day, not knowing if it's my last. I imagine the one reason my shit hasn't been packed up for me is the ironclad employment agreement I signed, although he no doubt has his attorneys trying to find a loophole. Bet he's regretting buying SER about now.

That thought crushes me even more.

A glance at the digital clock shows it's 6:30 a.m. Usually, I would have the entire weekend planned with Zel, but I've been so preoccupied this week, I can hardly think about making it through the next minute, let alone plan days in advance. I've been a horrible mother these past few days and that needs to stop.

Taking a deep breath, I tuck down all the personal shit I'm dealing with, focusing on my daughter.

"So, what do you want to do today?" I ask, feeling marginally better.

"I want to take pictures. Can we maybe take a walk down to the lake?" My daughter the artist. She's incredibly talented in so many ways. In addition to being artistic, she has uncanny people skills, like her father. I always thought she was an old soul in a little body.

She is my sun. My world revolves around her.

"Sure. Sounds great. What else?"

"Maybe have lunch with Aunt Mira?" she hedges.

I chuckle lightly. Hazel doesn't miss a beat. When Mira dragged me back to her condo, the tension was as thick as sludge. Zel made herself scarce so Mira and I could talk. The first thing Mira told me when Zel left the room was that she hasn't been intimate with Connelly. I did believe her, but that didn't squelch my jealousy at the closeness I felt between the two of them. I have a very hard time believing a womanizer like Connelly could just be "friends" with a female and not hit on her. But I didn't ask because I didn't want to know. I was already in too much pain.

"I can see if she's free."

My baby looks up at me with Connelly's eyes. My breath hitches at her question. "And maybe she can invite her pretty friend, Connelly?"

"Zel, I...I don't know. He's probably a very busy man." And he's made it pretty clear the last thing he wants to do is see me, let alone spend an awkward hour with me.

She props herself up on her elbow, face in her palm, turning very serious. "Mommy, I think he's the one."

"Who's the one?"

"Mira's friend, Connelly," she says brightly.

I try to speak, but have to stop several times before I can barely whisper, "What one is that, sweetie?"

"The one we've been waiting for."

Oh God. Tears well so fast, they're overflowing before I have a chance to stop them.

"Why would you say that, Hazel?"

She flops down on her back, blinking at the ceiling. "You're going to think it's weird."

I match her position and catch her hand in mine, giving it a squeeze. "I promise I won't."

"I dreamed about him. Well, his eyes anyway."

"You dreamed about your fat—" I catch myself before I reveal the secret I've held inside for ten years. I need to tell Hazel, but I was hoping to talk to Connelly first to see how he wanted to handle it. I don't want to give her false hope if he wants nothing to do with her and with each day that passes it becomes more painfully clear I made the right decision all along.

"You dreamed about Connelly?"

"Yes. A lot."

Shit. I don't even know how to respond. She's practically rendered me speechless. "What makes you think it was him, Ladybird? It could have been anyone. And dreams are just—"

"Pretend. I knew you would say that, so that's why I didn't tell you."

"I'm sorry," I respond contritely. "I do believe you." After a few beats of silence, I add, "Why do you think it's him? Connelly?"

Her little shoulders rise. "I just know. I don't know how to explain it." Turning her head toward me, she says excitedly, "Did you see his eyes, Mommy? They're hazel, exactly like mine. Just like my name."

You were named after the thing I loved most about him. Even if I wasn't 100 percent certain when she was born that she was his, I'd hoped. In my heart, she always would have been. That's the only outcome I would accept.

I nod mutely, biting my lip to keep from bawling.

"Why are you crying?" She brushes away the drops tracking down my face, choking me up even more.

"I just love you so much," I manage to say. Her face brightens. It instantly makes me feel better.

"Do you believe me? About Connelly?" she asks almost pleadingly.

I smile softly, moisture blurring my vision. "Of course I do. It's right to trust your gut feelings."

A brilliant smile lights up her face, driving much-needed warmth into my frigid soul. "I think so, too, Mommy. And I have a good feeling about him."

I tug her to me for a hug, kissing her red-covered crown. "Me too," I croak halfheartedly, not sure I believe my own words.

I can live with Connelly disappointing or hurting me. It's hard; I won't deny it. I'll never love another. I'll never marry. I'll never grow old with someone by my side. Fine. I'm an adult, I've made my own bed and I will lie in it, suffering the consequences, whatever they may be.

What I won't tolerate, however, is him disappointing our daughter. She's entirely innocent in this charade I've played. I won't have him taking out his anger on her in any way, shape, or form. She already believes in a man she's met for all of ten seconds and while I still hold out hope that they can have a relationship, that that's what *Connelly* will want, if he doesn't, I don't want her heart torn to ribbons by him the way he did mine.

"Hey, how about banana pancakes?"

Excitement dances in her eyes. Zel is a pancake fiend. She'd eat them for every meal if I let her.

"Can I make the batter?"

"Of course. I'll even let you flip them."

"Really?" She jumps to her knees and bounces up and down.

I laugh. Sliding out of bed, I grab a robe from the back of my door. I slip it on and tie the sash tight. "Really."

Grabbing her hand, we head to the kitchen. A few minutes later with the concoction made, we pour four small blobs on the hot griddle. I rest against the counter, just taking her in as she impatiently keeps lifting up the edges to see if they're ready.

As she chatters away about Connelly, Connelly, Connelly, I stop paying attention. She's absolutely enthralled by him when all I can think of is that I'll do anything I have to in order to protect her from being hurt by my mistakes. Or by a father who may not even want her.

And out of everything, *that's* the toughest pill to swallow. I can't place too much faith in Connelly. I did that once before and got third-degree burns.

Once again, I strengthen my fortress, brick by brick, steel beams and girders. The walls are battle weary, the structure unsteady in a stiff wind, but I've done it before and I'll do it again. I have no choice. I never do. I have someone more important than myself to think about.

I have Hazel.

Chapter 23

Nora

"Hey, haven't seen much of you around lately," Brad says when I enter the break room to get my lunch from the fridge. Yogurt. It's about all I can stomach these days.

Despite my anxiety, Zel and I had a great weekend. Mira couldn't make lunch on Saturday, but on Sunday, we met at a place in the burbs called Butcher & The Burger, which was ranked in the top ten in the Chicagoland area for their burgers. The two bites I could choke down were fabulous, but the mood was brought down because the entire time, Zel grilled Mira about Connelly, particularly when Mira told her Connelly isn't married. My daughter is now obsessed with trying to set me up with her father. It would be almost comical if it weren't so ironic.

"Had my head down." I feed the soda machine two one-dollar bills. I could really use a glass of wine, but drinking during work hours is somehow frowned upon, so Diet Coke it is.

"Are you okay, Nora?" Brad asks lowly from

behind me. When his hand runs down my bare arm, I close my eyes, willing the tears away.

"Not really, but I'll be fine."

"It's Colloway, isn't it?"

Spinning around, I quickly case the room to ensure we're alone before pinning him with a glare. "He's your boss now, Brad. Give him a little respect." I have no idea why I'm defending Connelly, but Brad's consistent digging at him is starting to get under my skin. Regardless of Connelly's and my personal issues, Brad's behavior is inappropriate.

"I knew it," he announces, a cross between angry and concerned. He takes a step into me. I back up against the cool machine. "Did he hear me in your office? About Hazel?"

I shake my head, not wanting to talk about this with him. The ease with which Brad drew that conclusion in the first place only reaffirmed my need to tell Connelly about Hazel. I should have told him that night in his office as originally planned instead of spreading my legs and inviting him inside. I'm not sure if the outcome would have been any different, but it sure as hell couldn't have been worse.

Brad looks contrite. "Good. I'm sorry. I was out of line. I just..." He lowers his voice to barely above a whisper. "I just care about what happens to you, Nora. It kills me to see you unhappy."

My eyes mist against my wishes.

"Fuck, Nora," he groans seconds before I'm enfolded in his arms. I should pull away. I shouldn't be taking comfort from anyone, but I need it so badly, all I can do is hang on while I try desperately to pull myself together. "Tell me what I can do."

"I wish I could," I whisper. Taking a deep breath, I pull against his hold and he lets me go. I wipe the tears that leaked. Looking up, I see sympathy I didn't earn. "Brad, please leave the Connelly thing alone. You don't know the whole story and he's not the bad guy here. I am."

His face hardens. "I—"

"No. I don't want to hear another word about this. About him. This is between Connelly and me. I don't want you putting your job in jeopardy because of me."

"Fuck my job, Nora. Jesus Christ, is that what you really think I should be worried about here?" he rants a little too loudly.

I huff, looking around to see if anyone has wandered in. Thank God I see no one but us. "Stop it. You don't mean that. Brad, please. I need you to back off. Please do it for me."

His lips thin. Reluctantly he nods. "Fine. But I'll be here if you need anything. And just so you know, I don't give a shit about a fucking job. I would do anything to protect you, Nora, and I'm not afraid to take on someone like Colloway to do it."

I try to smile. It's nothing more than show. "I appreciate your indignation on my behalf, Brad, but it's not warranted. I assure you."

I grab my soft drink and, with yogurt in hand, exit the space that's seemed to grow smaller by the second, leaving behind the man who wants me more than anything while continuing to pine away for the man who will never want me again.

As I round the corner to my office, I'm stopped short when I see Connelly exiting it. Our eyes clash and my legs almost give at what I see.

Indifference.

Anything else I could have handled.

Rage.

Confusion.

Bitterness.

Even disgust.

But his indifference toward me is probably the one thing that could have completely broken me.

And now I know.

His eyes roll to my nutritious lunch and then back to my face. Still, the coldness remains. I nod in acceptance, then brush my way past him into my office. After setting my things on the desk, I take a deep breath before I face him.

"I would appreciate it if you could not ask security to usher me out. I'll leave quietly." Finding a new job will be another story as it's doubtful Wynn Consulting will give a glowing reference, but that's a problem for another day.

His brows crease as he stands in my doorway like there's some magical voodoo barrier he can't cross now that I'm inside. "What?"

"Security. I don't want all that attention. I'll leave without any fuss. I just need a few minutes to pack."

He looks utterly confused. "Security? What are you talking about, Nora?"

"I assume you're here to terminate me."

If I thought his indifference was bad, I was wrong. The sneer that turns the mouth that worshipped me only days ago is ugly and mean.

"You think now I know I have a daughter you've kept from me for ten years that I would send you away? No fucking way, Nora. You won't get that lucky. You're staying right here."

My jaw clenches. I can do nothing but take his wrath. It's been more than a week since I've seen Connelly. We haven't exchanged two words since the blowup and I was hoping that time would help him cool off a bit, but if anything, he's angrier.

"Okay. Then how can I help you?" I ask tightly.

The steps he takes into my office look like it pains him. The closer he gets to me, the more it pains me, too—to be so near yet to know a chasm of hurt and perfidy will keep us forever apart.

The bed I've made for myself is full of sharp nails and cut glass. It hurts like a bitch, but I refuse to feel sorry for myself. I have to take my medicine like a good girl, even if the poison each jab injects slowly strangles my insides.

Without a word, he throws a single piece of paper down on my desk. I rush to catch it before it skitters off the corner. I take a minute to look it over before raising my watery eyes to his.

Then he simply turns and leaves, and as much as I try to hold in my sob, I can't. Sinking down into my rolling chair, I stare at the document in my hand from the DNA Diagnosis Center.

Appointment date/time: September 27, 4:15 p.m.

Appointment office: Oak Park, IL

Appointment for: Nora Cantres (mother)
Hazel Cantres (minor)
Connelly Colloway (purported father)

Appointment reason: Paternity testing. Expedited results available within twenty-four hours by courier.

The rest of the document reviews the simple procedure—a buccal swabbing—and what to bring to the appointment. Birth certificates, government-issued IDs, and so on. It describes how to read the results: DNA markers, probability of paternity value, and combined paternity index value. It's all mumbo jumbo to me and wholly unnecessary. I know Connelly is Hazel's father, but he wants definitive proof. I can't blame him for that. I expected it, even.

But the thing that has me in a near panic, almost unable to breathe, is the description at the bottom about their "chain of command" process to ensure the results are 100 percent accurate. Because of their tight "chain of command" procedures, their results are legally defensible in court for things such as child custody, child support, immigration, and more. The only two words I can focus on in that entire sentence are "child custody."

Does Connelly plan to take me to court? Try to get custody of Hazel? Take her away from me?

303

Would he be so cold and vengeful to *do* that to me? To Hazel?

Oh, fuck. Never, in a million years, did I think Connelly would fight me for our daughter. If he wants to be part of her life, I will provide unfettered access to her. I will no longer try to keep him away from her or vice versa, but what never crossed my mind is that he'd want more than that. That he'd want her and *I'd* be the one fighting to keep her.

I don't know how long I sit in my office staring at a page full of words that could completely change life as I know it. I don't know what his endgame is and because he won't talk to me, I may not until I'm served court papers by some attorney's lackey. I don't want to jump to conclusions as this could be nothing more than a simple DNA test to verify paternity, but that innate motherly instinct rears up, sensing an immediate threat to her young.

And when a mother protects that which she grew in her womb and has a bond, which can't possibly be understood outside a mother-daughter relationship, fangs drop, claws unleash. Her thoughts turn focused, her aim deadly. She's a warrior without the training, running purely on instinct and sheer grit, failure not an option. A mother will fight anyone, anytime, anywhere to protect her offspring.

Even if that person is the child's father.

Chapter 24

CONN

The second I walk through the entrance of the DDC, I spot Hazel and Nora sitting in the sterile waiting room. I hang by the door just watching them. Hazel's doing something on a tablet. Nora looks pissed and anxious.

The tears in her eyes as she read the DNA appointment letter yesterday were excruciating to see, yet part of me wanted to revel in them. It's like the cool water of her anguish soothed the hurt just a tiny bit. And how fucked up is that?

Regardless, I can't stop the twinge of guilt that pricks its way through my veins. I handled my interaction with her poorly yesterday. I know that and I was kicking my own ass even as I turned and walked silently out of her office.

But had I stayed...had I said a single word, I would have slammed her door shut and taken her violently over her desk, showing her just how deep my hurt runs. The heady combination of her perfume and natural essence wafted across her desk, slapping me in the face, making my craving for her burn white-hot. It's like she has some sort of fucking spell knit around me that I can't find a way to break. As it was, I had to force my body away from hers. With each footfall in the opposite direction, I left another piece of me behind.

I have missed her so fucking much these past few days, my soul physically aches. I feel like I'm suffocating without her. This pain is ten times worse than any I have ever felt.

I'm digging deep for forgiveness here, because we have a daughter to raise whether we do it together or not, but I'm finding that well bone-fucking-dry. And to be honest, that scares me. Forgiveness is one of my biggest strengths. If I don't have that, what do I have?

Hazel spots me and tugs on her mother's sleeve, excitedly pointing in my direction. Nora looks sexy as hell in her pale silk pink blouse and navy pencil skirt. The strappy navy heels she's wearing make her calves look even more toned—like carved marble. I want to drop at her feet, spread her legs, and graze my teeth all the way up them to her honeyed center. I want to spend hours making her mindless, forgetting this shit between us.

Christ. I scrub my face, trying to take the lascivious thoughts away with one swipe of my hand. If only it were that easy.

When Nora's hot balls of fire land on mine, I start moving forward. The looks on the two females that belong to me couldn't be more contrasting. Hazel is lit up with surprise and elation. Nora is lit, but with something altogether different. Fury and indignation.

"What are you doing here, Connelly?" my daughter asks sweetly as I take a seat next to her. I look to Nora for direction and she just smirks, raising one brow in challenge.

Ah...so I'm hung out to dry. Guess I sort of deserve that for just springing this on her without so much as a discussion on how to handle this whole testing with Hazel ahead of time. I realize I have no idea what Nora would have told Hazel as to why she's here, about to get her mouth swabbed.

Guess I already made my first of many fuck-ups as a parent.

"What are *you* doing here?" I retort. Another glance at Nora has her looking away, pure annoyance on her face.

"It's something for school."

"School?" I ask, genuinely wondering what ruse Nora used.

"Yep. Kids are getting sick and they need to make sure I'm not infected before I go back tomorrow."

"Ah." I sweep my eyes back to Nora's and she's intently watching my reaction, her face now passive.

"So, what are you doing here?"

I track back to Hazel and smile warmly. "Same."

"Really?"

"Yeah, really. Quite a coincidence, huh?" I chuckle.

"Sure is." When she smiles at me I am absolutely blown away. Breathless. I can literally feel myself falling in love with this little wisp. I already know I will follow in a long line of fathers whose daughters have them wrapped around their pinkies. I feel the strings being pulled taut already.

I get an almost overwhelming feeling that I should abandon this entire DNA testing idea because I know in my heart this sweet girl is mine. I'm not sure I could stand to find out that she's not. Strangely, I want her to be mine with everything inside me.

But I have to know. Definitively. For a whole host of legal reasons, I need to be absolutely certain. My brothers have been gently suggesting I get an attorney. Although I know they're right, I just can't make myself take those drastic measures yet.

Clearing my throat, I ask, "So, Hazel, you like ladybugs?"

"I love them. Just like my mommy. She has one tattooed on her neck, but she says I can't get one until I'm at least eighteen." Hazel gives Nora a warm smile, which she returns.

"Your mother has a tattoo?" I have had my tongue all over her entire body and I never saw any ink. "Where?" I want to ask Nora, but I'm not sure she'll tell me, so I direct my question to Hazel.

"Her neck. Her hair covers it up."

"Ah." I wonder why the thought of running my tongue over an insect makes my dick twitch. I look to Nora. She refuses to look back.

Hazel's next question drags me from my dirty thoughts. "How did you know I like ladybugs?"

She follows my eyes to the bracelet she's still

wearing. It looks worse for the wear and I wonder how long it's been circling Hazel's delicate wrist. Hazel quickly covers it as though she's done something bad.

"It's okay, Zel." Nora tugs her close with one arm around her shoulders and Hazel buries her face in her mother's chest.

"Did I miss something?" I ask in confusion. When our eyes connect again, it's different now. Softer, as if we've both called a momentary truce but are still on the defense, waiting for the next volley. I hate it.

"She, ah...she knows she's not supposed to wear it." I can tell Nora's getting uncomfortable with where this conversation is headed. I can't stop myself from pressing, though.

"Why? It's a pretty bracelet," I challenge tritely. Yep, that was a low blow, but I couldn't hold in the biting words.

Breathing deep, she clams up and looks away. We sit there for close to a minute in silence. I don't think I'll get an answer when Hazel's small voice pipes up. My lungs seize at her answer, and a little of the resentment I've held on to disintegrates.

"It was a gift to her from my daddy. It's special and she doesn't want it broken on accident."

Nora's newfound interest in her nails keeps her eyes from mine. Before I can ask Hazel any questions about where her daddy is, a woman dressed in scrubs is calling us back. She's holding a clipboard and greets us cordially, ushering us all in the back where they quickly, but very efficiently validate our documentation. Gathering our individual samples, they place them in tamper-resistant secure packaging right in front of us. The whole thing takes us all less than fifteen minutes.

Looking like just a regular family, we walk together to the exit. I hold the door open for Hazel and Nora, who barely spares me a glance. Hazel's talking a mile a minute about ladybugs and how they are beetles, not insects, and how not all ladybugs have spots and how they come in lots of different colors and how her mommy nicknamed her Ladybird because her mommy was nicknamed Ladybug. I'm not sure yet how I feel about the last part. I only know I'm not ready to examine it yet.

"What are you doing?" Nora asks coming to a stop as we walk across the parking lot.

"Walking you girls to your car. Can never be too careful," I grab on to her elbow, pulling her forward, making sure she's beside me before I reluctantly let go.

"Hey, Connelly," Hazel sings while skipping just ahead of us. "My mommy isn't married and doesn't have a boyfriend."

"Hazel Mirari," Nora spits. I start to laugh. She's clearly trying to set her mom and me up on a date. I inanely wonder how many times she's done this before. And if it's worked. My laughter dies.

"What?" She turns back toward us and shrugs. "It's true."

"Well, we don't need to broadcast it to the world," Nora grits as we reach her red Focus.

"I'm not, Mommy. I'm just broadcasting it to Connelly," she replies innocently.

"Oh my God," Nora mutters under her breath. "I'm sorry."

"Don't be." When I open Hazel's door for her, I'm rewarded with a beaming grin. I am enthralled by every smile, each word.

"Thanks," she says politely. I wait until I'm sure she's inside and right before I shut the door, Hazel tells me, "Did you know that my middle name means miracle?"

I catch Nora rolling her eyes before opening her own door. I crouch down so we're eye level. "No, I did not. It's a really pretty name, just like Hazel."

"Mommy said I'm her miracle because I almost—"

"Okay, Zel, that's enough oversharing. I'm sure Connelly has to get back to work or something."

"No." I grin. "I really don't."

"See, he doesn't," she tells Nora smugly. Turning her attention to me, she asks, "Did you want to come over for dinner?"

"Oh my God. Hazel. Stop." Nora raises her voice, which I guess to Hazel means business, because she goes silent and sulks in the seat of the car with her arms crossed.

I want to say yes, if for no other reason than to spend time with my daughter. Learn new tidbits about Nora she's so willing to share. But I also know I'm not quite ready to spend that much time with Nora acting like a family that hasn't been torn apart by her machinations. "Ah, I can't tonight, Hazel. But some other time, okay?"

That perks her right back up. "Really?"

"Yeah, really." I look to Nora. She's watching

our interchange intently. I wish I could tell what she's thinking. Having no idea whether Nora has told Hazel she works for me, I don't mention it, leaving them with a vague, "I'll see you both around."

I stand and reluctantly shut the car door, sealing them inside together, while I'm on the outer fringe once again. I step out of the way, watching them back out and drive away. I'm so lost in thought I almost miss Hazel excitedly waving at me through the window. I wave back.

When they're out of sight, I walk slowly to my car replaying every piece of information Hazel gave me over the last few minutes, wondering what she was about to say when Nora cut her off. It's only after I shut myself inside my own hunk of steel that I realize I'm smiling. That I'm already a planning a life I'm not sure is mine yet for the taking.

My smile drops in a hot second. Once again, hurt and bitterness take up residence inside me, but this time, it feels ever so slightly less burdensome. I think I even feel my well fill up with a few trickles of absolution.

It may not be a lot, but something's better than nothing.

Chapter 25

Nora

"Thank you, Mr. Gamby. We'll be in touch."

I hang up from my fifth phone interview today. I have three more and a late-day staff meeting. It's not quite 2:30, yet I'm already exhausted.

Connie, my assistant, pops her head in. "Nora, Mr. Colloway would like to see you in his office."

Irritation stirs. He all but ignores me and now he's summoning me to his office through my admin? Well, he can damn well wait.

"I have an interview in five minutes. It will have to wait."

Her eyes pop like she's one of those squeeze dolls. And I'd just squeezed. "Uh, he said it doesn't matter what's on your calendar—you need to come now."

I sigh heavily. What I'd like to do is send back my own message that he can't just demand I drop every-fucking-thing whenever he wants, CEO or not, but I don't. There's no reason to get poor innocent Connie involved in our personal mess.

"I'll need you to reschedule my interview with—"

"Taken care of. I've cleared your calendar for the rest of the day, per Mr. Colloway's instructions."

Clenching my jaw, I rise from my chair and make my way to the elevator, punching the button for the thirty-second floor so hard I break a nail. All too soon, I'm approaching his office. Lydia, his assistant, rises from her desk when she sees me.

"Hi, Nora. Go on in. He's expecting you." I search her face, replay the tone in her voice to see if I can get a feel for what I'm about to walk into. It's blank.

"Thanks," I mumble.

Connelly's door is shut. I stand there for a moment staring at the wood that separates us, realizing my heart is racing with trepidation. I feel a flush creeping up my neck and try to stop my pits from sweating. I'm not sure what I expect when I finally pluck the courage to turn the knob. It certainly isn't what I find inside.

Connelly's sitting at his round conference table—the same one he set lavishly with freezer crap. I shove that memory aside because he's not alone. To his left is an older, pretty woman. She's dressed in a sharp black business suit with conservative matching pumps. Her golden hair is pulled back severely in a bun. Fashionable thick black glasses complete her librarian ensemble.

Only I know she's no librarian.

"Nora," Connelly says crisply as he rises. Once again, he's in complete control of his emotions, but I'm about to fucking lose it. This is a goddamned ambush and he had the audacity to do this at work. How completely irresponsible of him to air our dirty laundry here. "This is Cynthia McNamara. Cynthia, Nora Cantres."

I barely spare a glance at the pristine woman, who is now also standing beside Connelly. I ignore her, not even bothering with pleasantries. A throat clearing to my right pulls my attention to a man I hadn't noticed before.

"I need your signature, ma'am," he says, thrusting a manila envelope into my hands before handing me a pen. Holding a clipboard, he points to a signature line. I have no idea what I'm signing, but I have to imagine it's the results of the paternity test we took two days ago. I guess they were true to their word about a quick turnaround.

After the courier leaves, Connelly waves for me to sit. I want to kick him in the nuts. Tell him to fuck off, but I need to pick my battles. Besides, I think maybe I'll need to be seated when I hear whatever he has to tell me with his attorney present.

Nodding to the packet in my hand, he tells me quietly, "The results." That's when I see a matching one in his, which is still sealed. "I wanted to wait for you."

While that should provide me some measure of comfort, it doesn't. It incenses me. "But we needed an audience?"

Jaw tight, he replies, "I thought it best to have my attorney present to discuss next steps if the results were positive."

Hurt, betrayal, loss, and despair would have brought me to the ground had I been standing. I hate the way I'm feeling inside. My emotions threaten to consume me whole. My eyes begin to water against my wishes.

After Connelly's interaction with Hazel the other day, I saw a different side to him, even thought maybe I saw some threads of forgiveness in his eyes, in his tone, in the brief glances he gave me.

Guess I was wrong.

My lips turn up in a sneer. "Well, shame you didn't afford me the same courtesy."

"Nora," he starts before I cut him off with a wave of my hand.

"I don't want to hear it. Let's just get this over with."

Using my thumb, I slide it under the gum of the flap and pull out a single sheet of paper. I scan the page for the only data point that matters, finding it a quarter of the way down.

Probability of Paternity: >99.99%

I stare at that number until it blurs together into a giant blob. I feel such intense relief and happiness in that moment I let a sob escape. I always felt Hazel was Connelly's, but to have it confirmed provides such a sense of rightness I hadn't realized I needed until right then.

But then the direness of the situation slams back into me. My relief quickly morphs to undiluted rage and profound sadness.

Connelly hates me. *He has every right to*, I remind myself.

With unchecked tears rolling down my face, I

lift my eyes to his and see pure joy. For just a split second that throws me off track, but then I steer myself back on the bumpy road.

His attorney starts talking. The only word I hear is "custody."

Oh. *Fuck.* No.

"I won't let you take her from me," I put out there. My voice is hard, unyielding.

Lawyer girl opens her mouth to speak again when Connelly places his hand on her arm. She snaps it shut. I hear her stark white teeth clash and I secretly hope she chipped one.

"Take her from you?" he replies incredulously. "I don't want to take her from you, Nora. I would never do that. You're her mother. I only want my equal time with her."

My anger deflates, leaving me with nothing inside but a deep ocean of bleak sadness that now falls in endless streams.

"I would have given that to you, Connelly. I would give you anything you asked for. I know you have no reason to think otherwise but I do want our daughter to know you. I know I was wrong to keep this from you. I was wrong to keep you from Hazel and her from you. I know that now."

My eyes shift to Cynthia before landing back on him. I stand, clutching the results in my hand. "I understand the need to protect yourself legally. I do, but I don't appreciate being ambushed at work and I sure as fuck don't appreciate having an outside party be witness to such a private moment. You took something that should have

317

been reserved for the two of us and you demeaned it by having her here."

"Where are you going," his loud voice booms as I make my way to the door.

"To secure my own legal counsel." I pivot and he's so close I almost run into him. Fucker. "You didn't need to do this," I say in a low, resigned voice.

"How was I supposed to know that?" he clips. "I have no idea what I *am* supposed to be doing here, Nora. My entire world has been shaken and stirred. My head hasn't stopped spinning for nine fucking days."

I shake my head, not knowing how to respond because mine has too. "I know it was foolish, but for Hazel's sake, I'd rather hoped we could have figured that out together. I know now that's not possible."

When I turn back toward the door, this time, he lets me leave.

Chapter 26

Nora

The doorbell chimes melodically. It would be soothing under any other circumstance. Not today, though. Today it signals the second half of my atonement. Zel is practically vibrating with excitement as she runs to answer it. I, on the other hand, am shaking with anxiety. Nerves have twisted my insides until they hurt. I hope my daughter doesn't hate me, too, after today.

After I left Connelly's office the other day, I couldn't breathe the same air as him. I ended up leaving work early for the day, something I never do. Sitting in the parking lot, I called Mira and cried. After she spent ten minutes graphically detailing how she was going to systematically cut off his balls slowly and painfully before starting on other important body parts, she made a few calls, getting me the name of a family law attorney. She's female, she's bloodthirsty, and she only takes on mothers as clients. I spent an hour late in the afternoon with Ms. Hilary Parks of Parks, Smith, and Woodford and sent her name and contact information to Connelly that night via text.

I didn't expect to talk to Connelly directly again. I thought we'd impersonally communicate through e-mail and couriered letters from our respective legal representation, organize drop-off dates and times, and stay in our cars while Hazel shuffled between us. It sickened me this is where we seemed to be headed. It was an unhealthy relationship for all involved. One that would be hard for Zel to understand. She is such a loving, caring, and forgiving human being.

But he surprised me by stopping by my office the next morning, apologizing for how poorly he'd handled things. Again. It was a strained conversation, emotions still running high on both sides. We agreed that we'd table the attorneys for now. Try to work things out amicably. Ms. Parks very outspokenly disagreed—but my life, my decisions. I never wanted to involve her anyway. I just felt I had no choice.

So here we are. Three days later. It's time to tell Hazel about Connelly being her father. We agreed to do it together. When I suggested it, he jumped all over it. I was grateful because I'm not sure I can do this alone.

I have no idea how Hazel will react. All I've told her about her father over the years when she's asked is that sometimes fathers or mothers can't be with us the way we want, but that I know her father loves her very much. I have never said one disparaging word to Hazel about Connelly. No matter what happens between us, I never will.

Voices draw closer to the kitchen. I take in a shaky breath, letting it out gradually.

"Mommy, Connelly's here," Hazel hums from behind me.

Drying my hands, I swivel from the sink to face them. I have to hang on to the counter behind me when our eyes connect. Hummingbird wings flutter against the insides of my belly. He looks so damn edible in his fitted dark-wash jeans and black pinstriped button-down. It's untucked and the cuffs are rolled, giving a casual yet sexy air about him.

God, I love him so damn much it pains me.

"Hi," I practically wheeze.

"Nora." He tips his head in greeting. It's stilted, awkward. I hope Hazel doesn't notice.

"Mommy, can I give Connelly a tour?" My baby girl's eyes are twinkling like holiday lights, so she's apparently none the wiser about the tension that's running like electric currents between her parents.

"Not now, Ladybird. After dinner, maybe. Why don't you show Connelly where he'll be sitting, okay?"

"Sure!"

Grabbing Connelly's hand, Zel excitedly drags him to the kitchen table, pointing to his place. I thought it best if we keep things pretty informal, so I made a simple meal of baked fish, salad, and crusty French bread. Luckily for me, Zel likes fish and I know what a health nut Connelly is. I ridiculously debated for an hour on wine. Wine, no wine. Wine, no wine. Finally, I ended up setting white wine glasses out, but now I'm wondering if that was such a good idea. I guess it's too late to pull them off now.

"I hope mahi-mahi is okay?" I set down a platter containing the seafood, along with the bowl of salad. Hazel has already placed the basket of bread on the table.

"It's fine, Nora. Thanks." He's short. His smile seems forced.

It makes me ache, this awkwardness between us. Is this how it will always be from now on? Painted-on smiles? Fake pleasantries? Barely leashed animosity?

I feel like crying. I paste on a smile instead.

"Mommy, can I say the prayer?"

"Sure, Zel." I chance a quick glance at Connelly to see he's utterly fascinated with her.

Hazel folds her hands and squints her eyes shut. "Thank you for the food we eat. Thank you for the world so sweet. Thank you for the birds that sing. Thank you God for everything. And thank you for having Connelly here for dinner," she adds at the end, throwing me a look that already begs forgiveness in case it would make me upset.

It's silent for a very long heartbeat before Connelly chuckles, which makes Hazel giggle, and pretty soon the tension has completely fizzled because we're all laughing loudly.

The meal goes by quickly and, much to my surprise, comfortably. Hazel keeps the conversation going single-handedly. She talks about her new school, the photos of trees and a bird in flight she took last weekend, and a new friend she made this week named Callie. If there's one thing that Zel excels at more than taking pictures and designing, it's talking.

Hawk barking at the door gets our attention. He knows we're eating and he's missing out on table scraps. I normally let him run around but I think he could sense my nerves. He's been hugging my leg all damn day, afraid to leave me for a second.

"You have a dog, Hazel?"

"Yep. We got him from the Humane Society in our old home."

Connelly gives me a look that may border on warm. I try to return it, but feel my bottom lip quiver.

"Do you like sports, Connelly?" Hazel asks, drawing the conversation back to her.

"Sure do." He smiles, pushing his empty plate away.

"Do you like hockey?"

Uh oh. I know for a fact Connelly is a die-hard Red Wings fan.

"What all-American male wouldn't like hockey?" he feigns with a wink, which makes her giggle again. She hasn't stopped grinning since she found out he was coming over.

"Who's your favorite team?" she asks excitedly.

"The only one worth anything. The Wings, of course."

"The Wings?" she groans while rolling her eyes. Her disappointment is clear. I have to work to hold in a laugh.

"Oh no. Don't tell me you're a Blackhawks fan?"

Connelly asks, choking on Blackhawks like it's a dirty word.

"All the way."

He laughs, shaking his head. "You do realize that the Wings have won nearly double the cups as the Blackhawks, right?"

His stats are futile. Hazel has a binder full of her own. They start winging fan-filled mud, nicely of course. I have a feeling this back-and-forth bantering could go on for hours, neither of them giving an inch.

I start to clear the table while they each try to convince the other about the error of their ways for their NHL team selections and am surprised when Connelly stands to help. We all move around the kitchen in synch like we've done this a hundred times before. I have to tamp down the feeling of rightness. I know it won't last.

When we're done, Hazel asks again if she can give Connelly a tour. I want to say yes so we can delay the inevitable.

"Maybe in a few minutes. Connelly and I," I pause casting him a quick glance, "we, uh, have something we need to discuss with you."

Her eyes volley between the two of us as if she senses something in our lives is about to significantly change. "Okay."

Connelly agreed to let me take the lead with this conversation, but if I don't get some air about now, I may pass out. "How about let's sit on the patio." I pick up my liquid courage, walk to the glass sliding doors that lead to the enclosed backyard, and step outside.

Hawk runs right up to me and demands to be petted. I comply. He follows me over to the patio furniture as I sit. He stands protectively in front me, not really growling at Connelly, but not warmly welcoming him either. Hawk relaxes a bit when I start scratching behind his ears but never lets down his guard.

I've racked my brain about what I'm going to say to my ten-year-old. I decide the best approach is to be as honest and direct as possible. That's the way Hazel and I have always been with each other, except for this one thing. And she's mature enough to handle the truth.

Once we're settled, Hazel and me on the loveseat, Connelly in a lounger across from us, I focus my attention on my daughter and start.

"Hazel, first I need to apologize because I wasn't quite truthful the other day when we went to get that test."

Her brows crease. "But I thought you were always honest with me? 'Honesty is the best policy' you always say."

I choke on my guilt. So much guilt. "I made a mistake, Ladybird. I'm so sorry."

She grabs on to my hand and tells me it's okay. So forgiving. I hope she still feels that way in five minutes. It takes a few beats before I can go on. "I love you more than all the stars in the sky. Nothing will ever change that. You know that right?"

She nods.

"Do you remember what I've told you about your daddy?"

Her eyes now flick to Connelly and stay there.

She knows exactly what I'm about to tell her. I feel like I'm going to barf.

"Hazel," I gently prompt. When she finally tears her eyes away from her father and back to me, my breath hitches. I don't see anger or blame or even confusion. I see...*hope*. And a thousand times more than Connelly's acceptance, I need Hazel's. I need to know I'm not going to lose her over this secret I've kept.

"Is Connelly my daddy?" her small voice asks.

My eyes fill so fast I can't see. Now it's my turn to nod silently and a few of them spill. Her attention lands on her father once again. For the first time since we sat down, I allow myself to look at Connelly. Leaning forward in his seat, elbows on his knees, hands clasped between his legs, he has a gentle smile on his face as he raptly watches our exchange. He's trying to hide it, but he's as nervous as I am.

"I know this is kind of coming out of the blue and I know you probably have a lot of questions. I promise we'll take as much time as you need..."

My words fade into the background, trailing off when Hazel rises and walks over to Connelly. She stands there for eons as they view each other in a new and different light.

Father to daughter.

Child to parent.

Blood to blood.

Relief is palpable, and I know everything will be all right with Hazel and me when she throws her arms around Connelly's neck in acceptance. It's a tender moment I will never forget until I close my eyes for the final time. Connelly's frozen for all of two seconds before he wraps himself around her tiny frame, holding her tight.

His eyes connect with mine. My hand flies to smother my sobs when I see tears glistening in the sunlight. *Thank you*, he mouths silently. All I can do is nod.

"Wanna tour now? Wanna see my drawings?" she asks, bouncing up and down in front of him. He looks to me for permission. I silently give it.

"Sure. I'd love that, Hazel."

"Mommy, do you wanna come, too?"

"No," I choke on a whisper. "Don't you have any questions you want to ask first?"

Her eyes roll to the sky, but don't come back to me. They land on her father. "Can I call you Daddy?"

A strangled noise escapes me.

"You can call me whatever you're comfortable with, Hazel." When I hear his voice crack it almost ruins me.

"I want to call you Daddy," she replies enthusiastically.

This is the single best trait about Hazel. She is *the* most accepting person I have met, whether it be child or adult. She doesn't question, she doesn't argue. She has mentioned her father only a handful of times since she was old enough to understand he wasn't with us. Every time, she just accepted my vague answer that he couldn't be, but it wasn't his fault. Now that he is here, she's not questioning why, she's just accepting that he is. I love her all the more for that.

Hazel gets halfway inside before she turns around and runs back to me, enveloping me in an enthusiastic hug. "I knew he was the one, Mommy. I just knew it," she whispers in my ear. I don't even try to stop the water cascading freely down my face.

Hazel rejoins Connelly and holds out her hand for him to take. They connect for the first time as father and daughter, walking inside with the biggest grins on their faces I could possibly imagine.

My heart has never been so full, yet so profoundly empty at the same time.

Chapter 27

CONN

"Hey, what's up?"

"Nothing," I lie. I've been sitting at the end of Nora's street for almost fifteen minutes. I'm supposed to be there in five for my first outing with Hazel. I'm nervous as hell and need some encouragement. With the exception of Nora, I have always been confident, but I find I'm having the same insecurities now about my daughter. What is it about the Cantres women that makes me question myself?

"Isn't tonight the first night with your daughter?" my twin prods.

"Yes."

"What do you have planned?"

Because I didn't want to ask Nora, making it appear as though I didn't have a fucking clue what I was doing—which I don't—I talked to Ella instead. Like she has so much more expertise than I do, but she also knows my daughter so I thought she'd be a solid second source.

She suggested taking Hazel to Millennium Park,

so that's what I'm going to do. After we walk around, I'll grab us a bite to eat. Then we can picnic on the grassy lawn. It's a beautiful fall day and with a sweater, hopefully she'll be fine. Maybe I should make her bring her winter coat, just in case.

"Millennium Park."

"That should be fun."

"Yeah."

"One-word answers." Asher pauses. "It's going to be fine, Conn. You know that, right?"

"Yeah," I reply softly, *hating* the fact I'm this unsure about myself. Hazel was a ball of excitement after Nora and I talked to her a few days ago. She spent an hour going through all of her artwork and another hour showing me her photographs. Ella was right. She's incredibly talented. And grounded. And mature. And funny. She's incredible, period.

"Do you want Alyse and me to meet you?"

"No. Nora and I agreed that it just be us for a few weeks until Hazel acclimates. She seems to be handling it well, but we just don't want to push things and overwhelm her."

"Makes sense." Another pause. "You know, out of any of us brothers, I always thought you'd make the best father."

Snorting in disbelief, I ask, "Why?" I'm not sure how he could think that when I didn't even think I wanted kids until days ago.

"Because you're the closest in personality to Dad. You inherited his patience and level head. He did his best teaching by being a great role model and that's you, Conn. You're going to fuck up, because I'm sure being a parent is hard, but we reaped the benefits of great parents, so some of that had to rub off on you. Hell, I'm hoping it rubbed off on me."

And this right here is why I called my twin. He always makes me feel better.

"Maybe you're right."

"There's no maybe about it. I'm just thrilled that you'll be doing all the learning before me. That way you can give me tips and keep me from making the same mistakes."

I chuckle. "I'm sure I'll fuck up plenty."

"I'm sure you will, too. But that doesn't mean you won't be a good dad, Conn. It just means your kids will learn how to apologize."

If there was one thing our father was good at, it was acknowledging when he'd screwed up. Our father was the best role model a kid could ask for. Both my parents were. I want to be that for Hazel. And I can tell how good of a mother Nora is. Even if she has kept my daughter from me all these years, there is no disputing her love for Hazel.

"Thanks, Ash."

"Anytime. Now, stop dragging your feet and go spend time getting to know your daughter."

I disconnect the call, start the car, and drive the short distance to Nora's house feeling much better. The door flies open before I even reach it. Standing there with an ear-to-ear grin on her face is Hazel.

My God in heaven, she is magnificent.

Nora stands just a few feet behind her looking

so fucking beautiful it kills me. I acknowledge her with a slight dip of my head, my heart speeding up for all sorts of different reasons. Anger. Lust. Punishment. *Love*. Her deceit is unimaginable, yet...yet I still need her. I fucking *need* her with an untamed wildness that seems to quadruple daily.

I've purposely stayed away from her for the past couple of weeks, except when we had to talk about business or Hazel. And there are always people around. If I get even a second alone with her, I'm not sure I'll be able to keep from stripping her raw and raining the worst pain she's ever felt before lavishing the most intense pleasure she can handle over every square inch of her. I want to spank her ass until she has tears of remorse running down her face before I fuck her until we both pass out. I can't reconcile the opposing things I want to do to her. I've never been so torn.

But I have to push all those emotions to the back of my mind right now and focus only on my daughter. I'm still too raw to deal with anything else.

"Hi, Daddy!" Hazel throws her arms around my waist, hugging me tight.

Suddenly I wonder why I was so nervous.

"You got your camera?" I ask, matching her smile. I'd sent Nora a text, asking her to make sure she brought it.

"Got it." She holds up a nice, but inexpensive Nikon. I already know for Christmas I'll be getting her the next step up. One complete with interchangeable lenses for better shooting. Hell, I won't even wait until Christmas. I have ten Christmases to make up for. Birthday's, too.

"You need a jacket, though. It could get chilly."

"I'll be fine in this." She pulls at her light, long-sleeve rainbow sweater.

"Zel, take your jacket." Nora hands her a yellow zip-up hoodie, which Hazel accepts with some reluctance.

"Ready?" I ask, holding out my hand for hers.

"Ready." She grins, lacing her small fingers with mine.

My gaze sweeps up to Nora who looks as if she may start crying any second. I shove away the guilt that makes me feel. "I'll have her home by eight-thirty."

"Sounds good," she says softly. "Have a good time, Ladybird."

"I will," Hazel shouts behind her as we make our way to my car.

"I like that you open my car door," she announces after I settle in the driver's seat and pull on my own safety belt.

"Well, any man worth his salt opens a car door for his lady. Remember that," I wink.

She grins, easily accepting my first bit of fatherly advice. "I will."

Huh. I take a deep, relaxing breath as we back out of the driveway and head back toward the city. I may end up being okay at this father thing after all.

Chapter 28

CONN

We walk over the lush grass of the pavilion. There are no performances tonight, but it's a nice night in the city and there are plenty of people milling around. Many have their blankets spread out, having the same idea I did. Everyone knows these nice days will be winding down as fall's crisp air is sucked down from the north. Pretty soon, the snow will be falling once again.

"This is sooooo cool," Hazel murmurs.

"It is, isn't it?" I've honestly never stopped to appreciate this area. But Hazel...she is in absolute awe. She's not taken that camera from her eye since we set foot in Millennium Park. Right now, she has it pointed up and is snapping rapid-fire pictures of the stainless steel ribbons that crisscross over the 7,000-acre lawn and stand over a hundred feet above us. It's incredible how they look as if they're suspended.

So far, we've walked the gardens, watched the fountains, and strutted around the Bean, an iconic draw for both visitors and locals. The Bean is a

Chicago landmark that's shaped like an oval and made from highly polished steel. The twelve-foot arch on the base of the structure provides a nice area to walk under and its mirrored surface is a dream for photographers to capture great pictures of the reflection of downtown Chicago. Hazel spent fifteen minutes taking snapshots from different angles.

I've finally convinced her we need to eat, so we grab a couple of hot dogs and sodas from Park Grill and try to find "the perfect" spot to sit. I keep pointing out to plots of grass beneath us but nothing seems to satisfy her. I think she just wants to case the entire span of this huge lawn until she's exhausted or her digital card is full. I hope that card fills up soon.

"How's this spot?"

At last, she takes the plastic away from her face and grins. "You're hungry, aren't you?"

I start laughing. "Starved."

She points to the tiny pile of dirt coating the grass right by my feet. "There's an ant hill there."

"Good point. We don't want to have ants crawling on our food."

"And we don't want to kill them either. Did you know ants can lift twenty times their own body weight? If I was as strong as an ant I could pick up a car!"

I am in utter amazement of this girl. *My* girl. So much like her mother with trivial facts. "Wow. An impressive fact I did not know. Well if they're that strong, couldn't they just pick us up and move us if we sat on them?"

"Daaaaddy," she chastises, hand on hip. Secretly loving my new title, I chuckle and grab her hand, taking a few steps ahead. Searching the grass, I see no sign of ants.

"Here?"

She carefully peruses the ground before deeming it acceptable. We spread the thin blanket I've been carrying and sit. I hand her a hot dog, which she quickly unwraps. When she takes a bite, she moans.

"Good?"

"I love hot dogs," she says around a mouthful of bread and meat. "Do you?"

"Eh. I'm more of a fish guy." Actually, I can't stand hot dogs. They're nothing but processed animal parts.

"I like fish, too."

"I know." I bop her on the nose. She giggles.

While we eat, we talk about school and moving. She says she loves it here, but misses her old nanny and friends. I tell her about my brothers and the fact she has two cousins with one on the way. That lights her up. She's already begging to meet them. I tell her I'll talk to her mother and work out a time soon. Then I talk about her grandma and tell her stories about her grandpa. She's sad she won't get to meet him. So am I. She asks me about my job and squeals when I tell her our company owns a plane. Unlike her mother, she likes to fly. After I tell her that her mom works for me, she just grins mischievously.

It's light, easy conversation. She doesn't ask hard questions and for that, I'm grateful because I don't know how I'd answer them.

When we're done eating, we lay back on the blanket, staring at the silvery structure above us. She grabs my hand, holds it tight. It reminds me of when I took Nora to the country club my parents belonged to for Memorial Day fireworks. We lay on the bank of Orchard Lake on a blanket similar to this one and held hands as colored lights exploded over our heads. Three days later, Hazel would be conceived.

Fuck.

My heart suddenly feels too heavy for my chest, but Hazel saves me from spiraling into despair without even knowing it.

"Daddy?"

I turn my head toward her. She does the same so now I'm staring into my own eyes, my own image. "Yeah, sweetie?"

"I'm glad we moved to Chicago," she tells me.

I swallow the knot in my throat. To think that I almost didn't get to meet this wonderful little beauty who is so much like me is uncanny. "Me, too, Hazel."

Then she slams me with a doozie. Probably my first of many. "Do you love my mommy?"

Jesus. So much it's fucking excruciating. But how do I answer that loaded question without giving our daughter hope there's a future for the three of us when I don't know if there is? With everything else I'm feeling for Nora at the moment, without a doubt I love her just as much as I hate her, so I answer honestly, I guess.

"Very much, but sometimes love isn't enough, Hazel."

A soft smile turns her mouth up. "But sometimes it is," she says with such maturity and wisdom it fucking astounds me. Then she turns her attention back to the sky, leaving me to replay what she said over and over and over.

As we lie quietly next to each other, I have to wonder if the very thing that drove us apart— *her*—could also be the very thing that pulls us back together. At this point, it's a toss-up.

Chapter 29

Nora

"How's everything going?" my sister tentatively asks.

I'm not sure how she wants me to answer. There's thick tension between Connelly and me. We've avoided each other as much as possible these past few weeks. Well, I should say he's avoided me. He's still very angry and hurt. Rightfully so. I wish we could talk and clear the air, but his body language is pretty clear. *Stay the fuck away.* Zel senses it, too. Every time we're in the same room she tries to lighten the mood, bless her big heart.

The arrangement we have for sharing our daughter is working right now, but pretty soon I know it won't be enough for Connelly. There are no overnights yet, no discussion of holiday sharing, and no plans about what we'll do come summertime.

That's when I wonder what he'll do, what sort of legal action he'll take. I try to put myself in his place. I'm sure I'd want to do the same thing. Protect myself legally. I just hope when that time comes, it can be amicable. One day, he briefly mentioned child support, but I brushed him off. I told him if he wanted to buy Zel things, he certainly could, but that we've managed fine without his money all this time and don't need it now. I could tell it angered him, but he let it go. At least for now. I know that won't last.

"Honestly, I'm feeling like my future balances on the edge of an unevenly sharpened knife. I never know if the next step will slice me apart or grant me another reprieve," I reply at last.

"I'm sorry, Nora. I know all of this is hard. For everyone. I want you to know I don't judge you. And I'm not taking sides."

Tears well. "Thanks, Mira."

Last Saturday, when Connelly had Zel, Mira and I had lunch, which led into dinner, and I ended up having to rush home by eight o'clock to be sure I was here when Connelly dropped her off. I told Mira things only my mother knew. She listened, she supported. One of the pluses of moving here is that I finally feel as though I have a family again outside of Carl. I wish I'd had her as a confidant growing up.

"Have you...have you talked to him?" I hate asking but I'm dying to know.

At the other end of the line, I hear her take a swallow of something before answering. "Just once. He called and asked where he should take Hazel for their first outing."

Ouch. That pricks.

"I think he's been avoiding me. Probably the whole sister thing and all."

"I'm sorry. I know you two are close." I'm insanely jealous, but I'd never tell Mira she couldn't be friends with Connelly. Besides, you don't *tell* Mira anything. She'd do whatever you told her not to just to spite you anyway.

"Nah. He'll come around. He just needs some time, Nora. It was a big shock. Let him absorb it for a bit, okay?"

"I know." I swallow my tears. "God, Mira, I miss him so much. I know we weren't back together very long, but I felt whole like I never had and I...I just miss him so damn much. I miss the way he looked at me with so much heat and love and devotion. I feel lost. I feel like I'll never have that again and I know I don't deserve it, but I still want it."

"Have you tried to talk to him? Tell him how you're feeling?"

"No," I sniffle, dabbing my eyes with a tissue. "I'm trying to give him some space."

My phone beeps indicating I have an incoming call.

Carl.

"Hey, I gotta go. I'll call you later this week to work out a time to take Hazel."

"Can't wait. I love that little girl. Call me if you need me. Anytime."

"Will do. Thanks, Mira. Love you."

"Love you, too."

I click over to answer Carl's call just in time.

"Hey," I say, stretching my sweater tighter against the wind that's picked up. It's definitely fall in the heartland. I take a quick look through the glass patio doors into the kitchen and note that Zel will be home within the half hour from her night with Connelly. Tonight, she had quite a bit of math homework to do, so Connelly's getting exposed to all parts of parenting. Math is not Hazel's strong suit, hence her tutor.

"Hey, Ladybug. How are you?"

On the edge of despair trying not to look down.

"I'm good," I reply on autopilot, but he must hear the tears in my voice.

"Nora. What's the matter, sweetheart? Everything going okay at Wynn?"

This is one conversation I've avoided for the past three weeks. I know I need to tell Carl about Connelly, about our past, about the fact he's Hazel's father. I also know it won't be an easy one because it will hurt him that I've not confided in him before this. The biggest reason, though, is that I just don't want him to be disappointed in me.

"Nora? Do you need me to get on a plane? Beat the shit out of someone?"

My laugh is watery. "You would, wouldn't you?"

"Damn straight I would. I'll ruin anyone who has hurt my girl." He laughs. I don't. I'm afraid in this case, I'm the one who's done all the hurting.

"I have something I need to tell you."

"Sounds big."

I swear if I hadn't heard loving encouragement in his tone, I would have chickened out. Again. But it's exactly what I need in order to tell the only other man I love what I've done.

"It is," I whisper.

Then I fill my lungs with bravery and begin.

Chapter 30

CONN

If you had to pin me down, make me give you one word that would best describe how I've felt without Nora all these years, that word would be: yearning. She's a hunger I could never fill. A thirst I could never quench. An ache I could never soothe. As full as my life has always been, I've still had this shadowy hollowness inside of me that only her light has ever been able to penetrate.

When I saw Nora for the first time, she stirred something in me I'd never felt before. I was downright besotted and I fell in love so damn fast it would make your head spin. Every cell in my body was inextricably drawn to her, screaming for her. I never even tried to fight it because I knew I'd already lost. I was hers.

I remember in AP Psych, the one class we had together in our senior year, I'd watch in fascination as she'd repeatedly tuck her hair behind her ear, even though it hadn't fallen out. And when she was concentrating hard on something, she'd unconsciously trace her lips with her index finger. Around and around. It was hypnotic and sexy as hell.

During those months when I was young and cocky and I tried to get her to talk to me, to pay attention to me, hell, simply to acknowledge my very fucking existence, I yearned. I ached. I craved everything about her. Her smile. Her light. Her devotion. I wanted it all. It drove me mad that I couldn't have her.

I asked myself repeatedly...was it the chase, the game, the win? What was it that made me want her like nothing I'd wanted before? But every time I came back to the same answer.

Nora was my kismet. She was my destiny. She was mine.

I've done little else over the last few weeks but think. My mind is at war with my heart. Hell, my heart is at war with itself. It's exhausting. I'm not sure you could find a man on earth more conflicted than I am right now.

On one hand, the time I've spent with my daughter has been incredible. Surreal, actually. I'm completely and totally in love with her already. She has me wrapped tightly and she knows it.

The day after we told Hazel about me, Nora and I worked out a schedule where I take her for a few hours two nights during the week and one day on the weekend. I spent all day with her last Sunday at the Children's Museum. We had an absolute blast in the tinkering lab, but Hazel was naturally drawn to the Artabounds Studio so we spent most of our day there. Before we left, I bought a season pass so we could go back as many times as she wants.

We've been taking it slow. I agreed to those terms, but damn if it's not enough for me. I want and *need* more. I want to spend every free minute with Hazel.

Which brings me to the other hand.

I'm in emotional agony over what to do about Nora. I love her madly and deeply. I feel dead inside without her...without her laugh or her touch or her challenging mouth. I need her to feel alive again, but I'm still so fucking hurt it's difficult to even breathe. Pain stabs me fresh each time I see her, knowing everything I've lost and everything that's been taken away from me.

The question I've been wrestling with for weeks now is how can I possibly overcome her betrayal? How can I trust her again? How can we build a future together? I want to. Jesus, I want to with everything in me. I just don't know how.

Which is why I'm here. In Detroit. Sitting in my mom's kitchen at eleven thirty at night. I drove up on the spur of the moment tonight right after work. I didn't even bother to stop for a change of clothes. I always keep a few extra things here anyway.

"Sorry to just show up unannounced." Maxwell, our eleven-year-old golden cockerdoodle, sets his head expectantly in my lap. Upon his silent command, I rub the perm-like curly hair between his ears, watching his chocolate eyes drift shut.

"You don't have to apologize for needing your mother, Connelly." She reaches across the table and takes my hand.

I've known I had a daughter for over a month

now, but I haven't yet talked to my mom about her. I know, I know. I'm close to my mother, all of us boys are, but telling her over the phone just didn't seem right and I was too fucked in the head most of the time to get my jumbled thoughts out anyway.

"So you heard, huh?" Guess I couldn't expect my brothers to keep their mouths shut. The danger of having such a close-knit family is that you don't get a lot of privacy.

Her smile is sad and weary. "It accidentally slipped."

"Who told you?"

"Now, Connelly, you know I'd never tell you that."

"Asher and his big fu— mouth." I almost swear but catch myself just in time to halt Barb Colloway's verbal lashing for cussing. She just chuckles. I know I'm right.

"Your brothers mean well. They love you very much."

"Yeah." I know. "I'm sorry, Mom. I just...it's been a lot to deal with."

"I can only imagine. But you don't have to deal with it alone. Lean on the people who love you, Connelly."

"I'm trying."

"So, want to tell me about it?"

"I'm not sure where to start."

"The beginning's always a good place." Her reply is soothing and full of encouraging love.

When I raise my gaze to my mother's, I immediately know I should have made this trip weeks ago. I haven't even said a word and I already feel better, the burden a little less to handle on my own. Maybe by the time I leave here I'll have more clarity.

"Well, you remember Nora." She nods, and during the next hour, I launch into my story. Every sordid, dirty detail of it, including my own betrayal of Nora back when I was nineteen. The cheating, the pregnancy scare, the loss of that life, and how relieved I was. She prompted me with questions along the way, but for the most part, I just talked. She just listened. It was cathartic.

When I was done, my mom sat there in silence, pondering all I'd told her. Staring out the window into the night sky. I was blown away when she finally spoke.

"I'm going to tell you something I've never told another soul, Connelly, some of it not even to your father, and I'd appreciate it if you kept this between us. It's not something I'm proud of."

"Okay," I reply slowly, stretching out the word. I'm not at all sure I want to hear what she has to say. I have a feeling it's very personal and I don't know if can handle being saddled with someone else's secrets right now. I already feel like a two-ton truckload of them sits on my own chest, weighing me down.

"A few months before I met your father I dated this man named Brent for a few months. I thought I knew what love was, but I was clueless until I met your father. Anyway, Brent and I broke up, and three weeks later, I met Frank Colloway." The stars in my mom's eyes shine brightly when she talks about my father. They were every couple's barometer for a perfect marriage. But as they dim when she continues purging her secret, now I'm certain I don't want to hear it. "You already know your father asked me to marry him just a few months after we started dating. What you don't know is that we broke up for a short time because...I'm ashamed to admit I cheated on him. With Brent."

"Mom," I groan. "I do not need to hear this."

"No. You do. It's relevant, I promise." Inhaling a lungful of air, she continues. I can feel how hard this is for her. "Your dad and I got back together and shortly afterward I found out I was pregnant."

What. The. Actual. *Fuck*? My mother? Saint Barb? Cheated? Pregnant? Did I fall through a black hole in the universe? What does a son even say to that?

"What—"

"I lost the baby. At ten weeks I had a miscarriage. Your father knew about the baby, of course, and I told him I was certain it was his, but even I couldn't be sure. And he knew it. I always thought my penance for that great sin I committed against your father was the loss of that child. I mourned for months. It took almost two years before I'd try again and then it was almost a year before we got pregnant with Gray and Luke."

I'm speechless. This is not something you need to hear about your parents.

"Why are you telling me this, Mom?"

Except I already know.

348

Everybody makes mistakes, even those close to sainthood.

Everybody deserves redemption, no sin too great.

Even my mother.

And where would my family be if my father hadn't forgiven my mother? We wouldn't. I scrub my face in complete disbelief, my mind racing.

"Do you love her? Nora, I mean?" she adds, unnecessarily clarifying her question, ignoring mine.

Do I love Nora?

No. It's so much more than a simple four-letter word. It's a shared connection, a twining of our marrow, our cells, our very essences. It's concrete and rooted and unbreakable. But is it enough?

"To my very bones. I am her. She is me."

"Then get off your ass and get her back."

Once again, I stare at my mom in utter shock. Secret revelations? Cursing? It takes me a while to get my bearings back to respond.

"I'm so mad, Mom. I'm not sure I can forgive her," I confess almost in a whisper. "I'm not sure there's a future for us anymore. I think it's too late."

She nods, turning down her mouth like she's disappointed in me. "Do you know why I put my own sins on this very table for you to judge?"

"I..." This feels like a trick question. Even your own mother tries to trip you up sometimes. I think for a minute on what she's trying to tell me. "It's a story about Dad, not you. It's about forgiveness."

"Yes." She beams just as she did when I came

home with the first-place ribbon in the sixth-grade science fair. "Had he chosen not to forgive me, I wouldn't be sitting here with you now, because there wouldn't be a you. Instead of letting that mistake tear us apart, we let it drive us closer together. He was it for me like I was for him."

She pauses, taking my hand between hers and makes sure I'm listening to each and every word. "Holding on to resentment is like wearing cement shoes, Connelly. It weighs down your entire being. Body, mind, and spirit. It will drag you down into the bowels of bitterness, and that's a lonely place to spend your life. Everyone makes missteps, son. Everyone deserves forgiveness, a second chance. Even Nora. You have every right to be mad at her for what she's done and I'm not telling you that you don't. What I'm telling you is it's time to start getting over it. Forgive her and free your heart to love her. You are full of so much love, Connelly, just like your father. If that love belongs to Nora, then you owe it to yourselves, and your daughter, to try."

I reach out and tug her to me so she doesn't see the moisture fogging my vision.

"Time is not guaranteed to us, Connelly," she whispers in my ear. "Don't waste any more of it holding on to needless resentments. It's never too late. You both made mistakes. Don't make any more."

We both made mistakes. She couldn't be more right.

"Thanks, Mom." I squeeze her tight as my throat works to swallow my racing emotions.

"Anytime. Now it's time for this old woman to hit the hay. I have a breakfast date in the morning."

I laugh, kissing her forehead as we stand. "And would that date be with one Bob Monroe?" Bob Monroe, Luke's fiancée's father, and my mother have been "dating" for months now. I think they're both past the point of trying to say it's anything but that.

"It would indeed," she beams, starting toward the stairs. Maxwell follows.

Again with the beaming.

"Are you happy, Mom?"

She stops halfway, turning back around. "I loved your father, Conn. More than I ever thought possible. And when he died, I accepted that I'd lived a happy and full life with my soul mate and that you only get one of those in a lifetime. Sometimes, though, we do get second chances."

I nod, unable to speak. No one wants to see my mom happier than I do. She's such an incredibly amazing woman with a wealth of love to give. I'm glad she found someone else who is worthy to accept it.

She smiles softly. "And when we're blessed with another chance at happiness, well...it would be foolish to squander it, don't you think?"

As she walks up the creaky stairs, I get the distinct impression she's no longer talking about her and Bob Monroe.

Chapter 31

CONN

I knock on the door and wait. When she doesn't answer right away, I knock again. I rarely just pop over unannounced but I needed to see her. I need someone to talk to.

At last, I hear her footfalls and the light shining through the peephole dims. When she hesitates I don't think she's going to let me in. Then the door opens.

"Hey."

"Hey." Her smile is sympathetic and I know things between us will be okay. Other than the first date with Hazel, I haven't talked to Ella since the day I stood in her apartment and looked upon my daughter for the first time. Things were too awkward, given the fact she's Nora's sister and Hazel's aunt. If she's anything like my family, family sticks together. Period.

I give her sweat-clad body a quick once-over, but it's different now than all the other times before it. All I see is the sister of the woman I'm in love with, not the beautiful one I've been attracted to all this time. "You busy?"

"Nah. Come on in." She steps aside to let me enter. "You want a beer?"

"I'd love one. Thanks."

I take a seat on her plush white couch. Soon enough, Ella returns with two cold brews in her hand. She sits on the other end, tucking her bare feet beneath her.

"No hot date tonight?" I ask, taking a long swallow.

"Just with my hand."

That makes me choke and I spray hops and barley all over myself. "Jesus, Ella." I set the bottle down and wipe myself off.

She smirks. "Hmmm, guess things have changed between us, huh?"

I sigh heavily, knowing she's right. Normally we'd banter back and forth off each other for a good fifteen minutes over a comment like that, most of it sexually charged, yet I just practically chastised her for it. It feels more than wrong to even think about doing that now. "I guess they have."

It's been a whole week since I talked to my mom. Another week of thinking, soul-searching. Another week without Nora in my arms or my bed. Another week of bitter loneliness. I'm starting another interminable weekend without her. At least I get to spend the day with Hazel on Sunday.

"I'm glad, you know."

"Glad about what?" I pick up my beer and lean back, putting my feet up on her coffee table. She

353

scrunches her forehead in annoyance but doesn't tell me to take them down, so I don't.

"That nothing happened between us." She drops her gaze briefly. "I wouldn't be able to look at Nora if it did and...well, I need her in my life. Hazel, too. So..."

So do I, I think. Jesus, so do I.

"I've missed you, Ella. I've missed talking to you."

"Me too, playboy, but Nora's my sister and I..."

When she leaves her sentence hanging, I rescue her. "It's okay. You don't have to explain. I get it. You don't want to watch her get hurt."

"I don't want to watch *any* of you get hurt, Conn. I care about all three of you. A lot."

"I don't know what I'm supposed to do, Ella. Tell me what to do," I beg quietly.

This is why I came here. My mom gave me so much to think about, but I still feel a little lost and I guess I was hoping to gain some insight from the person closest to Nora besides Hazel. Hell, I should be talking to Carl, not Ella, but there's no way in hell I can do that. He'll probably gut me, then sink my empty shell to the bottom of the Ohio River.

"No can do, amigo. Only you can figure this out, Conn."

"This is such a pile of shit," I mumble, letting my head fall against the cushions behind me.

"You know," she starts, "My grandpa ran a cattle farm in rural Iowa. When I was growing up, my mom would drop me off there for three weeks out of the summer. I loved my grandparents, but I used to hate going there. They made me get up early, like at the ass crack of dawn, and do all kinds of chores. The one I hated the most was cleaning out Deguello's pen."

"Deguello? What the hell is a Deguello?" I'm from Detroit. We don't have farms there.

She looks at me with a twinkle in her eye. "Not what. Who."

"Okay, who the hell is Deguello?" And what the hell does he or she have to do with my current predicament with Nora?

"Deguello was my grandpa's prize bull. He was treated like a fucking king, let me tell you. I half expected to see him draped in a purple velvet cape when I got to his pen. Anyway, my job in the morning was to scoop his shit. From the age of twelve to sixteen part of my summer ritual with my grandpa was to scoop cow crap."

I start howling with laughter until tears run down my face. I cannot imagine this prissy woman sitting next to me hauling cow dung.

"Anyway," she shouts loudly, trying to shut me up. "You can imagine how much I complained about that. So one day I asked my grandpa why we had to scoop up Deguello's shit—I used that exact word mind you—and he stopped me from what I was doing and said, 'You may see shit, Mirabella, but do you know what I see?' I knew he was about to tell me something insightful, something I'd remember until the day I died."

"What did he tell you," I prod when she hesitates, knowing she's about to pass down the same insight to me that I'll also remember until the day I die.

"He said 'I see vegetables on a family's dinner table that will feed their kids the nutrients they need to grow up strong and healthy. I see the energy I need to run my lights and heat my water and power my entire farming operation. I see gold, Mirabella. And if all you see is a pile of shit, then you're missing an entire world of lost potential and opportunities.' Then he went back to work like we hadn't spoken a word."

"He sounds like a good grandpa," I say eventually, cutting through the silence around us as I digest the words she just spoke.

"He was."

Was. I didn't miss her sorrowful use of past tense.

"So...you're saying my shit pile is really a gold mine then?"

We laugh for a couple of minutes before sobering again. Ella reaches over and takes my hand. "Twenty-four karat."

A burn starts in my eyes. I blink it away. "I love her, Ella."

"I know."

"God, I miss her. My entire being aches without her." I'm in fucking agony.

"So does hers."

I swivel my head and look at her. "Yeah?"

"Yeah," she replies softly with a sad smile on her face.

Sitting back, she quietly nurses her beer. I've learned more about Ella in these last few minutes than I have in the year that I've known her. I wonder what else is lurking under the layers she uses to keep herself protected?

"You've never told me stories about your childhood before."

She looks thoughtful before answering, "That's because before, you were just the hot guy next door who kept unsuccessfully trying to get into my bed."

I smile. It was true. At first. "And now?"

One shoulder comes up. "Now you're family."

Family. Regardless of where Nora and I end up, there is that.

She squeezes my hand once before letting go. "Feel better?"

I nod slowly. "Getting there."

She curls her fingers and blows on her knuckles before pretending to shine them. "I have a gift like that."

A light chuckle escapes. "Thanks, Ella."

"Anytime, playboy. Anytime."

Chapter 32

Nora

We walk into the upscale wine bar in downtown Chicago shortly after nine. There's soft music playing. The lights are low. An oblong maple bar sits smack dab in the middle of the spacious room, providing the perfect centerpiece for the alcoves on the outer edges that contain plush couches and mismatched chairs. This entire place is perfect for small groups to gather or intimate enough for a couple to have after-dinner drinks. It seems like a place Connelly would have taken me.

Jesus, Nora. Stop torturing yourself. You're his child's mother. Nothing more.

"There they are," Kam excitedly points, dragging me across the hardwood flooring, my heels clicking as I jog to keep up with her.

"They? I thought it was just the two of us."

Damn her. Kam is famous for dragging me along to more than one party unannounced. I've felt like the awkward third wheel more than once. I didn't want to come out tonight, but I didn't have a valid excuse either since it's Saturday night and

Hazel sweet-talked her way into spending the night with Mira. Besides, Kam was absolutely relentless. She doesn't like to be told no.

"Kam…" I moan, trying to stop her.

She pivots and grabs my shoulders, shaking me slightly. "Look. You need to get out and make friends, maybe even get laid. And I know how close you like your circle. If I told you, you would have said no."

I huff. The getting laid part is true. The making friends part is debatable.

"Now. Paste on a big smile and be your sweet self."

"Fine," I acquiesce. It's too late now, anyway. "But I'm leaving early."

"Yeah, yeah."

Seconds later we arrive in front of a group of stunning women, and…Landyn. *Huh?* I stand there, confused, as Kam runs around giving hugs to her friends. Landyn squeezes through the melee and throws her arms around me.

"What are you doing here?" she asks in my ear.

"Uh, I could ask you the same."

She points to a jaw-dropping gorgeous brunette. "Addy's my aunt and also my soon-to-be cousin-in-law, I guess. That's kind of weird," she mumbles.

I'm sure my face scrunches up in utter confusion, but before I get a chance to ask any more questions, Kam is once again pulling me by the arm into the middle of the group as everyone settles back in their seats.

"Guys, this is Nora Cantres. Nora, meet Livia

Colloway, Alyse Colloway, Addy Monroe, soon-to-be Colloway, and of course you already know Landyn."

Frozen.

That's me.

And not the carefree "Let It Go" *Frozen* either.

I suppose had I confided in Kam about my epic fuckup with Connelly and Hazel I wouldn't have gotten myself into this situation. She probably thinks she's doing me some big favor by introducing me to his family so Connelly can win back the "redhead who broke his heart." She's a big believer in fairy-tale endings.

I quickly weigh my options.

Tuck tail and run or square my shoulders and make the best of it.

I'm so damn tired of running.

"Nice to meet you," I say, holding out my hand to Addy. They're each polite, which I guess is more than I could have hoped for. I've hurt their brother-in-law terribly and it's natural to protect your family. When I get to Livia she doesn't take my hand, but stands instead, enfolding me in her arms. You could have blown me over with a puff of air.

"It's nice to finally meet the woman who brought Conn to his knees," she whispers in my ear. "Congrats. Welcome to the family, Nora."

"But I'm not—"

"You will be. Once he gets his head out of his ass."

She's obviously the optimist of the bunch.

Sitting down, she pats the open space between

her and Kam, indicating I should take it. Not wanting to be rude, I do. I feel an instant kinship with this woman already. Her warmth puts me at ease and the other women quickly follow suit. I can see why Connelly's brothers fell in love with them. I'm suddenly grateful Hazel will have them in her life, even if I may not.

"Did I miss something?" Kam leans over and asks quietly. Guilt, my very best friend, assails me again. Kam has known something is wrong, but she has respected my need to sort things out in my own head before talking to her.

"Yes, but I'll tell you later. I'm sorry, I should have told you by now."

"No worries, Lucy. We're good." My nonjudgmental friend. She has my back to the end. I love Kamryn so much.

Over the next hour or so, I learn all sorts of interesting facts about the Colloways. Gray and Livia have been married not quite a year and have four-month-old twin boys, Grant and Cash. Alyse is Livia's sister and Asher's wife. They were just married this past July and she's expecting at the end of February. Addy is engaged to the elusive Luke, Gray's twin. I never had a chance to meet Luke as there was some rift between him and his family by the time I met Connelly. They're getting married in Maui in April. They all laughed about how Gray unintentionally paid for their honeymoon through a gift he gave Addy for helping him win Livia back.

And the story about how Landyn is Addy's niece, but also the Colloway boys' cousin is beyond bizarre. Novel worthy. And I thought my life was fucked up. I will give Landyn credit, though. She sure has her act together for all the shit she's been through. I have a feeling what I've learned, though, only scratches the surface of what lies beneath. For all of them.

"So, Nora, how is Hazel adjusting?"

I look at Addy, wondering if she's trying to bait me, but she's not. She's genuinely interested. "She's pretty laid back, so she's adjusting very well, actually. She loves her new school and has made a lot of new friends already. She's so excited to be in the city with her beloved Blackhawks. She's a hockey nut."

"Hockey? She's ten, right?"

I laugh. "Yes. My godfather is into hockey, so I think that's where she picked it up."

"When do we get to meet her?"

I face Livia not wanting to look at Kam. She's not stupid. I'm sure by now she's figured out the connection. "We're taking things a little slow, letting her adjust to the whole news first. But soon."

"Good. I'm excited to get to know her. The Colloways are a pretty close-knit bunch, in case you didn't know."

"I do," I reply hoarsely. "And you won't be able to keep her away once she gets her hands on Grant and Cash. She loves babies." Zel has begged me for years to have another baby, even if we adopt. She wants a sibling so bad. I guess she'll have to settle for cousins instead.

"So how are things between you and Connelly?" Alyse asks. "He's pretty tight-lipped around us."

Hmmm...let's see. Awkward. Tense. Uncomfortable. Lonely, actually. Very, very lonely. Glancing at Kam who's riveted to what I'll say, I settle for, "Amicable." Which is also not untrue. Connelly's been nothing but polite to me during our brief interludes. Polite like one would greet their dry cleaner or hairdresser or a police officer pulling you over for speeding.

Very fucking polite.

"He'll come around. Asher's working on him." She winks conspiratorially.

Before I can tell her that earth has a better chance of being taken out by a meteor than us reconciling, a familiar form catches my eye. And what I see burns me. Shreds me to pieces. If I looked down, I would not be at all surprised to see my heart beat through the gaping hole in my chest.

It's Connelly.

And he's not alone.

I've been emotionally barren for the last eleven years. Slowly freezing to death without the love of the only man I've ever wanted. I have Hazel, yes, but having the love of your child is incomparable to having the love of your soul mate.

Seeing Connelly with another woman attached to his arm is like a hot blade slicing through that frozen tundra and carving out the remainder of my iced-over heart. So many things have happened that should have squashed my hope of getting back together, but I'm too stubborn to take the hints. Or stupid. Now, any shred of irrational hope I've held on to all these weeks crumbles into dust, choking me on the caustic particles.

I want to look away, but I can't. I'm riveted to the train wreck happening right before me.

I watch them wander over to the bar. He pulls out a chair for her. She gazes at him in awe as if he's one of the seven wonders. He takes a seat next to her. She scoots closer. He orders her a drink. She won't take her eyes off him. He gifts her with a panty-melting smile that crushes me. She runs her fingers playfully on his forearm. I can hardly breathe.

I hate her fucking guts. I hate knowing he's out on a date with another woman. I hate that she's touching him when it should be me. I hate that he's not mine anymore. But more than anything, I hate that I just refuse to accept it.

It's been close to two months now since Connelly and I have been intimate and all this time, I've wondered if he's been with other women. I'd hoped against hope, not able to stomach the thought of his hands skimming someone else's curves or his unmatched sexual talents making them weep with pleasure. It's one thing to *think* he may be with another woman...it's quite another to see it with my own two eyes.

Feeling something on my arm, I turn to Livia who has a sad, sympathetic smile on her face. I realize I have no idea how long I've been staring.

"I have to go."

As I get up, though, Addy spouts, "You mean go get your man back from that blonde slut, don't you?"

"No." I shake my head. "No. He doesn't want me. Clearly."

"Nora." Addy stands, gripping my shoulders. "He's a man. And men are...well, their egos are made of tissue paper. His pride is wounded and he's licking it. That's all."

"But what I did, Addy...it's unforgivable."

She smiles like I'm missing something. "Nothing is unforgivable, Nora. You're human. You made a mistake. You owned up to it. Stop beating yourself up about it and woman up. Do you want Conn? Yes or no?"

"More than anything."

"Then go fucking get him and make him listen to you." She stares at me, eyebrows quirked in a dare. An hour is barely enough time to get to know someone but what I can pick up about Addy already is that she's tenacious and full of fire. I like her. Tremendously.

"Okay. Yes. You're right." I want Connelly. It's time I fight for him.

Before I lose my courage, I straighten my shoulders, beginning to close the twenty-five feet that separate Connelly and me, wishing it were more. I have no idea what I'm going to say when I just saunter up to him as if I have every right to him. *"Hey, fancy seeing you here? Who's your slut? I mean, date?"* I think it will take everything in me not to punch blondie in her pixie face or gouge her eyes until they run with scarlet tears. I hope she has one hell of a major medical plan. She may need to cash in on that bad boy tonight. I've never struck another human being in my life, but all I feel is murderous the closer I get to them now that I can hear her high-pitched, fake laugh.

But my nonplan blows up in my stunned face when I'm within five feet. My skin heats and tightens and I swear I hear the collective gasps of the group I just left as the whole thing unfolds before my watery eyes.

Time slows—each drawn-out frame dramatically playing out.

Connelly turns his head.

The curvaceous seductress cups his face.

She leans up.

Shuts her eyes.

Plants an I'm-as-easy-as-my-dress-makes-me-look kiss on his full lips.

Which he returns.

The sand we bury our heads in sometimes is hot and dark and suffocating, but necessary for our emotional survival. Bring on the smothering darkness again, I beg of you.

Instead of making a beeline for them, I walk right on past and make one toward the door. Damn good thing I had my purse with me. I'm not sure I could have made that walk of shame back to the table to retrieve it.

Once I step outside, I see no cabs waiting by the curb, so I quickly make my way toward the end of the block, wishing like hell I'd held my ground and told Kamryn I needed to clean grout tonight instead of letting her talk me into coming out.

I fling my arm in the air, hailing a ride back to the loneliness of my three-bedroom suburban rental when I hear a rumbly male call my name. I look down the street to see Connelly jogging toward me at the same time a yellow cab comes to a screeching halt by my feet, missing my toes by barely an inch.

Ignoring the loud voice gaining on me, I start to open the back passenger door when it's slammed shut from behind. Then I'm being spun around and pressed against the cold metal.

"Where's Hazel?" *Of course.* He's worried about our daughter, not me. The crushing blows keep pounding relentlessly into me.

"She's with Mira. Hazel wanted to spend the night with her."

"What the hell are you doing here?" he asks angrily. *He's* angry? *He's* the fucking one that's angry?

"Oh, I'm sorry. I didn't realize we were sharing our social calendars with each other now. I guess I missed the entry about your little tryst tonight with the golden sprite. My bad," I bite sarcastically.

"Nora." He blows out a frustrated breath. "It's not what it looked like."

"Really? Was she showing you firsthand how to tie a cherry stem with your tongue, then?" I glare at him.

He looks away guiltily. My anger rushes out of me like a valve that was turned on full blast. I just feel...empty. I hang my head, so damn tired of this emotional roller coaster I've been unwillingly riding for the last few weeks. I want off that fucker.

"I don't want to do this anymore, Connelly." I sound defeated. I think I am. I guess I needed a good dose of reality. Well, I got a big healthy, bitter spoonful tonight. I'll never forget the acrid taste.

His finger slides under my chin. He forces it up. "What don't you want to do anymore?"

"Any of it. I don't want to do any of this anymore. I'm so tired of it all."

"So am I," he replies flatly. His eyes roam my face. I feel as though he's cataloging every feature. Everything about his body language says he still wants me, yet he's so goddamned irritatingly calm. It's both confusing and exciting.

"Hey lady," a foreign voice booms. "You getting in or what?"

I answer yes at the same time Connelly yells the exact opposite.

"Don't you need to get back to your *date*?"

I sound like a whiny sixteen-year-old who just caught her boyfriend making out with another girl. Guess I don't really care.

"She is not my date." He enunciates each word. Fingers pinching my bicep, he starts dragging me down the pavement. Away from the bar. Away from my ride. I struggle until I hear tires squeal, indicating the cab has taken off in search of a paying fare. I rip my arm from his hold, unable to stand his touch without wanting it more places than just there.

"Oh, that's right. You don't date. You just fuck," I spit. Increasing my pace, I scan the street for another cab, needing to get the hell out of here before I say something else I'll regret. I want off the damn ride, but I don't know how to make it stop.

I spot a white cab turning the corner, headed

my way. Before I can throw my hand back in the air my back meets a hard, unyielding structure and Connelly's mouth crashes to mine, swallowing my cry. I try to push him away. He shackles my wrists and pulls them over my head, pinning me against the building with his broad, masculine body. My leg unconsciously finds its way around his thigh, opening me so his arousal nestles perfectly in the V of my body.

God, how I want him even though I just saw him with another woman.

What the hell is wrong with me?

"Nora, Jesus I have missed you." Wet lips trail along my jaw. His sharp teeth nip my throat, pulling a long, needy moan from me. Next thing I know my hand is in his and we're walking at a clipped pace once again down the street. I know exactly where we're headed. This wine bar is just two blocks from Connelly's building, which made it convenient for me when I left Mira's.

We're silent on the five-minute walk. When we get to the elevator and step in, a female voice calls for us to hold the door. In walks a gorgeous blonde. Her hands are full of groceries and she doesn't look up when she asks us to push the button for floor eight.

Connelly tenses, but reaches forward and punches it anyway. The elevator starts to ascend. At that moment, blondie chooses to glance up. When her eyes land on Connelly, they steel, then bounce to me, to our twined hands, and back to Connelly before finally stopping on mine.

The corner of her lip sneers up. "I hope you brought a snowsuit."

"Excuse me?" I stutter.

"A snowsuit." She slips her eyes back to Connelly before finishing. "To ward against the frostbite. He'll fuck you, then fuck you over. He's as cold as the Antarctic."

"Lorna," he warns on an angry rumble.

The steel box I'm now suffocating in slows to a stop, the chime indicating we've hit the eighth floor. "What?" she challenges with raised, angry brows. "The female race needs to band together against bastards like you." And with that, she exits without so much as a look back to witness the destruction she's left behind.

Of course. Another scorned woman. *Two women in one night at that.* Jumping into any icy lake in the middle of January in the Antarctica would have felt better than this right here. I don't know what the hell I was thinking coming back with Connelly. Thinking this could work. Thinking he could be faithful.

There was no thought. Clearly.

Connelly will be a great father to Hazel. Seeing them interact and the love he has in his eyes for her, I have no doubt about that now. But that's all he'll ever be. Her dad. Not my lover. Not my husband. Not my anything, except a past I'll have to painfully relive each time I see him.

I start to reach for the lit panel, my index finger grazing the one for the lobby when Connelly shoves me against the wall and takes my mouth with his. It's punishing, demanding. A clear statement.

I want to sink into this. Into him. Into this fantasy I can't seem to shake. But we will never be because of so many reasons and this back and forth between us is just too damn hard to slog through anymore.

Everything in me protests the loss of his lips on me when I tear away. Except my brain. She's the only one thinking clearly. Finally. I try to push him back but it's like a feather moving Mount Everest. Impossible. "Get away."

Powerful muscles keep me pinned while strong hands frame my face. Connelly's determined eyes bore into me. His chest heaves, but the rest of him is in complete control. "Fuck no. I've stayed away too long, Nora. No more. You're coming home with me and we're going to talk."

Talk.

Right.

That smarts a little, but I have no time to whip out my calendar and schedule a mutually agreeable date because the elevator reaches the thirty-fourth floor and I'm being dragged out. Hands still twined, we're on the move again, walking into his condo in short order. Once I hear the door click shut behind us, my nerves flare.

———

"Drink?" Connelly asks in a short tone, heading to the kitchen.

"No, thank you." I need to keep a clear, sharp mind or else I'll get lost in him again. I can't do that anymore. My heart can't take the whiplash.

Connelly grabs a glass from the cupboard and fills it with water before returning to where I'm standing. His voice is even, level, and sincere. "I needed to get out of my condo to think. I ran into Heidi on the way into the bar. She asked if she could join me while she waited for her friends to arrive. I thought it would be rude to say no since I was by myself."

Oh. I drag in a breath. It tastes of sour jealousy. "She clearly wanted you."

A wry smile tips his lips. "I'm not really sure how you want me to answer that, Nora."

"I guess it's rhetorical. And the other?" I tack on, my brows hooking upward.

At least he has the sense to look sheepish. When he doesn't answer, I don't press. I already know anyway and I also know I'll just have to fucking get used to it. I'm sure I'll see him with plenty of women in the future. None of them me.

Sighing, I walk to his bay of windows, gazing into the night sky that I love so much. I see a few bright stars twinkling, but mostly I see blackness, the lights of the city drowning out the beauty of the Milky Way. I feel that way inside. The consequences of my decisions cover me like a thick, wool blanket. Very little light shines through. "I didn't like her lips on yours," is out of my mouth before I can tamp down the green-eyed monster.

"I didn't either, princess." My eyes fall closed at his endearment as his warm breath scatters across my neck. "I haven't been with anyone since

I first laid eyes on you back in that conference room at SER, Nora. I haven't *wanted* to. I want you to know that."

Relief makes me shaky. I wish that changed things between us. I'm afraid it doesn't, though. "We need to talk."

"I know," he answers quietly.

"I'm sorry, Connelly. So very sorry. I know it will never be enough, but I want you to know how much I regret my decision. I understand you'll never be able to forgive me and I'm not asking you to. I know I don't deserve it. I can't forgive myself. I just...I want you to know how truly and deeply full of regret I am." His reflection in the glass blurs as I let the tears carrying my sins flow.

Gently turning me to face him, I can barely stand the anguish on his face. "Why, Nora? Just tell me why?"

"I saw you. The night of your birthday, I came to surprise you and I saw you with her, having sex. I heard her moaning your name, Connelly. I saw everything."

His eyes float shut. A pained look crosses his face before his head drops. "Jesus, Nora. I...I made a fucking huge mistake. I don't even remember it. I was so drunk."

That makes two of us. On all counts.

I continue, needing to purge. "I was devastated so I reacted out of spite. I know it was wrong but I slept with somebody else and when I ended up pregnant I was so in shock I wouldn't even accept it for weeks. Then I—" Shit this is hard. "I came to see you right before you left for college," I finish on a whisper that tastes of bile. I tried to do the right thing early on. It just blew up in my face. The shrapnel that hit me that day bled hot for years.

"You did?" His brows scrunch together. "When?"

I have to force my swallow down. My skin feels so tight it could split open any second. "Mid-August. You were at open gym shooting hoops. I waited outside the building trying to gather up the courage to talk to you—to tell you everything—when I saw you and Alan come out. I was just about to step around the corner when I overheard Alan say how you'd dodged a bullet with Meredith and the baby."

"Oh fuck," he breathes. His hands come up to cover his face. They're trembling.

"And you agreed," I utter softly, the ache of that statement still a fresh wound in my heart. "You said—and I quote—'there's no fucking way a baby is in my future plans.'"

"Nora," he croaks. He drops his hands and lifts his gaze to mine. It's fraught with naked, glistening pain. My own eyes fill back up. "It...fuck, it would have been different with you. I *loved* you. She was just...she was nothing."

I bite my lip, bobbing my head up and down a few times, not knowing how to respond to that. When you're an eighteen-year-old girl who is pregnant by a guy who cheated on you—who got *another* girl pregnant at the same time—leaving him behind is your one and only option.

But of course, I'm no better. I did exactly the same thing. And then I kept it from him. At least I knew all of his indiscretions. I didn't give him the same courtesy.

"That's why you didn't go to Dartmouth like you'd planned. You were pregnant."

I feel my head nodding, but mostly I just feel numb. I need to stay that way to get through this. Not able to look at him while I tell the rest of my story, I head to a stuffed armchair and sit, talking to the floor as I continue. This is, by far, the hardest thing I have ever had to do in my entire life. Even harder than burying my parents.

"I had a rough pregnancy. I had spotting early and ended up on bed rest. Went into premature labor a couple of times, but Hazel didn't want to wait any longer, I guess, and she was born almost four weeks early. She had some respiratory issues and they had to transport her to a children's hospital. Six days after her birth, she contracted an infection and nearly died. She was there for twenty-nine days before they finally released her."

"Jesus, Nora." He's quiet for a moment. "Her middle name? Miracle?"

I nod once.

"Is she okay now? I mean, does she have any residual health issues?" He sounds wrecked.

"She has moderate asthma. She has to limit her physical activity or she goes into coughing fits and can't catch her breath. I think that's one of the reasons she loves photography and design so much. While everyone else was running around, playing outside, she sat on the steps and doodled. But she never complained. She never does. About anything."

He takes a seat on the loveseat, on the edge closest to me. "She's fantastic, Nora."

"She is," I whisper brokenly. "She's incredible. My little miracle." I swallow hard past the lump in my throat, continuing on. "Anyway, shortly after I brought her home, my mom was diagnosed with cancer. I had to take care of both her and a newborn. I drove Mom back and forth to her chemo appointments. I lost track of how many times she ended up in the ER. And Hazel was sick a lot because of her weakened immune system, so I had that to deal with on top of watching my mother slowly and painfully die right before me."

"Fuck," he curses softly. "I hate this. I hate that I wasn't there to help you. To help with Hazel. To help with your mother."

It's not your fault, I think but don't say.

"The guilt ate me raw every day, Connelly. The more Hazel grew, the more I knew she was yours. The more I knew you needed to know. The more it didn't matter what had happened in our past. I, ah..." I take a long, deep fortifying breath. "After my dad died, I did a lot of soul-searching. I essentially grew up without a father and I knew it was unfair of me to put that same thing on Hazel. I'd made the decision you needed to know and was halfway to Chicago two years back."

When I brave a glance at him, all I see is profound sadness. I almost stop and just leave. I don't, though. I need to gut this out.

"I stopped at a convenience store to get gas and some food. I was up at the counter paying when I saw it." I pause. He looks broken because he knows exactly what I saw. "You were on the front cover of a rag."

A heavy sigh escapes him as his gaze falls to the floor again. The headline of that damning article will never leave me.

Chicago Playboy Denies Knocking up Stately Socialite.

He mutters a string of curses under his breath along with, "It wasn't me."

"Yes. I know that now," I reply just as quietly. I remember the intense relief when he told me he didn't have children, followed immediately by the intense shame that he did. He just didn't know.

"I feel like destiny pushed us together but worked like a tireless bitch to pull us back apart." His voice is thick and strained.

I huff a half laugh. Yeah. I feel the same way.

"None of it matters anyway, Connelly. What I did was wrong. I am solely to blame here. Not you or destiny or some rich bimbo who tried to pin down the unattainable playboy. It was all me."

He leans forward, settling himself in the pose I love so much. Legs wide, elbows on knees, hands falling between his spread thighs. So damn manly and sexy. "See, that's the same thing I've been trying to tell myself for the past few weeks. That all the blame falls on you. But it doesn't, Nora. Not *all* of it, anyway. I may not remember that night, but I damn well remember everything that followed. I should have called you. I *wanted* to. I just..." The pause is pregnant, full of grief. "I didn't know how to tell you how massively I'd betrayed you." I bite my trembling lip, hard, keeping the

377

waterworks at bay. "I fucked up, too, and I can't sit here and cling to my righteous indignation anymore."

I look away. Swallow awkwardly. It doesn't matter what he did. Nothing I say can justify my actions. "I had so many excuses. I was always able to rationalize my decision."

"Like my Macy's-worthy revolving door?" he asks a little bitterly, eyes swinging my way.

My smile is fleeting. "Partly, yes." I can't deny the truth, but I can't let him believe that's the main cause either. "But the biggest reason was simply that I was afraid to tell you. That bad decision in the beginning kind of snowballed. The more time that passed the harder it became to face. It's like this lie you hold on to with everything in you and the tighter you hang on, the more your grip becomes frozen and the harder it is to just speak the truth, to admit you were wrong. That was me. I was frozen with fear. I kept telling myself I was doing the right thing, even though deep down I knew I wasn't. There are so many things I'd do differently if I could." I pause briefly before adding, "but I can't."

Silence encases us, sitting heavy. Connelly stares at the floor, his head hung low. He runs his fingers through his hair several times until the unruly locks stand on end. I wonder if our conversation is over. If the silence is my cue to go. After ages of no noise but our soft breathing and whispering regrets, I decide it is, so I make to stand when his hand shoots out and curls around my wrist.

Jaw locked tight, he slides from the couch to kneel in front of me, taking my face between his hands. "Do you forgive me, Nora?"

I start shaking my head, confused. "What do *I* have to forgive?"

"We *both* fucked up. Yours was not trusting me enough, but I didn't trust in us enough, either. You were right back in Cincinnati when you said I had a bruised high school ego. I should have gone after you. Fought for you. Fought for us. Hell, I should have never attended that party and been on a plane to Baltimore instead of sulking like a spoiled brat. I need to know if you forgive me, too."

"I did a long time ago," I whisper unevenly.

His tongue snakes out to catch a lone drip of water tracking down my face before bringing his soft lips to meet mine. Salt and sorrow linger long after he pulls away.

"I'm tired of the baggage, princess. It's too fucking heavy to carry anymore. I need to let it go."

I nod in agreement, not really understanding where this is going or what he's saying.

"Do you still love me, Nora?" His eyes bounce back and forth between mine, anxious.

I bring my hands to his face, cupping his scruff-covered jaw. "I'm not capable of loving anyone else, Connelly."

His steely gaze bores into mine, reaching into that plane that has only ever been reserved for him. "Neither am I. I'll do whatever you need. *Be* whatever you need. Say whatever you want to

379

hear, but I want to be part of your lives, Nora. No matter what. Yours and Hazel's."

I hate the hope building inside. "Part of our lives how?" Hazel's, I understand. Me, however? That's still not clear.

"Selfishly, I want it all. But if that's not possible, I guess in any way you'll let me."

My head is buzzing. When I stumbled behind him to his apartment, I never fathomed he'd be telling me he wants a life with me. With *us*. We have this insane burning chemistry, yes, but could there be more after all we've been through?

"How can you possibly forgive me?" I ask on a choked breath.

In one swift move he's sitting in the chair I was just occupying and I'm straddling his semistiff erection. "How can I not? I've been hollow inside without you. We've missed so much, Nora. I can't bear the thought of missing another second without the two girls I love most by my side."

Relief swims inside me. I'm hardly able to believe what I'm hearing. I don't know if I'll wake up tomorrow and find this has all been a dream. But if it is, I plan to live fully with my head in the clouds of delusion before reality rips me violently to her bosom once again.

"I love you." My voice is nothing but a hoarse wisp of air.

"I love you, princess. So much." His eyes turn positively molten and his voice drops two octaves. "I need to be buried deep inside you, Nora. So fucking deep you feel like you've finally come home."

I already am home.

As soon as he speaks that last word our lips are fused together in a fit of unrestrained passion. We fumble with our shirts, tearing them off in our madness. I hear buttons ping against the end table. My bra goes flying. His hands knead my breasts. His fingers pluck at my nipples. Then he's dipping his head and I'm crying out when he bites one hard before sucking even harder.

"Fuck yes, you taste so good," he croons as he makes his way to the other one. My fingers dig in his hair and I let my head fall back as he feasts, devours, and drives me to the edge of madness.

I'm begging him to ease the ache deep in my center when I hear his husky voice say, "Stand up."

I scramble to my feet, ready to surrender to his every whim.

"Peel those jeans down those sexy legs, Nora. And make it fast." He's making quick work of his own denims, popping the button and loosening the metal teeth enough so he can slip his hand inside. He palms his cock and brings it out to play, smiling ever so slightly.

I want to watch him pleasure himself, but I want him to fuck me more than I want to see his come ribbon his stomach. In seconds, my pants and soaked lace are kicked to the side along with my shoes. I'm now completely bare, waiting. Hardly able to breathe.

"I want that pussy on my mouth," he tells me darkly, making no move to stand or kneel or slide to the floor beneath me. So I crawl onto his lap, hold on to his shoulders, and run the juices of my arousal up and down his dick, never taking my eyes off his. His scratchy jeans abrade my inner thighs, which makes it all the more arousing.

Watching Connelly turn into raw fluid energy beneath my touch is heady and mind-blowing. I feel powerful for a single second until he grumbles, "Enough," and all the power shifts back to him.

Drawing me up his body, he drags his hot tongue down my trembling stomach until my knees are perched on the top of the chair on either side of his head. It's ridiculously hedonistic and sexy to have my splayed pussy just inches from his mouth. Thank God I waxed last week.

When Connelly gazes up the line of my body my sex clenches. Hard. And when that wicked smile turns his mouth up I gush so much I feel a trickle of need now smearing the insides of my thighs. "I'm going to eat you until your voice is ruined."

"Oh God," I breathe. My legs already burn from the position I'm holding.

His deft fingers spread me open. Running a single finger through my slit, he rumbles, "Nora, so damned ready for me. Always. Christ." Another rush of liquid seeps out. Then his tongue darts out and circles my clit so lightly, so teasingly. My legs give way, but strong arms wrap around the backs of my thighs to keep me from falling.

"Connelly, please," I beg, undulating my hips, trying to get what I need from him. My sex is empty. I need something. Anything to quench this fire culminating.

"You want to coat my tongue like you just did my cock, don't you, Nora?"

My yes is swallowed up in a lust-induced fog when he lowers his head between my spread thighs and devours me in an openmouthed kiss. In one long lick from back to front, his tongue unravels me. Tears me apart. Within moments, I'm moaning and writhing uncontrollably under his talented mouth. In under less than two minutes, I'm coming apart at the seams, moaning for him over and again.

My muscles liquefy. When his hold releases, I slide down his torso in a sated heap, ready to sleep. But he has other plans. Controlling my body with incredible ease, he places me on his lap and drives inside me in one smooth, ruthless thrust. I gasp at the fullness, feeling something I didn't think I'd ever feel again.

Perfection.

Peace.

Whole.

"Hell, yes. You're mine," he grunts in my ear, pumping like a man unhinged. "Mine, Nora."

His declaration tears free the brittle threads that have held me together. He painstakingly unravels me thoroughly and completely so he can put me back together again, stitch-by-stitch, the way I was always meant to be. Joined to him. I was *his*. I *am* his in a way I've never been able to comprehend. My body responds to his nearness, setting my soul free and making me sigh in contentment.

"Always. I'm yours," I pant.

"I've...missed...you...so...damned...much." Each word is rumbled in time with the ferocious stab of his hips. "So fucking tight and hot. Squeeze my cock, baby." His groan is long and broken when I obey.

Burying my head in the crook of his neck, I cry out as his thrusts become more urgent, more uncontrolled. My entire body shakes. I am a wild, reckless, hot twisted mess.

"Ah, Nora. God, I can't hold back." I feel him swell right before he stiffens. His grip tightens to the point of bruising. His head falls back at the same time my name cascades out on the most erotic moan I have ever heard. That, combined with the wash of his seed deep inside, sets off my own fireworks. The rush of rapture firing through me is almost blinding. I bask in the heady glow as long as I can before gravity tugs me back to reality.

As we come down from our intense high, my body trembles against his and he holds me closer. He never stops whispering kisses over my chilled flesh when he withdraws and carries me silently through his condo to his bedroom. He cleans me reverently. He comforts thoroughly. Tucking me into him, he draws the sheets over us and strokes my sweaty hair.

"Sleep, sweet girl," he rumbles against the crown of my head.

I want to. I'm absolutely exhausted. Emotionally and physically. I can't, though, without saying one last time, "I'm—"

"I forgive you," he interrupts. "I forgive you, Nora. We can't rewrite history. We can't change our decisions as much as we wish otherwise. We have to live with our mistakes, but we don't have to let them rule our future. I want to start over. I want to bury this and make the life with you and Hazel that we should have had. That I *want* to have now."

His plea is heartfelt and sincere, not full of blame. It tears at me somewhere deep down. I tip my face up to meet his eyes. "You can really forgive me? After all I've done?"

"Yes. I didn't realize that I could do nothing *but* forgive you until I saw you run out of that bar. Every step you took away from me was like a fresh wound to my soul, Nora. It's taken me a while, and I'm sorry for that, but as someone wise recently told me, hanging on to resentment is like wearing cement shoes. I don't want to look back on my life and realize I'd drowned with them on. I don't want to lose you again. I told you, princess, that baggage is too heavy and I'm tired of carrying it. All I want, all I *need* is you and Hazel."

"Is this real?" I whisper the same question he did just weeks ago. My head is a jumble.

His face is soft and loving. Stroking my cheek, he says, "As real as it gets, baby."

He rolls me on top of him and frames my face. "Never leave me again."

Slowly, a smile creeps across my face. "I thought you said never say never."

A smirk curls those beautifully swollen lips of his before he says, "In this particular case, I think never is appropriate, wouldn't you agree?"

Grinning, I say, "I do."

"I'm thinking about tying you to my bed, just to make sure you stay put," he says, his tenor low and gravelly.

"You've tied many a woman to your bed, have you?" I ask teasingly, but the thought makes jealousy stir.

"I don't let women in my bed, Nora." I almost laugh before the earnestness of his tone catches up with me. It's then I realize that Connelly and I have been treading a parallel path. I've not had many lovers while he's had too many, but the one thing we've had in common is our inability to be emotionally intimate with anyone else. We've both lived lonely lives, just in very different ways.

"So I would be a first?" I push.

It's dark, but I still see his sincere grin. "You seem to be the first with a lot of things. The only, in fact."

"Okay then, I'm definitely game." My voice comes out sultry and needy at the thought of being the only woman completely at his mercy.

Chuckling, he pulls me down for a drugging kiss before draping me over him once again. "Sleep for a while, princess. You're going to need it. Because my goal before the sun breaks is to make you come so many times you lose count."

I try to tell him that I don't need sleep; I'm ready to start losing count now. But when I open my mouth, a yawn sneaks out instead and my eyes shut before I can tell them why they should stop. I feel like I haven't slept in a month. As I drift toward unconsciousness, I hear Connelly whisper that he loves me. His arms squeeze protectively, keeping me safe. Keeping me his.

My journey has been long and tumultuous, but I know I've reached my final destination.

It only took me eleven lonely years to arrive.

Chapter 33

CONN

Lord, she is impossibly beautiful. And mine.

Sitting on the edge of the bed, I watch Nora sleep. Dark lashes rest against her fair skin. They remind me of inky fans. Her breaths are shallow and even. Lips still kiss-swollen. She's more peaceful than I've ever seen her.

She belongs here. In my bed. In my life.

It feels right.

I know some people will scratch their heads at my decision to forgive Nora. Even adamantly disagree with it, thinking her punishment should be perpetual. She kept me from my daughter and my daughter from me. Yes, it was an egregiously bad decision, but I also know in my heart of hearts at the young, immature age of nineteen, knowing she slept with someone else and wasn't sure if Hazel was mine would have been too raw, too ego bruising, and absolution would have been impossible, regardless of my own mistakes at the time.

The thing is, mistakes aren't measured in

ounces and pounds, the scales tilting in favor of one or the other. If they do, that's called a grudge and your side will always weigh more, holding you back, keeping you down. You will lose, even though you'll think you're winning.

So, no. Her sins are not heavier than mine or vice versa. Hers are no less deserving of forgiveness than my own. Our errors in judgment are exculpated by compassion, understanding, and empathy. But most of all, unconditional love. It's far easier sometimes to play judge and jury and condemn without understanding than to do our own soul-searching.

When I saw Nora walk out of that bar misunderstanding what she thought she'd witnessed, I saw my future leave with her. It took me until that very moment to know beyond a shadow of a doubt that I had no choice *but* to forgive her. My soul has screamed for her all these years. She's opened my eyes to all of the things in my life I've been missing but refused to acknowledge. Love, companionship, comfort in the arms of someone who actually gives a shit about you and your well-being.

But regardless of how forgiveness plays into our situation, there is no future without Nora. We share a child. We share responsibilities. We will forever share a life whether together or apart. And I tried to picture it with her floating in the periphery. I pictured her eventually meeting and falling in love with somebody else. I envisioned her pregnant with another man's baby. I saw myself forever pining for her like I've already been doing for so many years. And it gutted me. Ruined me.

My mom was right, and not just about removing baggage.

Nora owns my love. She's my beginning and ending, the whole space in between. My forever.

So whether anyone agrees with my decision is completely irrelevant. I know this place, right here, right now, with Nora sharing my bed is what's right for me and my family. I just hope she can forgive herself.

Nora shifts and I glimpse a hint of her dark pink areola peeking out from the covers. My cock swells. The urge to drag down the sheet that's covering her and take her again is raw and pulsing. Her moans and pleas from the many ways I wrung the last ounce of pleasure from her body last night still echo loudly in my ears.

"Ready for number five?"

"Five, huh?" She sighs in contentment. "I didn't think that was possible in one day, let alone one hour."

"That sounds like a challenge, princess."

"It wasn't. Trust me."

"Too late."

I stopped keeping track at seven. Nora's brain had turned to sated mush far earlier. I want to wake her, but I won't. As it is, I think I woke her about every two hours all night long because of my inability to control my insatiable desire for her. These last few weeks without her have been hell.

With a heavy sigh, I pull on some gym shorts and exit the bedroom. When she wakes, we need to talk about getting our family back together. Permanently. I want the three of us living under the same roof. I want access to my girls twenty-four seven and I don't plan on wasting any more time. I have no idea how Nora will react, but I have no intent on letting her say no. I've never been more resolved about what I want.

I'm in the kitchen, starting to pull the things together I'll need to make crepes when my cell rings.

"Up awful early, aren't you?" I quip, unable or unwilling to hide my good mood.

"It's after eleven already. I'd hardly call that early," my twin replies.

"Is it really?" I hadn't even bothered to look at the time yet.

"Talked to Mom yesterday."

"Yeah?" I want to tell Ash about my reconciliation with Nora, my grand plans for the future. Ash has been nothing but supportive of whatever I decide, but he's been the one who's pressing hardest on me to give Nora a second chance. I've found that a bit odd, given the fact that Asher's not the forgive-and-forget type. We couldn't be more opposite in that regard. I think perhaps his wife has something to do with his newfound change of heart.

"Yeah. About fucking time you told her," he chastises on a loud breath.

"Imagine my surprise when she already knew."

"Knew what?" he feigns.

"You're so full of shit, Ash."

"This is not news, brother," he drawls. Asher is shameless, as always.

I chuckle, unable to help it. I love him unconditionally anyway, even if he does butt his nose into my business when it's not welcome. I think back to when I practically forced him to call his ex, Natalie, so he could break free of her invisible hold. He needed to in order to give Alyse all of him. *Hmmm.* Two peas in a pod, I guess.

"So, did she help provide some clarity?"

"Doesn't she always?"

"Yes, asshole. That's why I've been telling you to talk to her."

A noise from the hallway draws my attention.

"Jesus," I breathe lightly. Nora's standing in the opening of the kitchen wearing the royal-blue button-down I had on last night. There's a single button holding the two halves together. The one that's straining just below her voluptuous breasts. I'm quite sure I've not seen a sexier sight than a scantily clad Nora in *my* shirt. No woman has ever worn my clothing. I would barely let a female in my place, let alone in my attire. On the spot, I decide I want to see Nora in it every day.

"What?" I ask Ash when I realize he's still talking.

"I said what are you going to do?"

"What am I going to do?" I repeat Ash's question slowly while holding my woman's burning gaze. I answer, speaking to my brother, yet every word is meant only for her. "I'm going to reunite my family. I'm going to be the father Hazel needs. I'm going to be the man Nora deserves. I'm going to marry her and have loads of babies."

With every word I speak, her eyes grow wider. Her mouth falls open a little farther, and my grin gets cockier.

"You can have the land," I add before he has a chance. He won, fair and square and I could give a flying fuck. Everything I need is standing right in front of me. Well, except for my daughter.

"Nah. I don't want it."

"What?" I respond in surprise. "You've been giving me shit about that for months. Now you say you don't want it?"

Nora glides toward me, her gate sure and elegant. She looks to be floating an inch above the floor. Her face has turned from that of surprise to pure hunger and my cock goes rock hard in one point three seconds. I need to get Ash off the damn phone. Right. Fucking. Now.

"All I ever wanted was for you to be happy, Conn. It sounds like you are."

I stifle a groan when Nora's lips skate across my neck to my shoulder. I fist her hair when her teeth find my flat nipple and clamp down. I have to remember to breathe when she grabs my stiffness through loose fabric.

"Besides I don't want to pay the taxes on a land worth over a mil," he chuckles darkly.

What? Is he still talking?

"I gotta go." I throw my phone on the counter, hoping I've disconnected. "Nora, baby, what are you doing?" I rasp when she drops to her knees. Nails scrape my flank on her downward descent before my shorts pool around my ankles. The sting is sweet. Addicting.

My head falls against the cupboard when her breath trickles hot across my straining dick, washing me in scorching desire.

"Fuuuuck," I hiss. Every muscle in my body tenses when her tongue teasingly circles my throbbing tip. Rounding me several times first, she groans when she finally takes me shallowly inside her warm mouth before repeating the entire provocative process again. Gripping the base of my cock, she squeezes hard at the same time she gently fondles my balls. I jerk, almost losing it.

Christ Almighty. I've had plenty of women do this for me over the course of the last few years, but nothing has felt like this. Nora's mouth is pure, unadulterated perfection. It's as if she knows exactly what I like and how I like it, but this is the very first time I've had the intoxicating pleasure of her mouth on me.

I try holding back.

I want to let her take the lead.

I want to let her set the pace.

I want to fuck her mouth slowly, drawing out my pleasure. Feel every euphoric tingle as it crawls up my spine.

But my wants mutate into frantic need the second she drags my rigid length all the way to the back of her throat and moans. Her hum is a mind eraser. All my good intentions were just destroyed with her swallow.

"Nora, shit."

Fingers twine, caught in her fiery strands. My

hips pump with sure strokes, and I have just one goal in mind. The flawless suction of Nora's mouth pushes me to the edge hard and swift. Embarrassingly fast. I'm a coiled solid mass of nothing but sensation.

"So fucking good," I rumble in exquisite desperation as she expertly works me into an absolute frenzy.

I need to slow down, savor this, but it's far too late. My orgasm is already barreling down on me with a violence I can't stop. I want to come down her throat, watch her take every drop of me, but the urge to mark Nora's naked flesh with my seed is crude and primitive, a necessity I can't resist. I pull out of her heat, rip my shirt she's wearing open, and fist my cock as I finish myself off all over her gorgeous, heaving tits with a throaty rumble.

"That was hot," she murmurs a little shyly, her face flushing even more. My hand is still wrapped tightly around her long hair, tipping her head up so her eyes never leave mine. I grudgingly unwind the tangled fingers as I relax the others still squeezing the life out of my dick.

"That was unexpected," I say with a smirk, dropping my gaze to the strings of milky white now decorating her puckered nipples. I reach down to swirl the cooling sticky substance around her nub with my index finger. She shivers. When my eyes sweep back up, I add, "And undeniably hot."

I grab a paper towel, reluctantly handing it to her as I help her to her feet. She has to yank it from my hand, laughing. "Want me to rub it in and skip a shower?" she teases.

"Would you?" I reply. Seriously.

Her happiness radiates off my walls, the melodic notes squeezing my heart. I watch in disappointment as the evidence of my virility is wiped away with a few flicks of her wrist. My frown makes her eyes light up with delight.

"No, but I *would* let you do it again," she saucily breathes against my mouth before wrapping her arms around my neck and kissing me slowly. My dick stirs again.

"I will take you up on that, princess."

"Who were you talking to?" she asks tentatively, watching me closely.

I wrap my arms around her waist, pulling her into my already stiffening cock. She trembles a tad and I grin. God, I will never get enough of her. I feel like a horny eighteen-year-old again. "Ash."

"Did you mean it? What you said?"

Looking deeply into her eyes, I confess simply, "Every word, Nora."

"I feel like I need to pinch myself," she whispers, water filling her eyes.

"I am sure I can help you out with that." There are plenty of places on her I'd like to pinch before soothing the bite. I swoop down, taking her mouth in a scorching kiss and am getting ready to throw her down on my kitchen table so I can eat my kind of breakfast when I hear her stomach grumble.

"I need to feed you," I groan, leaning my forehead against hers. We both work to catch our breaths, which had taken off in anticipation of yet another sweaty workout.

"I can wait." But her belly disagrees. Loudly.

With a quick kiss, I unwind her from me and tug the two parts of hanging fabric together so her magnificent body does not tempt me. "Go shower while I make breakfast for us, princess."

She hesitates.

"What is it?" I ask, feeling her worry.

"I..." When she looks away for a moment, I already know this conversation is going places I'm not going to like. "I just think we should take things slow. With Hazel, I mean. If for some reason this doesn't work out between us, it would crush her."

Oh hell no. Fuck. No.

"No."

"Connelly," she starts to protest.

"Stop." She does only because I don't give her a choice with my fingers now clamping her lips closed. "Let's talk about this after we've eaten, okay?" Little does she know there will be no discussion. Period. By the end of this week, I *will* be living with her and Hazel in her rental until we can figure out where we'll move permanently. I love my condo and will hate to be away from my brothers, but the heart of the city is not the best place to raise a ten-year-old. I may not know a lot about kids yet, but I do know that.

"Okay," she acquiesces. She sees my resolve, but I know she's steeling herself for a fight to protect our daughter. I commend her for that, though it also stings she thinks I would do that to her. To them. Deep down, I hope she knows I would never hurt them.

Placing a kiss on her temple, I swat her on the ass so hard she squeals. "Off to the shower with you now so I can cook. You're a distraction."

"I love you, babe," she purrs in my ear. I feel a sting on my lobe. Before I can react she's run halfway across the kitchen.

"Nora," I growl, "you're gonna pay for that, princess."

"I was hoping you'd say that," she throws insolently over her shoulder, sashaying down the hall and out of my sight.

It's official.

Both of my girls have me wrapped completely and thoroughly around them.

I'm whipped.

And I'm decidedly okay with that.

Chapter 34

Nora

I take my time under the hot spray, reliving every single second of the past twelve hours, still not able to believe I haven't fallen into some alternate universe where all of your dreams turn into reality. Any minute I expect to see tiny fairies with tiny magical wands flying around by their tiny wings. I feel like if I blink a second too long or take too deep of a breath this will all just disappear and I'll be waking up alone in my bed once again.

Connelly wants me.

He forgives me.

He wants to be a family.

He wants to *marry* me.

Marry. Me.

I saw the hurt in his eyes when I told him I wanted to go slow. I used Hazel as an excuse, but I think I'm protecting myself just as much. I would break completely if this didn't work and I didn't lie that Hazel would be crushed. She's already hinted several times about us all living happily ever after.

The crazy girl has even picked out names for her fantasy siblings. I've tried to gently redirect her without crushing her burgeoning hope, but she refuses to listen. She's adamant about a future with Connelly. She's been surprisingly more mature about this entire thing than either her father or me.

I guess my young-in-age but mature-at-heart daughter had foresight I couldn't even imagine.

Last night, I felt the weight of every burden I've carried alone for so long being lifted one by the one with each word I spoke. I felt like I could take a deep, cleansing breath for the first time in years. I got everything off my chest that I'd always wanted to say. I unloaded every sin, every worry, every mistake. I vomited it all.

Except one.

That one I hope he never discovers. That's the one I fear would crush him the most. That may even be the most unforgivable sin of all.

Chapter 35

CONN

I heard the water turn off just minutes ago. I've stood here over the heat of the stove for the last fifteen minutes fantasizing about Nora's naked body in my glass shower stall, hot water sluicing down her curves, greedily hugging the perfect lines of her body. I envisioned her cupping her pussy and kneading her full breasts as she washed the final remnants of my scent away.

The caveman in me takes over at that thought. I need to mark her again. I inanely wonder if my brothers all feel like this about their women. I make a mental note to discreetly ask them next time we're together.

As I impatiently wait for Nora to return so I can feed her and fuck her, in that order, the doorbell rings. I quickly assess what I'm wearing—green and white baggy gym shorts and nothing else—and decide it will be fine. It's probably Ash anyway.

I fling open the door expecting my brother's face to be staring back at me but have to drop my surprised gaze on my little girl standing there instead.

"Hazel? What are you doing here?" I glance down the hallway to see Ella's nowhere to be found. I'm suddenly angry. "Where's your aunt?"

Hazel ignores my outburst and breezes through the entryway.

"Are you just wandering the halls by yourself?" I demand as I follow her to the kitchen.

"Daddy, I'm ten years old. Actually, I'm closer to eleven now than ten. I'm not a baby. You know I can babysit *actual* babies when I'm eleven?" I'm a bit taken aback at the chastising grumble that comes from her little mouth. She's a miniature version of her mother.

"Of course you're not. I didn't mean to imply you were a baby. I just...does Ella, I mean Mira, know where you are?"

A little eye roll accompanies her answer. "Yes."

"And she let you come here by yourself?"

"You mean, did she let me walk down the *hallway* by myself?"

I feel like a fish gasping for air, my mouth opens and closes so many times while no words come out. This is a side of my daughter I've yet to see. Then she gives me a little smile, which is more like a smirk, and I'm hooked once again. "Okay, point taken."

Hazel lazily hops up on a chair at the island. Her eyes pop at the feast I've laid out for Nora and me. Fresh fruit, including blueberries, strawberries, raspberries, and sliced bananas accompany homemade crepes and hand-whipped cream. I'd honestly planned to eat most of my meal off of Nora, but I guess that will have to wait.

Suddenly I understand the perils having children has on your sex life. That just makes me all the more resolved to be creative because Hazel's mother and I are just getting started with all of the wicked sins I will be lavishing on her. If that means breakfast in our bedroom at two in the morning, then so be it. I don't need much sleep anyway.

"Hungry, Ladybird?" I ask with a grin.

"Famished!" she replies excitedly as she balances on her knees in her seat. She told me last week she loves it when I use her nickname, so I've tried to use it as often as possible.

I fill a plate with two of the French pancakes and start to pile some fruit on when I realize I don't know what she likes. "Anything I shouldn't add?"

Her little nose wrinkles up. "No raspberries. I don't like the seeds."

"Neither do I." I wink, drawing a giggle from her. "You probably don't like whipped cream, either, right?" The withering look I get makes my heart melt. "I'll take that as a yes, then."

Setting the meal in front of her, I add, "Sorry I don't have any nuts. I'm allergic." Sometimes I forget about all the things people eat nuts on, crepes being one of them.

Her gaze snaps to mine. "You are?"

"Yep," I nod, grabbing my own plate to fill. "Have been since I was a baby."

"Me too," she whispers in awe. Our eyes lock

403

and I feel something unnamed pass between us. I think maybe it's unconditional love.

"We have a lot in common, yeah?"

She just bobs her head and silence envelopes us.

"I knew when we moved here that something good was going to happen to us."

"You did? Why?" I take a seat next to her, giving her my full attention.

"Do you believe in signs?"

I dip my head in agreement, thinking about all the signs that have been right in front of me, which I've ignored.

"Me too. I saw my good luck sign the night we moved here."

"What's your good luck sign, Hazel?" I think I know what she'll say. She's wearing it around her wrist even now, but I'm shocked at her explanation.

"A dragonfly."

"I thought it was a ladybug?"

"Ladybugs are good luck too, but..."

"But what?" I prod at her hesitation. I reach for her small hand, taking it in mine. "You can tell me anything, Hazel."

"But so are dragonflies. And Mommy told me once that dragonflies are creatures of water, just like my daddy."

I frown, not understanding what either she, or Nora, would have meant by that, but my brilliant girl clears it up for me quickly. Apparently she's inherited a love of all things philosophical like her mother.

"The sign, Cancer, is a water element. So I just knew when I saw a dragonfly stuck in my window on the first night we moved in that you were here." She looks at me briefly before continuing. "And Mommy once told me that my daddy was a water sign like me. Pisces. And that's why I was born so early, so I could be like him."

My breath stops. My eyes actually tear.

A sniffle from the corner of the room draws my attention away from Hazel. When my gaze clashes with Nora's, I fly into action without even thinking. Next thing I know her face is between my fingers, her lips meshed with mine. I kiss her and kiss her and kiss her until I remember our girl is nearby, watching. I'm not sure what the protocol is for showing affection in front of your child, but if it's anything other than acceptable, I'm changing the damn rules.

"There is no you, Nora. There is no me. There's just us. Do you understand? Just us."

"Yes."

I am demanding and she is sweetly compliant. It makes me so fucking hard when she surrenders to me like this. Remembering our daughter is looking on, I will my dick to at least a semihard state, grateful for my loose shorts, and chance a glance at Hazel. She is beaming from ear to ear. I expected disgust or maybe even apathy, but pure joy radiates from her like sunlight on a brand new day.

"It okay with you if I move in this week, Hazel?"

I hear Nora's gasp, but I couldn't care less. I want Nora. I want Hazel. I want them forever. I don't plan on asking permission to piece my fractured family back together.

"Yeah!" she yells jumping off the chair and into my arms.

When my eyes slide back to Nora, she's just shaking her head, but a grin that looks just like Hazel's is painted on her face.

Love can hurt and heal. It can break and mend. It can be the loneliest place on earth or fill you will such a sense of completeness you feel like you're going to ignite.

With both my girls in my arms, I'm on fucking fire.

Chapter 36

Nora

For weeks now things have clicked along smooth as glass. Connelly didn't wait a week to move in. He loaded up his car with a few days' worth of clothes that Sunday night when he took us home. He's been with us ever since.

Hazel is in heaven and I do believe I am right there with her.

He'll drop casual hints here and there about marriage, but he's yet to come outright and ask me. At first, I was a little miffed, but I think I'm okay with it now. I know I don't need a piece of paper to make our relationship true and real.

"Knock, knock."

I would recognize that voice anywhere. He's been avoiding me like the plague lately.

"Come on in, stranger."

Brad saunters inside. Leaving the door open, he takes a seat across from me. My desk separates us, but he feels so far away it may as well be the Grand Canyon. It makes my heart hurt.

"Yeah, sorry about that," he replies awkwardly, throwing one leg over the other.

"I've missed you," I tell him lowly.

His eyes have been wandering everywhere, avoiding contact with mine. I taste good-bye suspended in the air.

"Again, sorry."

"Why do I feel like you're not here to talk about business?"

When his grays latch on to me, all I see is sorrow. He takes one long breath and before he speaks, I already know what he'll say. "I wanted to tell you in person that I've handed in my resignation."

"Brad, no...Why?"

He half snorts, half laughs. "Nora, do you really need to ask?"

Suddenly angry, I lean back in my chair and cross my arms. "Yes, I really do *need* to ask."

His eyes turn to steel and his jaw tightens. "Fine. You already know, but since you're making me say it, I'm not going to hold back. I can't watch you with *him*, that's why. I don't think you comprehend how in love with you I am, Nora, and I can't witness firsthand *him* living the life that *I* want with you. That's fucking torture. Daily. Fucking. Torture. It's one thing to know I can't have you. It's another thing entirely to know someone else does."

"Brad," I start with compassion, "you knew there couldn't be anything between us. I've made that very clear. I've never led you to believe otherwise."

His eyes flit away briefly. "I know." His resigned voice just about breaks me. I hate that my friend is hurting because of me and there's nothing I can do about it. "I just always held out hope, like I imagine you did with him."

Now it's my turn to look away. I don't know what to say. I'm sorry seems appropriate, but I'm not. I'm sorry he's *hurting*, but I won't apologize for being with Connelly, where I'm meant to be.

"You don't have to leave, Brad. Not because of this."

He smiles sadly. "I do. Reverse the roles, Nora. If he were with someone else, what would you do?"

That's a stupid question. I would rip her fucking eyes from their sockets.

I try a different tactic. "Connelly won't accept your resignation."

His mouth turns down. "He already did."

After a silent stare-off, I croak, "I'm sorry."

His head bobs back and forth as he stands. "Don't be sorry, Nora. I've only ever wanted to see you happy. I'd just hoped it could eventually be with me, but you're where you're supposed to be. And so is Hazel."

I swallow thickly.

"You are happy, right?" I hate the small thread of hope he has in his voice.

"Very."

He nods once sharply, turning around one last time before he leaves. "You call if you ever need me, yeah?"

"Of course I will."

I'm still watching the space Brad just vacated

409

trying to work through my mixed emotions when Connelly steps through my doorway. The look on his face says it all.

"You heard, didn't you?"

"Yes," he replies. Unrepentant, I might add.

I want to chuckle, but I'm still reeling a bit, sad to be losing a good friend even though it's selfish of me. "You followed him here, didn't you?"

Connelly shuts my door and closes the scant distance between us. I squeak when he picks me up out of my chair and sets me on my desk like I weigh nothing. He stands between my legs and holds my head still with his large hands. "Yes, I did. And I won't apologize. He was going to make one final play for you."

"He was telling me good-bye," I argue.

"Nora, even you aren't that obtuse."

My lips curl, remembering how I called him that at the welcome party a few months ago.

"You clearly haven't learned the rules of personal space yet," I whisper hoarsely, unable to concentrate on anything now but the flames of desire dancing in his eyes.

He dips his head, skimming my jaw with his nose before sucking the sensitive skin underneath hard. "Princess, I know the rules. I simply choose not to follow them when it comes to you."

My core gushes for him, like it always does, but he groans and pulls away before I have a chance to even reach for the simple mechanics that are keeping him from me.

"I want you," I moan, my hands going to his waist.

"Jesus, I want to fuck you and tattoo every inch of you so every fucking man on this planet knows you belong to me." He's growly, possessive. I love it.

"Feeling the need to mark your territory?"

"Yes," he answers shamelessly, his lips a hair away from mine.

"Then do," I urge.

He drops his forehead to mine on a painful groan. "I wish I could, baby. I admit, I have another reason for being here. It's work related." At my pout, he grins and adds, "But we'll definitely pick this up later. Doesn't Hazel have photography lessons tonight?"

I nod.

"Good. I haven't fucked you on the back patio yet and I plan to remedy that."

"God, Connelly." My heart rate surges at his sinful words. The prospect of doing something so wicked excites me.

Resigned to the fact that I need to wait until later to assuage the burning in my center, I ask, "So what did you need?"

"Alred called this morning."

I immediately stiffen. In my entire career, I have never come across a more blatant chauvinist than Alred Kinnick. Most men at least *attempt* to hide their bigoted opinions, but he seems to go out of his way to showcase them like he's proud of his small dick and even smaller mind.

"You do realize I can't do my job if he calls you every time he needs something, right?"

"I'm sorry, Nora. Can't teach an old dog new tricks, I guess."

411

"Well you can put the bitch down, then," I mumble snidely under my breath. His chuckle eases the sting of the situation a little. I have given *Alred* no less than a dozen highly capable candidates for his CEO position over the past two months and he picks each one apart. God help the person who does pass his unreasonable scrutiny.

"He has a new candidate he'd like *us* to talk to."

Us. Of course.

"Who?"

"Alan Johansen."

I swear by all that's holy, every molecule of oxygen was just sadistically sucked out of my hundred-twenty-square-foot office space.

"Alan?" I can't breathe.

"Yeah, he's the CEO at a midsized investment firm in Maryland. Kinnick got wind of him somehow and is intrigued. As luck would have it Alan's in Chicago for the next few days speaking at a conference and he has time for dinner tonight. I've already talked to him and we'll be meeting at The Met at seven."

I open my mouth, unsure of what's going to come out other than oh-hell-to-the-fucking-no, when he speaks over me. "I already talked to Gray. Landyn is going to take Hazel to their place after school, so we'll just spend the night at my place since we'll probably get in late. I guess I'll have to fuck you on the patio another time."

I ignore his joke.

"Connelly—"

I'm once again cut off, this time with a quick kiss. "I gotta run, princess. I'm already late for meeting with Ash. It will be great to catch up with our third, won't it?" he adds excitedly.

Our third. The tripod of Dowling High, us three. Where Connelly went, so did Alan, so we spent a lot of time together.

Once again I'm left staring at nothing but air, my mind still spinning on the tilt-a-whirl.

I haven't seen or heard from Alan Johansen in over a decade. The last I've seen of my one-time good friend was the horrifying morning I woke up in his arms the night after Connelly's birthday party. The last time I talked to him was a week later to make sure he understood how much of a mistake I'd made when I begged him not to tell Connelly about either us or the fact that I'd seen Connelly with someone else.

Alan was the one who'd helped me plan the surprise visit for Connelly's birthday. Alan was the one who picked me up from the airport and drove me to his house when my flight was delayed by four hours because of severe thunderstorms in Baltimore. Alan was the one standing beside me as we watched a beautiful brunette writhe on my love's naked body.

And Alan, the third in our tight little unit, a boy I loved but was not in love *with*, was the one who intimately comforted me after I'd drunk myself into a black stupor.

He is my biggest mistake. My deepest regret. And the one unforgivable betrayal Connelly can never discover.

Chapter 37

CONN

To say that the tension at our quiet table could be cut with any type of knife, dull or sharp, would be an understatement. Alan will hardly take his eyes from Nora and Nora will barely acknowledge his existence. It's starting to make me wonder what the fuck is going on here. Whatever it is, I don't like it.

I'm reminded of my conversation with Gray on the dock a couple months back.

"Did he like Nora?"

"Who?" I ask, thoughts still clouded by yesterday's mistakes.

"Alan."

Alan. Yes. I'm pretty damn sure he was in love with her, too. "Who wouldn't like Nora? She was a dick magnet."

"And you trusted the friend who's been jealous of you your entire life not to say anything to a girl he also liked? Who you won over him?"

"So, Alan, how's Lydia?" His fucking *wife*.

Dragging his gaze away from my Nora, my friend of twenty-five years looks at me. "She's good, man. Spends her days taking tennis lessons and getting spa treatments. Just what every wife of a CEO should be doing."

"Wow, Alan," Nora's razor-sharp voice cuts in. "I didn't take you for such a misogynist. You'll fit right in at Kinnick Investments."

"Nora," I chastise, unable to believe how she's acting.

I think I may hear her apologize under her breath, but can't be sure. *What the fuck is going on?*

Alan just laughs, clearly oblivious to her ire. "Temper still matches her hair, I see," he jokes, but nobody laughs. This little reunion is not going at all like I'd planned. I expected a relaxing night of moseying down memory lane, but now I wish I hadn't agreed to this meeting. All I want to do is get Nora back to my place so I can spend a couple hours enjoying how right she feels underneath me before we get Hazel.

I redirect our conversation back to business so I can get this over with. "You interested in this challenge, Alan?"

"Hell, yes. It's a great opportunity. Alred Kinnick is an investment God. This would be a dream job."

"No issues relocating?"

"Not in the least. The wife has some family in Louisville, so this would be closer for her. And no kids to worry about. Yet." He winks.

Nora remains unusually quiet as we spend the next hour discussing the position, the job requirements, and the challenges of working for Alred Kinnick. No matter how brilliant he is, the fact remains Alred's an epically fucked-up bastard and working for him would not be an easy feat, even for someone who appears to worship him.

We pass on dessert but take coffee when the conversation turns more personal. And uncomfortable.

"Do you remember that epic birthday party I threw you after graduation, Conn?"

Alan pointedly eyes me with something I can only decipher as hostility. He's deliberately throwing me under the bus in front of Nora.

Alan and I have stayed in touch over the years, often catching up when we're both back home over the holidays or whenever he happens to be in town or I'm on the East Coast. But as with everyone else, life gets busy and we don't talk as often as we used to.

When we spoke earlier today, though, we spent a few minutes catching up on events over the past year. I brought him up to speed on my brothers, my nephews, and my mom's new man. I told him about my recent acquisition of SER and reuniting with Nora. I left out the part about our daughter because I didn't feel it necessary to air our dirty laundry to the world, but I got the impression from him even through the phone that he was surprised. And envious, even though he's married to a very beautiful, very young, twenty-three-year-old sexpot.

"Excuse me," Nora says, her voice tight. Standing, she throws her napkin down before heading in the direction of the ladies' room.

"What the fuck are you doing, Johns?" I demand, reverting to my old high school nickname for my best friend. I glare at him, simmering. I hate how my cool veneer is cracking, but fuck, he's pissing me off. That was an unnecessarily intentional low blow.

"What? Just wanted to talk about old times. Don't be so goddamned touchy, Colloway."

My eyes slide in the direction Nora just took, then back to Alan. I study him quietly trying to piece together what he's conveying with his body language and cryptic, almost caustic words. The edges of this jumble are jagged but are starting to slowly smooth out. And I don't like how they fucking sound clicking together.

"You knew she knew, yet you never said anything. Why?"

A hard sneer twists Alan's lips. His eyes shine in victory, but I have no idea what he thinks he's won. *I* have Nora. "You don't know, do you?"

"Know what?" I'm getting pretty fucking tired of his games and rhymes. This is not the friend I once knew. Correction...*thought* I knew.

"Oh, this is almost too good," he chuckles before taking a sip of his hot coffee.

"Stop talking in fucking circles and spit out whatever it is you want me to know."

"Whose idea do you think the surprise was? Who do you think drove her to my house? Who do you think *comforted* her when she found her *boyfriend* all drunk and hopped up on Molly in bed fucking some whore?"

Nothing in that sentence made sense. Not. A. Thing. There's so much I needed to dispute, but the only word I could latch on to was "comfort."

The puzzle snaps in place with a deafening sound. The earth shudders below me as if a massive earthquake just ripped through the city. Or my world.

"I was devastated, and I reacted out of spite."

Mother. Fucker.

Gray was right. Alan wanted everything I had. He always did. And when he didn't get it, he set out to make sure I didn't have it either.

My stomach churns with disgust and my blood boils with an anger so raw, so potent, so all-fucking-consuming, it takes me over completely.

Next thing I know Alan's fleshy throat is between my fingers, his back plastered against the thick glass wall that separates him from life and certain death, should it give way. I vaguely feel a sting on my hands and arms, his nails ineffectively digging into me for purchase. Through the unadulterated hatred now clouding my vision and my common sense, I hear my name being called.

I squeeze harder.

"You fucking set me up," I seethe, my spit flying in his face. "You got me drunk, fed me drugs, and sent some whore to fuck me so Nora would see the whole goddamned thing because you wanted her. Didn't you, you sick fuck?"

He shakes his head, but his effort is weak. I see the life draining from him. I tighten my hold.

I. Want. Him. Dead.

"Then you took advantage of her. You fucking used her in your sick, twisted mindfuck of a game. All because of what? Because she loved *me*? Wanted *me*? You ruined me! You destroyed her! Do you have any fucking idea what you did?" I roar so loudly I swear I feel the floor shake.

It's not the floor.

It's me.

I faintly hear people yelling and screaming, but one word registers. Just one. The only word I think could bring me out of my murderous haze, keeping me from spending the next ten to twenty getting ass raped.

Hazel.

I immediately sense Nora. She's crying. Pleading with me to let go. Telling me to think of Hazel and how she needs her father.

I drop Alan like a flaming hot sack of shit.

He's already taken too much from me. I won't let him take anything else.

The second I let him go, she's in my arms, wrapping every single limb around me. She's sobbing uncontrollably and squeezing me so hard she may leave marks. I welcome them. They will remind me of all we've lost, but more importantly, all we've found again.

"I'm sorry, baby. I'm sorry," I choke out. So fucking sorry for so many things, the least of which was not recognizing a traitor in our midst. The person who knew me since the age of five and was supposed to be my friend worked against us, skillfully ripping us apart. My chest heaves as I work to get my blood pressure back under control.

I look to my left to see Miles, the restaurant manager and a good friend, nod once in understanding before snapping into motion, trying to rein in the current chaos.

My gaze sweeps down to the floor, landing on Alan's prone form. He's holding his throat, which is no doubt tender and will carry evidence of his betrayal for weeks to come. His eyes are filled with guilt. He's not physically dead like I'd wanted, but he's now dead to me.

The damaged boy I once knew apparently grew up into an even more damaged man, taking things away from Nora and me that can never be replaced. His jealousy and cunning ruined so many lives, perhaps even his. It's painfully obvious to me that he's still in love with Nora.

My thoughts fill with vengeance—of ruining his life, his career, his very own marriage—but the moment it lands, it disappears. He's not worth the effort and karma is always kindest to people like him. He'll get his due, just not by my hand. I have other, far more important things to worry about than getting my revenge. Besides, I think the fact that I'm holding the woman we both love in my arms is revenge enough.

I start to walk away, Nora still wrapped around me like a vine when I hear Alan rumble through what I hoped was a permanently damaged windpipe, "I didn't...sleep with...her. I...swear. I just...let her...think that."

At that, Nora cries even harder, burying her head in my neck. If he thinks his long-overdue admission makes it better, it doesn't. In fact, it makes this entire fucked-up situation far, far worse. He let her believe a heinous lie for so many years. A lie that forever changed all of our lives.

As I look down into the face of my ex-best friend for the very last time, I see genuine remorse. I see honesty. I see his silent plea for forgiveness.

Too bad it's eleven fucking years too late.

And I'm fresh the fuck out of forgiveness.

Chapter 38

CONN

"I was wondering when you would show up," Carl Steele says, eyes twinkling before he takes a long swallow of his Bud Light draw.

"You know, Carl, I've been on to you this whole time." I watch him, taking a pull of my own beer.

Unbeknownst to Nora, I flew into Cincinnati for lunch with the former owner of SER, but I plan on being home in time for a date tonight with the Blackhawks and Red Wings. Hazel and I have front row tickets. She's been strung tight for a week in anticipation. That girl can trash talk even better than my brothers, I think. Trouble is on the horizon with her, I can already tell. I'm not much of a gun carrier, but I think I need to invest in a shotgun and learn how to use it. There's not much a boy finds sexier than a girl who can talk sports with him and match him stat for stat.

The penance of my past womanizing comes in the form of a beautiful, rambunctious almost eleven-year-old. I'm sure I'll be blessed with about four more girls to round out years of atonement.

"This *whole* time, son? I'm not so sure about that."

I admit it took me a while to put everything together, but it only took a few times of meeting with Carl before I noticed the subtle similarities between him and Nora. The way they both crinkled their noses as they silently formed an argument in their head. The way the shade of his eyes matched hers almost exactly. The fact both of their hearts are as wide and deep as the ocean. But the thing that gave Carl away was his unabashed pride in Nora.

There is no mistaking the love of a father for his daughter. I should know.

"When did you know?" I ask. Curiosity has gotten the better of me, but that's not the real reason I'm here.

"When did I know you were Hazel's father?"

I nod, a slight smile on my lips.

Across the wooden table, he pins me with a thoughtful gaze. I wonder what he sees. Does he see someone worthy of his daughter? Of his granddaughter? Or does he simply see a ruthless businessman who has a sordid, playboy past? I hope it's the first two, but I fear it's the latter. And if that's the case, I know I've earned it. But for some reason, he still wanted me to be with Nora anyway, so that has to count for something.

"When your face showed up in *Forbes* a few years ago."

I laugh and shake my head. "You're pulling my leg."

"I'm not." He pauses, thinking over his next words carefully. "I remember you, you know. I knew you recognized me the first time we met about the acquisition. I could tell you couldn't place me, but I've never forgotten the boy who made my ladybug's heart run like a race car."

I'm speechless.

Almost.

"So the whole sale was..." *A setup on his part to push Nora and me back together?* And here I thought I was holding the golden ticket. All along it was Carl.

"Yep. You played into my hands beautifully, Connelly. Sam Makey was always in my pocket, not yours," he winks, a big-ass grin on his face.

"What about the gambling? The stock market shit?"

He shrugs. "What about it?"

"Was that all a farce, too?" That's one of the reasons I knew Carl needed to sell SER. Another card in my hand, a tidbit I'd heard from...Sam Makey. *Fuck. Me.*

"I've made some bad decisions for sure, but let's just say I've made a couple of *decent* investments as well."

"You're fucking kidding me." I'm stunned. Utterly. I was played by the savviest player I've ever come across and I was none the wiser.

"Nora's always been a little stubborn, in case you didn't already know that," he tells me sarcastically. "She needed you. Hazel needed her father. You both needed a push. I just happened to have all the right cards at the right time for once and I played them."

We fall silent as I digest everything he just told me.

"Why all the push and pull during the sale? Why all the crazy demands? You tried to stop this more than once."

"I think you know the answer to that, son. You may have been the man she never got over, but you're also the one who broke her in the first place. It was my job to put you through your paces. Make sure you were willing to do anything for her. Change your lifestyle for her. For my Nora. For your daughter. I knew if you were, everything else would work itself out between you two." He takes a swig of his beer before continuing. "When I saw war in your eyes in that boardroom, I knew you'd stop at nothing until you had her. I saw a man uncompromising and resolute. I knew then you were worthy. Had I not seen that, we wouldn't be sitting here today."

Except he's wrong. I would have stopped at nothing to get Nora, sale or no sale. "I would have found another way had you not sold me SER."

"I know," he smirks.

"I'm...wow. I'm impressed, old man. Well played."

Carl just laughs. A full, hearty belly laugh.

"You knew I would win," I say, more than a little amazed. I was so cocky at first, so overconfident and I doubted myself, doubted us, many times over the past few months, but Carl always knew. He believed even when I didn't.

His head dips and he answers softly, "If you're meant to be with someone, it's a shame not to."

"Sounds like experience talking."

Carl clams up, finishing his beer on a long chug. I move on to the real reason I'm here, but I'm not done discussing this topic. It's not lost on me that Nora being unaware Carl is her real father is just like me not knowing about Hazel. True, he's been a part of her life, but not in the way he should have been. Hazel's been in the dark all these years about my true identity, but so has Nora. How she can't see that this man in front of me is her flesh and blood is beyond me.

It's as clear to me that he's her father as it is to Carl that I'm Hazel's.

"I'm going to ask Nora to marry me. I want your blessing."

"You don't need my blessing, Connelly. But if you feel like you need it, you have it."

I didn't expect anything less, but now's my time to move in for the kill.

"I thought it was customary to ask the father of woman you want to marry for permission."

I'm not sure I could have surprised Carl more than if I'd sat here telling him I was a transvestite.

"Her father's passed away, son. You know that."

"No, the man who didn't deserve that title is dead. Her real father is alive and kicking and still very much a part of her life, but for some fucking reason, he's wearing a mask."

"Connelly," he growls. "Let it go. It's not your business."

It's my turn to laugh, but it's full of disbelief instead of humor. Oh, the irony. He pushed Nora and me together because of Hazel, but he refuses to own up to his own mistakes and be part of Nora's life the way he should.

"Oh, it *is* my fucking business, all right. These

are *my* girls we're talking about. Their happiness is *my* responsibility. I am their protector now. I will not keep this from her, Carl. There are no more secrets between us. Nora needs a father. Hazel needs a grandfather. Time to man up."

He shakes his head slowly. "It's too late. I can't...it's...it's too late." The sound of defeat just plain pisses me off. I imagine I sounded much like this when I was sitting across from my mom only weeks ago.

"No, you're wrong," I tell him adamantly, remembering my mother's words. "It's never too late. You don't want to be on your deathbed with regrets, Carl. This would be the pinnacle of regrets, not coming clean with her. She deserves to know."

"She'll never forgive me...or her mother."

There's a story here I ache to understand, but it's not mine. It's Carl's and Nora's. And he couldn't be more wrong. If anyone will understand the angst he's feeling, it's my soon-to-be wife. If anyone can forgive him, it's her.

"Wrong again." My tone is so harsh, his gaze sweeps up to mine for the first time since we've started this difficult conversation. "She's walked in your shoes. If there's anyone who will forgive you, Carl, anyone who will understand, it's your own daughter."

He nods as understanding dawns on him.

"It's never too late," I add again. "Never. I'm the poster child of second chances."

Chapter 39

Nora

"Been a lot of change this year, Ladybug."

"Yes, a lot," I agree. So much I have to not think about it most days or it's overwhelming.

New city, new job, new life. New chances at true happiness.

I found out our high school best friend was a psychotic turncoat who deviously plotted to keep Connelly and me apart. Oh, and bonus, that I never did sleep with him as he'd led me to believe. It all makes sense now. My lack of memory, no evidence of our indiscretions, no soreness between my legs, and most of all, his insistence about the whole surprise remaining top secret.

And, finally, in the biggest plot twist of all, my father isn't dead but has been with me all along, guiding me, loving me, being the supportive father figure that mine never was.

When Carl came to see me last week, I immediately knew something was wrong. I thought he was going to tell me he'd lost every cent he had or that, God forbid, he was dying. But as soon as he divulged his secret love affair with my mother, everything clicked. The same temperament, the same ideals, the same love of life. I was more like him than I ever was my father. Things went too far the one and only night he and my mother were together. I was conceived and none of them ever spoke about it, but they all knew I was Carl's, not my father's.

It makes so much more sense now—how my father let Carl have so much leeway in our lives. When I questioned Carl about why my mother didn't just divorce my father and marry him, all he would say was that my mother loved my father, too. I guess I'll never know the complications of their love story, and I'm not really meant to. What I do know is that Carl loved a woman who loved him back but they couldn't be together.

Carl hasn't admitted it to me and Connelly refuses to say, but I know he set up the whole sale of SER so Connelly and I wouldn't make a similar mistake. That's the selfless love of a parent for their child.

"She's going to be after you for a brother or sister pretty soon," my father says, throwing his arm around my shoulder, pulling me close. We watch Hazel dote on Grant and Cash like a little mother hen. She even tried her hand at changing their diapers, and when she found a little surprise in one, she handled it like the true champ she is. She's going to make a great big sister.

Laughing, I reply, "She already is. Daily."

I have to admit, I was nervous about today. I haven't eaten much this week leading up to

Thanksgiving. It's the first time I have seen Barb Colloway since Connelly and I reunited. She came to Chicago a couple of weeks ago, but I was out of town for a business meeting and missed seeing her. Truth be told, I wasn't sure I was quite ready anyway. Regardless of Connelly's forgiveness and the wrongs that were done to both of us so long ago, I still carry a tremendous amount of guilt. I'm working through it, but that doesn't disappear overnight.

Now I know where Connelly gets his capacity to forgive: his mother. The second I walked through that door, she had me in her arms, whispering how glad she was to see me again and how happy I make her son. I held it together. Barely.

"You get that CEO spot filled yet for Kinnick?"

I snort. "Finally. Last week. In my seven years of doing this job, that was the most difficult man I've ever worked with. I've already made it known to Connelly that in a few years when this next CEO is fired, I will not work on his replacement."

"Bet you're glad to have that behind you."

"No truer words have been spoken."

I hear commotion to my right and see that Connelly and his brothers have returned from their annual game of HORSE. Connelly looks absolutely victorious.

"I don't know why I even bother to play that stupid game with you every damn year. You're unbeatable," Asher grumbles. Alyse throws her arms around him, planting a big kiss on his cheek before whispering something in his ear that makes his eyes fall half-mast with desire. He lifts her so her legs wrap around him, even with her growing belly, and walks out of the kitchen.

Well then. Guess Ash will be getting a consolation prize that will make his loss sting a little less.

"Hey there," Connelly murmurs against my neck before snuggling me in his arms.

"You won, I take it?" I almost moan when he lightly nips my lobe.

"As if there was any question." So cocky. Good thing he has me to keep him in line. His eyes flit to my dad before landing back on me. "Let's take a walk, princess."

"Where? It's about thirty-two degrees outside. If I can see my breath, I'm out."

"The dock."

"It's cold," I whine.

"Then put on a coat." He laughs, tapping my nose with his finger. I almost refuse, but he looks earnest.

"What about Hazel?"

"She's a big girl. She'll be fine for a few minutes. Besides, you'll probably have to pry her fingers off of those babies to get her to go anywhere. She's quite a doting cousin."

I tear up watching Hazel in the rocker singing Cash a lullaby. "She loves kids."

"I know," he whispers, wrapping his arms around my waist from behind. "I intend to give her lots of them to babysit, so we'd best get started on that. I'm not getting any younger, you know."

I tilt my head back and latch on to the most breathtaking eyes I'm sure were ever made. The love floating in them is tangible. It touches me everywhere.

Kissing the tip of my nose, he grabs my hand and pulls me toward the door, yelling that we'll be back in a bit. I try to catch Zel's attention to make sure she's heard but see her grinning at Connelly, a secret passing between them. They seem to have a lot of those these days.

Hazel and I have been on our own so long, I thought it would be an adjustment to have Connelly in our house and lives twenty-four seven. It's not. Other than experiencing the occasional cold, wet ass from falling into the toilet when the seat's left up, it's been relatively smooth sailing.

I'm ashamed to admit it, but I also thought it may be an even bigger adjustment to have her affections split between the two of us. But just as a parent has the capacity to infinitely love all their children, so do kids. I've seen Hazel grow and blossom in ways I've never dreamed of. The way you only can when you have a father or father figure.

Bundled in our winter jackets, Connelly takes my ungloved hand in his and we head around the left side of the house, down the dull, now hibernating grass. Dry blades crunch under our feet with each step. The air is crisp, a few flakes already floating aimlessly from the overcast sky. I see my breath with each exhale and the cold burns my cheeks already.

Nearly a foot of snow is forecast by morning. Zel is already planning an epic snowman-building competition tomorrow with her aunts and uncles, all of whom are on board. Guys against girls, of course. Looks like she inherited the competitive gene from the Colloways, too. She's in absolute heaven with her newfound family. I pinch myself often to be sure I'm not dreaming.

A few short minutes later, we're standing at the end of the Colloway dock, hand in hand, gazing out on the peaceful, glass-top lake. The view is simply breathtaking even in the chill of winter. Oak, maple, and ash trees have shed most of their leaves, but full, lush evergreens and pines add color to the picturesque landscape.

"Do you know when I fell in love with you, Nora?"

I gaze at his profile as he stares out into the majestic scenery before us. It's sometimes hard to believe this beautiful man is mine.

"No."

"It was the week after you'd started at DH. I was building up my nerve to talk to you..."

"You? Building up nerve? Now that I don't believe. You were awfully cocky when you slid next to me in the lunchroom that day like you already owned me."

He looks at me then and the fierceness in his hazels makes me choke on my laugh. "It's true. I may have covered my nerves with bravado, but it made my stomach clench every time I thought about approaching you. I was utterly smitten from the first time my eyes landed on you, Nora. I knew you belonged to me, but I couldn't understand how or why I felt that way."

"Oh," I whisper softly.

"You were walking down the hall between classes and I could tell you were late and flustered. Mary Hartfield, that jealous cow, stuck her foot in your way, tripping you. Your books and papers went flying, but you managed to catch yourself pretty cleanly on your hands. I thought to myself, this is divine intervention. Now, I'll have a reason to talk to this bewitching creature without sounding like I'm coming on to her. I was almost to you, but Ronnie Pulman beat me to it, that bastard."

A slight smile tilts my mouth. I remember the incident, and I remember thinking that the fact my face nearly made BFFs with the hard linoleum floor was no accident.

Connelly wraps me in his embrace once again before continuing. "I stood not ten feet away and watched you gift him with the most magnificent smile I'd ever seen. I had never been jealous over a girl before, Nora. I knew if I had these unfamiliar feelings of wanting Pulman's blood on my hands for just pulling a simple smile from you that I was doomed. And I didn't give a shit, either. *That's* when I felt it. You handled yourself with such grace and poise and confidence and I instantly, instinctively knew I wanted those traits in the woman I would marry, even though I'd never given that a single thought before."

My eyes promptly water. "Connelly..."

He runs his hands gently from the crown of my head down before stopping at my cheeks. My icy hair is pressed against my ears and face.

"You were my first, Nora. In everything. My first love, my first lover, my first heartbreak."

"Your first lover?" I ask, my brows pinching together.

"Yes," he replies adamantly. "I should have told you back then, but I was kind of embarrassed. I wanted it to be perfect."

"It was," I murmur, overjoyed about the fact that I was his first just as he was mine.

"I agree." His voice is just as soft.

"I think more important than being first, though, is being last."

A few tears slide from the corners of my eyes while I maintain my silence, hanging on every one of his breaths.

"You were also my last love, my last heartbreak, the last woman I let into my life in any meaningful way. We've had so many good memories right here on this dock, Nora." He looks around us, eyes lingering on his childhood house in the distance before engaging me again. "I want to add another one."

Taking my shaky, numb hands in his steady ones, he steps back and swings our joined limbs slightly, making me laugh.

"Do you know why a man prostrates himself to ask the woman he loves to marry him, princess?"

My throat closes—it's so constricted I can't speak, so I just shake my head. The wind has picked up and is whipping my loose hair around. The white flakes in the strong gust melt on my exposed skin when they land. I no longer feel them.

"It's because she has all the power. It's symbolic, I think, to look *up* at the woman who owns everything he is. His heart, his thoughts, his happiness, his future. The other half of his soul."

I bite my lip, hard, trying to hold my shit together when he bends, placing one knee on the weathered boards beneath our feet.

"*You* are the life I want, Nora. You *are* my life. Period. I want to go to sleep every night and wake up every morning with you in my arms. I want to kiss your neck when you get ready for work and hear you moan in pleasure. I want to hear you yell at me to put the toilet seat down. I want to sit on the patio and watch our kids play and fight in the backyard. I want to make a million new memories with you so that when we're eighty and sitting on the patio watching our grandchildren play and fight in the same yard as our children, we can reminisce on the fifty amazing years we've had together with goofy smiles on our faces."

I think I shed a new tear for each romantic and heartfelt word he pours out.

"I want to be your husband, Nora. God, I want that more than anything. You own me completely and thoroughly until the day I die, but *I* can only be complete when I'm yours. I love you so much. Marry me, princess." Choked full of emotion his eyes glisten in the cold winter air. He's one step away from breaking down, just like me.

Connelly stuffs his hand in his pocket. My watery gaze drops when he pulls out a very stunning and very large step-cut ruby, platinum, art deco engagement ring. I immediately recognize the repurposed jewel in the filigree castle setting, now surrounded by dozens of tiny round diamonds.

It was my mother's.

She wore it on her right hand for as long as I could remember. I coveted that ring. I studied it endlessly as a child, each unique facet. And whenever I would ask where she got it, she would only tell me it came from someone special.

She'd willed it to Carl when she passed away.

Click. Another piece of my life soundly falls into place.

The cold dissipates, leaving me warm and fuzzy. Falling to my knees on the hard wood, I pull his lips to mine, whispering, "Yes, yes, yes."

"Babe," he mutters between ravenous kisses, "let me put this on you before I drop it between the slats and the lake sucks it up." He takes my left hand, sliding the cold metal onto my ring finger. Where it will forever stay.

"I wanted to give you something as unique and spirited as you are, but I also wanted it to mean something. I hope you don't mind..."

"I don't. It's perfect, Connelly. Thank you for doing this for me."

His smile is sheepish. "It was partly Carl's idea. When I asked him if he had anything I could use, he selflessly offered this up and being the bastard that I am, I took it."

"I think I was always meant to have this. Just not until my mom felt it was right." I wince, the hard surface biting into my kneecaps.

"Come on." Connelly helps me up. He sneaks a hand underneath my coat, placing it on my stomach. "I want you swollen with my baby," he says, his voice husky.

"You do, huh?" An involuntary shiver racks me. Connelly holds me closer.

"I mean it, Nora," he whispers in my ear. "I want to marry you tomorrow and I want babies the next day."

I want more kids just as badly, if not more, than Connelly. But I want that to be a decision we make together. When the time is right for us.

My head falls to his shoulder. "I don't think it quite works that fast."

"I can make all kinds of magic happen, baby." I feel his smile against my temple when he kisses me.

"I thought you weren't a sorcerer?"

"Have a few tricks up my sleeve," he jokes.

"Has Hazel been working on you?"

He tugs my hair until our eyes meet. A soft smile spreads his full pink lips, which lower to meet mine. God, I'd give anything to have him naked and taking me fast and rough right now.

"And if she has?" he breathes against my mouth.

"Who knew such a strong man could bend like hot iron with a single flick of an eyelash?"

"Like mother, like daughter."

"Touché."

Dipping low, he presses his lips reverently to mine. He craddles my face and takes control, tilting me so our mouths slant perfectly together. Sweeping his tongue inside, he slowly makes love to my mouth the way I hope he'll be doing to me later in the guest house.

"God, I love you, Nora," he murmurs against my cheek, "so damn much."

This right here is what I've wanted since the moment I laid eyes on Connelly Colloway when I was seventeen. To belong to him. To be his wife. To live our days and nights together: loving, fighting, being. Even after the past few weeks of blissful happiness, I still wake up some days wondering if I've dropped into a dream. It takes all of two seconds to realize I'm not when I feel Connelly's strong, powerful arms surround me, holding tight like I'll vanish any second. I think he feels the same way I do: he may wake up and I'll be *his* dream. But I'm not. He's not. *We're* not. This is as real as it gets. I'm so euphoric my chest feels like it may crack from the fullness most days.

"I love you so much I can hardly breathe sometimes."

It's not until now that I realize snow's starting to fall hard. The large flakes have gathered in his black hair and on the shoulders of his navy peacoat. He looks divine. "It's you and me now. You, me, Hazel, and all the siblings we can give her." Dropping his voice to a sultry timber, he declares, "I plan on starting tonight, I want you to know. I'm going to fuck you until it's physically impossible for me to continue."

That familiar tingle between my legs starts burning. "Promise?" I tease, knowing full well we can't make a baby yet. And so does he.

"Oh hell yeah," he promises darkly. "If it wasn't so cold, I think I'd bend you over and fuck you right here."

I wrap my hand around the thickening bulge in

his pants and gaze up at him with what I know is mischief in my eyes. "I think I'd let you."

"Nora," he rumbles, fingers covering mine, squeezing hard. "Do not tempt me." I giggle right before a blast of frigid air hits me. "Come on. Let's get back. You're shivering."

With one more fast kiss and grins plastered on our faces, we hurry back to the house the same way we came, hands locked. The temperature has dropped about five degrees, the wind is gusty, and a thin white glaze now blankets the ground.

The moment we set foot in the kitchen, nine sets of eyes stop what they're doing and turn our way. Even the twins quiet down. The only set I'm glued to, however, is our daughter's. They're bright with anxious anticipation, darting back and forth between her dad and me.

She knew.

Connelly confirms it when he smirks and shrugs his shoulders. "You don't think I'd ask you to marry me without our daughter's okay, do you?"

"You said yes?" her little voice squeaks as she bounces up and down.

Before answering, I look around the room, realizing two things.

Everyone knew what that little walk was about, and I feel like the luckiest woman on earth to be able to share this special moment with a family that loves my daughter and me unconditionally. And now they're our family. *Our family.*

Standing side by side with my soul mate, I marvel at the obstacles we've overcome. We've both made mistakes. We've both been wronged. We're both imperfect but perfectly perfect for each other.

That's the thing about a soul mate, though. They know you. All of you. The good, the bad, the dark and ugly scarred parts of you, yet they love the entire package regardless. And with my entire family surrounding us, I couldn't feel more loved or accepted for all of my perfect imperfections.

A grin overtakes me as I look into my daughter's angelic face. "I said yes."

The entire kitchen erupts in chaos.

"About fucking time," I hear Luke say over the melee right before Barb yells at him for swearing in front of little ears, to which he just laughs.

Then we're encased in arms and congratulations and tears. When Connelly reaches for me, I slide easily into his hold.

I love this family. I love their boundless love. I love their unwavering loyalty. I love their dedication, commitment, and support of each other. I love that Hazel and I are now part of their crazy, flawed, tight little unit.

Most of all, I'll love this man next to me with every part of my being until I take my last breath.

It may be over eleven years in the making, but I'd say that Connelly and I have more than earned the overflowing joy that's spilling out of this room.

Just goes to prove: Never say never.

Epilogue

Eighteen months later...

CONN

"I don't understand how *I'm* being punished for *your* dream, fireball," Luke's loud, gruff voice booms.

"Because...because you just *are*," Addy responds tightly. Luke has her locked in his arms but she's trying to squirm away. She squeals and I presume he's found a ticklish spot. Addy Colloway is like a rabid animal sometimes. Wild and unpredictable. And I thought Nora had a quick temper. She's got nothing on Luke's wife and he's even subdued her somewhat. I can only imagine what their bedroom is like when he's taming her.

"What's that all about, princess?" I ask my lovely wife, nodding toward Addy and Luke. She's sitting next to me, unhappily I might add. I made her get off her feet and rest like she's supposed to. I almost put the kibosh on this Memorial Day party, the first one in our new Lake Forest home, but Nora insisted. Her insistence came complete with real tears, so I was forced into this little barbecue or would have been forced to live with the consequences.

I'm a smart man.

"Addy had a dream that Luke had an affair with Halle Berry, so she's refused to let him watch any movies with her in it."

"Uh oh." I chuckle. "The X-Men series is one of his faves."

"Exactly," she smirks.

"I think she's overreacting a bit, don't you? I mean, Luke can control a lot of things about Addy, but her dreams aren't one of them." I turn my gaze, meeting Nora's. She's scowling. "Or maybe not." That puts a smile on her gorgeous face. I grab her hand and bring it to my lips, brushing them across her knuckles.

One thing I quickly learned about the women in this family...they're stuck together like superglue, even Hazel. You don't cross. You don't question. You don't argue. You just agree. Life is easier that way. Everyone has learned this little trick except Luke. He still pushes Addy constantly, but then again that's their thing.

Hazel pops out the front door, face stuck in her new cell phone. She's been begging for one for six months and I finally caved. Imagine that.

"Ladybird, you cleaned your room, right?"

"Yep," she answers, not looking away from the screen for an instant as she bounds down the wooden porch steps.

"Hazel."

She stops midstep and turns back. "Yeah," she responds guiltily.

443

"Your room?"

"Yes, Daddy. My room is clean."

Eye twitch. Shuffle step. She's getting better, but she'll never best me. I arch a knowing brow.

"Fine." She stomps back up the stairs. I hold out my hand as she passes by. Her phone drops in my palm. Her mother and I laugh and her little feet pound louder.

"And be quiet. The baby's sleeping!" I yell behind her, tucking the mind-sucking contraption in my back pocket.

"She's doomed. She knows she'll never get away with anything with you as her father."

"Well, at least I have that going for me," I mumble.

Our daughter has hit the age of twelve and apparently something happens overnight when girls turn twelve. Before, you couldn't go anywhere without them attached to your hip; now you're the bane of their precious existence. You were once the smartest human being on earth, and now you suddenly have nothing but air between your ears. You used to be the light of their lives, but now you're darkness they have to suffer through.

Nora assures me it will eventually pass. In five years or so.

My mother assures me we all pulled the same shit to some degree, but it was around the age of fourteen instead. Being a parent of a preteen is damn hard work.

"You feeling okay?" I ask.

"I'm fine, Connelly. Jesus, stop smothering me."

I'm not sure who I feel more sorry for at the moment: Nora or myself. Her hormones are raging. One minute she's like sunshine. Bright. Happy. Warm. The next, she's turned into Medusa. I'm sure I see snakes swirling in her hair and I have to work hard to dodge their poisonous strikes. I'm stuck with two unpredictable women. My forecast of penance has finally come true.

But today's a good day. A happy day. A day of family celebration. Everyone I love is here. My whole life under one roof, including Nora's father and my mom and her "boyfriend." And because it's a good day, I'm not going to let chemicals win this fight.

Picking up a protesting Nora, I settle her on my lap until her fight leaves. I gently grab her chin between my thumb and forefinger and lift her face to me.

"Better get used to it, princess. I will spend the rest of my life smothering you. Worrying about you to exhaustion. Loving you to annoyance." I move my hand to her swollen belly, six and a half months ripe with our baby girl.

Yep...penance.

She places her hand on top of mine, hooking our fingers together. "Everything is fine, Connelly. I swear. You're being overprotective."

"No cramps?"

"Nope."

"No spotting?"

"None for weeks. Want evidence?"

"Maybe." My chest stings where she swats me

good. Little does she know I'm not playing. "I'm not going to apologize, sweetheart. Our baby girl has to bake a while longer."

"I know," she agrees quietly.

Nora and I got married in a small, private ceremony just weeks after we were engaged, with just our family in attendance. Neither of us wanted to wait or plan an unnecessarily elaborate wedding and the only people we wanted as witnesses were those who meant the most to us. Then we started the lengthy process of having my name added to Hazel's birth certificate as her biological father—a painstaking procedure but well worth the effort in the end.

During this entire time, we embarked on building our new home and arguing about when we were going to have more kids. Nora hedged. She was nervous. She'd had a bad pregnancy and bad delivery with Hazel. She was worried she'd have a repeat. When we finally decided six months into our marriage to give it a go, little did we know that we'd have such difficulty getting my swimmers past the goal line. Turned out Nora had developed some endometriosis, so we went the medical intervention route. At last, after almost six months of shots and visits and procedures...success.

But then her fears came true. Nora started having problems similar to when she was pregnant with Hazel. She had pretty severe morning sickness and developed light spotting at ten weeks. Went into false labor once at the four-month mark. We thought we were going to lose the baby. Things were touch and go for a while and she was on complete bed rest for several weeks. Then, like divine intervention, the spotting stopped, the cramps went away, and her OB said as long as she took it easy, she could be up and around.

To be safe, she's taken a leave of absence from work until after the baby's born. It's been hard for her, but I'm not unhappy in the least. Her sole goal right now is to take care of our children while I take care of her.

"I love you, Nora Colloway." I hook a finger under her chin and tip her head to the right angle so I can kiss her.

"I love you back, Connelly Colloway," she replies against my wet lips before pressing hers to them again.

"Hey, mind if I run a quick bath?" Ash interrupts looking completely disheveled, a filthy dirty, dripping one-year-old in his arms. Alyse is right behind him, calm as a cucumber, cooing at their daughter whose legs are flailing as she giggles. "Lila landed in a mud puddle before I could stop her."

I want to laugh, but I know I don't dare. I'll be him this time next year.

Ah, fuck it.

"Go ahead. Yuck it up, brother. You'll get your due."

"Looking forward to it," I reply, meaning every syllable. "Hey, see if Hazel wants to help. She loves that stuff."

"Will do."

Ash and Alyse head inside just as my mom and Bob plod up the steps, taking the chairs next to us.

Nora tries to get up, but I stop her. She glares. I laugh. Life is good.

"How's the mother-to-be doing today?" my mom asks Nora, patting her lovingly on the leg.

"Good, Barb. Thanks for asking." I hear the smile before I see it.

"How come you're sweet to her but sour to me?"

"Just the way it is, son," my mother answers for my wife. She and Nora giggle, like they have an inside joke, while Bob shrugs his shoulders in an empathetic gesture.

"This has been a great day, Conn. We should make this a tradition," Bob says, grabbing hold of my mom's hand. My mother is glowing...like a newlywed. But they aren't yet, although we hope they will be soon. Bob has been trying unsuccessfully to convince Barb Colloway to marry him. All us kids have given her our blessing, knowing it's what Dad would have wanted. I think she'll cave soon.

"I think we will, Bob." I nod.

"Your sister able to make it for dinner, Nora?" Bob asks. Even though everyone knows Ella isn't technically Nora's sister now, no one acknowledges it, especially Nora and Ella. To them, they will always be sisters.

"She said she'd try." I don't hold out hope Ella will show. I don't know what's going on with her lately, but she's been conspicuously absent and it's upsetting Nora. I try to stay out of "sister stuff," but I'll have to get on Ella about that. I don't want Nora under any stress whatsoever. I kiss Nora's temple. She snuggles closer.

We fall quiet and I take a deep breath full of sublime gratitude.

With my wife and unborn child in my arms, we sit on our wraparound porch and I gaze out at the backyard. There, Gray and Livia push their giggling boys on the massive swing set big enough for a park. At three months along, Livia is barely showing, pregnant with just one this time. Gender still unknown.

Luke and Addy battle it out with lawn darts while three-month-old Charlotte naps in the crib upstairs.

Carl, the self-professed Master Griller, is cooking up brats and burgers, insistent that I take care of Nora while he takes care of the food. I didn't put up too much of a fight.

Landyn is even here, arriving a short time ago. She's part of the family after all, in so many ways, so it's not a surprise she's spending the day with us. What is the surprise, however, is who she brought with her: Cooper Jensen. They look a little friendly, too. I had no idea she was dating anyone, let alone Mr. Jensen. I'll have to dig into that more another day. Right now, all I want to do is revel in being with my family.

"All right, food's up!" Carl yells, prompting my mom into action. She runs inside to get the side dishes while Carl sets a giant platter on the twelve-foot custom outdoor table we had made for the patio, just for get-togethers like this.

Nora goes to follow her. I clamp her to me. "Just a minute."

She glares at me with ire in her gleaming green eyes. My redhead is firing up again. "I can carry a salad, you know."

I hold in a snicker. "Yes. I know."

"Then let me up."

"In a second. Answer a question first."

She cocks her head. "The answer is yes."

"You don't know the question yet," I tell her, chuckling.

"Then it's a definite no."

Laughing, I pull her close and whisper, "Are you happy, Nora?"

Tipping her head and softening her face, she presses my scruffy cheeks between her tiny hands, kissing me so slow and so soft I immediately harden. It's been weeks since I've rocked inside her inviting heat. Sex is a no-no right now, but it's forced us to be creative. Let's just say we've eaten a lot of late-night meals off of each other, discovering several new erogenous zones.

"Bursting with it. You?"

"Blissfully content," I reply, bringing her mouth again to mine. The truth is, I've never been fucking happier in my entire life, every day better than the last.

"Hey, you two lovebirds, food's getting cold," Livia yells. A glance in her direction shows we're the last ones to the table.

I groan, wanting only to spend some naked time alone with my wife. "Why did we do this again?" I grumble, only half kidding.

"Come on, lover boy." Standing, she grabs my

hand, yanks me up, and wraps herself around me. "You'll have plenty of time to keep me naked in bed since your mom is taking Hazel tomorrow for the next two weeks."

"Mmm, how could I forget?" I nibble her neck, thinking of the many places we have yet to christen in the house.

"Come on." She takes me by the hand, leading me down the steps. Her sexy ass, which has filled out nicely with her pregnancy, is what really pulls me forward. "Let's go have another first."

"Sounds perfect," I reply, a smile the size of Texas on my face.

As I slide into an empty space at the table, Nora by my side, I take a moment to let my gaze meander over my family. Food is passed. Laughter rings. Voices get progressively louder. Grant cries when he drops his sippy cup on the ground. It's utter chaos, but I'd give everything I own to experience this single second over and over again.

The Colloway boys have all battled tirelessly for our second chance at love and family and futures with women who almost slipped through our fingers. Women who were *always* meant to be ours. It hasn't been easy. Each of us has had our own obstacles to overcome...our own demons to slay...our own souls to search.

As I told Gray a few months back, though, nothing worth winning is ever easy. Nothing worth having comes without sacrifice, wounds, or scars. And nothing worth holding on to comes without paying the ultimate price: your very soul.

But if you're with the right person, you won't even know that piece of you is missing because that space is not dark and empty.

It's whole and complete: filled with your other half.

~ The End ~

My musical inspiration for writing
Destination Connelly

"Sorry" by Art of Dying
"Breathe Into Me" by Red
"Room To Breathe" by You Me At Six
"Pieces" by Red
"Your Love Is a Song" by Switchfoot
"Gave It All Away" by Red
"Apologize" by OneRepublic
"From Where You Are" by Lifehouse
"Start Again" by Red
"Breaking Inside" by Shinedown
"Never Be the Same" by Red
"Not Strong Enough" by Apocalyptica
"Mystery of You" by Red
"Fight to Forget" by Red
"Wait For Me" by Theory of a Deadman
"Yours Again" by Red
"Stay" by Rihanna
"Part That's Holding On" by Red
"Say It" by Evans Blue
"Casual Sex" by My Darkest Days
"Thread" by Flyleaf
"Secrets" by OneRepublic
"Best Is Yet to Come" by Red
"Second Chance" by Shinedown

Other works by K. L. Kreig:
The **Regent Vampire Lords** series:

Surrendering
Belonging
Reawakening
Evading

The Colloway Brothers series:

Forsaking Gray
Undeniably Asher
Luke's Absolution
Destination Connelly

Have you met the other Colloway brothers yet? If not, start at the beginning of a series reviewers are raving about!

"This series is absolutely amazing. Brilliant. Intense. Passionate. Suspenseful. K. L. Kreig really brought her all when she introduced us to the Colloway brothers."

~ Renee Entress's Blog

"The Colloway brothers are some of the most swoon-worthy, panty-soaking, endearingly flawed men in contemporary romance today. They are full of grit, intelligence, and sex appeal that will leave you breathless and begging for more."

~ Rachel Caid,
Author of the *Finding Home* series

Forsaking Gray

by K.L. Kreig

Available Now

Chapter 1

Livia

I see him across the room. I'm utterly breathless.

My heart races.

My stomach flutters.

My soul disintegrates into a pile of scattered ashes once again.

I'm a complete fucking mess. No muscle will obey my command to move, even my eyelids. They refuse to take away his image for even a second.

Why is he here?

I shouldn't be taking this risk. I shouldn't be openly ogling him, but I can't look away. Holy mother of perfection...he's everything I remember and more. As breathtaking as the very first time I laid eyes on him. He's every woman's fantasy, probably men too. I see other women watching him and I want to scratch their eyes out. Some blatantly stare, as I do. Some sneak sly glances so their spouses or dates won't notice.

Foolish.

Of course their dates notice a textbook male specimen such as him in the room. All other men are busy pissing in a circle around their women to ward him away.

As if sensing my weighty stare, his eyes lock with mine. Neither of us moves.

The woman dripping off his arm, hanging on his every word, seems oblivious to our connection. Every sound fades away as we stare into each other's eyes from across the ballroom. Eyes I'm all too familiar with but haven't seen in what seems like a lifetime. Eyes that haunt me.

God, I miss him with a raw ache that intensifies daily.

"Wow, look at that fine piece of ass. He's fuckable," whispers one of my best friends, Kamryn, following my stare.

The best of my life.

He starts across the room in my direction, his date all but forgotten as he leaves her in his dust. She's calling after him, but he simply waves his hand in dismissal, not bothering to look back. His angry eyes never leave mine, his full lips drawn in a tight thin line.

Oh shit. Time to go.

"Kam, I'm not really feeling well, sweetie. I'll call you in the morning after my interview." I'm frantic to escape. I turn to leave, heels clicking as I quickly walk toward the exit. Kamryn practically runs to keep up.

"Let me call my driver for you, hon."

I call over my shoulder as I race toward my escape. "No, no. It's fine. There are plenty of cabs out front. I'll just hop in one and be home in no time. Really, it's fine."

Her grip is like an iron fist around my arm as she maneuvers me back to face her. Kam frowns, clearly not believing the blatant lie I threw her way. Whatever. Over her shoulder I estimate he's just fifty feet from where we now stand and moving at a clipped pace. As if by divine intervention, he's stopped by a buxom blonde whose nipples are ready to fall out of her slutty dress any second. One deep breath and pop, they're free. He shakes her off, heading in my direction once again. Can't blame her for trying.

Crap, Livia. Get. Out. Now.

"I think I may be sick, Kam. I'd really like to get home before I lose those little shrimp thingies I just ate." Not so much of a lie this time. My stomach *is* doing somersaults.

I turn and flee. I hear Kam call after me, but keep going this time. Making it to the safety of a cab before *he* reaches me is paramount.

Damn Kam and her insistence that I wear her four-inch Louboutin heels. So what if the fire engine red is a perfect complement to my also borrowed black leather strapless sheath. The shoes are still half a size too small and pinch my feet, making a hasty escape nearly impossible.

I should ditch the damn things like Cinderella. I

bet she didn't even 'lose' her glass slipper. She was no doubt trying to escape this supposed Prince Charming because he was an arrogant asshole, and it fell off in her urgency to get away. In traditional antifeminism fashion, a man weaved an elegant story about how much better a girl's life would be with a boy in it. He would swoop in and save her from her persecuted life and they would live happily ever after.

Bullshit. All of it.

There is no happily ever after. Not for me anyway. That childish fantasy was ruthlessly shattered over five years ago.

I make it out of the ballroom, down the stairs and have the front hotel door halfway open when a strong hand clamps down on my shoulder, effectively stopping my forward movement. An electric current runs through my body and I feel him everywhere. His hand may as well be between my legs for all my body cares.

Damn you, Louboutin and your impractical shoes.

"Hello, Livia," a deep sensual voice drawls behind me. His voice and touch combined almost make my knees buckle. After all these years, he still has the same effect on all of my senses like the day we met. He sounds the same, albeit a bit more grown up. And a *lot* more sexy.

Jesus, I don't think I can do this.

You can do this, Livia.

You have *to do this.*

Be cold.

Be unaffected.

Lie.

I take a deep breath, will the tears back, and steel myself before turning to face him.

"Hello, Gray. Fancy seeing you here." *Holy...breathe, Livia, breathe.* I am almost taken aback by how utterly gorgeous he is. He had been stunning across the room and he was always beautiful, but up close he's like a golden angel sent directly from heaven—or hell—to tempt me. His face is no longer boyish, but all man, complete with the sexiest scruffy whiskers I have ever seen. This is more than a five o'clock shadow, but not quite a full beard. I'm a sucker for scruff. Especially on Gray, but he's never worn it like this. It's downright sinful.

Double damn.

"What are you doing here, Livvy?" *Livvy.* I haven't heard that name in over five years. It sounds so damn good I want to weep.

Dig deep, Livia...maintain the façade you've perfected so very well.

"I came for the same reason you probably did: the animals." Bravo for me. I sounded very confident...and very *stupid*. My internal head is shaking at me sadly.

He says nothing, remaining stoically silent, his eyes searching mine for the truth.

Subject change, before he asks too many more questions, for which I'll have to build lie on top of lie. I've told so many lies I need a cheat sheet to keep track of them all. "So, why are you in Chicago?"

His penetrating gaze makes me even more nervous than I already am, and I start to squirm. I never intended to run into anyone I knew here, let alone him. I would have never let Kam talk me into this stupid fundraiser otherwise.

Shit. Shit. Shit. This is so not good.

"I took over my father's company, and we moved the headquarters from Detroit to Chicago last year."

He lives here? In Chicago? My mind is spinning. I'm trying to process the fact that my ex-fiancé lives in the same city as I do and that he took over his father's company already. I didn't remember Frank being that old. I shouldn't be engaging him in conversation, but I can't help but ask, "Did he retire?"

"No. He died." I gasp and my heart sinks.

"God, I'm sorry Gray, I had no idea. Your dad was a wonderful man." He was like a father to me, more so than my own, who essentially sold me to save his own life. I loved that family. They were like my own until they weren't anymore.

"Of course not, Livvy. How could you possibly when you fucking disappeared over five years ago, without a trace, without a call, without a forwarding goddamn phone number?" His retort is ripe with barbs, and it stings the way it was meant to. I deserve some of his ire yes, but not all of it.

Gray has no clue the living nightmare I've endured. What I did for my family or for him. And it will stay that way. I have to get away from him before I do something stupid, like spill my guts. He is my past, and as much as it deeply pains me, he has to stay that way. Too much has happened in the last five years that I simply can't overcome. I am damaged goods now, and Gray would never want me if he knew the truth. I need to get the hell out of here before I break down. I can't keep the tears back much longer.

"I have to go. It was nice to see you again, Gray." I need to get out of here before I throw myself at him and beg for his forgiveness. Because even though I don't quite deserve it, a small part of me desperately craves it. Gray is my first love. The only man I will ever love. And that young, naïve woman now buried deep inside me will hold tightly to the memory of her first love with her last dying breath. It's all that has gotten me through the worst days of my life.

And it's all I have left.

I spin to leave when a strong hand pulls me back once again. Every time this man puts his hands on me, I bend to his will, and right now I feel like a torch has been set to my bones and they are far too pliable. My eyes flit between it and his ever-so-handsome face. He gets the gist and lets go.

Although his voice has softened, his annoyance clearly rings loud when uttering his next words. "How can I get ahold of you, angel? I'd like to have dinner. Catch up."

My heart skips a beat. I haven't heard that endearment in so long, I have to blink back the tears threatening to fall. I *want* to agree. I nearly do. But then, common sense slams back into my frontal lobe at a hundred miles per hour. If I spend time with Gray, he'll pepper me with questions.

Questions he has *every* right to have answered. But those are answers I won't give. I can't. He can never know.

Gone is the young, naïve, rosy-colored glasses woman he fell in love with. Gone is the carefree, idealistic woman he asked to be his wife. What stands in her place, instead, is a cynical, horribly used, and hopeless one. Shattered beyond all repair.

"I can't," I whisper. Then I do turn and flee. Luckily, there are several cabs waiting out front and I hop in the first one, yelling at him just to drive. As I turn around, I see Gray standing on the sidewalk, breathing hard, watching me drive away. Déjà vu cuts me like a sharp knife and I begin to sob silently. These are the first tears I've allowed myself to shed in four and a half years.

Once again, I am leaving the only man to ever make my stomach flutter and my heart race. The man who pursued me relentlessly for that first date by returning for six straight nights to the pizzeria I worked at until I said yes. The man I dreamed of having children with. Growing old with. The only man I have and ever will love.

All because of *him*. Always because of *him*. As with every day for the past five years, I curse the day Peter Wilder set foot into my life. And I curse my father for bringing him there.

Excerpt of

Undeniably Asher

by K.L. Kreig

Available Now

Alyse

A quick glance at the clock shows it's almost noon. I ready myself for my next meeting, wondering what the hell Asher Colloway thinks he's trying to pull and why he didn't just put his name on my calendar instead of his holding company. Clearly he's trying to surprise me.

Well, the surprise is on him. Not only do I know it's him I'm meeting with, I know that he asked for client references, and I know he's already called each and every one of them. We're a small office and Heather keeps nothing from me, not to mention we like to give our clients a heads up when we know they'll be called by a potential customer.

The thing is, I have no idea what he would possibly want to hire my small firm for, but since I'm desperate for revenue, I can't *not* take the meeting. I have more to think about now than just my pride. I have three employees counting on me to feed and clothe themselves and their families. That's a heavy burden.

I thought about having Al sit in, but decided

against it. I already know Asher and he knows me, so having another male in the room isn't a necessity. Besides, a little part of me is thrilled to spend a few hours alone with him, even if we are just discussing business. *Okay, a* big *part of me.*

I managed to close one deal earlier this week and am waiting to hear back from the other client, hopefully by the end of the day. That one doesn't look too promising as we're a bit apart on pricing for our services. I have a small office and can't afford to be quite as flexible as other, larger firms that have more capital to work with. Another thing I did not take into consideration when I jumped into this dream of mine headfirst. *Ugh.*

My speakerphone squawks, and Heather's voice floats through. Her normally quiet, soft demeanor has clearly been ratcheted up a few degrees, because she actually sounds excited. I can hear the smile in her voice. Yes, Asher Colloway will do that to a woman, at least any straight one. "Ms. Kingsley, your noon appointment is here."

Ms. Kingsley? Heather hasn't addressed me as Ms. Kingsley since our first interview, and even at the end of that meeting she was calling me Alyse. I keep the laugh from my voice as I respond, "Thank you, Heather. Please send Mr. Colloway in." Once I disconnect I do chuckle. Heather usually has me on speakerphone when she buzzes my appointments in, so Asher's little surprise has just been turned around. *Ha! Boo-yaa!*

I'm still laughing when Asher opens my door. The moment my eyes land on him, though, it stutters a slow death. My gaze slowly travels down his insanely fit body and I realize he's watching me watch him, but I don't care enough to stop.

He's absolutely breathtaking in his fitted charcoal suit and crisp white shirt, which he's left open at the throat, sans tie. And the tiny bit of chest hair I see peeking through against his golden skin makes me water in more than one place. I've never seen him in anything but jeans and henleys or polo shirts, but *hot damn* if he doesn't look even more mouthwatering when he's dressed up. My entire body feels warm and tingly, inside and out.

I gravitate toward men with dark looks.

Dark hair.

Dark whiskers.

Dark eyes.

Dark personality.

Asher Colloway fits that bill to a perfect "T." At a little over six feet, he's tall, at least for me since I hover around the five-foot-four mark, give or take a half inch on a good day. And he's downright beautiful. All of the Colloway brothers could effortlessly grace the cover of a magazine, but Asher is different. He's a guy you could easily get lost in before your brain catches up to remind you why you shouldn't. He has an aura about him that's nothing short of magical and when you look at him, a spell is woven that you can't escape. You don't want to.

When I met him for the first time at seventeen, I thought he was the best thing since sliced bread. I even thought I was in love with him, but we were in very different places in our lives. Then I met Beck and I moved forward instead of looking back.

Now, though...now, I can honestly say that at twenty-nine, Asher *is* the sexiest man I have ever laid eyes on, hands down.

I want him. Desperately.

And desperation makes you do stupid, stupid things.

"Get your fill yet?" A smug smirk turns up one corner of his kissable mouth.

Damn him. I have absolutely no snarky comeback to that, because I've been openly ogling. I only hope I don't have drool dripping down my chin. I nonchalantly reach up to check, faking a cough.

"Why the secrecy?" I ask, changing subjects, not taking my eyes from him.

He closes the door before taking a seat in the chair across from my metal desk, throwing one foot onto the opposite knee. He steeples his fingers in front of his chin. The arrogant glint in his dark eyes makes me want to drop to my knees in front of him, unzip his pants, and wipe it off.

"You knew it was me."

I knew Asher had taken over as CEO for his father's company—I *may* have asked Livia what the Colloway brothers were up to after she'd reunited with Gray. In preparation for this meeting, when I researched GRASCO Holdings and found that CFC fell under them, I was irritated at first that Asher wanted to catch me cold. I never attend a client meeting without doing my homework first, especially since I'm fighting for the very existence of ARK Consulting. But then I quickly decided to turn the tables on the self-assured SOB.

Knowing that I would be meeting with Asher today, I've dressed particularly sexy in a short nude pencil skirt paired with a sheer royal-blue blouse and a matching low-cut cami underneath. Definitely not how I would dress for a normal client meeting, but I went all out for Asher. I let a slow smile turn my lips as I sit back in my black vinyl chair and casually cross my legs.

Asher's eyes follow my leisurely movements and widen at the expanse of bare thigh I'm now showing. He may have even seen a flash of the nude thong I'm wearing from his position. His heated gaze rises, capturing mine, and I have to actually talk myself into breathing, trying to remain unaffected by the intense desire he clearly wants me to see. It's not working too well.

"It may surprise you to know that I do know how to use the Internet," I finally manage to bite sarcastically.

"You haven't changed a bit, Alyse."

"I beg to differ," I retort, knowing full well life has made me more cynical and closed off.

He rewards me with a small smile, which almost melts me on the spot. He's like the sun. Warm. Inviting. Only more deadly if you spend too much time in his presence. He's quiet for several beats, his eyes assessing me deliberately. "I like a woman with fire."

"Do you?" I cross my arms, unsure where this conversation is headed, but it's not about business anymore. I don't miss how his eyes linger too long on my now-exposed cleavage.

"Yes." He uncrosses his leg and leans forward,

elbows on spread knees, hands clasped. His want-filled gaze burns my cocky attitude to ashes. "It makes her complete submission all the sweeter."

A flash fire of heat scorches my lady parts. My mouth drops open temporarily before I think to close it. Asher is so good, so smooth, and I am *waaaay* out of my league trying to trade barbs with him.

"What are you doing here, Asher?"

He leans back again, resuming a casual position, a slight smirk on his face. His eyes twinkle like stars and I find myself getting lost in them again. "Besides getting you wet?" he drawls roughly. Even though he's spot-on, his assumption angers me. I open my mouth to protest when he interrupts. "You still with Popeye?"

Huh? It takes me a minute to figure out what he means. *Finn.* I stare at him in complete and utter shock for several moments. Then, I can't help it. I laugh. I've never been around a man who has kahunas as big as Asher Colloway. He was always direct, but in the years since I've seen him, he's sharpened it considerably. It's refreshing and unsettling at the same time.

I shake my head, still chuckling, but he's stony silent. His desire has now clearly morphed into annoyance, which makes me laugh even harder. "And if I say yes?"

"Are you?"

I almost decide to lie just to see how he'll react. Anger isn't the type of response I want from Asher, though. I'm not really sure what I do want, but I know it's not that. "No."

As fast as his annoyance came, it went with my admission.

"Did you come here to question my relationship status? You could have just hopped on Facebook for that, saved yourself the drive." I uncross my legs and lean on my forearms, the coldness from the steel desk seeping into my exposed pores through the thin fabric. It's November in Detroit and very cold, but I still can't regret my choice of wardrobe after seeing the appreciation in both Asher's eyes and slacks.

"Because it's not official until it's Facebook official, right?"

"Right," I drawl. "So, back to my original question. Why are you here?"

"I want to hire you."

I assumed when he was calling references that was his angle. I'm thrilled, but at the same time, disappointed. I need this job, but I also want Asher, even though that's not the best of ideas. And I can't have both.

*Why?...*a little voice whispers.

Because it's kind of a faux pas to sleep with your clients, I tell that little slut.

"For?"

"There's someone embezzling within my company. I want them found and stopped and prosecuted." He pulls an envelope out of a folder he set down on the edge of my desk earlier. "Our outside audit firm completed our annual audit and found a discrepancy in the books, but they aren't equipped to take it further. We need someone who has expertise in ferreting out things like this, whose techniques will hold up in a court of law. I know you've worked on cases before where your work has supported a legal case."

True. I live to bring down white-collar thieves. My dad was a thief; he just stole our childhood from my sister and me instead of a corporation or business. I think that's one of the reasons I went into this field to begin with. "Is this a past or ongoing issue?"

"I have reason to believe it's ongoing, but of course I can't be sure."

"Do you have any suspicions?"

"Yes. Unfortunately nothing solid, though."

I look down, unsure of how I should approach this. I don't want to talk myself out of a job, but I want to be up front as well. I don't doubt my ability in the slightest, but CFC would be, by far, the biggest client I've worked on, and this project could possibly take months, given my small staff depending on how deep the embezzlement is buried. "You do know I haven't worked on a project for a company your size yet, correct?"

He nods, staying quiet.

"Okay. Let me look this over and work up a proposal and a timeline for your review. I can have it to you by mid-next week. Then we can meet again, discuss any questions you might have, and negotiate terms."

"No."

My brows draw together in confusion. "No, what?"

"No. I told you I want to hire you. *You*. I've

already done my research. I don't need to review anything."

I'm taken aback for a moment. "I could rob you blind. My fee may not even be competitive with the other firms you're considering."

"I'm already being robbed blind. And you won't. Whatever your fees, whatever your terms, I'll agree to them. I want the best, Alyse." He pauses before he adds, "I hear that's you."

Huh? This is by far the weirdest client prospect meeting I've ever had. I have to wonder what the catch is, because this seems too good to be true. "Uh, oookay."

"I want you to start on Monday."

It's the Wednesday before Thanksgiving. I think for a minute, cataloging our current projects. I was planning to take this new client I just secured, but I can give that to Al. Tabitha still has at least two weeks on her current project, and I'll have to come in now on Friday to wrap up a few loose ends and do some paperwork. "I can make that work."

He's silent, studying me. "One more thing. And it's nonnegotiable."

I smirk. "I'm not sleeping with you." *Even though right now I can think of nothing else but your hot, wet tongue worshipping every inch of me.*

Laughing, he leans forward, his forearms on my desk, his face mere inches from mine. I want to lean back, yet not at the same time, so I don't. Once again, Asher invades my personal space. I can't stop the big breath I take, inhaling his manly, spicy scent. It's all I can do to keep my eyes from rolling back in my head.

He doesn't miss it either. I'm getting the distinct feeling he doesn't miss any of my bodily reactions to his inebriating presence. When he finally speaks, his voice drops several octaves to panty-melting sexy. "Good. Because I'm looking forward to fucking you instead."

Holy balls. His blistering stare and egotistical words light a blaze deep within my belly. If I was wet before, I'm positively drenched now. And mute. Very, very mute. On account of the fact that my mouth is now bone-dry and all thought has fled my desire-clouded brain.

His next words pull me out of the sexual haze he has trapped us in. It's a place I could imagine myself staying. Forever. "I need you at headquarters during the audit. In Chicago."

I blink a few times to clear my mental fog, letting his words register. Being onsite during an audit is pretty standard, at least part of the time, but this will be a big audit and could take months. I bill for lodging and meal expenses, but the thought of spending months in a hotel and shuttling back and forth on the weekends to Detroit is less than appealing. On the other hand, it gets me closer to Livia. Hell, who am I kidding? I'd shuttle back and forth to San Francisco if there were a paying client there.

"You have offices here in Detroit, right?"

"Yes, but I need to keep this as quiet as possible. CFC is not all that big, so the fewer people who know about you, the better. I need you in Chicago. There's a secluded office available on my floor."

The thought of being near Asher daily does

funny things to my insides. More than it should. More than I want. "That's going to be pretty costly for you," I murmur. *And me*, I think, in more ways than one.

He leans back slightly and I'm able to take a deep breath for the first time in long minutes without inhaling him. His unique fragrance is clouding my mind, my judgment.

"I have another proposal."

I roll my eyes, leaning back in my chair. His magnetic pull makes it hard to do even that.

I am in so much trouble.

"I'm not staying with you, either."

"Now, Alyse, why do you insist on ruining all my fun?" he quips, winking.

I smile, but remain quiet. Even if he would be so bold to suggest it, he would have to know I'd never accept.

"Okay. If you won't stay with me, then we have an executive apartment that's not being used. It's fully furnished and close to the office. The building has a nice gym and a couple of restaurants. It's not terribly fancy, but it's better than a hotel."

"I—I don't know, Asher." I'm hedging, but the second his proposal left his mouth I already made up my mind. If I had a place that felt like my own, I could stay there most weekends instead of driving back to Detroit, where there was really nothing left for me except bad memories and ghosts from my past that won't seem to let me out of their unyielding grip.

He gets comfortable again before continuing his sales pitch. "It's in the same building as Livia and

Gray, so you'll also be close to your sister. I know you're helping with their shotgun wedding and wouldn't it be convenient to be able to hop in the elevator and pop in on her? Of course, I would probably call ahead first, because..."

He leaves his insinuation hanging and we both laugh, lightening the mood.

As I pretend to think about it for a couple of minutes, his intense gaze never leaves mine. I can feel him willing me into acquiescence. I almost break a smile, but that would be giving him too much and right now I need to hold parts of me back, because I can already tell Asher will demand everything from me. And then some. Certain girlie parts are already begging me to submit, submit, submit.

Seeing Asher again a couple of months ago triggered something inside me. Made me remember my girlish dreams when I was eighteen and in love with Beck. Dreams that have been too painful to remember, but now that I do, I want them desperately. To be honest, it made me remember what I felt when I almost gave myself to a young Asher Colloway.

I want bone-deep love, a family, happiness, and a man that will worship me. I thought Beck was the man who would give me everything, but he's dead and apparently wasn't the man I thought he was at all.

Finn certainly wasn't that man.

And I don't think Asher Colloway can give me any of those things either. I'm not sure he can give *any* woman that.

Pleasure? No doubt.

A future? Not likely.

He's nearly thirty, never been married, and is clearly a player. I want more than that now. God knows I *deserve* more than that. As much as I'm attracted to him, sleeping with him is probably the dumbest idea to ever cross my mind, yet my conviction not to needs a lot of reinforcement.

I refocus on the reason we're having this discussion in the first place. Keeping my business afloat. "Okay. I accept your terms."

His smile blinds me, and all thoughts I just had about why I should stay away from this man float out of the room on a cloud of pure lust.

Yep, my conviction needs a lot of work.

A. Lot.

Prologue

December 27

LUKE

Enjoying the view of her toned bare thigh with each step she takes, courtesy of that nice high slit in her dress, I watch her sashay over to where I'm leaning against the bar. She orders a Corona Light from the bartender, tapping her perfectly manicured pink nails against the cool granite while she waits.

I've been watching her with that jackass photographer for the last hour, getting progressively angrier by the minute, not quite understanding why. She's smokin' hot, yes, but I have absolutely no claim on her. Not that I wouldn't mind a little sample. Or fifty.

Confusingly, it's the same reaction I had when I saw her in his arms last Friday night. The urge to introduce his face to a cement wall was so great, had she not been drunk off her ass, I may not have been able to resist.

She'd be a handful for any man to juggle, no doubt in bed and out, and picture boy, Cooper Jensen, isn't even close to enough man for her. It will take a strong hand to control her, make her submit, and God himself help me, that's all I've thought of since I laid eyes on her for the first time months ago. I want to hear her raw voice sobbing my name while I have her pinned helplessly underneath me. Who knew that Eric's sister was so fucking sexy? Probably why he kept her under wraps all those years ago.

Addy Monroe is like a wild horse. Untamed, full of fire, even feral if you get her riled up enough. I had a small taste of that last weekend after Gray's bachelor party when we stopped by the bar where the girls were having their own celebration. I saved her from herself by confiscating their almost-empty bottle of Patron. Every heated word she spat tugged straight on my cock, and by the time I left with her passed out in my arms, I was rock hard. Let's just say it was a long fucking night all around.

I want her. Not that I *deserve* her. She's untainted, unlike me. I have so many fucking stains, industrial-strength cleaner couldn't remove them all. But I'm not looking for a relationship; I'm looking for a good fuck. I'm looking for oblivion.

Liar, my conscience loudly whispers.

Fuck off, I tell him, even louder.

I discreetly adjust my hardening dick. "No

tequila tonight?" I feel the smirk on my face, but don't know if she sees it or not. I'm trying to refrain from looking at her as I will my own body into submission.

"Unrequited love sucks, doesn't it?" she replies with a bite before taking a sip of her beer straight from the bottle. I love a woman who isn't too prissy to drink her alcohol from the actual container it's served in. More than that, I love a woman with a smart, feisty mouth.

"I have no idea what you're talking about, sweetheart."

I flick my eyes over to see hers stray to Gray and Livia across the ballroom and her lips upturn in a sly smirk. "Whatever you say. I'm pretty much the subject matter expert on that shit."

She turns and leans her back against the bar, mirroring my stance. We're both silent, watching the happy newly married couple with drinks in our hands. The more I think about what she said, the more it plain pisses me off.

Yes, I care deeply for Livia. I have for years. No one can possibly understand what I watched her go through and what I had to suffer through myself. How that bonds two people on a totally different plane.

But even if Livia could have been mine, I know her heart will always belong to Gray. I could never interfere with that. Wouldn't. Besides, I've done enough to my family without intentionally trying to steal my brother's girl. I do have a few shreds of decency left that I'm trying desperately to hold on to. They're wound so tightly around my fingers, they're cutting off the circulation, but I'll be damned if I'll let them go.

Regardless of what Addy may think, I'm genuinely thrilled for them both. After what she's been through, *no one* deserves happiness more than Livia. But fuck, I won't deny watching them get married today was hard. Harder than I thought it would be, and it's not because I still want her. I gave up on that notion years ago, even if my heart didn't quite get the memo.

No...it was hard because the love that hovers above them like a bright golden halo is sickening. What's even more sickening is that as I watch them, I'm envious. I want *that*, only the logical part of me knows I'll never have it. I push those feelings of optimism that keep bubbling to the surface down deep into the muck again. I may have moved past the worst times of my life, but in no way do I kid myself that I'm worthy of a woman's love or acceptance of who I am and the things I've done.

So tonight I need to forget.

About Livia.

About my tainted past.

About all the things I now want but will never get.

And I think Addy Monroe is just the woman to do that, even if it can only be for a few minutes. My dick hardens painfully whenever I set eyes on Livia's best friend, the little sister of *my* best friend Eric, and I have to be honest...she's the only one who's stirred it for quite some time now. I've wanted this spitfire since the minute I saw her

479

shaking the tits and ass God so graciously blessed her with at the bar when I first came back to Chicago in September to protect Livia from our sordid past.

"Maybe fifteen minutes in the back will wipe that smirk off your face," I whisper as I lean sideways toward her. In my peripheral, I see her head turn to me.

"Wow, a whole fifteen minutes, huh? I think I'll have to take a rain check on that offer, Rico Suave." She spins on her heels to walk away from me.

Oh, hell no.

Next thing I know, her body is pressed against mine, held in place by a firm palm to her neck and another circled around the trim waist I've wanted to squeeze all night.

Sweet Jesus and Mary, she feels fantastic. I have to suppress the groan that wants to escape from somewhere deep inside—it would give her too much power over me and control is what I need to wrestle from her, inch by agonizing inch. My lips are at her ear, grazing the tender flesh with each word I rasp.

"Sweetheart, I can spend the next fifteen *hours* lavishing untold pleasure and blissful pain all over and inside every single inch of your delectable body until you beg for me, *cry* for me, to stop."

The way her breath hitches has my cock pleading to ram into her over and over. Uncaring who may see, I release her waist and grab her hand, bringing it between our bodies, forcing it to my shaft with my hand on top. Guiding her, I squeeze, moving our twined fingers up and down the length of me. She moans and my eyes close at the image of sinking my cock slowly between her red-glossed clever lips.

Nipping her lobe harshly, I grate, "Let's start with that smart mouth of yours, shall we?"

Babbles...

This is bittersweet. The end of a series, which I spent months conceptualizing and writing. Each story, while very different, carried the same overarching theme: forgiveness, second chances, and alpha men who knew what they wanted from the word go. What would life be without those? I can't tell you how much these brothers mean to me and how much I've enjoyed sharing them with you. I hope they will forever be a part of your lives, just as they will be mine. Who knows...maybe somewhere down the road, we'll meet them again. I have a couple spin-offs in mind. We'll just have to see where they may go.

If you noticed my musical inspiration, you may nave noticed a theme. I wrote this entire series to Red, a band I happened to stumble across on Octane one day—a Christian rock band, I would come to find out later! Their words spoke to me exactly as if these characters did. Their feelings became my characters' emotions. Give them a listen, maybe. They're awesome and their lyrics are meaningful.

The stats I gave around lung cancer are all true, sadly. It's such an underdiscussed disease and so very hard to detect until it's almost too late. A nonsmoker, my mother-in-law, Alice, died of lung cancer at a horribly young age of sixty-seven. And she was also the inspiration for Barb Colloway. She was a selfless, amazing woman, the likes of which I doubt I'll ever meet again. Her life left an impression on so many and I can only hope to be half the woman she was. I miss her every single day.

Writing a book is a solitary process. Producing it, however, takes a village and I have so many people to thank.

Nikki, your fantastically tight editing blows me away. Your education on comma placement is endearing but wasted! You're worth every penny I pay you. **Heather**, your friendship, support, and encouragement on down days is always the kick in the pants I need. **Rachel**, my sounding board, you may like Miller Light, but I can look past that one little character flaw. Love you to pieces, my friend. **Angie, Desirae, Trena, Kay Su, Michele, Sophie, Tina** and countless other blogger friends who have reached out to me individually about these boys. Thanks for your unconditional support and pimping of me. It doesn't seem like enough, but it's all I have.

Friends, family, bloggers, authors, betas, pimpers, and most importantly MY READERS: if you had a hand in this, if you supported me in any way, shape, or form, you know who you are and you know I thank you from the bottom of my heart. I am nothing but sincerely, eternally grateful for your belief in me.

Finally, after forty some years, I have found my true passion in life. I may never be a best seller, I may never win writing awards, I may never be able to make a true living at doing what I love, but I don't even care. Every message and each e-mail I get from someone who wanted to personally reach out to me and praise me for how my work touched them in some way is *truly* a surreal feeling and *that's* why I do this. Because you all encourage me. For that, I thank you.

For the love of God...help an author out! LEAVE A REVIEW on Goodreads, Amazon, or wherever. Even one or two sentences or simply rating the book is helpful for other readers. Reviews are critical to getting a book exposure in this vast sea of great reads.

About the Author

This is the hardest part...talking about myself.

I'm just a regular ol' Midwest girl who likes *Game of Thrones* and is obsessed with *Modern Family* and *The Goldbergs*. I run, I eat, I run, I eat. It's a vicious cycle. I love carbs, but there's a love-hate relationship with my ass and thighs. Mostly hate. I like a good cocktail (oh hell...who am I kidding? I love *any* cocktail). I'm a huge creature of habit, but I'll tell you I'm flexible. I read every single day and if I don't get a chance...watch the hell out, I'm a raving bitch. My iPad and I: BFFs. I'm direct and I make no apologies for it. I swear too much. I love alternative music and in my next life, I want to be a badass female rocker. I hate, hate, hate spiders, telemarketers, liver, acne, winter, and loose hairs that fall down my shirt (don't ask, it's a thing).

I have a great job (no...truly it is) outside of writing. My kids and my husband are my entire world and I'd never have made it this far without them. My soul mate husband of over twenty-eight years provides unwavering support and my two grown children know the types of books I write and they don't judge their mom anyway (and my daughter is a beta reader even...yes, that can be awkward...very).

I'm *sincerely* humbled by each and every like on my Facebook page or sign up for my newsletter or outreach from someone who has read and loved my books. I still can't get over the great support. The romance book community is a wonderful and supportive one. I've made more friends since I started this journey than I've made in my life and I'm a pretty affable person. It's surreal. I'm pretty sure it always will be.

In short, I am blessed...and I know it.

If you're a stalker, the first step is to admit it. After that, you can find me in a lot of places, all of which I use with irregular frequency.

In this day and age, with so many great authors and so many new releases, it's challenging to keep up with it all, so if you don't want to miss when my next book is releasing, sign up for my newsletter found on my website. Promise, no spamming and you'll only get it when I have something important to say.

Website: http://klkreig.com